ULTIMATE BESTIARY

-The Dreaded Accursed-

5TH EDITION COMPATIBLE

Legal

Nord Games denies wholeheartedly and unreservedly any claim that this book has been transformed by dark ritual and terrible sacrifice into a vessel for the authors' immortal souls. However, ensuring that this book remains in good condition, and out of the hands of exorcists should be the owner's highest priority, for unrelated and normal reasons.

Credits

Authors: Lou Fryer, Ralph Stickley

Lead Designer: Isabel Beis

Proofing: Lou Fryer, David Gibson, Emma Stickley

Art Director: Ralph Stickley

Layout and Typesetting: Chris van der Linden, Ralph Stickley

Illustrators: Joel Chaim Holtzman, George Mason, Karen Petrasko, Takashi Tan, Sam White

Additional Contributors: David Gibson, Jack Harding

Project Management: Ralph Stickley

Character Creation: Lou Fryer, Chris Haskins, Ralph Stickley

Brand and Marketing: Chris Haskins, Megan Roy

Table of Contents

Foreword

I write this around Christmas. The nights are long, and it is a good time for ghost stories. In my experience, it is also the time of year to reflect on what exactly it is I *do* for a living, if only to refine the explaination for those well-meaning relatives who inquire about, "that... writing thing(?)" each Christmas. *It's a bit like a video game, except you don't need a computer... not exactly a board game, no, more like a story, but all the characters are played by the readers... yes, a bit like Lord of the Rings, I suppose... did you want a refill on the port? Why don't I go and sort that out for you?*

It's been years now, and I've still not got the formula nailed down.

Oh, and what's this now? Do excuse me, it being Christmas (and this being London), a spirit has just appeared at my window. At once a child and a withered elder, topped with a comedy horned helmet. Calls itself the Ghost of Nord Past. 'Scuse me for a mo'.

Taking my hand, it shows me a vision of a familiar bespectacled man, younger than me and, regretfully, a little skinnier. He sits in the passenger seat of a minivan that struggled to get to Sequoia National Forest, and is struggling even more to make it back. They are discussing the driver's idea for a book—a collection of in-depth characters to use as NPCs in the shiny, new 5th Edition of D&D. As soon as they get back to the driver's house, they will start writing it. It's a nice diversion from the man's day job for the next few months.

Another ghost. Bear with...

Big fella this time, beardy and jovial, with an even bigger comedy horned helmet. The Ghost of Nord Present, apparently. I'll go and know him better.

On our travels, we see that Nord Games is on its sixth book now (and even more card decks), and is a proper company with an office, and employees, and everything. More than that, there are thousands of people reading and, apparently, *enjoying* the work they are putting out. In fact, the man feels so proud and grateful for everything that has been accomplished that this is the second time he's written about it in a foreword. I'm a little worried that the spirit is about to show me two ragged and wolfish children called Smugness and Self-Indulgence.

Thank goodness there is little chance of that.

You won't believe it; someone else at the window. Did the music suddenly get all ominous, or is that just me? Who could that be, then?

Let's find out together...

-Ralph Stickley

December 2019

Instructions

As with all of the *Game Master's Toolbox*, this book is here to make your job a little easier, so you can focus on creating awesome adventures for your players, and not have to devote time, for example, on working out the finer points of mummy biology.

The main body of the book is split up into the main undead and accursed creatures, each of which has a rundown of its origin, and a wealth of stat blocks running the gamut from the lowliest zombie, to the most frightful of master liches.

At the back of the book, you'll find additional stat blocks for animated objects associated with one or more of the monster types, rules for playing as accursed beings, and maps to use in encounters with these creatures.

As well as all that, you can use the encounter tables within the main chapters while running the game itself, to give a bit of variety at a moment's notice.

Acknowledgements

We'd like to say a massive thank you to all of our Kickstarter backers. Without you veritable horde of gamers, we wouldn't be able to do what we do. We hope you have as much fun using this book as we did making it!

A Preface

Life is such a fragile thing.

This momentary and perfect balance of body, spirit, and soul is both a blessing and a curse. Remove or compromise but one, and life is no more.

Yet does the zombie suffer, stripped of soul? Does the wraith mourn its long-forgotten body? This is a curse only of the living, this knowledge of ourselves, for knowledge engenders fear: fear of what might await us.

But is this burden not also our blessing? Is fear not a peerless motivator for greatness? Our time is brief, we must do well with it, and quickly. We must learn, and embrace our fear.

Once more, I have delved into the annals, and compiled firsthand accounts, excerpts, and notes concerning the undead and accursed, combining them with my own conclusions and summations. I hope they prove worthwile and instructional.

The lesson, I hope, is a simple one:
our time is finite, and the wise would not ask for more.

Addendum: During the course of my research, as I began the process of investigating sources, I was approached by a stranger, his scarred and rough-hewn face a terrible sight of fury and woe. He clutched a worn packet of papers in his good hand; the other, I noticed, was atrophied and claw-like. Wordlessly, he thrust the papers into my grasp, some ragged, some spattered with what could only be blood. Before I could ask for more details, he was gone. I have inserted the stories contained within throughout this book, where I hope they will be elucidatory.

GHOSTS

The woman is weeping. She has been weeping for centuries. The diaphanous smoke of her body trails off to nothingness, drifting gently in a non-existent breeze. Her face is a mask of grief, twisting into a grotesque caricature. The sobbing builds to a howling crescendo, a piercing shriek of pain and confusion as, all around her, the world warps, rotting and eroding in the gale of her emotion as if itself crying out. In a moment, the wind dies, and the woman is weeping. She will weep for centuries.

Where does the soul travel after death? To the depths of damnation? To sit by the side of the gods and feast eternally? This may be so for the truly wicked, or the exemplary heroes; the majority of mortals must however, at least for a time it would seem, wander. Most ghosts are simply the echoes of these wandering souls, drifting through the world, seldom visible, until…what? Some claim that such a ghost will pass on only when all who knew of it in life have died, others say that it must find its way through the twisting snarls of the ethereal to find its way to the afterlife. Dwarves say that when all the mountains have been ground to dust, all dwarven souls shall pass on to paradise together. Whatever the truth, the ghosts do not tell, if ever they knew it themselves.

Ghosts tend to possess the same personality traits they did in life, though it is not uncommon for their personalities to become tinged with melancholic longing for either the life they had or the release of the afterlife. Others are driven mad, consumed by the emotion of their death at the expense of all other feelings; such ghosts might appear to wear the face of a deceased loved one but, in truth, are nothing but tormented shades.

A ghost's appearance is closely tied to its emotions and its reasons for lingering. While ghosts normally resemble the living person around the time of their death, their appearance warps when under stress or when the ghost experiences strong emotions. A riled ghost (or one whose unfinished business is an angry one) might gradually morph to take on the appearance of their own violent death, becoming more and more horrifically exaggerated as the emotions grow and grow, with no physical body to restrain them. The ghost of an old man whose one regret was never confessing their love to a childhood sweetheart, being fixated on this moment, might appear almost solely as they did as a youth.

ORIGIN

Those who died with unfinished business, were struck down in a terrible passion, or whose deaths were accompanied by a particularly resonant emotion (anger, betrayal, fear, or pain being the most common); any of these may break the natural order of things. Such traumatic instances leave an imprint on the material plane, a portion of the deceased soul's personality with all but the most prevalent emotions at the time of death dampened. The rest of the soul passes on but, tethered by the lingering fragment, is unable to rest. If the ghost is able to find closure, the fragment becomes untethered from the world and is able to rejoin the remainder to be whole and at peace.

Formed of soul essence and sheer force of will, ghosts have the ability to overpower the soul of a living creature and exist within their body. While a ghost is able to possess anyone with weaker will than itself, those with some sort of link to the ghost are easier targets: those who have acquired items the ghost owned in life, blood relatives, those who dabble in ethereal magic and, particularly, those whose lives mirror that of the ghost itself. Whatever host the ghost chooses will typically retain some sense of the ghost's character for a time after their possession, whether it be a missing piece needed to puzzle out its motivation, or a sobering sense of its relentless fury. Possession can take place over the course of months or years, with the ghost taking control so slowly the victim does not realise until it is too late, or it can be as quick a process as it is unsubtle. Rarely, a benign ghost will use this ability to directly and efficiently guide another towards fulfilling its business while leaving them in control of their actions. More commonly, malign ghosts will possess a person entirely, leaving them aware of their body's actions, but unable to do anything to stop them.

While forcibly exorcising ghosts is a possibility in areas where they have become a problem, there is always the chance of it returning after a time, adding vengeance against the banisher to its agenda. A less risky, and more permanent, solution can be fulfilling whatever business that ties it to the world. Should a ghost understand and trust a promise made to help it achieve its aims, it will probably do no harm to the promise-maker though, should they fail, or make their oath in bad faith, the ghost's attacks will surely be redoubled. If its business is completed – whether it be finding and reuniting it with its lost remains, exacting revenge upon its betrayer, or declaring love to its betrothed – even the most violent and irrational of ghosts will have a moment of clarity and calm, before fading away with the momentary knowledge that it is going on to rest.

ENVIRONMENT

Ghosts tend to be restricted to the area in which they died, though how far their hauntings extend can vary dramatically; a ghost may be constrained to one room, one forest clearing, or an entire moor, seemingly dependant upon the circumstances surrounding the ghost's death as well as the issue it is attempting to resolve. Rarely, ghosts haunt an individual, following them wherever they go; this is usually the case for those betrayed by a close friend or lover.

A ghost can have a variety of effects on its environment, from a simple chill in the air, a vague sense of unease, or more specific hauntings. The circumstances of a ghost's death often seep into the surrounding area; blood will ooze from the walls around a murder victim, food will appear to turn to dust around a starved child, choking ash will fill the air around one who died in a fire, and so on. These apparitions, while alarming, are usually purely spectral, harmless in nature and, for the most part, not consciously controlled by the ghost in question, instead flaring up or dying down in response to its emotional state. However, some ghosts have the power to focus these effects sufficiently to do mortals harm, as well as to control relevant objects in their environment.

Particularly willful ghosts are able to manifest items, clothing, and even simulacra of living creatures as they wish. Animals significant to the ghost's life or death commonly accompany them - most often dogs or horses. While not truly the lingering soul of an animal in actuality, these creatures behave in much the same way, except for their unwavering loyalty to the ghost in question, as manifestations of their memory and extensions of their will.

"What I don't get is why come back, you know? Whassa point of comin' back if you ain't gonna enjoy nuffin'?
Dunno about you, but there ain't no business important enough - and I mean no business - important enough... for me to finish... that would convince me come back and not be able to 'ave a big bowl of me mum's hot pot and a pint of (*hic*) Rosie's Best Bitter."

-Martyn Rode, Farmhand

Roleplaying Ghosts

Ghosts can vary wildly in demeanour, from fairly pleasant - if somewhat morose - souls, whose business may be as benign as uncovering some final piece of research or seeing that their descendants live happily, to darker spirits with unfinished business of horror and death. Perhaps worse are those whose beings have become detached from their consciousness. With no memory of their former selves, or what tethers them to the material, they simply rail against the living, with tormenting flashes of memory and purpose only serving to taunt them.

The longer a ghost exists, the less coherent it is likely to grow. Over time, the emotional remnant tethering the ghost can grow more and more extreme to the point that it devours any nuance to its character. A ghost which began vengeful against a particular individual might, over decades and centuries, devolve into an avatar of unbridled rage so inarticulate it cannot comprehend its reason for lingering, let alone convey it to others.

Even the friendliest ghost has a constant, painful awareness of its own death. The existence of a ghost is a miserable one, only made tolerable by working towards their unfinished business. Ghosts can become desperate, hopeless, and psychotic if their goal seems impossible, and pathetically grateful should some living soul agree to help them. Over centuries of undeath, they can become entirely numb to their condition, caring not for what happens to them or, conversely, their resentment toward the living can stew, heightening their hatred and jealousy.

Combat Tactics

A ghost's emotional state and the nature of its unresolved issues will greatly affect its attitude about, and behaviour in, combat. A rational ghost will likely avoid direct confrontation, preferring to appeal to any would-be combatant's logic; if their intent is to get rid of the ghost, the path of least resistance is to aid it in fulfilling its task. Such a ghost may resort to possession, visions, and other tricks in order to coerce, threaten, or sway the uncooperative to their way of thinking.

Many ghosts, however, are quite mad. Without a lucid concept of its unfinished business, it will likely violently defend its solitude, and any living beings who come across it should count themselves lucky to be simply scared away.

Ghost Encounters

d8	CR	Encounter
1	3	**Lost Love:** 1 Horrific Countenance, 1 Possessive Consciousness
2	5	**Ill-fated Kennel:** 1 Horrific Countenance, 3 Phantom Hounds
3	7	**Tragic Siblings:** 1 Lingering Waif, 1 Haunted Doll
4	10	**Endless Dance:** 1 Dreadful Spirit, 2 Horrific Countenances, 4 Possessive Consciousnesses
5	13	**Fateful Hunt:** 1 Relentless Haunt, 1 Phantom Steed, 4 Phantom Hounds, 1 Animated Longbow
6	15	**Tormented Orphanage:** 1 Dreadful Spirit, 5 Lingering Waifs, 2 Living Dolls
7	16	**Damned Prison:** 3 Tortured Souls, 1 Possessed Armor
8	21	**Haunted Manor:** 1 Relentless Haunt, 2 Dreadful Spirits, 1 Lingering Waif, 4 Phantom Servants, 2 Phantom Hounds, 1 Living Doll, 1 Ghostly Stagecoach

PHANTOM SERVANT

Medium undead, any alignment

Armor Class 13
Hit Points 13 (3d8)
Speed 0 ft., fly 30 ft.

STR	DEX	CON	INT	WIS	CHA
8 (-1)	16 (+3)	10 (+0)	8 (-1)	13 (+1)	16 (+3)

Damage Resistances acid, fire, lightning, thunder; bludgeoning, piercing, and slashing from nonmagical weapons
Damage Immunities cold, necrotic, poison
Condition Immunities charmed, exhaustion, frightened, grappled, paralyzed, petrified, poisoned, prone, restrained
Senses darkvision 60 ft., passive Perception 11
Languages the languages its creator knows
Challenge 1 (200 XP)

Ethereal Sight. The phantom can see 60 feet into the Ethereal Plane when it is on the Material Plane, and vice versa.

Incorporeal Movement. The phantom can move through other creatures and objects as if they were difficult terrain. It takes 5 (1d10) force damage if it ends its turn inside an object.

ACTIONS

Multiattack. The phantom can use its Frightening Visage. It then attacks with its Blood-Chilling Touch.

Blood-Chilling Touch. *Melee Spell Attack:* +5 to hit, reach 5 ft., one target. *Hit:* 10 (2d6 + 3) necrotic damage.

Etherealness. The phantom enters the Ethereal Plane from the Material Plane, or vice versa. It is visible on the Material Plane while it is in the Border Ethereal, and vice versa, yet it can't affect, or be affected by, anything on the other plane.

Frightening Visage. One creature within 60 feet of the phantom, that isn't undead and can see it, must succeed on a DC 13 Wisdom saving throw, or be frightened until the end of the phantom's next turn. If a target's saving throw is successful, or the effect ends for it, the target is immune to this phantom's Frightening Visage for the next 24 hours.

Some ghosts are able to split away parts of their spirit to act independently, though still under the ghost's control. These fragments, known as **phantom servants**, should really be thought of a way for the ghost to spread its influence and accomplish multiple tasks simultaneously, rather than beings in their own right.

Please make sure tankards are washed PROMPTLY and THOROUGHLY. Arteus is clearly upset by mess and clutter, and I don't want to spend another day cleaning up the common-room and scrubbing blood out of the walls. YES, it is hypocritical that he wrecks the place when he's upset. NO, there is no value in trying to point that out to him.

—note posted behind the bar in The Famous Spirit taproom

HORRIFIC COUNTENANCE
Medium undead, any alignment

Armor Class 12
Hit Points 35 (10d8 - 10)
Speed 0 ft., fly 40 ft.

STR	DEX	CON	INT	WIS	CHA
5 (-3)	15 (+2)	9 (-1)	10 (+0)	13 (+1)	16 (+3)

Saving Throws Con +1
Damage Resistances acid, fire, lightning, thunder; bludgeoning, piercing, and slashing from nonmagical weapons
Damage Immunities cold, necrotic, poison
Condition Immunities charmed, exhaustion, frightened, grappled, paralyzed, petrified, poisoned, prone, restrained
Senses darkvision 60 ft., passive Perception 11
Languages the languages it knew in life
Challenge 2 (450 XP)

Ethereal Sight. The countenance can see 60 feet into the Ethereal Plane when it is on the Material Plane, and vice versa.

Incorporeal Movement. The countenance can move through other creatures and objects as if they were difficult terrain. It takes 5 (1d10) force damage if it ends its turn inside an object.

ACTIONS

Blood-Chilling Touch. *Melee Spell Attack:* +5 to hit, reach 5 ft., one target. *Hit:* 10 (2d6 + 3) necrotic damage.

Etherealness. The countenance enters the Ethereal Plane from the Material Plane, or vice versa. It is visible on the Material Plane while it is in the Border Ethereal, and vice versa, yet it can't affect, or be affected, by anything on the other plane.

Horrifying Visage. Living creatures within 60 feet of the countenance, that can see it, must succeed on a DC 13 Wisdom saving throw, or become frightened for 1 minute. A frightened target can repeat the saving throw at the end of each of its turns, ending the frightened condition on itself on a success. If a target's saving throw is successful, or the effect ends for it, the target is immune to this ghost's Horrifying Visage for the next 24 hours.

The wight returns for fear of death,
The lich for lore thereof,
The rev'nant to revenge itself,
The ghost, alone, for love.

-popular rhyme

PHANTOM HOUND
Medium undead, any alignment

Armor Class 14
Hit Points 22 (5d8)
Speed 0 ft., fly 40 ft.

STR	DEX	CON	INT	WIS	CHA
8 (-1)	18 (+4)	10 (+0)	2 (-4)	14 (+2)	14 (+2)

Damage Resistances acid, fire, lightning, thunder; bludgeoning, piercing, and slashing from nonmagical weapons
Damage Immunities cold, necrotic, poison
Condition Immunities charmed, exhaustion, frightened, grappled, paralyzed, petrified, poisoned, prone, restrained
Senses darkvision 60 ft., ethereal scent 60 ft., passive Perception 12
Languages —
Challenge 2 (450 XP)

Ethereal Sight. The phantom hound can see 60 feet into the Ethereal Plane when it is on the Material Plane, and vice versa.

Ethereal Scent. The phantom hound automatically senses the presence of any creature within 60 feet, that isn't a construct, in the Ethereal and Material Plane. This sense does not allow the hound to discern the location of these creatures, only their presence and number within range.

Incorporeal Movement. The phantom hound can move through other creatures and objects as if they were difficult terrain. It takes 5 (1d10) force damage if it ends its turn inside an object.

ACTIONS

Multiattack. The phantom hound can use its Frightening Howl. It then attacks with its Blood-Chilling Bite.

Blood-Chilling Bite. *Melee Spell Attack:* +4 to hit, reach 5 ft., one target. *Hit:* 12 (3d6 + 2) necrotic damage.

Etherealness. The phantom hound enters the Ethereal Plane from the Material Plane, or vice versa. It is visible on the Material Plane while it is in the Border Ethereal, and vice versa, yet it can't affect, or be affected, by anything on the other plane.

Frightening Howl (1/Day). The phantom hound emits a ghostly howl. Creatures within 60 feet of the hound, that aren't undead and can hear it, must succeed on a DC 12 Wisdom saving throw, or become frightened until the end of the hound's next turn.

Animals, on the whole, lack the awareness necessary to remain in spectral form after death, though there is nothing to prevent them doing so otherwise. Spectral hounds are well-established, and there is reason to believe that at least some of them are the genuine impressions of once-living creatures (as opposed to the extensions of a lingering humanoid spirit given canine form), perhaps driven by those same loyal instincts which will compel a still-living dog to pine at his dead master's grave until the day they themselves perish.

Spectral cats, on the other hand, are practically unheard of. It is thought that, as even the meanest street-cat comports itself with such a sense of royal self-importance, no cat feels there is anything in the mortal realm worth remaining for.

-Roniel Vaas, 'Denizens of the Ethereal'

Possessive Consciousness
Medium undead, any alignment

Armor Class 12
Hit Points 35 (10d8 - 10)
Speed 0 ft., fly 40 ft.

STR	DEX	CON	INT	WIS	CHA
5 (-3)	15 (+2)	9 (-1)	10 (+0)	13 (+1)	16 (+3)

Saving Throws Con +1
Damage Resistances acid, fire, lightning, thunder; bludgeoning, piercing, and slashing from nonmagical weapons
Damage Immunities cold, necrotic, poison
Condition Immunities charmed, exhaustion, frightened, grappled, paralyzed, petrified, poisoned, prone, restrained
Senses darkvision 60 ft., passive Perception 11
Languages the languages it knew in life
Challenge 2 (450 XP)

Ethereal Sight. The consciousness can see 60 feet into the Ethereal Plane when it is on the Material Plane, and vice versa.

Incorporeal Movement. The consciousness can move through other creatures and objects as if they were difficult terrain. It takes 5 (1d10) force damage if it ends its turn inside an object.

Actions

Demented Touch. *Melee Spell Attack:* +5 to hit, reach 5 ft., one target. *Hit:* 10 (2d6 + 3) psychic damage.

Etherealness. The consciousness enters the Ethereal Plane from the Material Plane, or vice versa. It is visible on the Material Plane while it is in the Border Ethereal, and vice versa, yet it can't affect, or be affected by, anything on the other plane.

Reconstitute. The consciousness rolls again to recharge its Possession ability.

Possession (Recharge 6). One humanoid, that the consciousness can see within 5 feet of it, must succeed on a DC 13 Charisma saving throw, or be possessed by the consciousness; the consciousness then disappears, and the target is incapacitated and loses control of its body. The consciousness now controls the body, but the target is still aware of its surroundings. The consciousness can't be targeted by any attack, spell, or other effect, except ones that turn undead, and it retains its alignment, Intelligence, Wisdom, Charisma, and immunity to being charmed and frightened. It otherwise uses the possessed target's statistics, but doesn't gain access to the target's knowledge, class features, or proficiencies.

The possession lasts until the body drops to 0 hit points or takes an amount of radiant damage from a single hit equal to the consciousness' current hit points. The possession also ends if the consciousness is turned, or forced out, by a *dispel evil and good* spell or similar effect, or the consciousness ends the effect as a bonus action. When the possession ends, the consciousness reappears in an unoccupied space within 5 feet of the possessed creature. The target is immune to this consciousness' Possession for 24 hours after succeeding on the saving throw, or after the possession ends.

Do you think a loved one has fallen foul of ethereal possession? Remember SPIRIT:

Suspect – a suspicious mind is more difficult to fool

Placate – acquiesce to the wishes of the possessed, unless doing so would bring harm to yourself or others: you may resolve the spirit's unfinished business on your own

Inquire - ask questions only the possessed would know the answer to

Remain calm – do not let the possessor know you are onto it, or mean it harm

Investigate – any additional information you can give as to the nature of the creature will be useful

Tell the relevant authorities to engage a specialist

If you suspect a ghost is attempting to possess you, report to the authorities for immediate exorcism. May the gods have mercy on you.

-excerpt from the pamphlet, '"Why Is Granny Floating?": A Guide To Ghosts in Your Home'

PHANTOM STEED

Large undead, any alignment

Armor Class 14
Hit Points 32 (5d10 + 5)
Speed 0 ft., fly 60 ft.

STR	DEX	CON	INT	WIS	CHA
8 (-1)	18 (+4)	13 (+1)	2 (-4)	14 (+2)	14 (+2)

Damage Resistances acid, fire, lightning, thunder; bludgeoning, piercing, and slashing from nonmagical weapons
Damage Immunities cold, necrotic, poison
Condition Immunities charmed, exhaustion, frightened, grappled, paralyzed, petrified, poisoned, prone, restrained
Senses darkvision 60 ft., ethereal scent 60 ft., passive Perception 12
Languages —
Challenge 3 (700 XP)

Ethereal Sight. The phantom steed can see 60 feet into the Ethereal Plane when it is on the Material Plane, and vice versa.

Ethereal Trample. If the phantom steed uses the Dash action, and moves at least 30 feet in a straight line through another creature's space, it can make one attack against that creature with its Cold Hooves as a bonus action.

Ethereal Mount. Creatures with both the Incorporeal Movement and Etherealness abilities can use the phantom steed as a mount. When such a creature controlling the steed uses its Etherealness ability, the steed enters the other plane along with it.

Incorporeal Movement. The phantom steed can move through other creatures and objects as if they were difficult terrain. It takes 5 (1d10) force damage if it ends its turn inside an object.

ACTIONS

Multiattack. The phantom steed can use its Frightening Scream. It then attacks with its Cold Hooves.

Cold Hooves. Melee Spell Attack: +4 to hit, reach 5 ft., one target. Hit: 12 (3d6 + 2) necrotic damage.

Etherealness. The phantom steed enters the Ethereal Plane from the Material Plane, or vice versa. It is visible on the Material Plane while it is in the Border Ethereal, and vice versa, yet it can't affect, or be affected by, anything on the other plane.

Frightening Scream (1/Day). The phantom steed emits a ghostly whinny. Creatures within 30 feet of the steed, that aren't undead and can hear it, must succeed on a DC 12 Wisdom saving throw, or be frightened until the end of the steed's next turn.

Lingering Waif

Small undead, any alignment

Armor Class 15 (see Sympathetic Armor)
Hit Points 70 (20d6)
Speed 0 ft., fly 30 ft.

STR	DEX	CON	INT	WIS	CHA
4 (-3)	14 (+2)	10 (+0)	9 (-1)	13 (+1)	17 (+3)

Damage Resistances acid, fire, lightning, thunder; bludgeoning, piercing, and slashing from nonmagical weapons
Damage Immunities cold, necrotic, poison
Condition Immunities charmed, exhaustion, frightened, grappled, paralyzed, petrified, poisoned, prone, restrained
Senses darkvision 60 ft., passive Perception 11
Languages the languages it knew in life
Challenge 5 (1,800 XP)

Aura of Abandonment. Any humanoid that starts its turn within 60 feet of the waif must succeed on a DC 14 Wisdom saving throw, or become charmed. The charmed creature perceives adult humanoids as hostile and malevolent. At the end of each of its turns, an adult charmed humanoid can repeat the saving throw, ending the effect on itself on a success. If an adult creature succeeds on its saving throw, it is immune to this waif's Aura of Abandonment for the next 24 hours.

The effect can be removed by a *dispel evil and good* spell or similar effect. It ends for all creatures affected by this waif's Aura of Abandonment, if the waif's unfinished business is resolved. Simply destroying the waif is not enough to break the effect.

Ethereal Sight. The waif can see 60 feet into the Ethereal Plane when it is on the Material Plane, and vice versa.

Incorporeal Movement. The waif can move through other creatures and objects as if they were difficult terrain. It takes 5 (1d10) force damage if it ends its turn inside an object.

Sympathetic Armor. The waif adds its Charisma modifier to its armor class.

Actions

Blood-Chilling Touch. *Melee Spell Attack:* +6 to hit, reach 5 ft., one target. *Hit:* 13 (3d6 + 3) necrotic damage.

Etherealness. The waif enters the Ethereal Plane from the Material Plane, or vice versa. It is visible on the Material Plane while it is in the Border Ethereal, and vice versa, yet it can't affect, or be affected by, anything on the other plane.

Reactions

Desperate Scream (Recharge 5-6). When the waif is targeted by an attack, harmful spell, or similar ability, it can emit an ear-piercing scream that resonates with a wave of psychic energy. Each creature within 30 feet of the waif, that can hear it, must make a DC 14 Wisdom saving throw. On a failed save, a creature takes 22 (5d8) psychic damage and is stunned until the end of their next turn. On a success, the creature takes half as much damage and isn't stunned.

The souls of those who died from neglect or abandonment, **lingering waifs** project a feeling of mistrust towards adults—those who should have cared for it in life—transforming them, in the minds of those affected, into the evil monsters they appeared as to the waif. The influence of a waif can cause children to become reclusive, or flee their homes, perhaps becoming waifs in turn. While an adult will cease to be affected once the ghost is put to rest, a child might never fully recover.

A waif's tether to the world of the living typically revolves around its guardians, whether it be avenging itself upon its abusers, or seeking to reunite with absent parents.

DREADFUL SPIRIT

Medium undead, any alignment

Armor Class 14
Hit Points 88 (16d8 + 16)
Speed 0 ft., fly 40 ft.

STR	DEX	CON	INT	WIS	CHA
8 (-1)	19 (+4)	12 (+1)	11 (+0)	15 (+2)	18 (+4)

Saving Throws Con +4
Damage Resistances acid, fire, lightning, thunder; bludgeoning, piercing, and slashing from nonmagical weapons
Damage Immunities cold, necrotic, poison
Condition Immunities charmed, exhaustion, frightened, grappled, paralyzed, petrified, poisoned, prone, restrained
Senses darkvision 60 ft., passive Perception 12
Languages the languages it knew in life
Challenge 8 (3,900 XP)

Ethereal Sight. The spirit can see 60 feet into the Ethereal Plane when it is on the Material Plane, and vice versa.

Incorporeal Movement. The spirit can move through other creatures and objects as if they were difficult terrain. It takes 5 (1d10) force damage if it ends its turn inside an object.

ACTIONS

Multiattack. The spirit can use its Horrifying Visage. It then attacks with its Blood-Chilling Touch.

Blood-Chilling Touch. *Melee Spell Attack:* +7 to hit, reach 5 ft., one target. *Hit:* 21 (5d6 + 4) necrotic damage, or 28 (7d6 + 4) necrotic damage, if the target is frightened.

Etherealness. The spirit enters the Ethereal Plane from the Material Plane, or vice versa. It is visible on the Material Plane while it is in the Border Ethereal, and vice versa, yet it can't affect, or be affected by, anything on the other plane.

Horrifying Visage. Creatures within 60 feet of the spirit, other than undead, that can see it must succeed on a DC 15 Wisdom saving throw, or be frightened for 1 minute. While frightened in this way, a target has disadvantage on saving throws against possession by the spirit. A frightened target can repeat the saving throw at the end of each of its turns, ending the frightened condition on itself on a success. If a target's saving throw is successful, or the effect ends for it, the target is immune to this spirit's Horrifying Visage for the next 24 hours.

Possession (Recharge 6). One humanoid, that the spirit can see within 5 feet of it, must succeed on a DC 15 Charisma saving throw or be possessed by the spirit; the spirit then disappears, and the target is incapacitated and loses control of its body. The spirit now controls the body, but the target is still aware of its surroundings. The spirit can't be targeted by any attack, spell, or other effect, except ones that turn undead, and it retains its alignment, Intelligence, Wisdom, Charisma, and immunity to being charmed and frightened. It otherwise uses the possessed target's statistics, but doesn't gain access to the target's knowledge, class features, or proficiencies.

The possession lasts until the body drops to 0 hit points or takes an amount of radiant damage from a single hit equal to the spirit's current hit points. The possession also ends if the spirit is turned, or forced out, by a *dispel evil and good* spell or similar effect, or the spirit ends the effect as a bonus action. When the possession ends, the spirit reappears in an unoccupied space within 5 feet of the possessed creature. The target is immune to this spirit's Possession for 24 hours after succeeding on the saving throw, or after the possession ends.

TORTURED SOUL
Medium undead, any alignment

Armor Class 14
Hit Points 88 (16d8 + 16)
Speed 0 ft., fly 40 ft.

STR	DEX	CON	INT	WIS	CHA
8 (-1)	19 (+4)	12 (+1)	11 (+0)	15 (+2)	18 (+4)

Saving Throws Con +4
Damage Resistances acid, fire, lightning, thunder; bludgeoning, piercing, and slashing from nonmagical weapons
Damage Immunities cold, necrotic, poison
Condition Immunities charmed, exhaustion, frightened, grappled, paralyzed, petrified, poisoned, prone, restrained
Senses darkvision 60 ft., passive Perception 12
Languages the languages it knew in life
Challenge 8 (3,900 XP)

Ethereal Sight. The tortured soul can see 60 feet into the Ethereal Plane when it is on the Material Plane, and vice versa.

Incorporeal Movement. The tortured soul can move through other creatures and objects as if they were difficult terrain. It takes 5 (1d10) force damage if it ends its turn inside an object.

ACTIONS

Multiattack. The tortured soul can use its Horrifying Visage. It then makes two attacks with its Prisoner's Chains.

Prisoner's Chains. *Melee Spell Attack*: +7 to hit, reach 15 ft., one target. *Hit:* 13 (2d8 + 4) necrotic damage. If the target is a creature, and the tortured soul doesn't have two other creatures charmed, it must succeed on a DC 15 Charisma saving throw, or be charmed by the tortured soul. While charmed in this manner, the creature is restrained, even if normally immune to the restrained condition. If the tortured soul moves, charmed creatures move with them, remaining a maximum distance of 15 feet away from the tortured soul.

The charm effect ends if an effect, other than the tortured soul's own movement, moves the tortured soul more than 15 feet away from the charmed creature or vice versa. At the end of each of its turns, a charmed creature can repeat the saving throw, ending the effect on itself on a success.

Etherealness. The tortured soul enters the Ethereal Plane from the Material Plane, or vice versa. It is visible on the Material Plane while it is in the Border Ethereal, and vice versa, yet it can't affect, or be affected by, anything on the other plane.

Horrifying Visage. Creatures within 60 feet of the tortured soul, other than undead, that can see it must succeed on a DC 15 Wisdom saving throw, or be frightened for 1 minute. A frightened target can repeat the saving throw at the end of each of its turns, ending the frightened condition on itself on a success. If a target's saving throw is successful or the effect ends for it, the target is immune to this tortured soul's Horrifying Visage for the next 24 hours.

Necromancers typically favor corporeal undead, trusting to the brawn of a zombie, or the obedience of a skeleton, to do their bidding. However, sometimes the spirits of the dead are enthralled, either as servants, bridges to the ethereal, or as sources of power to tap for ongoing rituals. The chains of these **tortured souls** bind them to service, preventing them from possessing living beings, but enabling them to ensnare the spirits of their enemies.

RELENTLESS HAUNT
Medium undead, any alignment

Armor Class 15
Hit Points 121 (22d8 + 22)
Speed 0 ft., fly 40 ft.

STR	DEX	CON	INT	WIS	CHA
8 (-1)	21 (+5)	12 (+1)	12 (+1)	15 (+2)	20 (+5)

Saving Throws Con +5
Damage Resistances acid, fire, lightning, thunder; bludgeoning, piercing, and slashing from nonmagical weapons
Damage Immunities cold, necrotic, poison
Condition Immunities charmed, exhaustion, frightened, grappled, paralyzed, petrified, poisoned, prone, restrained
Senses darkvision 60 ft., passive Perception 12
Languages the languages it knew in life
Challenge 12 (8,400 XP)

Ethereal Sight. The haunt can see 60 feet into the Ethereal Plane when it is on the Material Plane, and vice versa.

Incorporeal Movement. The haunt can move through other creatures and objects as if they were difficult terrain. It takes 5 (1d10) force damage if it ends its turn inside an object.

ACTIONS

Multiattack. The haunt can use its Horrifying Visage. It then attacks with its Blood-Chilling Touch. Alternatively, the haunt can make two Fling Object attacks.

Blood-Chilling Touch. *Melee Spell Attack:* +9 to hit, reach 5 ft., one target. Hit: 26 (6d6 + 5) necrotic damage.

Fling Object (Requires Possessed Object). *Ranged Weapon Attack:* +9 to hit, range 50 ft. (measured from the object's space), one target. *Hit:* 13 (2d8 + 5) damage if the object is Medium, 11 (2d6 + 5) damage if the object is Small, or 7 (1d4 + 5) damage if the object is Tiny. The damage type depends on the shape of the object. If the object has sharp points, it deals piercing damage, if it has a cutting edge, it deals slashing damage, otherwise the object deals bludgeoning damage. Weapons and pieces of ammunition always deal the type of damage that they would deal when wielded normally. A flung object is no longer possessed.

Etherealness. The haunt enters the Ethereal Plane from the Material Plane, or vice versa. It is visible on the Material Plane while it is in the Border Ethereal, and vice versa, yet it can't affect, or be affected by, anything on the other plane.

Horrifying Visage. Creatures within 60 feet of the haunt, other than undead, that can see it must succeed on a DC 17 Wisdom saving throw, or be frightened for 1 minute. A frightened target can repeat the saving throw at the end of each of its turns, ending the frightened condition on itself on a success. If a target's saving throw is successful, or the effect ends for it, the target is immune to this haunt's Horrifying Visage for the next 24 hours.

Object Possession. The haunt possesses up to six Medium or smaller objects of its choice, that are in the Material Plane, within 60 feet of it that are not being worn or carried. Each object remains possessed until the haunt relinquishes possession of it, leaves the Material Plane, or the object is more than 60 feet away from the haunt. The haunt can independently move each possessed object up to 40 feet in any direction immediately after using this ability, or as an action on subsequent turns. While possessed, objects can be suspended in the air. Additionally, after possessing objects, the haunt can choose to make one Fling Object attack as a bonus action.

The haunt can never possess more than 6 objects at once. If the haunt uses this ability again, while possessing objects, it must choose any number of objects to relinquish in order to be able to possess any others.

Possession (Recharge 6). One humanoid, that the haunt can see within 5 feet of it, must succeed on a DC 17 Charisma saving throw, or be possessed by the haunt; the haunt then disappears, and the target is incapacitated and loses control of its body. The haunt now controls the body, but the target is still aware of its surroundings. The haunt can't be targeted by any attack, spell, or other effect, except ones that turn undead, and it retains its alignment, Intelligence, Wisdom, Charisma, and immunity to being charmed and frightened. It otherwise uses the possessed target's statistics, but doesn't gain access to the target's knowledge, class features, or proficiencies.

The possession lasts until the body drops to 0 hit points or takes an amount of radiant damage from a single hit equal to the haunt's current hit points. The possession also ends if the haunt is turned, or forced out, by a *dispel evil and good* spell or similar effect, or the haunt ends the effect as a bonus action. When the possession ends, the haunt reappears in an unoccupied space within 5 feet of the possessed creature. The target is immune to this haunt's Possession for 24 hours after succeeding on the saving throw, or after the possession ends.

LEGENDARY ACTIONS

The haunt can take 3 legendary actions, choosing from the options below. Only one legendary action option can be used at a time, and only at the end of another creature's turn. The haunt regains spent legendary actions at the start of its turn.

Reconstitute. The haunt rolls again to recharge its Possession ability.

Fling. The ghost makes one Fling Object attack.

Deathly Strafe (Costs 2 Actions). The haunt moves up to half its flying speed. If it passes through another creature's space, it can make an attack with its Blood-Chilling Touch against the first hostile creature it passes through.

Possess (Costs 3 Actions). The haunt uses its Possession ability. It can only use this legendary action if use of its Possession ability is available.

My Esteemed Editor,

While it was not the story you were looking for, I have found one nonetheless. Should it be of interest to the Gazette's readers, I will now relate the circumstances that acquainted me with the monster hunter, Thaddeus Loach.

Having arrived in the provinces, as you requested, I found the war done, the people content, and a dearth of stimulation. However, having been told by your honored self to return with a story or not at all (for which you displayed an obvious preference), I seated myself in a parochial tavern by the name of The Tavern (for the village had but one), paid for a watery ale (for their wine selection was "both"), and reflected on my misery.

It was around my third tankard of the stuff that a local halfling, sunburnt from the fields, sauntered over with unearned confidence and asked, gesturing with a grubby paw at my quill and ink, if I was "one o' them fancy writer types". As I began to respond, he continued with what he, no doubt, considered a knowing smirk to his fellows back at his table. "'Cause if'n it's a real story you be lookin' for, go to the old farmhouse up on the hill." He offered to guide me, proffering a stubby hand for payment, but I declined, confident as I was in my ability to find my way around a village whose notable buildings could be counted on one hand and still have fingers enough 'tae pick yer hooter' (to borrow an earthy, dwarven phrase).

The farmhouse, as it transpired, was a fire-gutted ruin, home to a few intrepid sparrows and little else, truly notable only for its being the sole stone structure in the village (the rest being wattle-and-daub). Within the wreckage of collapsed beams and ashes, in what might have been a dining room, was a rough cairn, a colourless and papery bouquet of what might have been wildflowers propped up against it.

"He put them there," said a voice in the back of my head. "After."

I immediately knew this unbidden thought to be true, much as one accepts, unquestioningly, the logic of a dream (my unconscious mind was, perhaps, emboldened by the ale, poor as it was). Looking back, it seems obvious that the thought was not my own. At the time, the distinction was lacking.

It was as I reached down to investigate the flowers closer that the room briefly caught fire.

This, I knew with the same certainty, was no illusion or trick, and nor was that same voice which I now heard shrieking in mortal agony, melding with my own as the flames began to lick my cracking, bubbling skin.

Consciousness returned to me piece by piece in a fog of confused memory. I did not truly take in the images at the time, but Thaddeus introduced me, after the fact, to the process of automatic writing, which follows.

A curt dismissal, an outstretched stubby hand, a falling lantern, her ladyship rises from her desk to tell me I shall never be worthy of her son, the flame catches on bone-dry rushes, an infant howls, "What could you possibly offer him that we could not?", a tiny fist clutches in vain at my shawl, an ink bottle shatters on the floor of a jolting cart, the love of my life avoids my eye as the world bursts into flames.

I moved slowly, I recall, my mind sluggishly trying to keep pace, like trying to run through treacle while suffering from a bad head cold, and all in flashes, like a half-remembered night of drunkenness. I remember picking up the knife (though I don't remember where from), I remember dragging my feet along a road as it turned from rutted mud to paving slabs, I remember the glimpse of a familiar door, and starting towards it, when a rough hand grabbed my shoulder, turning me.

"Your child. Here," growled a voice. I grabbed at what they offered, hungrily, and felt as though I had simultaneously emerged from the surface of a deep, cold lake, and been punched very hard in the stomach. My vision cleared, revealing a pair of vomit-covered boots, and a crudely stitched doll, stuffed with sticks, clutched in my hands.

"Keep hold of that. Mistletoe and hazel. Some powdered silver," explained the stranger. "Simple charm. Should buy us a little time, but not much."

"Time?"

"You were headed towards the house?" he barrelled over my attempt at a question.

"I–"

"Let's pay them a visit. And don't worry about the boots. They've seen worse."

The stranger seized me by the arm and marched me towards the door of an old manor house that had recently seemed very familiar for reasons which now escaped me. He gave the door a sharp rap. After what felt like minutes (my head was still swimming), the door was opened by a man who had bid farewell to his fifties some time ago, and whose threadbare robes had, perhaps, not been changed since. Though apparently unfamiliar both to myself and my new companion, I felt a lurch in my chest at the sight of him as he peered at us and, again, the sensation of cold depths rushing up to meet me. Fearing I might vomit again, I remained silent.

My companion glanced between the two of us, as if working out a sum, before greeting the old man and asking if his father was at home.

"You can talk to him if you wish." The man's manner of speech suggested an upbringing of some privilege. "He seems to enjoy the company, but he doesn't speak much himself these days, and what he does say makes less and less sense."

He led us through the hallway which, like the man himself, gave the impression of much-diminished grandeur, and into the parlour, where a high-backed chair sat facing the fire beneath a moth-eaten boar's head.

"Some people to see you, father," the man bellowed towards the chair as we approached. The chair gave no reply. We drew closer, and could now see the wizened form seated upon it: an ancient, shrunken figure whose skin (shot through with blue veins, like a good cheese) looked to have been made for someone considerably larger, staring slack-facedly into the dwindling fire.

As his gaze turned absently to me, something sharpened in him, as if years suddenly melted away. The ghost of a young man flickered to life behind his clouded eyes, staring at me with stunned recognition. Again, cold depths rushed up to me, almost irresistible this time.

"Do you know what you have to do?" my companion murmured in my ear.

"What? No I–"

"Not you. I'm sorry, this might not be entirely pleasant."

With that, the doll was yanked unceremoniously from my hands, and I surrendered to the depths.

I am aware that I began to speak with a voice quite different from my own, but recall only a few fragments of what happened next (I relive them most nights, though cannot recall them past waking). Thaddeus related most of the following details, as one might describe the goings-on of birds in one's garden; a situation, to him, mildly interesting but, ultimately, of little consequence.

It seems that, as soon as the doll was taken out of my hands, the spirit that had lodged rent-free in my mind, took full control of my faculties and immediately started to shriek her indignation at the ancient figure in the chair.

"You took him from me!" I remember (or think I remember) her screaming. "You took him from me and you left me to die!"

The man recognized her immediately, as if I wasn't there at all. He shrunk back from her as she tried to strike him with my fists. Thaddeus held us back. He told me, after, that he had asked me (her?) if this was what I wanted, and told us to look at the man in the chair. I remember looking into his eyes, through hers. Behind decades of sadness and guilt, behind the broken, old man sat slumped in the chair, was a dashing youth full of sheer joy at seeing me again. Thaddeus told me of how my grip slackened on his arm. I stopped trying to fight my way to him. The man reached out a shaking hand towards me.

"Dorothea," he whispered, in prayer-like wonder. "Not a day goes by that I don't... I should have been stronger for you, denied them, not you... When I heard what happened after we... if it weren't for the boy... if it weren't for our son... I couldn't have gone on." He faltered, tears rolling down his wizened face, and then looked right back into my eyes.

"I'm sorry," he muttered. "I'm so, so sorry."

I came to, my hand resting on his. For a wonderful moment I felt entirely at peace, and then darkness took me. My companion picked me up like I was naught but a ragdoll myself and carried me out, telling the son that his father seemed to be feeling better and that maybe they should talk.

"What else did you say to him?" I asked, back in the same flea-bitten tavern I'd had the misfortune of arriving in earlier that day. Disoriented by the worst headache I had ever experienced (and I've had more than my fair share), I had allowed him to set me down on a bench and buy me a cup of something brown and wet which claimed to be tea.

"Told him who I was," he sniffed at the tankard in front of him, shrugged, and took a gulp.

"Right. And who is that, exactly?"

"Thaddeus Loach," said Thaddeus Loach.

"So you're some sort of ghost expert, Mr. Loach?"

"Thaddeus. Yeah, something like that. Sometimes it's ghosts."

Seizing immediately on the opportunity thus presented, I explained that I was in need of stories for the Gazette, and asked if I might accompany him on his next assignment, to chronicle his deeds for our readers. He grunted in what I can only assume was assent, though glanced down at his yet-unwashed boots.

One thing remained: I asked Thaddeus how he had explained our unusual conversation and my subsequent unconsciousness to the man's son.

"Told him you were absolutely steaming drunk and I had to get you home." The ghost of a half-smile crossed his weather-beaten face. "Too many spirits."

Ghouls & Ghasts

he stench hangs thick in the still air: putrefaction allowed to ferment and grow angry in the dank darkness. Wet gulping is punctuated by the cracking of old bones, as something gorges itself in the shadows. With a grunt, a hunched shape separates itself from the mound of carrion and turns, pale bulging eyes glinting with the dying light. Any semblance of humanity in the face is lost as the jaw gapes wider and wider: a jagged cavity of stinking rot and ravenous hunger.

Ever voracious, ghouls stalk the catacombs, battlefields, and charnel heaps to feast on rotting flesh.

Their physiology varies significantly but, on the whole, ghouls have pallid, translucent skin, with layers of muscle and bones glimpsed beneath, sometimes giving the impression of a corpse. Their fleshless limbs hold a deceptive, wiry strength, and their often-emaciated forms can swell considerably when gorged with flesh. Beyond these commonalities, individual ghouls can appear wildly different, as a result of their reproductive strategy, with some bearing fleshy wings, grotesquely hulking musculature, or even taking on a macabre semblance of human form.

Ghouls are reliant mostly on their sense of smell; they can pick up the scent of a carcass from miles away, and beneath several feet of earth. It is theorized they communicate to each other with pheromones; indeed, some use these pheromones as a natural weapon, producing a noxious odor which can incapacitate living creatures. However, most ghouls possess at least limited vision and, despite their hatred of the sun, those rare ghouls that are active during the day have been observed watching carrion birds in order to locate corpses. Despite common wisdom that suggests otherwise, ghouls are not harmed by sunlight; they simply prefer to forage under the cover of darkness.

Given a modest food source, a ghoul can be relatively benign, content to eat until the supply is exhausted before moving on to search for more. Being undead, they do not digest their meals in the usual sense, but the fermenting flesh aids in the development of larval ghouls. For this reason, if food is plentiful and they are allowed to gorge themselves, they become more of a threat, as their numbers swell. When plague and death stalk the land, ghouls are sure to follow, and the local populace learns quickly to burn their dead, or are overcome as the ghoul population expands.

ORIGIN

Though ghouls are undoubtedly undead, they are not the raised forms of corpses. Instead, they might be more accurately described as an entirely different form of life. It has been suggested that ghouls originate from another plane entirely, one where such life is common, and they have been drawn to ours through the cracks between worlds by the promise of food. Regardless of their origins, upon arrival, they spread quickly and can overrun an area in little time, if an infestation is not checked.

Ghouls reproduce by implanting a larva into a host body. While rotting corpses are preferred, ghouls are not fussy about the exact nature of the host, and some have even been known to make use of their paralyzing abilities to keep a living victim sedate in their lair (such forethought on the ghoul's part is, thankfully, rare). The larval ghoul absorbs their nutrients passively, at first, but soon develops jaws and begins feeding in earnest. The feasting ghoul matures quickly and so, when a lot of easy prey becomes available at the same time (for instance, after a battle), the ghoul population can explode almost overnight.

A curious quirk of ghouls, presumably due to their other-worldly nature, is their ability to gradually take on the physical, and even mental, traits of creatures that they feed upon. Additionally, the creature that serves as host for an implanted larva further shapes the ghoul that emerges from what's left of their harvested remains.

Over generations, this can alter different strains of ghoul dramatically. Ghouls have a marked preference for humanoid flesh, explaining their overall humanoid forms, but some differ from the norm, having gestated within significantly larger corpses, or those with unusual features, such as wings. After many generations of intelligent hosts, ghoul behavior can become more complex (these more cunning ghouls are sometimes distinguished as 'ghasts'), and some achieve near-human levels of intelligence, even gaining the power of speech and controlling their lesser brethren's development by providing them with specific foodstuffs, in much the same way livestock are bred for specific tasks.

A common myth is that a creature who indulges in cannibalism will, over time, become a ghoul themself. While mostly apocryphal, it is possible that a creature consuming the flesh of its own kind, where a ghoul has also fed, could ingest an amount of the ghoul's saliva (and, thus, their mutagenic properties) in a sufficient enough amount to trigger a physiological change over time.

ENVIRONMENT

Ghouls gather where there is a ready supply of flesh, and are able to derive nutrition from any flesh, no matter how decayed, even gnawing at old bones, long bereft of meat. They are tolerant of other ghouls, and group together where there is ample food, but will wander their separate ways when the supply runs low.

Ghouls prefer the dark. When they find outdoor food supplies, they will den during the day in a nearby cave, or burrow, and emerge to feed at night. When they find, or drag, a source of food to a sheltered underground location, they will feed day and night, only stopping when threatened, out of food or, most worryingly, ready to implant larvae. A ghoul's lair is strewn with splinters of bone from its feeding, and may contain the paralyzed bodies of its victims (or what remains of them) if it is in good enough condition to breed.

Most commonly associated with graveyards, crypts, and mausoleums, ghouls can also be found wandering the wilds. Wandering ghouls must resort to hunting and eating fresh meat more often than their more sedentary kin, and some develop a taste for it.

Rumors have always existed of ghoul cities, with tales of towers of bones, and living beings relegated to livestock. While feasible, given the existence of intelligent ghouls, the first-hand reports are rare and jumbled; clearly coming from minds too disorganized to give a full report of their experiences, if they ever even happened. Rather than crafting settlements in our own world, it is entirely possible these tales come from glimpses of the ghouls' home plane which, assuming ghouls themselves are representative, would be enough to drive even the most ordered mind to madness.

ROLEPLAYING GHOULS

Ghouls are unsophisticated, and driven almost entirely by their supernatural hunger, but most are, at least, as intelligent as dogs, and some significantly more so. While this might lead some to hope that a ghoul can be reasoned with, the truth is that, more often than not, this intelligence merely makes them more efficient hunters, less likely to fall for the simple traps which would, for example, outwit a zombie. Most ghouls are able to speak, to an extent, though commonly only know a few, disjointed words (such as 'hungry', 'food', or 'yummy').

Ghasts are of a more sophisticated bent, though feeding is still their main drive. A recently-fed ghast might have the foresight to allow a small amount of food to escape its clutches for the promise of greater reward later, a level of planning beyond most of its underlings.

COMBAT TACTICS

Most ghouls will only seek out living prey when they are gorged enough to breed, and will otherwise stick to easier foodstuffs which will not fight back. Ghouls on the hunt will aim to ambush lone targets, aiming to quickly paralyse a victim and drag it back to their lair (or devour it on the spot, if the coast is clear), and are uninterested in fighting beyond that point, unless they are attacked in a manner that would stop their flight.

Ghouls show an animalistic survival instinct, and will generally flee if a foe puts up a significant defense, but may tail prey at a distance, especially if other food is scarce.

While they do not work together as such, ghouls are often drawn together to the same food sources, and are cunning enough to capitalize on the opportunity to attack as a group. Bands of ghouls will attempt to paralyze as many different targets as possible, and may squabble over the spoils, should they outnumber their prey.

The more intelligent forms of ghoul will often use their baser brethren much like attack animals, caring little for their wellbeing and happy to sacrifice them should it benefit the grander strategy. These ghouls tend to be more selective of their victims, choosing to devour or abduct those which would best suit their collective's evolution.

GHOUL ENCOUNTERS

d12	CR	Encounter
1	1	**Sparse Leftovers:** 7 Stunted Ghouls
2	2	**Meager Snack:** 1 Ghoul Gnawer, 5 Stunted Ghouls
3	3	**Macabre Picnic:** 4 Ghoul Gnawers, 3 Stunted Ghouls
4	6	**Bloody Lunch:** 1 Dread Ghoul, 6 Ghoul Gnawers
5	7	**Cave Carrion:** 4 Eyeless Stalkers, 2 Garghouls
6	10	**Twisted Supper:** 1 Nighthulk, 2 Garghouls, 1 Bilemaw Ghoul, 2 Eyeless Stalkers, 7 Stunted Ghouls
7	11	**Odious Dinner:** 3 Ferocious Ghasts, 6 Bitter Ghasts
8	12	**Horrid Meal:** 1 Ravenous Creeper, 2 Dread Ghouls, 5 Ghoul Gnawers
9	14	**Morbid Banquet:** 1 Ghoul Sophisticate, 3 Dread Ghouls, 2 Ghoul Gnawers, 1 Nighthulk
10	17	**Inviting Revelry:** 6 Infectious Raveners, 4 Bitter Ghasts
11	19	**Dread Feast:** 1 Noxious Devourer, 1 Infectious Ravener, 2 Ferocious Ghasts, 2 Nighthulks, 3 Bilemaw Ghouls
12	21	**Massacre's Spoils:** 1 Ghast Warlord, 6 Ferocious Ghasts, 3 Nighthulks, 6 Garghouls, 6 Bitter Ghasts

Stunted Ghoul

Medium undead, chaotic evil

Armor Class 11
Hit Points 9 (2d8)
Speed 30 ft.

STR	DEX	CON	INT	WIS	CHA
10 (+0)	13 (+1)	10 (+0)	4 (−3)	8 (−1)	4 (−3)

Damage Immunities poison
Condition Immunities charmed, exhaustion, poisoned
Senses darkvision 60 ft., passive Perception 9
Languages Common
Challenge 1/4 (50 XP)

Keen Smell. The ghoul has advantage on Wisdom (Perception) checks that rely on smell.

Actions

Bite. *Melee Weapon Attack:* +1 to hit, reach 5 ft., one creature *Hit:* 4 (1d6 + 1) piercing damage.

Claws. *Melee Weapon Attack:* +3 to hit, reach 5 ft., one target. *Hit:* 3 (1d4 + 1) slashing damage. If the target is a creature other than an elf or undead, it must succeed on a DC 9 Constitution saving throw, or be stunned until the end of the ghoul's next turn. Creatures that are immune to being paralyzed are immune to this ability.

Generations of poor feeding can lead to weedy and **stunted ghouls**; less of a physical threat, perhaps, but often starving and desperate.

Ghoul Gnawer

Medium undead, chaotic evil

Armor Class 12 (natural armor)
Hit Points 22 (4d8 + 4)
Speed 30 ft.

STR	DEX	CON	INT	WIS	CHA
12 (+1)	13 (+1)	12 (+1)	7 (−2)	11 (+0)	6 (−2)

Damage Immunities poison
Condition Immunities charmed, exhaustion, poisoned
Senses darkvision 60 ft., passive Perception 10
Languages Common
Challenge 1 (200 XP)

Keen Smell. The gnawer has advantage on Wisdom (Perception) checks that rely on smell.

Actions

Multiattack. The gnawer makes two attacks: one with its bite, and one with its claws.

Bite. *Melee Weapon Attack:* +3 to hit, reach 5 ft., one creature. *Hit:* 4 (1d6 + 1) piercing damage.

Claws. *Melee Weapon Attack:* +3 to hit, reach 5 ft., one target. *Hit:* 3 (1d4 + 1) slashing damage. If the target is a creature other than an elf or undead, it must succeed on a DC 10 Constitution saving throw, or be paralyzed for 1 minute. The target can repeat the saving throw at the end of each of its turns, ending the effect on itself on a success.

"They enter through the cracks, we are told, as rats will enter a kitchen, drawn by the crumbs. However, will rats not also flee a sinking ship? What wave are they running from, I wonder, and how long before it swallows us all?"

—Ylandro Movag, naturalist

Garghoul

Medium undead, chaotic evil

Armor Class 12
Hit Points 40 (9d8)
Speed 30 ft. fly 60 ft.

STR	DEX	CON	INT	WIS	CHA
14 (+2)	15 (+2)	10 (+0)	5 (-3)	12 (+1)	6 (-2)

Damage Immunities poison
Condition Immunities charmed, exhaustion, poisoned
Senses darkvision 60 ft., passive Perception 11
Languages Common
Challenge 2 (450 XP)

Keen Smell. The garghoul has advantage on Wisdom (Perception) checks that rely on smell.

Actions

Multiattack. The garghoul makes two attacks: one with its bite, and one with its claws.

Bite. *Melee Weapon Attack:* +2 to hit, reach 5 ft., one creature. *Hit:* 9 (2d6 + 2) piercing damage.

Claws. *Melee Weapon Attack:* +4 to hit, reach 5 ft., one target. *Hit:* 7 (2d8 + 2) slashing damage. If the target is a creature other than an elf or undead, it must succeed on a DC 10 Constitution saving throw, or be paralyzed for 1 minute. If the target is paralyzed, the garghoul can grapple it as a bonus action (escape DC 12) and the garghoul can't use its claws against another target. The target can repeat the saving throw at the end of each of its turns, ending the paralysis effect on itself on a success.

A rare strain, winged **garghouls** are, more commonly, predatory in their behavior, snatching away their paralyzed victims to devour at leisure.

Ghastly Ghouly, what do you hear?
I hear him shout and scream with fear.
Ghastly Ghouly, what do you smell?
I smell his blood and his guts as well.
Ghastly Ghouly what will you do?
Boil his bones for a ghoulish stew.
Ghastly Ghouly coming for you!

-counting chant for a children's game.
Ghastly Ghouly must keep their eyes closed and is roundly mocked until they can catch and 'eat' one of the other children.

EYELESS STALKER
Medium undead, chaotic evil

Armor Class 14
Hit Points 55 (10d8 + 10)
Speed 40 ft., climb 30 ft.

STR	DEX	CON	INT	WIS	CHA
13 (+1)	18 (+4)	13 (+1)	6 (-2)	14 (+2)	≤ (-3)

Skills Perception +6, Stealth +5
Damage Vulnerabilities thunder
Damage Immunities poison
Condition Immunities blinded, charmed, exhaustion, poisoned
Senses blindsight 30ft. or 10 ft. while deafened (blind beyond this radius), passive Perception 16
Languages Common, Undercommon
Challenge 3 (700 XP)

Keen Hearing and Smell. The eyeless stalker has advantage on Wisdom (Perception) checks that rely on hearing or smell.

Sightless Awareness. The eyeless stalker can make a Wisdom (Perception) check as a bonus action.

ACTIONS

Bite. *Melee Weapon Attack:* +4 to hit, reach 5 ft., one creature. *Hit:* 11 (2d6 + 4) piercing damage.

Claws. *Melee Weapon Attack:* +6 to hit, reach 5 ft., one target. *Hit:* 9 (2d4 + 4) slashing damage. If the target is a creature other than an elf or undead, it must succeed on a DC 12 Constitution saving throw, or be paralyzed for 1 minute. The target can repeat the saving throw at the end of each of its turns, ending the effect on itself on a success.

Blind ghouls are relatively common in deep cave networks, where constant darkness and rapid proliferation quickly make eyes useless.

We examined the skin and organs closely and, finding no evidence of barbs, stings, or any other vector for paralytic venom, nor specialized organs for the production of electricity, were forced to conclude that the ghoul's power of paralysis is magical in nature. It has been conjectured that ghouls can control their noxious scent, and a focused flare of stench can incapacitate a foe, but this hypothesis is unsatisfactory as it does not factor in elven immunity (given that elves are, on the whole, keen of senses, it would make sense for them to be more susceptible than most, were this the case).

As an aside, the stomach tissue was found to be incredibly elastic, able to distend to frankly ludicrous proportions and retain structural integrity. Tales of ghoulish gluttony are not exaggerated in this regard.

-Kassin Yan, student of anatomy, dissection notes

DREAD GHOUL
Medium undead, chaotic evil

Armor Class 15 (natural armor)
Hit Points 75 (10d8 + 30)
Speed 30 ft.

STR	DEX	CON	INT	WIS	CHA
15 (+2)	18 (+4)	16 (+3)	7 (-2)	13 (+1)	6 (-2)

Saving Throws Con +5, Int +0, Wis +3
Damage Immunities poison
Condition Immunities charmed, exhaustion, poisoned
Senses darkvision 60 ft., passive Perception 11
Languages Common
Challenge 4 (1,100 XP)

Keen Smell. The ghoul has advantage on Wisdom (Perception) checks that rely on smell.

ACTIONS

Multiattack. The ghoul makes two attacks: one with its bite, and one with its claws.

Bite. *Melee Weapon Attack:* +4 to hit, reach 5 ft., one creature. *Hit:* 11 (2d6 + 4) piercing damage.

Claws. *Melee Weapon Attack:* +6 to hit, reach 5 ft., one target. *Hit:* 9 (2d4 + 4) slashing damage. If the target is a creature other than an elf or undead, it must succeed on a DC 11 Constitution saving throw, or be paralyzed for 1 minute. The target can repeat the saving throw at the end of each of its turns, ending the effect on itself on a success.

Bilemaw Ghoul
Medium undead, chaotic evil

Armor Class 13
Hit Points 90 (12d8 + 36)
Speed 30 ft.

STR	DEX	CON	INT	WIS	CHA
13 (+1)	16 (+3)	16 (+3)	8 (-1)	14 (+2)	6 (-2)

Damage Immunities poison
Condition Immunities charmed, exhaustion, poisoned
Senses blind, tremorsense 30 ft., passive Perception 12
Languages Common, Undercommon
Challenge 5 (1,800 XP)

Keen Smell. The bilemaw has advantage on Wisdom (Perception) checks that rely on smell.

Actions

Bite. *Melee Weapon Attack:* +6 to hit, reach 5 ft., one creature. *Hit:* 10 (2d6 + 3) piercing damage, plus 9 (2d8) poison damage. If the target is a creature, it is grappled. Until this grapple ends, the target is restrained and the bilemaw can't use its bite against another target.

Claws. *Melee Weapon Attack:* +6 to hit, reach 5 ft., one target. *Hit:* 8 (2d4 + 3) slashing damage. If the target is a creature other than an elf or undead, it must succeed on a DC 14 Constitution saving throw, or be paralyzed for 1 minute. The target can repeat the saving throw at the end of each of its turns, ending the effect on itself on a success.

Bile (Recharge 5-6). The bilemaw spews black bile in a 20-foot cone. Creatures in the area must make a DC 14 Constitution saving throw, taking 27 (6d8) poison damage and becoming poisoned for 1 minute on a failed save. On a success, the creature takes half as much damage and isn't poisoned. While poisoned in this way, a creature has disadvantage on saving throws against being paralyzed.

An amalgam of traits from various sources, **bilemaw ghouls** constrict live prey with their prehensile tongues while toxins in their saliva wear away at their defenses.

NIGHTHULK
Large undead, chaotic evil

Armor Class 13 (natural armor)
Hit Points 76 (9d10 + 27)
Speed 40 ft.

STR	DEX	CON	INT	WIS	CHA
19 (+4)	10 (+0)	17 (+3)	2 (-4)	9 (-1)	6 (-2)

Damage Immunities poison
Condition Immunities charmed, exhaustion, poisoned
Senses darkvision 60 ft., passive Perception 9
Languages understands Common, but can't speak
Challenge 6 (2,300 XP)

Keen Smell. The nighthulk has advantage on Wisdom (Perception) checks that rely on smell.

Thrash (1/Turn). The nighthulk gains advantage on a single melee weapon attack roll this turn. If the attack hits, it deals double damage.

ACTIONS

Multiattack. The nighthulk makes two attacks: one with its bite, and one with its claws.

Bite. *Melee Weapon Attack:* +7 to hit, reach 5 ft., one creature. *Hit:* 18 (4d6 + 4) piercing damage.

Claws. *Melee Weapon Attack:* +7 to hit, reach 5 ft., one target. *Hit:* 13 (2d8 + 4) slashing damage. If the target is a creature other than an elf or undead, it must succeed on a DC 13 Constitution saving throw, or be paralyzed for 1 minute. The target can repeat the saving throw at the end of each of its turns, ending the effect on itself on a success.

While **nighthulks** can arise spontaneously where ghouls feast on the flesh of oxen, apes, or other muscular beasts, they are most common where a more intelligent ghoul, or ghast, guides their development to aid their own dominance.

Ghouls as attack dogs, my foot! Not content with merely gorging on the flesh of corpses I had yet to raise, the wretched things started work on my zombies, and a fine feast they had for themselves too, before I was able to quell them.

–Silsaethyn Drakenir, necromancer

Ghoul Sophisticate

Medium undead, neutral evil

Armor Class 16 (natural armor)
Hit Points 165 (22d8 + 66)
Speed 30 ft.

STR	DEX	CON	INT	WIS	CHA
15 (+2)	20 (+5)	17 (+3)	11 (+0)	15 (+2)	13 (+1)

Saving Throws Con +7, Int +4, Wis +6
Skills History +4, Perception +6, Persuasion +5
Damage Immunities poison
Condition Immunities charmed, exhaustion, poisoned
Senses darkvision 60 ft., passive Perception 15
Languages Common
Challenge 10 (5,900 XP)

Connoisseur. Whenever the sophisticate hits a living humanoid with its bite attack, it regains a number of hit points equal to the damage dealt by the attack.

Deadly Fencer. The sophisticate's rapier attacks deal an additional 1d8 damage (included in the attack).

Keen Smell. The sophisticate has advantage on Wisdom (Perception) checks that rely on smell.

Actions

Multiattack. The sophisticate makes three attacks: one with its rapier, one with its bite, and one with its claws.

Rapier. *Melee Weapon Attack:* +9 to hit, reach 5 ft., one creature. *Hit:* 14 (2d8 + 5) piercing damage.

Bite. *Melee Weapon Attack:* +9 to hit, reach 5 ft., one creature. *Hit:* 15 (3d6 + 5) piercing damage.

Claws. *Melee Weapon Attack:* +9 to hit, reach 5 ft., one target. *Hit:* 12 (3d4 + 5) slashing damage. If the target is a creature other than an elf or undead, it must succeed on a DC 16 Constitution saving throw, or be paralyzed for 1 minute. The target can repeat the saving throw at the end of each of its turns, ending the effect on itself on a success.

Legendary Actions

The sophisticate can take 3 legendary actions, choosing from the options below. Only one legendary action option can be used at a time, and only at the end of another creature's turn. The sophisticate regains spent legendary actions at the start of its turn.

Attack. The sophisticate makes a rapier attack.

Passe Arriere. The sophisticate makes a melee attack, with disadvantage, against a target within reach, and then moves up to half its speed without provoking opportunity attacks from the target of the attack.

Bite (Costs 2 Actions). The sophisticate makes a bite attack.

Whether the **sophisticate** should be considered a ghoul or a ghast is a matter for debate. It is clearly a cut above the average ghoul in intelligence, and will manipulate lesser ghouls to serve its own agendas, but said agendas are still, primarily, the simple acquisition of food. Like a twisted, cannibalistic gourmand, sophisticates commonly have particular tastes when it comes to flesh, sending out their minions to abduct specific races, or individuals, they believe taste especially delicious.

RAVENOUS CREEPER

Medium undead, chaotic evil

Armor Class 16 (natural armor)
Hit Points 170 (20d8 + 80)
Speed 30 ft.

STR	DEX	CON	INT	WIS	CHA
17 (+3)	20 (+5)	19 (+4)	7 (-2)	15 (+2)	6 (-2)

Saving Throws Con +5, Int +0, Wis +3
Skills Perception +6
Damage Immunities poison
Condition Immunities charmed, exhaustion, poisoned
Senses darkvision 60 ft., passive Perception 16
Languages Common
Challenge 10 (5,900 XP)

Keen Smell. The creeper has advantage on Wisdom (Perception) checks that rely on smell.

ACTIONS

Multiattack. The creeper makes two attacks: one with its bite and one with its claws.

Bite. *Melee Weapon Attack:* +9 to hit, reach 5 ft., one creature
Hit: 14 (2d8 + 5) piercing damage.

Claws. *Melee Weapon Attack:* +9 to hit, reach 5 ft., one target.
Hit: 12 (2d6 + 5) slashing damage. If the target is a creature other than an elf or undead, it must succeed on a DC 16 Constitution saving throw, or be paralyzed for 1 minute. The target can repeat the saving throw at the end of each of its turns, ending the effect on itself on a success.

LEGENDARY ACTIONS

The creeper can take 3 legendary actions, choosing from the options below. Only one legendary action option can be used at a time, and only at the end of another creature's turn. The creeper regains spent legendary actions at the start of its turn.

Crawl. The creeper moves up to half its speed without provoking opportunity attacks.

Bite. The creeper makes a bite attack.

Claw (Costs 2 Actions). The creeper makes a claw attack.

In the frozen wastes, they tell of men who, in the sunless days in the depths of winter when the flesh of beasts is hard to come by, eat of their own dead. It is not an abomination to them, but a simple act of survival. Should the rumors be believed though, there are some who develop a taste for it. Not content with cold meat, they hunt the living, snatching them from their camps and dragging them into the icy night, never to be seen again.

Ghouls, of course, may be a part of the phenomenon, but one should not dismiss entirely the darkness which can be unlocked by desperation.

—Finthareal Ellanwe, 'Whispers from the Grave'

Bitter Ghast

Medium undead, chaotic evil

Armor Class 14 (natural armor)
Hit Points 33 (6d8 + 6)
Speed 30 ft.

STR	DEX	CON	INT	WIS	CHA
15 (+2)	15 (+2)	12 (+1)	11 (+0)	14 (+2)	8 (-1)

Damage Resistances necrotic
Damage Immunities necrotic, poison
Condition Immunities charmed, exhaustion, poisoned
Senses darkvision 60 ft., passive Perception 12
Languages Common
Challenge 2 (450 XP)

Keen Smell. The ghast has advantage on Wisdom (Perception) checks that rely on smell.

Stench. Any creature that starts its turn within 5 feet of the ghast must succeed on a DC 12 Constitution saving throw, or be poisoned until the start of its next turn. On a successful saving throw, the creature is immune to the ghast's Stench for 24 hours.

Turning Rage. If the ghast succeeds on a saving throw against an effect that turns undead, it falls into a frenzy until the end of its next turn. While frenzied, the ghast has advantage on attack rolls and saving throws against being charmed or frightened and effects that turn undead.

Actions

Multiattack. The ghast makes two attacks: one with its bite, and one with its claws.

Bite. *Melee Weapon Attack:* +4 to hit, reach 5 ft., one creature. *Hit:* 6 (1d8 + 2) piercing damage.

Claws. *Melee Weapon Attack:* +4 to hit, reach 5 ft., one target. *Hit:* 5 (1d6 + 2) slashing damage. If the target is a creature other than an undead, it must succeed on a DC 12 Constitution saving throw, or be paralyzed for 1 minute. The target can repeat the saving throw at the end of each of its turns, ending the effect on itself on a success.

Ferocious Ghast

Medium undead, chaotic evil

Armor Class 15 (natural armor)
Hit Points 90 (12d8 + 36)
Speed 30 ft.

STR	DEX	CON	INT	WIS	CHA
19 (+4)	17 (+3)	16 (+3)	11 (+0)	14 (+2)	8 (-1)

Saving Throws Con +6, Int +3, Wis +5
Damage Resistances necrotic
Damage Immunities poison
Condition Immunities charmed, exhaustion, poisoned
Senses darkvision 60 ft., passive Perception 12
Languages Common
Challenge 5 (1,800 XP)

Keen Smell. The ghast has advantage on Wisdom (Perception) checks that rely on smell.

Stench. Any creature that starts its turn within 10 feet of the ghast must succeed on a DC 13 Constitution saving throw, or be poisoned until the start of its next turn. On a successful saving throw, the creature is immune to the ghast's Stench for 24 hours.

Turning Rage. If the ghast succeeds on a saving throw against an effect that turns undead, it falls into a frenzy until the end of its next turn. While frenzied, the ghast has advantage on attack rolls and saving throws against being charmed or frightened and effects that turn undead.

Actions

Multiattack. The ghast makes two attacks: one with its bite, and one with its claws.

Bite. *Melee Weapon Attack:* +6 to hit, reach 5 ft., one creature. *Hit:* 13 (2d8 + 4) piercing damage.

Claws. *Melee Weapon Attack:* +6 to hit, reach 5 ft., one target. *Hit:* 11 (2d6 + 4) slashing damage. If the target is a creature other than an undead, it must succeed on a DC 13 Constitution saving throw, or be paralyzed for 1 minute. The target can repeat the saving throw at the end of each of its turns, ending the effect on itself on a success.

Ghouls gather in the low places, where the foulest humors pool. In their stinking lairs, they vomit up their spawn to hatch in corpses or in living folk; it matters not so long as they be unmoving. The spawn burrow deep and, loathsome foetuses they are, devour as they grow until, surfeited, they burst from these wombs of flesh to breed anew.

-Elbrecht Inske, 'Beasts of this World'

INFECTIOUS RAVENER

Medium undead, chaotic evil

Armor Class 15 (natural armor)
Hit Points 135 (18d8 + 54)
Speed 30 ft.

STR	DEX	CON	INT	WIS	CHA
19 (+4)	17 (+3)	17 (+3)	11 (+0)	14 (+2)	16 (+3)

Saving Throws Con +6, Int +3, Wis +5
Damage Resistances necrotic
Damage Immunities poison
Condition Immunities charmed, exhaustion, poisoned
Senses darkvision 60 ft., passive Perception 12
Languages Common
Challenge 7 (2,900 XP)

Keen Smell. The ravener has advantage on Wisdom (Perception) checks that rely on smell.

Scent of Hunger. Any humanoid creature that starts its turn within 15 feet of the ravener must succeed on a DC 15 Wisdom saving throw, or be charmed by the ravener for 1 minute. While charmed, the creature is overcome by a hunger for the flesh of the living that clouds all of its other mental capacities. The charmed creature must use all of its movement to move toward the nearest paralyzed or unconscious humanoid, or humanoid corpse, along the shortest available safe path, and use its action to attempt to eat the humanoid. For each turn the charmed creature spends eating, the targeted humanoid takes 1d6 piercing damage.

If the charmed creature is not aware of any humanoid corpse or paralyzed or unconscious humanoid within 120 feet, it must instead attack the nearest humanoid, other than itself, with the intent to kill and eat the target.

At the end of each of its turns, a charmed creature can repeat the saving throw, ending the effect on itself on a success.

If a creature succeeds on the saving throw, or the effect ends for it, the creature is immune to the ravener's Scent of Hunger for 24 hours.

Turning Rage. If the ravener succeeds on a saving throw against an effect that turns undead, it falls into a frenzy until the end of its next turn. While frenzied, the ravener has advantage on attack rolls and saving throws against being charmed or frightened and effects that turn undead.

ACTIONS

Multiattack. The ravener makes two attacks: one with its bite, and one with its claws.

Bite. *Melee Weapon Attack:* +7 to hit, reach 5 ft., one creature. *Hit:* 13 (2d8 + 4) piercing damage.

Claws. *Melee Weapon Attack:* +7 to hit, reach 5 ft., one target. *Hit:* 11 (2d6 + 4) slashing damage. If the target is a creature other than an undead, it must succeed on a DC 13 Constitution saving throw, or be paralyzed for 1 minute. The target can repeat the saving throw at the end of each of its turns, ending the effect on itself on a success.

Rather than simply being nauseating, the pheromones of the **infectious ravener** drive those around it into a frenzy, briefly granting them a ghoul-like hunger for flesh.

Noxious Devourer
Medium undead, chaotic evil

Armor Class 16 (natural armor)
Hit Points 204 (24d8 + 96)
Speed 30 ft.

STR	DEX	CON	INT	WIS	CHA
20 (+5)	19 (+4)	19 (+4)	12 (+1)	15 (+2)	9 (-1)

Saving Throws Con +8, Int +5, Wis +6
Skills Perception +6
Damage Resistances necrotic
Damage Immunities poison
Condition Immunities charmed, exhaustion, poisoned
Senses darkvision 60 ft., passive Perception 16
Languages Abyssal, Common
Challenge 12 (8,400 XP)

Keen Smell. The devourer has advantage on Wisdom (Perception) checks that rely on smell.

Stench. Any creature that starts its turn within 15 feet of the devourer must succeed on a DC 14 Constitution saving throw, or be poisoned until the start of its next turn. On a successful saving throw, the creature is immune to the devourer's Stench for 24 hours.

Turning Rage. If the devourer succeeds on a saving throw against an effect that turns undead, it falls into a frenzy until the end of its next turn. While frenzied, the devourer has advantage on attack rolls and saving throws against being charmed or frightened and effects that turn undead.

Actions

Multiattack. The devourer makes two attacks: one with its bite, and one with its claws.

Bite. *Melee Weapon Attack:* +9 to hit, reach 5 ft., one creature. *Hit:* 18 (3d8 + 5) piercing damage.

Claws. *Melee Weapon Attack:* +9 to hit, reach 5 ft., one target. *Hit:* 15 (3d6 + 5) slashing damage. If the target is a creature other than an elf or undead, it must succeed on a DC 14 Constitution saving throw, or be paralyzed for 1 minute. The target can repeat the saving throw at the end of each of its turns, ending the effect on itself on a success.

Legendary Actions

The devourer can take 3 legendary actions, choosing from the options below. Only one legendary action option can be used at a time, and only at the end of another creature's turn. The devourer regains spent legendary actions at the start of its turn.

Crawl. The devourer moves up to half its speed, without provoking opportunity attacks.

Bite. The devourer makes a bite attack.

Claw (Costs 2 Actions). The devourer makes a claw attack.

"I have seen the bone spires, the clouds of white dust kicked up by bloodied feet. I have seen the pens of carrion under the scab-red sky. I have seen the feasts and festivals, the revelries of marrow, blood and bile, flesh and sinew. I have known hunger, and I have known that most horrible satiation."

-ravings of a vagrant, known only as 'Hunger'

Ghast Warlord

Medium undead, chaotic evil

Armor Class 18 (plate armor)
Hit Points 187 (26d8 + 104)
Speed 30 ft.

STR	DEX	CON	INT	WIS	CHA
20 (+5)	19 (+4)	19 (+4)	15 (+2)	17 (+3)	13 (+1)

Saving Throws Con +9, Int +7, Wis +8
Skills Insight +8, Perception +8, Persuasion +6
Damage Resistances necrotic
Damage Immunities poison
Condition Immunities charmed, exhaustion, poisoned
Senses darkvision 60 ft., passive Perception 18
Languages Abyssal, Common
Challenge 16 (15,000 XP)

Keen Smell. The warlord has advantage on Wisdom (Perception) checks that rely on smell.

Legendary Resistance (3/Day). If the warlord fails a saving throw, it can choose to succeed instead.

Stench. Any creature that starts its turn within 15 feet of the warlord must succeed on a DC 18 Constitution saving throw, or be poisoned until the start of its next turn. On a successful saving throw, the creature is immune to the warlord's Stench for 24 hours.

Turning Rage. If the warlord succeeds on a saving throw against an effect that turns undead, it falls into a frenzy until the end of its next turn. While frenzied, the warlord has advantage on attack rolls and saving throws against being charmed or frightened and effects that turn undead.

Actions

Multiattack. The warlord makes four attacks: one with its bite, one with its claws, and two with its longsword.

Bite. *Melee Weapon Attack:* +10 to hit, reach 5 ft., one creature. *Hit:* 18 (3d8 + 5) piercing damage.

Longsword. *Melee Weapon Attack:* +10 to hit, reach 5 ft., one creature. *Hit:* 9 (1d8 + 5) slashing damage.

Claws. *Melee Weapon Attack:* +10 to hit, reach 5 ft., one target. *Hit:* 15 (3d6 + 5) slashing damage. If the target is a creature other than an elf or undead, it must succeed on a DC 16 Constitution saving throw, or be paralyzed for 1 minute. The target can repeat the saving throw at the end of each of its turns, ending the effect on itself on a success.

Legendary Actions

The warlord can take 3 legendary actions, choosing from the options below. Only one legendary action option can be used at a time, and only at the end of another creature's turn. The warlord regains spent legendary actions at the start of its turn.

Attack. The warlord makes a longsword attack.

Coordinated Assault. The warlord, or one of its ghoul or ghast allies within 60 feet that can see or hear it, moves up to its speed. The warlord can't choose the same creature to move more than once between its turns.

Claw (Costs 2 Actions). The warlord makes a claw attack.

Particularly intelligent ghasts can amass quite a following of lesser ghouls, and often intentionally breed exotic strains. These **warlords** often hold delusions of grandeur, taking over castles, or complexes of ruins, as their lair.

My Venerated Editor,

Life on the road is not exactly the daring adventure I had hoped for, involving as it does rather more relieving oneself amongst bushes and developing blisters in previously unknown crevices of one's anatomy. Weeks bereft of featherbed, washbasin, and a good meal were beginning to wear on me. Thaddeus seemed no worse for it but, then again, Thaddeus had started the journey resembling nothing so much as a leather bag full of old meat.

When we began to pass fellow travelers on the road, I began to take hope, and when those travelers spoke of a local festival taking place in a nearby village, that hope blossomed into a glorious dream of artisanal cheeses, mulled wine, and some kind of roasted beast. Thaddeus was resistant to the idea until I suggested that, surely, in a gathering of such multitude, trouble was sure to rear its head. My companion's reluctance thus deftly swept aside, we rode on, towards this fabled land of plenty.

The initial signs were all rather encouraging; as we crossed a brook into the village, chickens scattering before us, we were confronted by a riot of activity. A band, accompanied by dancers, blared away, gamely attempting to mask their lack of practice with sheer enthusiasm. Stalls crowded every thoroughfare, packed with talismans, brightly woven blankets, ointments, oils, pigments, and, finally, clay bottles of what could only be wine.

I approached, already fishing in my coin purse for the few coppers I expected to pay for a provincial vintage, when the wine seller asked me, with something of a melancholy smile, who I was buying for.

"Why, myself of course, though I may give a sip to my traveling companion. A small one."

"Oh," she said, with perhaps a hint of offense, "this wine is not for the living."

Registering my confusion, she explained to me (as one might to a child) that the festival was known as 'The Turning of the Bones', an honoring of the dead that took place every three years, somewhat delayed, and therefore highly anticipated this time around, due to the war. Bizarrely, the high point of the ritual seems to be exhuming the corpses of their ancestors, changing their shrouds and clothing, washing and grooming them, and giving them offerings of food and drink. Truly, the minds of rustic folk continue to baffle me; the thought of inviting great-grandmother around for afternoon tea fills me with nothing but horror (although, in all fairness, she was an incorrigible harridan while alive; perhaps the tomb has improved her).

Thus informed, we allowed ourselves to be jostled by the crowd towards the village's disproportionately well-appointed cemetery; indeed, I suspected that the vast majority of the dead contained therein enjoyed better lodgings than their living kin. In front of one of the larger mausoleums, a matronly figure, distinguished by her robes and heavy chain as the local mayor, was in the throes of a welcoming speech.

"I stand now on the steps of the tomb where I too shall rest one day, and ask those who came before me for their blessing and their wisdom. While they are remembered, theirs is life eternal. The honor of beginning proceedings is, as always, theirs." Her attendants peeled off and descended the stairs into the tomb. "Though I'm sure my mother will have a thing or two to say about the delivery of my speech when she comes out later!" She smiled broadly, and there was a smattering of polite laughter; I got the impression that this was not the (already weak) joke's first outing.

As her attendants began to re-emerge, empty-handed, whispering urgently in the mayor's ear, a murmur began to ripple through the assembled crowd. This, it seemed, could not bode well. I turned to Thaddeus, only to see him striding forwards, the crowd parting before him, and I had little choice but to attempt to tag along (with muttered "excuse me…"s and, "I do beg your pardon…"s, which Thaddeus had declined to indulge in). The mayor seemed shaken and pale as Thaddeus approached, beginning to resemble a corpse herself, but was nodding enthusiastically and gripping Thaddeus' hand with both of hers by the time I caught up.

"I am a professional, milady. Whatever is going on, I'll–"

"*We'll* get to the bottom of–," I cut in. I offered my hand. It was declined.

"*Myself and my assistant* will see to it," Thaddeus finished. "Come on."

And, with that, the aides stepped aside, allowing us through the doorway and down the stairs, into the dark of the tomb. The sound of the crowd was immediately muffled by the pressing stone, and the air grew cooler as we descended. Thaddeus reached into his pack, extracted two faintly glowing crystals, and handed one to me. The gloom was cast back, revealing a large chamber, the walls lined with long, low alcoves which, presumably, were designed to hold the venerated bodies of the deceased and, in that regard, were failing spectacularly. A few bits of ragged cloth littered the floor but, otherwise, it was empty. A hole, draped with cobwebs and large enough to crouch into, gaped in the corner, like the waiting maw of a large fish.

Thaddeus immediately set to, poking and prodding among the alcoves, finally withdrawing his hand, to reveal a viscous slime coating the tips of his fingers. This he rubbed and sniffed in the manner of a sommelier, before wiping it on his jacket and proclaiming, "Ghoul spit. Careful with that. Don't get it in your mouth."

I began to protest that I could see no conceivable instance in which that might be a possibility, but Thaddeus had already moved to the far corner of the chamber, peering into the hole. Before the fear of what he was about to do could fully manifest, he ducked into the tunnel beyond and, once again, I was carried along in his wake.

The tunnel was damp and smelled of meat that had begun to turn. Its walls were flaking soil, marked with rough gouges where its excavator had ripped its way through. Before long, my hand, which had been tracing the wall of the passage, was thrown with a horrible lurch into the darkness of an intersecting passage and, glancing about, it quickly became clear that a whole warren of tunnels honeycombed the entire graveyard.

After a few minutes, we came to an open space, another tomb, simpler perhaps, but far larger. As we straightened up and willed the cramp to leave our legs, Thaddeus tapped me on the shoulder and gestured to the hunched figure we now unexpectedly shared a space with.

I had, I recalled, seen a ghoul in a travelling grotesquery in my youth. It growled and stank and frightened me dreadfully when it threw itself against the bars, though my brother insisted it was simply a man, shaved bald and with teeth filed to points. I began to suspect my brother was correct in his assertion; the creature before me was very little like a man indeed.

Its waxy skin, through which layers of greyish, inhuman muscle could be seen, was sagging and wrinkled, hanging in folds around its bulging eyes, and at the corners of its fang-lined maw. It looked more like a half-melted waxwork than a living creature as it stared at us, gulping in befuddlement at the intrusion.

"No wonder there are so many tunnels," I posited. "That thing's ancient, it could have been down here for centuries."

Thaddeus merely grunted suspiciously.

In an instant, the creature was gone, loping away down a passageway with speed belied by its withered form. Of more concern than its sudden escape was its howl that reverberated all around us, echoing and building. Wordless though it was the meaning was clear; a warning, and a call to arms.

Ghouls poured from every dank hole, a tide of nauseating flesh, spilling over each other in a chaos of limbs and gnashing teeth. I was rooted to the spot, barely able to comprehend the scene before me, let alone compose a fitting eulogy for my short adventuring career, when they stopped short, pacing and growling a perimeter some feet away (though, I can assure you, they were close enough that the stench was overwhelming - a truly unpleasant blend of spoiled meat and an animalistic musk all of their own). I turned to Thaddeus for guidance, only to find neither hide, hair, nor boots of him.

A figure made its way through the throng; more upright, its head held high on a bull's neck of corded muscle. It wore something which I might charitably describe as a toga, fashioned, it would seem, from the browning remnants of funereal shrouds. The other ghouls parted before it, some going so far as to bow their misshapen heads to the ground. Its face was horribly human until it opened its mouth, near splitting its head in two.

"Human." Its voice was marrow slurped from a splintered bone; a harsh, clacking gurgle.

I wasn't sure how it wanted me to respond. I bowed my head in what I hoped was a respectful gesture. "Yes?" I squeaked.

It seemed to find this amusing, its horrid maw splitting yet further until it vomited out a sickening shriek that, from context, I assume served as a laugh. It turned to survey its audience, circling my frozen form. As it passed by, the ghouls began to mimic its awful laugh, though there was no humor in their blank expressions. Once it had completed its circuit, it held out a claw for silence and turned its attention back to me.

"This human submits to us like they shall all submit! It dares not look into our eyes, for it knows they are everywhere. It knows not of how little time its kind have left on this world, of how they all shall soon fall to the mercy of The Shrouded One." It adjusted the ragged linen across its shoulders, which had begun to slip as its gesticulations grew wilder.

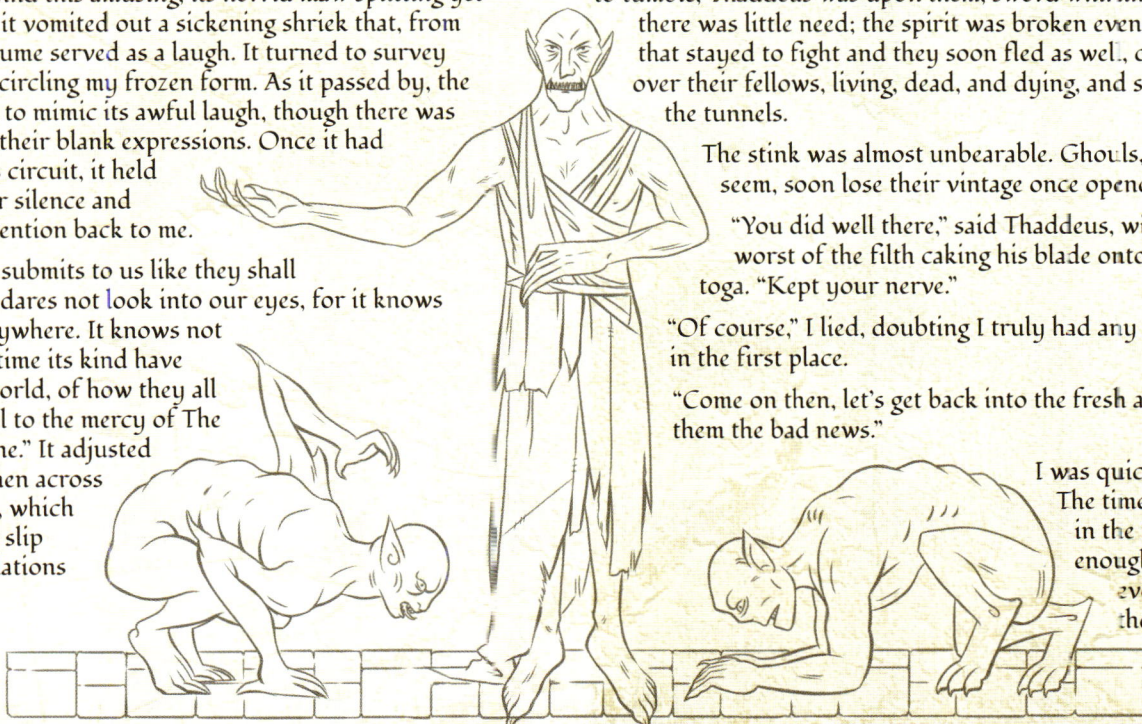

As I glanced up, I saw a dark figure stalking around the periphery of the chamber. Thaddeus held a finger to his lips.

"Erm," I began, defiantly. "We won't submit easily. We'll fight you."

"Fight, yes. Die, yes."

This seemed rather definitive but, for the first time in our adventures, I felt I had a role to play in the hunt (however minor), and Thaddeus needed more time.

"And then what?"

"Great feasting we shall have after the rising, once the world is cleansed. All those unworthy for the great host shall be our meat." The ghoul seemed to be growing impatient, and eager for its next meal.

"Well," I said, now desperate to fill time. "Some people are bland, aren't they? Very bland. Or sweet! A little sweetness is lovely, but some people I've met are positively saccharine. Many are too rich, I'm sure you'll agree. Some, though, are bitter, and sour, and tough as old boots, and for gods' sake Thaddeus, what are you waiting for?!"

Darting forward with a fluidity and grace quite unlike his usual demeanor, Thaddeus struck, a pouncing wildcat with a claw of quicksilver. The blade struck true and bit deep, near cleaving the beast's arm from its shoulder. It turned to him with a terrible shriek, its other arm already raising to slash its unseen assailant with ragged, filth-encrusted claws, but Thaddeus' sword flashed up to meet them. The surrounding ghouls seemed to boil over each other in their eagerness to defend their king but, before they could reach him, before its severed claws could even hit the ground, it was over; with another slash, Thaddeus removed the beast's head.

It fell to the dirt with a dull and final thud, frozen in an expression of indignant surprise and, with that, the fight seemed to go out of the ghoulish throng. Even as their king's corpse began to tumble, Thaddeus was upon them, sword whirling, but there was little need; the spirit was broken even in the few that stayed to fight and they soon fled as well, clambering over their fellows, living, dead, and dying, and scattering into the tunnels.

The stink was almost unbearable. Ghouls, it would seem, soon lose their vintage once opened.

"You did well there," said Thaddeus, wiping the worst of the filth caking his blade onto the ghoul's toga. "Kept your nerve."

"Of course," I lied, doubting I truly had any nerve to keep in the first place.

"Come on then, let's get back into the fresh air and give them the bad news."

I was quick to agree. The time we had spent in the tunnels was enough to make even me long for the road.

LICHES

The corpse moves with an elegance and precision belied by its withered form. Desiccated flesh clings tight to the contours of underlying bone. In the pits of its long-empty sockets, twin stars glow with inscrutable intelligence. As it raises a staff in a skeletal, ring-encrusted hand, power thrums, oppressive and heavy in the air. Its jaw opens, and words pour forth, ancient and terrible, harsh and profane, powerful and forbidden. It is without pity, without remorse, without soul.

Eternal life. It is a lofty goal, one sought by many. Few, however, possess the ability to achieve it, and fewer still are willing, desperate, or mad enough to pay the price. Those few who do may, through various roads, attain lichdom.

Liches hold an almost-legendary status in common myth, like dragons, as beings so far outside the average experience that they may as well not exist, so small are the chances of ever encountering one. While stories of eternal monarchs ruling as gods on earth may have their roots in the occasional lich who takes an interest in human affairs, they could just as likely be spun from the propaganda of some forgotten empire. Destroying a phylactery (or something resembling a phylactery in all but name) is a common quest for heroes of legend though, rather than the blood and ritual scrolls of reality, said item might contain the creature's still-beating heart, or something similarly fanciful.

ORIGIN

Liches are, invariably, powerful magic users who, through foul craft, have prevented their souls from passing to the afterlife by use of phylacteries. Most liches were learned and studious in life, coming upon the necessary rituals through decades of study and experimentation, but this is not the only path. Other liches may have been influential cultists, wielding the power of evil gods or even demon lords. Though it is more common for such people to be consumed, or at least controlled, by their master in death, some are able to strike bargains or twist their allotted power to lichdom. Rarer still are blight liches, who manage to pervert the magic of nature itself into fuelling their unlife. The multifaceted deities of nature seem united in their hatred for undeath, and it takes a singularly powerful individual to so confound them.

The rituals themselves vary in detail, much as the different practitioners of magic differ in the details of their craft. Most commonly, the would-be lich spends years on preparatory rites, gradually embalming their own body in a similar manner to mummification, while also regularly performing rituals (or continually performing one enormous ritual of many stages - reports differ), binding a portion of their soul to the mortal realm within a phylactery, an object used as a vessel to store and protect the soul fragment. The preparations culminate in the imbibing of a magical poison while also sacrificing a living soul. It is believed that the lich's partial soul and that of the sacrifice, passing on at the same moment, allows the portion the lich has tethered to remain unnoticed by the higher powers.

The nature of the sacrifice seems almost a matter of personal taste. For some, it is a simple means to an end, using whatever being can be procured most expediently. Others view the sacrifice as an integral part of the ritual, forever tying the two souls together, and will only bestow this dubious honor on a person of importance, whether it be a faithful servant, or a hated rival. The patron of a profane lich might require their sacrifice be a loved one, as a test of faith, while blight liches might ensure their sacrifice's blood is drunk by the thirsting roots of a twisted tree.

A phylactery commonly takes the form of a large locket or small chest, though any container will serve the purpose if properly prepared along with the lich's preparation of its own body. At the very least, the phylactery must contain some of the lich's blood, though small scrolls of binding and warding (sometimes written in said blood) are common as well. This preparation makes a phylactery more durable than appearances might suggest, and it takes powerful magic to truly destroy one. Only the most confident or foolhardy lich wears or displays their phylactery openly; most keep them sealed away separately, commonly behind several layers of traps, within a remote location, or even a bespoke pocket-dimension.

Doubtless, most liches would make their phylacteries truly inaccessible were it not for the need to keep them fuelled with fresh souls. The fragment of the lich contained within the phylactery constantly feels the pull of the ethereal, the inexorable call towards death, which all bodiless souls experience as the proper way of things. Sacrificed souls bolster the phylactery, forming a cage from which escape is impossible.

Without a supply of souls to sustain it, a lich will begin to deteriorate both physically and mentally, losing what limited grip it had on sanity to begin with as its soul fragment begins to bleed into the afterlife. However, as the physical shell weakens, the magic holding it together begins to exude, increasing the lich's potency, though diminishing their fine control over it. Some liches intentionally delay the necessary sacrifices in order to maintain this heightened power as long as possible. A soul will fuel the phylactery for roughly the duration of the individual's remaining lifespan, so the soul of a young elf would be of far greater value than that of, for example, an elderly human.

Environment

Liches tend toward self-importance and grandiosity. Secure in the knowledge that they shall remain in this form for eternity, and keen to ensure that eternity is spent in comfort, most liches construct grand domiciles for themselves either before commencing their transformation ritual, or over the course of centuries afterwards. While unable to enjoy many of the luxuries of their surroundings in the traditional sense, the very knowledge that they are surrounded by finery, moldering and cobwebbed as it may be, brings something close to joy.

Dependant on their aims, liches may also be found in more utilitarian environments. If, for example, a lich was bent on controlling a settlement in secret, it may reside in the local crypts (potentially expanding and connecting disparate tombs into a city-spanning network).

Regardless, a lich's lair is likely to be unwelcoming to the living. Apart from the occasional sacrifice to be made to the phylactery, most liches have no interest in dealing with the living or being disturbed by would-be heroes interrupting their work by attempting to slay them, and have no need to come and go themselves, so making their home inaccessible with traps and hazards is of no consequence to them. Even the décor, being chosen by an insane undead, is unnerving and off-putting to the living, tending towards the macabre and the profane.

Roleplaying Notes

Liches retain much of their former personality and interests, though there tend to be some commonalities. Most liches share a penchant for grandiosity and selfishness, though where this is simply true of the sort of individual who would seek lichdom, or a change brought about by the transformation is difficult to say. The extreme focus exhibited by liches does seem to be a part of their condition; a complete disregard for anything which does not pertain to their study or ambitions.

A universal trait shared by all liches is an all-consuming arrogance, a belief that they are a supreme and exemplary being. After all, a lich will have killed at least one person in order to extend their lifespan; older liches may have killed thousands and seen the price worth paying. Not all believe themselves on the path to godhood, but it is certainly not unheard of for such megalomaniacal ambitions to manifest.

Some liches may appear civil, and a very rare few even seem to enjoy company (after centuries of solitude, any novelty must be a boon). There are few beings a lich would deem as an equal, however, and it would take an uncommonly powerful spellcaster to earn anything approaching respect. The best most mortals can hope for is to be treated as a useful servant, as a lich's respect is generally coupled with jealousy, paranoia, and plotting, and those not deemed useful are simply fuel for the phylactery.

All liches are, understandably, paranoid about their only real weakness - their phylactery, and contingencies to protect themselves in the event it is discovered occupy a not-insubstantial part of their time. A lich's arrogance in its schemes will usually enable them to project a front of haughty detachment but, should their phylactery be directly and unequivocally threatened, they will quickly lose any façade of civility or composure.

Combat Tactics

Liches are rarely caught unawares, given that they rarely leave their lairs, and said lairs are invariably designed in such a way as to give them warning, should there be any intrusion. Most liches have had decades, or centuries, to plan contingencies for multiple situations, including having an escape route - preferably one which also destroys any interlopers and the chance of their work falling into the wrong hands, such as bringing down the entire structure on top of their heads.

Clever and ruthless, liches will capitalize on any opportunity granted to them, fighting with no sense of honor or mercy – if their defences are so compromised that they are physically attacked, it is vital that none live to tell the tale.

While neutralizing the threat is a lich's priority, they will take victims alive if the opportunity presents itself. This is far from an act of clemency; having a stock of fresh souls, ready to be sacrificed to the phylactery when the time is right, is a matter of simple practicality.

Lich Encounters

d8	CR	Encounter
1	8	**Corpse Retinue:** 1 Profane Lich Neophyte, 6 Human Zombies, 1 Dwarf Zombie, 2 Elf Zombies, 1 Ogre Zombie
2	12	**Unholy Study:** 1 Apocryphal Lich Initiate, 2 Skeletal Dogs, 4 Skeleton Archers, 4 Skeleton Infantry, 8 Human Zombies, 1 Troll Zombie
3	20	**Deathblight:** 1 Blight Lich Adept, 3 Skeletal Minotaur Warriors, 4 Orc Zombies, 6 Hobgoblin Zombies, 2 Zombie Bears , 2 Ogre Zombies, 1 Troll Zombie
4	20	**Spiritual Congregation:** 1 Profane Lich Adept, 1 Spectral Raven, 2 Hateful Wraiths, 2 Deadly Specters, 4 Traversing Specters
5	23	**Necrobestiary:** 1 Blight Lich Magus, 2 Spectral Ravens, 2 Skeletal Hill Giants, 1 Skelephant, 4 Zombie Bears, 3 Zombie Oxen, 8 Skeletal Dogs
6	24	**Dracocrypt:** 1 Apocryphal Lich Magus, 1 Skeletal Dragon, 1 Spectral Dragon, 2 Young Zombie Dragons
7	24	**Cryptlord's Entourage:** 1 Apocryphal Lich Master, 1 Ghostly Stagecoach, 1 Adult Zombie Dragon, 2 Deadly Specters, 4 Skeleton Soldiers on Skeletal Riding Horses
8	25	**Bone Court:** 1 Profane Lich Master, 1 Skeletal Minotaur Warlord, 2 Skeletal Minotaur Warriors, 2 Bone Horrors, 8 Skeleton Pioneers, 8 Skeleton Marksmen

Demiliches

As a lich's body deteriorates, its remains bristle with unchecked magical potency. As this process ravages the lich's body, it gradually turns into what is known as a demilich.

The following templates can be applied to any lich.

Lesser Demilich

- Once only the lich's torso, head, and arms remain, it is known as a lesser demilich. The following changes apply to the lich:

- The lesser demilich's size is Small . Its Hit Dice become d6s. As a result, its hit point maximum is reduced by its Hit Dice.

- The lesser demilich's walking speed becomes 5 ft., but it magically gains a fly speed equal to its former walking speed. The demilich can hover. If the demilich is prevented from flying, for any reason, it falls prone and can't stand.

- The lesser demilich has an additional spell slot of each spell level that is no higher than half the maximum spell level it can cast.

Greater Demilich

- A greater demilich's body is all but annihilated and only the skull remains, flaring with magical currents:

- The greater demilich's size is Tiny. Its Hit Dice become d4s. As a result, its hit point maximum is reduced by twice its Hit Dice.

- The greater demilich's walking speed becomes 0 ft., and it magically gains a fly speed equal to its former walking speed. The greater demilich can hover. If the greater demilich is prevented from flying, for any reason, it falls prone and cannot stand up or crawl.

- The greater demilich has an additional spell slot of each spell level it can cast.

- The greater demilich's spells don't require somatic or material components.

- **Ethereal Touch.** When the greater demilich uses its Decomposing Touch or Paralyzing Touch attack, it delivers the attack with an ethereal hand, formed by its magic. The greater demilich doesn't physically touch the target, and thus isn't subjected to any effects caused by touching the target.

- **Commanding Touch.** The greater demilich can't wield weapons. If it has the Commanding Warhammer action, this becomes a melee spell attack, using its spell attack bonus. It deals 4 (1d8) additional necrotic damage, in place of the normal bludgeoning damage, and is delivered by an ethereal hand, formed from its magic.

Transcendent Demilich

- The lich's body has been consumed by its magic and turned into an inferno of pure magical force, shaped into a deathly visage of hatred, and commanded by the soul still trapped within its phylactery. All changes from the Greater Demilich template apply in addition to the following:

- The transcendent demilich's fly speed is no longer considered magical.

- **Incorporeal Movement.** The transcendent demilich can move through other creatures and objects as if they were difficult terrain. It takes 11 (2d10) force damage if it ends its turn inside an object.

- The transcendent demilich becomes immune to the grappled, petrified, prone, restrained, and unconscious conditions.

- Spells of levels no higher than half the transcendent demilich's maximum spell level can be cast at-will.

- **Antimagic Weakness.** The transcendent demilich can be directly targeted by a *dispel magic* spell, as if it were a magical effect. Instead of being dispelled, the lich must make a Charisma saving throw against the caster's spell save DC. On a failed save, the lich takes 3d10 force damage, plus 1d10 for each spell level higher than 3rd, or half as much damage on a successful saving throw.

- If the transcendent demilich starts its turn within an *antimagic field*, it takes 58 (9d12) force damage.

- A creature under the effect of a *dispel evil and good* spell can make melee spell attacks against the transcendent demilich that deal 1d12 force damage per level of the spell to the transcendent demilich on a hit.

- Whenever one of the transcendent demilich's spells is successfully countered by a *counterspell*, it must succeed on a Charisma saving throw against the caster's spell save DC, or become incapacitated until the end of its next turn.

APOCRYPHAL LICH NEOPHYTE
Medium undead, neutral evil

Armor Class 16 (natural armor)
Hit Points 88 (16d8 + 16)
Speed 30 ft.

STR	DEX	CON	INT	WIS	CHA
9 (-1)	14 (+2)	13 (+1)	17 (+3)	15 (+2)	16 (+3)

Saving Throws Con +4, Int +6, Wis +5
Skills Arcana +9, History +6, Perception +5
Damage Vulnerabilities radiant
Damage Resistances necrotic
Damage Immunities poison
Condition Immunities charmed, exhaustion, frightened, paralyzed, poisoned
Senses darkvision 120 ft., passive Perception 15
Languages Common, plus up to five other languages
Challenge 7 (2,900 XP)

Legendary Resistance (1/Day). If the neophyte fails a saving throw, it can choose to succeed instead.

Rejuvenation. If it has a phylactery, the destroyed neophyte gains a new body in 4d10 days, regaining 1 hit point and becoming active again. The new body appears within 5 feet of the phylactery.

Spellcasting. The neophyte is a 6th level spellcaster. Its spellcasting ability is Intelligence (spell save DC 14, +6 to hit with spell attacks). The neophyte has the following wizard spells prepared:

Cantrips (at will): *acid splash, mage hand, prestidigitation*

1st level (4 slots): *detect magic, magic missile, shield*

2nd level (3 slots): *detect thoughts, invisibility, mirror image*

3rd level (3 slots): *animate dead, dispel magic, fireball*

Turn Resistance. The neophyte has advantage on saving throws against any effect that turns undead.

ACTIONS

Paralyzing Touch. *Melee Spell Attack:* +6 to hit, reach 5 ft., one creature. *Hit:* 7 (2d6) cold damage, and the target must succeed on a DC 14 Constitution saving throw, or be paralyzed for 1 minute. A creature can repeat the saving throw at the end of each of its turns, ending the effect on itself on a success.

Apocryphal Lich Initiate

Medium undead, neutral evil

Armor Class 16 (natural armor)
Hit Points 93 (17d8 + 17)
Speed 30 ft.

STR	DEX	CON	INT	WIS	CHA
9 (-1)	15 (+2)	13 (+1)	18 (+4)	16 (+3)	17 (+3)

Saving Throws Con +5, Int +8, Wis +7
Skills Arcana +12, History +8, Perception +7
Damage Vulnerabilities radiant
Damage Resistances necrotic
Damage Immunities poison
Condition Immunities charmed, exhaustion, frightened, paralyzed, poisoned
Senses darkvision 120 ft., passive Perception 17
Languages Common, plus up to five other languages
Challenge 11 (7,200 XP)

Legendary Resistance (2/Day). If the initiate fails a saving throw, it can choose to succeed instead.

Rejuvenation. If it has a phylactery, the destroyed initiate gains a new body in 2d10 days, regaining 1 hit point and becoming active again. The new body appears within 5 feet of the phylactery.

Spellcasting. The initiate is a 9th level spellcaster. Its spellcasting ability is Intelligence (spell save DC 16, +8 to hit with spell attacks). The initiate has the following wizard spells prepared:

Cantrips (at will): *acid splash, mage hand, prestidigitation*

1st level (4 slots): *detect magic, magic missile, shield*

2nd level (3 slots): *detect thoughts, invisibility, mirror image*

3rd level (3 slots): *animate dead, dispel magic, fireball*

4th level (3 slots): *confusion, dimension door*

5th level (1 slot): *cone of cold, scrying*

Turn Resistance. The initiate has advantage on saving throws against any effect that turns undead.

Actions

Paralyzing Touch. *Melee Spell Attack:* +8 to hit, reach 5 ft., one creature. *Hit:* 7 (2d6) cold damage, and the target must succeed on a DC 15 Constitution saving throw, or be paralyzed for 1 minute. A creature can repeat the saving throw at the end of each of its turns, ending the effect on itself on a success.

APOCRYPHAL LICH ADEPT

Medium undead, neutral evil

Armor Class 17 (natural armor)
Hit Points 117 (18d8 + 36)
Speed 30 ft.

STR	DEX	CON	INT	WIS	CHA
10 (+0)	16 (+3)	14 (+2)	19 (+4)	17 (+3)	18 (+4)

Saving Throws Con +7, Int +9, Wis +8
Skills Arcana +14, History +9, Perception +8
Damage Resistances necrotic; bludgeoning, piercing, and slashing from nonmagical weapons
Damage Immunities poison
Condition Immunities charmed, exhaustion, frightened, paralyzed, poisoned
Senses truesight 120 ft., passive Perception 18
Languages Common, plus up to five other languages
Challenge 16 (15,000 XP)

Arcane Dismantlement. Whenever the adept successfully dispels or counters a spell with *dispel magic, counterspell,* or a similar spell, it can make an Intelligence (Arcana) check against a DC equal to the spell's level + the spell save DC of the spell's caster. On a success, the adept recovers an expended spell slot equal to, or less than, the dispelled spell's level.

Legendary Resistance (3/Day). If the adept fails a saving throw, it can choose to succeed instead.

Rejuvenation. If it has a phylactery, the destroyed adept gains a new body in 1d10 days, regaining half its hit points and becoming active again. The new body appears within 5 feet of the phylactery.

Spellcasting. The adept is a 13th level spellcaster. Its spellcasting ability is Intelligence (spell save DC 17, +9 to hit with spell attacks). The adept has the following wizard spells prepared:

Cantrips (at will): *acid splash, mage hand, prestidigitation*

1st level (4 slots): *detect magic, magic missile, shield*

2nd level (3 slots): *detect thoughts, invisibility, mirror image*

3rd level (3 slots): *animate dead, counterspell, dispel magic, fireball*

4th level (3 slots): *confusion, dimension door*

5th level (2 slots): *cone of cold, scrying*

6th level (1 slot): *disintegrate, globe of invulnerability*

7th level (1 slot): *plane shift*

Turn Resistance. The adept has advantage on saving throws against any effect that turns undead.

ACTIONS

Paralyzing Touch. *Melee Weapon Attack:* +9 to hit, reach 5 ft., one creature. *Hit:* 10 (3d6) cold damage, and the target must succeed on a DC 17 Constitution saving throw, or be paralyzed for 1 minute. A creature can repeat the saving throw at the end of each of its turns, ending the effect on itself on a success.

Encrusted locket

Silver, emeralds, ivory

Notes: Seller claimed this was the phylactery of the lich known as The Eternal Queen. Hinges suggest a large interior space, though I have been unable to open it to attest to the story's veracity.

Seller claimed the lich was defeated, but I swear I can hear it whispering.

File for resale. Urgently.

—Quranis Kuilanya, antiquarian, personal inventory

APOCRYPHAL LICH MAGUS

Medium undead, neutral evil

Armor Class 17 (natural armor)
Hit Points 135 (18d8 + 54)
Speed 30 ft.

STR	DEX	CON	INT	WIS	CHA
11 (+0)	16 (+3)	16 (+3)	20 (+5)	18 (+4)	19 (+4)

Saving Throws Con +10, Int +12, Wis +11
Skills Arcana +19, History +11, Perception +10
Damage Resistances cold, lightning, necrotic
Damage Immunities poison; bludgeoning, piercing, and slashing from nonmagical weapons
Condition Immunities charmed, exhaustion, frightened, paralyzed, poisoned
Senses truesight 120 ft., passive Perception 20
Languages Common, plus up to five other languages
Challenge 21 (33,000 XP)

Arcane Dismantlement. Whenever the magus successfully dispels or counters a spell with *dispel magic*, *counterspell*, or a similar spell, it can make an Intelligence (Arcana) check against a DC equal to the spell's level + the spell save DC of the spell's caster. On a success, the magus recovers an expended spell slot equal to or less than the dispelled spell's level.

Legendary Resistance (3/Day). If the magus fails a saving throw, it can choose to succeed instead.

Rejuvenation. If it has a phylactery, the destroyed magus gains a new body in 1d10 days, regaining all its hit points and becoming active again. The new body appears within 5 feet of the phylactery.

Spellcasting. The magus is an 18th level spellcaster. Its spellcasting ability is Intelligence (spell save DC 20, +12 to hit with spell attacks). The magus has the following wizard spells prepared:

Cantrips (at will): *acid splash, mage hand, prestidigitation*

1st level (4 slots): *detect magic, magic missile, shield*

2nd level (3 slots): *detect thoughts, invisibility, mirror image*

3rd level (3 slots): *animate dead, counterspell, dispel magic, fireball*

4th level (3 slots): *blight, confusion, dimension door*

5th level (3 slots): *cone of cold, scrying*

6th level (1 slot): *disintegrate, globe of invulnerability*

7th level (1 slot): *finger of death, plane shift*

8th level (1 slot): *dominate monster, power word stun*

9th level (1 slot): *power word kill*

Turn Resistance. The magus has advantage on saving throws against any effect that turns undead.

ACTIONS

Paralyzing Touch. *Melee Weapon Attack:* +12 to hit, reach 5 ft., one creature. *Hit:* 10 (3d6) cold damage, and the target must succeed on a DC 19 Constitution saving throw, or be paralyzed for 1 minute. A creature can repeat the saving throw at the end of each of its turns, ending the effect on itself on a success.

LEGENDARY ACTIONS

The magus can take 3 legendary actions, choosing from the options below. Only one legendary action option can be used at a time, and only at the end of another creature's turn. The magus regains spent legendary actions at the start of its turn.

Cantrip. The magus casts a cantrip.

Paralyzing Touch (Costs 2 Actions). The magus uses its Paralyzing Touch.

Sense Weakness (Costs 2 Actions). The magus telepathically probes a creature it can see, within the range of its telepathy, for its strengths and weaknesses. The target must succeed on a DC 19 Charisma saving throw, or the magus learns of the target's damage vulnerabilities, resistances, and immunities, as well as condition immunities and the exact number of hit points remaining.

Frightening Apocrypha (Costs 3 Actions). The magus telepathically focuses a stream of forbidden knowledge on one creature it can see within 20 feet of it. The target must succeed on a DC 19 Wisdom saving throw, or become frightened for 1 minute. While frightened, the creature has disadvantage on Intelligence, Wisdom, and Charisma saving throws against the magus' wizard spells. The frightened creature can repeat the saving throw at the end of each of its turns, ending the effect on itself on a success. If a target's saving throw is successful, or the effect ends for it, the target has advantage on Intelligence, Wisdom, and Charisma saving throws against the magus' spells until the next time it fails to save against one of them, and is immune to the magus' gaze for the next 24 hours.

I look back now on the path down which I may have embarked, and I feel sickened. Some of you reading this, I know, will have idly wondered at the idea of lichdom, as I did. But stop to think of the cost. Not the cost to oneself, for I know many who would be willing to pay any price for knowledge, myself included. No, a lich does not come into being simply through force of will and manipulation of the higher magics; each lich sits upon a throne of death. Not only must they kill in order to attain lichdom, but they must do so regularly to maintain it.

Think of these poor wretches. These are siblings, parents, friends, and children. Each had dreams, wants, plans, flaws. Within their ranks were scholars and warriors, heroes and villains, each one of them, with their own unique experience and view, the world shall never hear from again. Hundreds of souls reduced to tinder in the furnace of one monster's ambition.

–Kofran Weima, from the open letter, 'Why I Turned From Lichdom', published in Magister's Monthly

Apocryphal Lich Master

Medium undead, neutral evil

Armor Class 18 (natural armor)
Hit Points 150 (20d8 + 60)
Speed 30 ft.

STR	DEX	CON	INT	WIS	CHA
11 (+0)	18 (+4)	16 (+3)	22 (+6)	19 (+4)	20 (+5)

Saving Throws Str +7, Dex +11, Con +10, Int +13, Wis +11
Skills Arcana +18, History +13, Perception +11
Damage Resistances cold, lightning, necrotic
Damage Immunities poison; bludgeoning, piercing, and slashing from nonmagical weapons
Condition Immunities charmed, exhaustion, frightened, paralyzed, poisoned
Senses truesight 120 ft., passive Perception 21
Languages Common, plus up to six other languages, telepathy 60 ft.
Challenge 23 (50,000 XP)

Arcane Dismantlement. Whenever the master successfully dispels or counters a spell with *dispel magic, counterspell,* or a similar spell, it can make an Intelligence (Arcana) check against a DC equal to the spell's level + the spell save DC of the spell's caster. On a success, the master regains use of an expended spell slot equal to or less than the dispelled spell's level.

Forbidden Revelations. As a bonus action, the master projects eldritch knowledge to all creatures within range of its telepathy, overloading their senses with incomprehensible revelations. Creatures in range, that understand at least one language, must succeed on a DC 19 Wisdom saving throw, or take 9 (2d8) psychic damage and have disadvantage on attack rolls and ability checks until the start of the master's next turn.

Legendary Resistance (3/Day). If the master fails a saving throw, it can choose to succeed instead.

Rejuvenation. If it has a phylactery, the destroyed master gains a new body in 1d10 days, regaining all its hit points and becoming active again. The new body appears within 5 feet of the phylactery.

Spellcasting. The master is a 20th level spellcaster. Its spellcasting ability is Intelligence (spell save DC 21, +13 to hit with spell attacks). The master has the following wizard spells prepared:

Cantrips (at will): *acid splash, mage hand, prestidigitation*

1st level (4 slots): *chromatic orb, detect magic, magic missile, shield*

2nd level (3 slots): *detect thoughts, invisibility, mirror image, ray of enfeeblement*

3rd level (3 slots): *animate dead, counterspell, dispel magic, fireball*

4th level (3 slots): *blight, confusion, dimension door*

5th level (3 slots): *cloudkill, cone of cold, scrying*

6th level (2 slots): *disintegrate, globe of invulnerability*

7th level (2 slots): *finger of death, plane shift*

8th level (1 slot): *dominate monster, power word stun*

9th level (1 slot): *power word kill, time stop*

Turn Resistance. The master has advantage on saving throws against any effect that turns undead.

Actions

Paralyzing Touch. *Melee Weapon Attack:* +13 to hit, reach 5 ft., one creature. *Hit:* 14 (4d6) cold damage, and the target must succeed on a DC 20 Constitution saving throw, or be paralyzed for 1 minute. A creature can repeat the saving throw at the end of each of its turns, ending the effect on itself on a success.

Legendary Actions

The master can take 3 legendary actions, choosing from the options below. Only one legendary action option can be used at a time, and only at the end of another creature's turn. The master regains spent legendary actions at the start of its turn.

Cantrip. The master casts a cantrip.

Paralyzing Touch (Costs 2 Actions). The master uses its Paralyzing Touch.

Sense Weakness (Costs 2 Actions). The master telepathically probes a creature it can see, within the range of its telepathy, for its strengths and weaknesses. The target must succeed on a DC 19 Charisma saving throw, or the master learns of the target's damage vulnerabilities, resistances, and immunities, as well as condition immunities and the exact number of hit points remaining.

Frightening Apocrypha (Costs 3 Actions). The master telepathically focuses a stream of forbidden knowledge on one creature it can see within 20 feet of it. The target must succeed on a DC 20 Wisdom saving throw, or become frightened for 1 minute. While frightened, the creature has disadvantage on Intelligence, Wisdom, and Charisma saving throws against the master's wizard spells. The frightened target can repeat the saving throw at the end of each of its turns, ending the effect on itself on a success. If a target's saving throw is successful, or the effect ends for it, the target has advantage on Intelligence, Wisdom, and Charisma saving throws against the master's spells until the next time it fails to save against one of them, and is immune to the lich's gaze for the next 24 hours.

I had been so sure. Decades of study, years of preparation, months of work, and I had been sure. The phylactery was ready, the potion brewed, and I was sure.

A lifetime condensed into one moment.

That moment, when the concoction first touched my lips, the sweetness of the belladonna, the muskiness of the venom, and the copper of the still-warm blood, for the first time in the process, I felt doubt.

Then came the pain. That terrible, rending pain. I fell to my knees. I wept like a child. I gasped, and sobbed, and collapsed upon the chest of my sacrifice, whimpering as the substance did its work. Her faltering, fading breaths soothed me, like a mother's embrace.

—Teb Tzaano, lich, personal notes

Blight Lich Neophyte

Medium undead, neutral evil

Armor Class 15 (natural armor)
Hit Points 104 (16d8 + 32)
Speed 30 ft.

STR	DEX	CON	INT	WIS	CHA
9 (-1)	12 (+1)	14 (+2)	15 (+2)	17 (+3)	16 (+3)

Saving Throws Con +5, Int +5, Wis +6
Skills Nature +5, Perception +6, Survival +6
Damage Vulnerabilities radiant
Damage Resistances necrotic
Damage Immunities poison
Condition Immunities charmed, exhaustion, frightened, paralyzed, poisoned
Senses darkvision 120 ft., passive Perception 16
Languages Common, Druidic, Sylvan, plus up to three other languages
Challenge 7 (2,900 XP)

Legendary Resistance (1/Day). If the neophyte fails a saving throw, it can choose to succeed instead.

Rejuvenation. If it has a phylactery, the destroyed neophyte gains a new body in 4d10 days, regaining 1 hit point and becoming active again. The new body appears within 5 feet of the phylactery.

Spellcasting. The neophyte is a 6th level spellcaster. Its spellcasting ability is Wisdom (spell save DC 14, +6 to hit with spell attacks). The neophyte has the following druid spells prepared:

Cantrips (at will): *guidance, poison spray, thorn whip*

1st level (4 slots): *detect magic, fog cloud, thunderwave*

2nd level (3 slots): *gust of wind, hold person, moonbeam*

3rd level (3 slots): *dispel magic, protection from energy, sleet storm*

Turn Resistance. The neophyte has advantage on saving throws against any effect that turns undead.

Actions

Decomposing Touch. *Melee Spell Attack:* +6 to hit, reach 5 ft., one creature. *Hit:* 14 (4d6) necrotic damage, and the target must succeed on a DC 14 Constitution saving throw, or become poisoned for 1 minute. While poisoned, a creature must succeed on a DC 14 Constitution saving throw at the start of each of its turns, or take 14 (4d6) necrotic damage. Once a creature succeeds on the saving throw, the effect ends for it.

BLIGHT LICH INITIATE
Medium undead, neutral evil

Armor Class 15 (natural armor)
Hit Points 110 (17d8 + 34)
Speed 30 ft.

STR	DEX	CON	INT	WIS	CHA
9 (-1)	13 (+1)	15 (+2)	16 (+3)	18 (+4)	17 (+3)

Saving Throws Con +6, Int +7, Wis +8
Skills Nature +7, Perception +8, Survival +8
Damage Vulnerabilities radiant
Damage Resistances necrotic
Damage Immunities poison
Condition Immunities charmed, exhaustion, frightened, paralyzed, poisoned
Senses darkvision 120 ft., passive Perception 18
Languages Common, Druidic, Sylvan, plus up to three other languages
Challenge 11 (7,200 XP)

Legendary Resistance (2/Day). If the initiate fails a saving throw, it can choose to succeed instead.

Rejuvenation. If it has a phylactery, the destroyed initiate gains a new body in 2d10 days, regaining 1 hit point and becoming active again. The new body appears within 5 feet of the phylactery.

Spellcasting. The initiate is a 9th level spellcaster. Its spellcasting ability is Wisdom (spell save DC 16, +8 to hit with spell attacks). The initiate has the following druid spells prepared:

Cantrips (at will): *guidance, poison spray, thorn whip*

1st level (4 slots): *detect magic, fog cloud, thunderwave*

2nd level (4 slots): *gust of wind, hold person, moonbeam*

3rd level (3 slots): *dispel magic, protection from energy, sleet storm*

4th level (3 slots): *blight, polymorph*

5th level (2 slots): *antilife shell, contagion*

Turn Resistance. The initiate has advantage on saving throws against any effect that turns undead.

ACTIONS

Decomposing Touch. *Melee Spell Attack:* +8 to hit, reach 5 ft., one creature. *Hit:* 14 (4d6) necrotic damage, and the target must succeed on a DC 16 Constitution saving throw, or become poisoned for 1 minute. While poisoned, a creature must succeed on a DC 16 Constitution saving throw at the start of each of its turns, or take 14 (4d6) necrotic damage. Once a creature succeeds on the saving throw, the effect ends for it.

Undead Beast Shape (2/Day). The initiate magically polymorphs into a beast with a challenge rating of 6 or less, and can remain in this form for up to 9 hours. While in this form, the initiate resembles a decomposing, undead version of that beast. The initiate can choose whether its equipment falls to the ground, melds with its new form, or is worn by the new form. The initiate reverts to its true form if it dies or falls unconscious. The initiate can revert to its true form using a bonus action on its turn.

While in a new form, the initiate retains its game statistics and ability to speak, but its AC, movement modes, Strength, and Dexterity are replaced by those of the new form. Additionally, it gains the special senses, proficiencies, traits, actions, and reactions (except class features, legendary actions, and lair actions) of its new form. The initiate can't cast spells with somatic components in its new form.

The new form's attacks count as magical for the purpose of overcoming resistances and immunity to nonmagical attacks. Additionally, when the initiate hits with a melee weapon attack in its new form, the target takes an additional 14 (4d6) necrotic damage and must succeed on a DC 16 Constitution saving throw, or become poisoned for 1 minute. While poisoned, a creature must succeed on a DC 16 Constitution saving throw at the start of each of its turns, or take 14 (4d6) necrotic damage. Once a creature succeeds on the saving throw, the effect ends for it.

"What's the point in living forever if you don't update your wardrobe every once in a while?"

—Mihaelia Rhamonos, vampire

Blight Lich Adept

Medium undead, neutral evil

Armor Class 16 (natural armor)
Hit Points 135 (18d8 + 54)
Speed 30 ft.

STR	DEX	CON	INT	WIS	CHA
10 (+0)	14 (+2)	16 (+3)	17 (+3)	19 (+4)	18 (+4)

Saving Throws Con +8, Int +8, Wis +9
Skills Nature +8, Perception +9, Survival +9
Damage Resistances cold, lightning, necrotic; bludgeoning, piercing, and slashing from nonmagical weapons
Damage Immunities poison
Condition Immunities charmed, exhaustion, frightened, paralyzed, poisoned
Senses truesight 120 ft., passive Perception 19
Languages Common, Druidic, Sylvan, plus up to three other languages
Challenge 16 (15,000 XP)

Circle of Rot. Whenever an undead creature is destroyed within 60 feet of the adept, the adept regains a number of hit points equal to twice the destroyed creature's CR.

Legendary Resistance (3/Day). If the adept fails a saving throw, it can choose to succeed instead.

Rejuvenation. If it has a phylactery, the destroyed adept gains a new body in 1d10 days, regaining half its hit points and becoming active again. The new body appears within 5 feet of the phylactery.

Spellcasting. The adept is a 13th level spellcaster. Its spellcasting ability is Wisdom (spell save DC 17, +9 to hit with spell attacks). The adept has the following druid spells prepared:

Cantrips (at will): *guidance, poison spray, thorn whip*

1st level (4 slots): *detect magic, fog cloud, thunderwave*

2nd level (3 slots): *gust of wind, hold person, moonbeam*

3rd level (3 slots): *dispel magic, protection from energy, sleet storm*

4th level (3 slots): *blight, polymorph*

5th level (2 slots): *antilife shell, contagion*

6th level (1 slot): *move earth, wind walk*

7th level (1 slot): *plane shift, reverse gravity*

Turn Resistance. The adept has advantage on saving throws against any effect that turns undead.

Actions

Decomposing Touch. *Melee Spell Attack:* +9 to hit, reach 5 ft., one creature. *Hit:* 17 (5d6) necrotic damage, and the target must succeed on a DC 17 Constitution saving throw, or become poisoned for 1 minute. While poisoned, a creature must succeed on a DC 17 Constitution saving throw at the start of each of its turns, or take 17 (5d6) necrotic damage. Once a creature succeeds on the saving throw, the effect ends for it.

Undead Beast Shape (2/Day). The adept magically polymorphs into a beast with a challenge rating of 8 or less, and can remain in this form for up to 9 hours. While in this form, the lich resembles a decomposing, undead version of that beast. The adept can choose whether its equipment falls to the ground, melds with its new form, or is worn by the new form. The adept reverts to its true form if it dies or falls unconscious. The adept can revert to its true form using a bonus action on its turn.

While in a new form, the adept retains its game statistics and ability to speak, but its AC, movement modes, Strength, and Dexterity are replaced by those of the new form. Additionally, it gains the special senses, proficiencies, traits, actions, and reactions (except class features, legendary actions, and lair actions) of its new form. The adept can't cast spells with somatic components in its new form.

The new form's attacks count as magical for the purpose of overcoming resistances and immunity to nonmagical attacks. Additionally, when the adept hits with a weapon attack in its new form, the target takes an additional 17 (5d6) necrotic damage and must succeed on a DC 17 Constitution saving throw, or become poisoned for 1 minute. While poisoned, a creature must succeed on a DC 17 Constitution saving throw at the start of each of its turns, or take 17 (5d6) necrotic damage. Once a creature succeeds on the saving throw, the effect ends for it.

BLIGHT LICH MAGUS
Medium undead, neutral evil

Armor Class 17 (natural armor)
Hit Points 153 (18d8 + 72)
Speed 30 ft.

STR	DEX	CON	INT	WIS	CHA
11 (+0)	15 (+2)	18 (+4)	18 (+4)	20 (+5)	19 (+4)

Saving Throws Con +10, Int +10, Wis +11
Skills Nature +10, Perception +11, Survival +11
Damage Resistances cold, lightning, necrotic
Damage Immunities poison; bludgeoning, piercing, and slashing from nonmagical weapons
Condition Immunities charmed, exhaustion, frightened, paralyzed, poisoned
Senses truesight 120 ft., passive Perception 21
Languages Common, Druidic, Sylvan, plus up to three other languages
Challenge 20 (25,000 XP)

Circle of Rot. Whenever an undead creature is destroyed within 60 feet of the magus, the magus regains a number of hit points equal to twice the destroyed creature's CR.

Legendary Resistance (3/Day). If the magus fails a saving throw, it can choose to succeed instead.

Rejuvenation. If it has a phylactery, the destroyed magus gains a new body in 1d10 days, regaining all its hit points and becoming active again. The new body appears within 5 feet of the phylactery.

Spellcasting. The magus is an 18th level spellcaster. Its spellcasting ability is Wisdom (spell save DC 19, +11 to hit with spell attacks). The magus has the following druid spells prepared:

Cantrips (at will): *guidance, poison spray, thorn whip*

1st level (4 slots): *detect magic, fog cloud, thunderwave*

2nd level (3 slots): *gust of wind, hold person, moonbeam*

3rd level (3 slots): *dispel magic, protection from energy, sleet storm*

4th level (3 slots): *blight, confusion, polymorph*

5th level (3 slots): *antilife shell, contagion, insect plague*

6th level (1 slot): *move earth, wind walk*

7th level (1 slot): *plane shift, reverse gravity*

8th level (1 slot): *earthquake, feeblemind*

9th level (1 slot): *shapechange, storm of vengeance*

Turn Resistance. The magus has advantage on saving throws against any effect that turns undead.

ACTIONS

Decomposing Touch. *Melee Spell Attack:* +11 to hit, reach 5 ft., one creature. *Hit:* 21 (6d6) necrotic damage, and the target must succeed on a DC 19 Constitution saving throw, or become poisoned for 1 minute. While poisoned, a creature must succeed on a DC 19 Constitution saving throw at the start of each of its turns, or take 21 (6d6) necrotic damage. Once a creature succeeds on the saving throw, the effect ends for it.

Undead Beast Shape (3/Day). The magus magically polymorphs into a beast with a challenge rating of 10 or less, and can remain in this form for up to 9 hours. While in this form, the magus resembles a decomposing, undead version of that beast. The magus can choose whether its equipment falls to the ground, melds with its new form, or is worn by the new form. The magus reverts to its true form if it dies or falls unconscious. The magus can revert to its true form using a bonus action on its turn.

While in a new form, the magus retains its game statistics and ability to speak, but its AC, movement modes, Strength, and Dexterity are replaced by those of the new form. Additionally, it gains the special senses, proficiencies, traits, actions, and reactions (except class features, legendary actions, and lair actions) of its new form. The magus can't cast spells with somatic components in its new form.

The new form's attacks count as magical for the purpose of overcoming resistances and immunity to nonmagical attacks. Additionally, when the magus hits with a weapon attack in its new form, the target takes an additional 21 (6d6) necrotic damage and must succeed on a DC 19 Constitution saving throw, or become poisoned for 1 minute. While poisoned, a creature must succeed on a DC 19 Constitution saving throw at the start of each of its turns, or take 21 (6d6) necrotic damage. Once a creature succeeds on the saving throw, the effect ends for it.

LEGENDARY ACTIONS

The magus can take 3 legendary actions, choosing from the options below. Only one legendary action option can be used at a time, and only at the end of another creature's turn. The magus regains spent legendary actions at the start of its turn.

Cantrip. The magus casts a cantrip.

Decomposing Touch (Costs 2 Actions). The magus uses its Decomposing Touch.

Shapechange (Costs 2 Actions). The magus uses its Undead Beast Shape.

Rot Absorption (Costs 3 Actions). The magus draws life energy from creatures around it, that aren't undead or constructs, causing the victims' flesh to wither. Creatures within 30 feet of the magus must succeed on a DC 19 Constitution saving throw, or take 14 (4d6) necrotic damage. The magus regains a number of hit points equal to half the total damage dealt.

Blight Lich Master

Medium undead, neutral evil

Armor Class 18 (natural armor)
Hit Points 190 (20d8 + 100)
Speed 30 ft.

STR	DEX	CON	INT	WIS	CHA
11 (+0)	16 (+3)	20 (+5)	19 (+4)	22 (+6)	20 (+5)

Saving Throws Str +7, Dex +10, Con +12, Int +11, Wis +13
Skills Nature +11, Perception +13, Survival +13
Damage Resistances cold, lightning, necrotic
Damage Immunities poison; bludgeoning, piercing, and slashing from nonmagical weapons
Condition Immunities charmed, exhaustion, frightened, paralyzed, poisoned
Senses truesight 120 ft., passive Perception 23
Languages Common, Druidic, Sylvan, plus up to four other languages
Challenge 23 (50,000 XP)

Blightbringer. As a bonus action, the master radiates a toxic aura. Whenever a creature begins its turn within 30 feet of the master, it takes 18 (4d8) poison damage. The aura remains active until the master uses a bonus action to end the effect.

Circle of Rot. Whenever an undead creature is destroyed within 60 feet of the master, the master regains a number of hit points equal to twice the destroyed creature's CR.

Legendary Resistance (3/Day). If the master fails a saving throw, it can choose to succeed instead.

Rejuvenation. If it has a phylactery, the destroyed master gains a new body in 1d10 days, regaining all its hit points and becoming active again. The new body appears within 5 feet of the phylactery.

Spellcasting. The master is a 20th level spellcaster. Its spellcasting ability is Wisdom (spell save DC 21, +13 to hit with spell attacks). The master has the following druid spells prepared:

Cantrips (at will): *guidance, poison spray, thorn whip*

1st level (4 slots): *detect magic, fog cloud, longstrider, thunderwave*

2nd level (3 slots): *gust of wind, hold person, moonbeam, pass without trace*

3rd level (3 slots): *dispel magic, protection from energy, sleet storm, water walk*

4th level (3 slots): *blight, confusion, polymorph*

5th level (3 slots): *antilife shell, contagion, insect plague*

6th level (2 slots): *move earth, wind walk*

7th level (2 slots): *plane shift, reverse gravity*

8th level (1 slot): *earthquake, feeblemind*

9th level (1 slot): *shapechange, storm of vengeance*

Turn Resistance. The master has advantage on saving throws against any effect that turns undead.

Actions

Decomposing Touch. *Melee Spell Attack:* +13 to hit, reach 5 ft., one creature. *Hit:* 28 (8d6) necrotic damage, and the target must succeed on a DC 21 Constitution saving throw, or become poisoned for 1 minute. While poisoned, a creature must succeed on a DC 21 Constitution saving throw at the start of each of its turns, or take 28 (8d6) necrotic damage. Once a creature succeeds on the saving throw, the effect ends for it.

Undead Beast Shape (3/Day). The master magically polymorphs into a beast with a challenge rating of 12 or less, and can remain in this form for up to 9 hours. While in this form, the master resembles a decomposing, undead version of that beast. The master can choose whether its equipment falls to the ground, melds with its new form, or is worn by the new form. The master reverts to its true form if it dies or falls unconscious. The master can revert to its true form using a bonus action on its turn.

While in a new form, the master retains its game statistics and ability to speak, but its armor class, movement modes, Strength, and Dexterity are replaced by those of the new form. Additionally, it gains the special senses, proficiencies, traits, actions, and reactions (except class features, legendary actions, and lair actions) of its new form. The master can't cast spells with somatic components in its new form.

The new form's attacks count as magical for the purpose of overcoming resistances and immunity to nonmagical attacks. Additionally, when the master hits with a weapon attack in its new form, the target takes an additional 28 (8d6) necrotic damage and must succeed on a DC 21 Constitution saving throw, or become poisoned for 1 minute. While poisoned, a creature must succeed on a DC 21 Constitution saving throw at the start of each of its turns, or take 28 (8d6) necrotic damage. Once a creature succeeds on the saving throw, the effect ends for it.

Legendary Actions

The master can take 3 legendary actions, choosing from the options below. Only one legendary action option can be used at a time, and only at the end of another creature's turn. The master regains spent legendary actions at the start of its turn.

Cantrip. The master casts a cantrip.

Decomposing Touch (Costs 2 Actions). The master uses its Decomposing Touch.

Shapechange (Costs 2 Actions). The master uses its Undead Beast Shape.

Rot Absorption (Costs 3 Actions). The master draws life energy from creatures around it, that aren't undead or constructs, causing the victims' flesh to wither. Creatures within 30 feet of the master must succeed on a DC 21 Constitution saving throw, or take 21 (6d6) necrotic damage. The master regains a number of hit points equal to half the total damage dealt.

It is of those who attain lichdom through their own study that we know the most. By their very nature, such individuals are those of a diligent, scholarly bent, and their rituals often contain a written component, to say nothing of personal writings and research. Hard facts are still scant, though, for they are also a suspicious breed, and fearful of pretenders.

But what of the others? Of the profane liches, some little is known, from that which we can piece together about the darker practices of death cults. Notably, they must prove themselves of such unique worth in life that they are granted complete freedom as an agent after death, rather than remaining answerable to their patron. To this end, a would-be lich will commit heinous atrocities in the name of their deity. History runs red with the deeds of such individuals, and the presumably low rate of success does little to deter these attempts. Such liches, it would seem, often ascend accompanied by a mass sacrifice of their disciples; a number of these unfortunates' souls are gifted to the deity as part of the bargain, and some are returned as mindless thralls to the newly-formed lich.

Records of the blight liches are near to non-existent. The druidic rituals, of which their magic appears to be a corruption, are kept hidden from outsiders, as a rule, and their twisting by the undead is a subject of particular shame and secrecy.

~Oto Gwanye, 'Mage: The Seduction of Power'

PROFANE LICH NEOPHYTE

Medium undead, neutral evil

Armor Class 15 (natural armor)
Hit Points 104 (16d8 + 32)
Speed 30 ft.

STR	DEX	CON	INT	WIS	CHA
14 (+2)	9 (-1)	14 (+2)	15 (+2)	17 (+3)	16 (+3)

Saving Throws Con +5, Int +5, Wis +6
Skills Religion +5, Perception +6, Survival +6
Damage Vulnerabilities radiant
Damage Resistances necrotic
Damage Immunities poison
Condition Immunities charmed, exhaustion, frightened, paralyzed, poisoned
Senses darkvision 120 ft., passive Perception 16
Languages Abyssal, Common, Infernal, plus up to three other languages
Challenge 7 (2,900 XP)

Legendary Resistance (1/Day). If the neophyte fails a saving throw, it can choose to succeed instead.

Rejuvenation. If it has a phylactery, the destroyed neophyte gains a new body in 4d10 days, regaining 1 hit point and becoming active again. The new body appears within 5 feet of the phylactery.

Spellcasting. The neophyte is a 6th level spellcaster. Its spellcasting ability is Wisdom (spell save DC 14, +6 to hit with spell attacks). The neophyte has the following cleric spells prepared:

Cantrips (at will): *guidance, poison spray, thorn whip*

1st level (4 slots): *detect magic, fog cloud, thunderwave*

2nd level (3 slots): *gust of wind, hold person, moonbeam*

3rd level (3 slots): *dispel magic, protection from energy, sleet storm*

Turn Resistance. The neophyte has advantage on saving throws against any effect that turns undead.

ACTIONS

Commanding Warhammer. *Melee Weapon Attack:* +5 to hit, reach 5 ft., one target. *Hit:* 6 (1d8 + 2) bludgeoning damage, plus 4 (1d8) necrotic damage, and the target must succeed on a DC 14 Wisdom saving throw, or be charmed by the neophyte for 1 minute. A creature can repeat the saving throw at the end of each of its turns, ending the effect on itself on a success.

PROFANE LICH INITIATE

Medium undead, neutral evil

Armor Class 15 (natural armor)
Hit Points 110 (17d8 + 34)
Speed 30 ft.

STR	DEX	CON	INT	WIS	CHA
15 (+2)	9 (-1)	15 (+2)	16 (+3)	18 (+4)	17 (+3)

Saving Throws Con +6, Int +7, Wis +8
Skills Nature +7, Perception +8, Survival +8
Damage Vulnerabilities radiant
Damage Resistances necrotic
Damage Immunities poison
Condition Immunities charmed, exhaustion, frightened, paralyzed, poisoned
Senses darkvision 120 ft., passive Perception 18
Languages Abyssal, Common, Infernal, plus up to three other languages
Challenge 11 (7,200 XP)

Legendary Resistance (2/Day). If the initiate fails a saving throw, it can choose to succeed instead.

Rejuvenation. If it has a phylactery, the destroyed initiate gains a new body in 2d10 days, regaining 1 hit point and becoming active again. The new body appears within 5 feet of the phylactery.

Spellcasting. The initiate is a 9th level spellcaster. Its spellcasting ability is Wisdom (spell save DC 16, +8 to hit with spell attacks). The initiate has the following cleric spells prepared:

Cantrips (at will): *guidance, resistance, thaumaturgy*

1st level (4 slots): *bane, inflict wounds, shield of faith*

2nd level (4 slots): *blindness/deafness, hold person, spiritual weapon*

3rd level (3 slots): *animate dead, dispel magic*

4th level (3 slots): *banishment, guardian of faith*

5th level (2 slots): *geas, insect plague*

Turn Resistance. The initiate has advantage on saving throws against any effect that turns undead.

ACTIONS

Commanding Warhammer. *Melee Weapon Attack:* +6 to hit, reach 5 ft., one target. *Hit:* 6 (1d8 + 2) bludgeoning damage, plus 4 (1d8) necrotic damage, and the target must succeed on a DC 15 Wisdom saving throw, or be charmed by the initiate for 1 minute. A creature can repeat the saving throw at the end of each of its turns, ending the effect on itself on a success.

Bane of Life (1/Day). The initiate presents its holy symbol and speaks a baleful command, chastising the living. Each creature within 30 feet of the initiate, other than constructs, fiends, and undead, must succeed on a DC 16 Wisdom saving throw, or be frightened for 1 minute, or until it takes any damage. If a creature with a challenge rating of 2 or lower fails its saving throw against this effect, it immediately drops to 0 hit points.

A frightened creature must spend its turns moving as far away from the initiate as it can. As its action, the creature can only use Dash actions, or to try to escape an effect that prevents it from moving. If it has nowhere to move, the creature can use the Dodge action.

"I transcended when your people hunted in the brush with stones. When men bent the first plough, I was more learned in the higher powers than any creature living. I have been worshipped as a god, my sacrifices clawed each other's eyes for the privilege of dying for me and, when they cast me out, I displaced all the monsters of their primitive mythologies. I have worn many names in my time, but all have been feared. More heroes than even I can recall have attempted to slay me, and all have failed. The dust of their forgotten bones could choke a nation. So tell me, child, what is it that makes you dare hope for victory?"

-The First, lich

Profane Lich Adept

Medium undead, neutral evil

Armor Class 16 (natural armor)
Hit Points 135 (18d8 + 54)
Speed 30 ft.

STR	DEX	CON	INT	WIS	CHA
16 (+3)	10 (+0)	16 (+3)	17 (+3)	19 (+4)	18 (+4)

Saving Throws Con +8, Int +8, Wis +9
Skills Nature +8, Perception +9, Survival +9
Damage Vulnerabilities radiant
Damage Resistances cold, lightning, necrotic; bludgeoning, piercing, and slashing from nonmagical attacks
Damage Immunities poison
Condition Immunities charmed, exhaustion, frightened, paralyzed, poisoned
Senses truesight 120 ft., passive Perception 19
Languages Abyssal, Common, Infernal, plus up to three other languages
Challenge 16 (15,000 XP)

Legendary Resistance (3/Day). If the adept fails a saving throw, it can choose to succeed instead.

Rejuvenation. If it has a phylactery, the destroyed adept gains a new body in 1d10 days, regaining half its hit points and becoming active again. The new body appears within 5 feet of the phylactery.

Spellcasting. The adept is a 13th level spellcaster. Its spellcasting ability is Wisdom (spell save DC 17, +9 to hit with spell attacks). The adept has the following cleric spells prepared:

Cantrips (at will): *guidance, resistance, thaumaturgy*

1st level (4 slots): *bane, inflict wounds, shield of faith*

2nd level (3 slots): *blindness/deafness, hold person, spiritual weapon*

3rd level (3 slots): *animate dead, dispel magic*

4th level (3 slots): *banishment, guardian of faith*

5th level (2 slots): *geas, insect plague*

6th level (1 slot): *create undead, harm*

7th level (1 slot): *plane shift, regenerate*

Turn Resistance. The adept has advantage on saving throws against any effect that turns undead.

Actions

Commanding Warhammer. *Melee Weapon Attack:* +8 to hit, reach 5 ft., one target. *Hit:* 7 (1d8 + 3) bludgeoning damage, plus 9 (2d8) necrotic damage, and the target must succeed on a DC 17 Wisdom saving throw, or be charmed by the adept for 1 minute. A creature can repeat the saving throw at the end of each of its turns, ending the effect on itself on a success.

Restore Undeath. The adept touches a willing undead creature, within 5 feet of it, and expends a spell slot to channel negative energy. The target regains 8 (1d8 + 4) hit points, plus an additional 4 (1d8) hit points for each slot level above 1st of the expended spell slot.

Bane of Life (2/Day). The adept presents its holy symbol and speaks a baleful command chastising the living. Each creature within 30 feet of the adept, other than constructs, fiends, and undead, must succeed on a DC 17 Wisdom saving throw, or be frightened for 1 minute, or until it takes any damage. If a creature with a challenge rating of 3 or lower fails its saving throw against this effect, it immediately drops to 0 hit points.

A frightened creature must spend its turns moving as far away from the adept as it can. As its action, the creature can only use Dash actions, or to try to escape an effect that prevents it from moving. If it has nowhere to move, the creature can use the Dodge action.

PROFANE LICH MAGUS

Medium undead, neutral evil

Armor Class 17 (natural armor)
Hit Points 153 (18d8 + 72)
Speed 30 ft.

STR	DEX	CON	INT	WIS	CHA
18 (+4)	11 (+0)	18 (+4)	18 (+4)	20 (+5)	19 (+4)

Saving Throws Con +10, Int +10, Wis +11
Skills Nature +10, Perception +11, Survival +11
Damage Vulnerabilities radiant
Damage Resistances cold, lightning, necrotic
Damage Immunities poison; bludgeoning, piercing, and slashing from nonmagical attacks
Condition Immunities charmed, exhaustion, frightened, paralyzed, poisoned
Senses truesight 120 ft., passive Perception 21
Languages Abyssal, Common, Infernal, plus up to three other languages
Challenge 20 (25,000 XP)

Legendary Resistance (3/Day). If the magus fails a saving throw, it can choose to succeed instead.

Rejuvenation. If it has a phylactery, the destroyed magus gains a new body in 1d10 days, regaining all its hit points and becoming active again. The new body appears within 5 feet of the phylactery.

Spellcasting. The magus is an 18th level spellcaster. Its spellcasting ability is Wisdom (spell save DC 19, +11 to hit with spell attacks). The magus has the following cleric spells prepared:

Cantrips (at will): *guidance, resistance, thaumaturgy*

1st level (4 slots): *bane, inflict wounds, shield of faith*

2nd level (3 slots): *blindness/deafness, hold person, spiritual weapon*

3rd level (3 slots): *animate dead, bestow curse, dispel magic*

4th level (3 slots): *banishment, divination, guardian of faith*

5th level (3 slots): *geas, insect plague, scrying*

6th level (1 slot): *create undead, harm*

7th level (1 slot): *plane shift, regenerate*

8th level (1 slot): *control weather, earthquake*

9th level (1 slot): *astral projection, gate*

Turn Resistance. The magus has advantage on saving throws against any effect that turns undead.

ACTIONS

Commanding Warhammer. *Melee Weapon Attack:* +10 to hit, reach 5 ft., one target. *Hit:* 8 (1d8 + 4) bludgeoning damage, plus 9 (2d8) necrotic damage, and the target must succeed on a DC 18 Wisdom saving throw, or be charmed by the magus for 1 minute. A creature can repeat the saving throw at the end of each of its turns, ending the effect on itself on a success.

Restore Undeath. The magus touches a willing undead creature, within 5 feet of it, and expends a spell slot to channel negative energy. The target regains 9 (1d8 + 5) hit points, plus an additional 4 (1d8) hit points for each slot level above 1st of the expended spell slot.

Bane of Life (3/Day). The magus presents its holy symbol and speaks a baleful command, chastising the living. Each creature within 30 feet of the magus, other than constructs, fiends, and undead, must succeed on a DC 19 Wisdom saving throw, or be frightened for 1 minute, or until it takes any damage. If a creature with a challenge rating of 4 or lower fails its saving throw against this effect, it immediately drops to 0 hit points.

While frightened, a creature must spend its turn moving as far away from the magus as it can. It can only use Dash actions, or actions to try to escape an effect that prevents it from moving away. If it has nowhere to move, the creature can use the dodge action.

LEGENDARY ACTIONS

The magus can take 3 legendary actions, choosing from the options below. Only one legendary action option can be used at a time, and only at the end of another creature's turn. The magus regains spent legendary actions at the start of its turn.

Cantrip. The magus casts a cantrip.

Commanding Warhammer (Costs 2 Actions). The magus attacks with its Commanding Warhammer.

Unholy Healing (Costs 2 Actions). The magus uses its Restore Undeath ability.

Profane Sermon (Costs 3 Actions). The magus speaks a portion of an unholy sermon. Creatures within 30 feet that can hear the magus, other than undead, must make a DC 21 Constitution saving throw, taking 9 (2d8) necrotic damage on a failed save, or half as much damage on a successful one. Additionally, undead creatures within 30 feet, that can hear the magus, regain 4 (1d8) hit points.

PROFANE LICH MASTER
Medium undead, neutral evil

Armor Class 18 (natural armor)
Hit Points 190 (20d8 + 100)
Speed 30 ft.

STR	DEX	CON	INT	WIS	CHA
20 (+5)	12 (+1)	20 (+5)	19 (+4)	22 (+6)	20 (+5)

Saving Throws Str +12, Dex +8, Con +12, Int +11, Wis +13
Skills Nature +11, Perception +13, Survival +13
Damage Resistances cold, lightning, necrotic
Damage Immunities poison; bludgeoning, piercing, and slashing from nonmagical attacks
Condition Immunities charmed, exhaustion, frightened, paralyzed, poisoned
Senses truesight 120 ft., passive Perception 23
Languages Abyssal, Common, Infernal, plus up to four other languages
Challenge 23 (50,000 XP)

Harbinger of the Grave. Creatures within 40 feet of the master regain only half as many hit points from spells, potions, and magic items.

Legendary Resistance (3/Day). If the master fails a saving throw, it can choose to succeed instead.

Rejuvenation. If it has a phylactery, the destroyed master gains a new body in 1d10 days, regaining all its hit points and becoming active again. The new body appears within 5 feet of the phylactery.

Spellcasting. The master is a 20th level spellcaster. Its spellcasting ability is Wisdom (spell save DC 21, +13 to hit with spell attacks). The master has the following cleric spells prepared:

Cantrips (at will): *guidance, resistance, thaumaturgy*

1st level (4 slots): *bane, detect magic, inflict wounds, shield of faith*

2nd level (3 slots): *blindness/deafness, hold person, spiritual weapon, zone of truth*

3rd level (3 slots): *animate dead, bestow curse, dispel magic, protection from energy*

4th level (3 slots): *banishment, divination, guardian of faith*

5th level (3 slots): *geas, insect plague, scrying*

6th level (2 slots): *create undead, harm*

7th level (2 slots): *plane shift, regenerate*

8th level (1 slot): *control weather, earthquake*

9th level (1 slot): *astral projection, gate*

Turn Resistance. The master has advantage on saving throws against any effect that turns undead.

ACTIONS

Commanding Warhammer. *Melee Weapon Attack:* +12 to hit, reach 5 ft., one target. *Hit:* 9 (1d8 + 5) bludgeoning damage, plus 9 (2d8) necrotic damage, and the target must succeed on a DC 20 Wisdom saving throw, or be charmed by the master for 1 minute. A creature can repeat the saving throw at the end of each of its turns, ending the effect on itself on a success.

Restore Undeath. The master touches a willing undead creature, within 5 feet of it, and expends a spell slot to channel negative energy. The target regains 10 (1d8 + 6) hit points plus an additional 4 (1d8) hit points for each slot level above 1st of the expended spell slot.

Bane of Life (3/Day). The master presents its holy symbol and speaks a baleful command, chastising the living. Each creature within 30 feet of the master, other than constructs, fiends, and undead, must succeed on a DC 21 Wisdom saving throw, or be frightened for 1 minute, or until it takes any damage. If a creature with a challenge rating of 4 or lower fails its saving throw against this effect, it immediately drops to 0 hit points.

A frightened creature must spend its turns moving as far away from the master as it can. As its action, the creature can only use Dash actions, or to try to escape an effect that prevents it from moving. If it has nowhere to move, the creature can use the Dodge action.

LEGENDARY ACTIONS

The master can take 3 legendary actions, choosing from the options below. Only one legendary action option can be used at a time, and only at the end of another creature's turn. The master regains spent legendary actions at the start of its turn.

Cantrip. The master casts a cantrip.

Commanding Warhammer (Costs 2 Actions). The master attacks with its Commanding Warhammer.

Unholy Healing (Costs 2 Actions). The master uses its Restore Undeath ability.

Profane Sermon (Costs 3 Actions). The master speaks a portion of an unholy sermon. Creatures within 30 feet that can hear the master, other than undead, must make a DC 21 Constitution saving throw, taking 13 (3d8) necrotic damage on a failed save, or half as much damage on a successful one. Additionally, undead creatures within 30 feet, that can hear the master, regain 9 (2d8) hit points.

There is a certain level of superiority, some might even say arrogance, inherent to the character of a spellcaster. After all, they are able to bend the very fabric of the world to their will in ways that most can only dream of.

Perhaps it is natural, in a way, for this to play upon the mind of a mortal. One might begin with the best of intentions: "Why, with my unique mind, I work wonders for the betterment of all," they might think. "But, when I am gone, what lesser being shall continue my work?"

They study, they experiment, they perform ritual after ritual, and a seductive thought takes root: the thought of immortality. After all, if they never die, their work continues; think of how the world might be if the great thinkers of the past were not snuffed out, but had millennia more to refine their ideas!

"What is one life," they begin to think, "when compared to all I could achieve?"

And, with that thought, they are lost.

For what is one life? What is a dozen? A hundred? A thousand? Compared to the infinity of greatness not yet achieved, they are the same.

Another thought begins to fester. What if their great works fall into the wrong hands? What if some other should use their effort and sacrifice to achieve the same goal? What guarantee could there be that any other would share their ideals? Think of how the world might be if the great monsters of the past were not snuffed out, but had millennia more to refine their ideas...

And so, the lich retreats. What right have others to their work? Is it not enough for these ungrateful fools that the work be done?

-Javros Bortz-Welling, from his lecture, 'The Lich and Its Ways'

After weeks without a reply, I can only conclude that my letters have been waylaid, or else the ideas within them are of such little interest to my editor that he does not deign them worthy of inclusion. I, however, recognize the great import of recounting such strange and heroic episodes in a collective memoir, for posterity if nothing else and, therefore, turn my sights to higher purposes than the pages of a seldom-read local paper.

I had given up on trying to explain the idea of my new book to Thaddeus. While he tolerated my tagging along, he didn't seem to see the worth of recording the experience for others. Truth be told, while he is certainly a worldly man, with a deep knowledge of his craft, I remain unsure as to whether he can actually read. As such, I had abandoned that course and steered the conversation towards his previous exploits, in the hope of scouting out potential material in a slightly more veiled manner.

"Got a taste for it, eh?" As a man of action himself, he naturally took my interest as a sign that I planned on taking up the trade. I believe he found this amusing.

"Erm. Something like that."

Over the next few rounds of ale, he regaled me with his various adventures hunting a particularly troublesome lich, who went by the sobriquet, 'The Maid of Sorrows'. Having missed the pleasure of her acquaintance in life by some five centuries, Thaddeus first encountered her around thirty years ago (he did not go into details, but I infer that he came off significantly the worse in the fight that followed). After that, they crossed paths several times, occasionally by sheer coincidence, though it seems they make a serious go at hunting one another down every few years, to varying levels of success. Only Thaddeus could have 'kill a maniacal lich' as a low-priority item on his to-do list.

"Been sitting on some information for a while. Reckon I know where she is. Reckon she might know a thing or two about this Shrouded One an' all."

"The Shrouded One?" I put in. "You mean that ghoul back in the crypts? I'm not sure he'll be much of an issue without a head."

"Nah, 's no ghoul name," Thaddeus said, as if explaining that the sky is not, in fact, green. "This Shrouded One's some greater power it was serving and, mark my words, The Maid'll be up to her elbows in it; once a necromancer, always a necromancer. Was going to wait 'til you'd cleared off but, as you're keen..."

Things were progressing quicker than I would, necessarily, have liked.

"So how are you going to kill her?" I asked, in an attempt to show willing and hide my nerves.

Thaddeus looked at me blankly, as if weighing up just how basically he would have to phrase his reply.

"I mean," I continued, trying to claw back what I could of my reputation, "she has her... phylaster-thingy, doesn't she?"

"Phylactery."

"Yes, that. So what's different this time?"

Thaddeus grinned, revealing yellowed teeth. It was equal parts endearing and horrifying, and it was clear he had been waiting for this cue for much of our conversation. With a small flourish, he dropped a dark ruby, the color of arterial blood, onto the table. It fell with a heavy thunk, like a slab of meat.

"Oh," I said.

We set off the next morning, and I quickly knew that the inn's mattresses, scratchy and straw-filled as they may have been, would be sorely missed in the coming days. We traveled for days into the wilderness, through tangled briar and twisting forest, until we reached the complex of ruins which marked our quarry's lair.

Bits and pieces of black stone littered the area; crooked pillars, bowing walls and, here and there, a leering, demonic face, worn smooth by time, all clogged with roots and vines, as if the forest itself was attempting to devour evidence of the deeds which had taken place there.

One structure in the heart of it all still stood; a leaning, crumbling chamber, which was perhaps once a vestry or anteroom (I admit, I am not yet familiar with the specific terminology regarding abandoned and forgotten temples of dark ritual). A faint light emanated from within. Thaddeus gave a nod and proceeded inside.

We found her kneeling in the centre of a rune-etched circle, whether one of her own design or one she had found there, I did not know. The room was littered with paraphernalia, both magical and mundane, some twinkling with gems and others emanating unearthly light; a tied bundle of small bones, a string of what might have been prayer beads, a jewel-encrusted headdress, a faintly glowing, golden orb. Her robes suggested some religious sect, with a light veil which did nothing to disguise the crumbling ruins of the face beneath. The twin stars of her eyes gave no hint of surprise as they glanced up at our entrance.

"You are nothing if not persistent, Thaddeus," she said calmly, as her hand went to the orb. "Haven't I killed you already?"

"Did your best. Killed *you* though."

"Twice. I had not forgotten." She got to her feet or, rather, an upright position, floating a few inches from the ground. "Are there any more flaccid jibes, or shall we get to the business at hand? Only, I'm rather in the middle of something."

"Seems like you're in the middle of a lot of things, Shrouded One," Thaddeus spat, accusatorially. "Didn't realize you were going by a different name these days."

She tilted her head a fraction, curious. "I go by many names to many people. I have lain shrouded and risen again."

"Thaddeus-" I began, but was cut off.

"Surely you've not come to disturb my peace and quiet with naught but a name."

"Ghoul mentioned power and death, and an army. Said 'The Shrouded One' would lead some sort of cleansing. Seemed like your kind of thing. I'm here to put a stop to it."

"You'll stop nothing. Even if you were to kill me today, I'd be back within a moon's turn."

"Wouldn't be so sure," replied Thaddeus, casting before him, one after another, the jagged shards of a shattered ruby, the color of arterial blood. They skittered across the floor, echoing in the dead silence which followed, sliding to a halt at the liches feet.

She glanced down only briefly, before fixing us with a piercing stare. She uttered a gutteral phrase and, as the orb's light flared to blinding levels, a wall of deep-red flame sprung up before her. At the same time, we were thrown back against the opposite wall with enough force to rain down dust and flakes of masonry from the ceiling. Thaddeus heaved himself to his feet; I remained on the ground with my probable concussion. Neither of them seemed to notice.

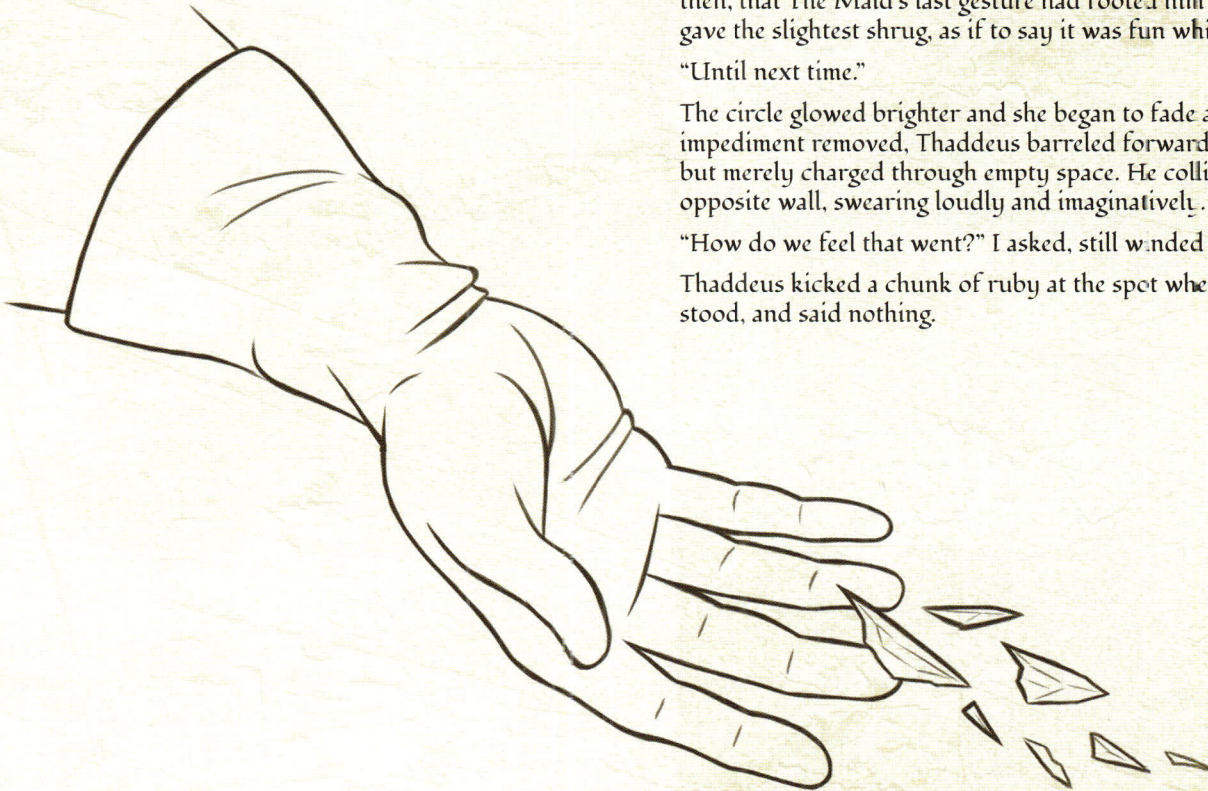

"I'm sorry to have wasted your time, Thaddeus," the lich shouted, now floating above the runic circle, which had begun to glow. Thaddeus darted behind a crumbling pillar as a bolt of crackling green energy shrieked overhead, taking a chunk of his cover with it. "I know nothing of any 'Shrouded One'," - she dodged a dagger thrown in her direction and countered with a thick cloud of noxious gas, which rolled across the chamber, flushing Thaddeus, coughing, from his refuge. "I am, however, excited to learn more," - she deflected an incoming crossbow bolt with a casual flick of her hand - "especially as it's got you so very hot and bothered." The lich extended a pointed finger as if to cast another spell and Thaddeus, his eyes locked onto her, tensed, ready to dodge. She relaxed with a mocking smile. "Yes, why not give something else a go at you? I'm sure whatever it is will be *very* interested to learn that you're on its tail, when I find it." Thaddeus remained stock still, staring daggers at her. I realised then, that The Maid's last gesture had rooted him to the spot. She gave the slightest shrug, as if to say it was fun while it lasted.

"Until next time."

The circle glowed brighter and she began to fade away. His impediment removed, Thaddeus barreled forward, sword drawn, but merely charged through empty space. He collided with the opposite wall, swearing loudly and imaginatively.

"How do we feel that went?" I asked, still winded on the floor.

Thaddeus kicked a chunk of ruby at the spot where she had stood, and said nothing.

LYCANTHROPES

The body spasms as the eyes darken into black pools, flashing in the moonlight. Bones crack and shift, growing like the limbs of a grotesque insect, twitching under the skin. Another convulsion, coupled with a cry of pain, turning into an animal roar as the face begins to lengthen, distorting with the skull beneath it. Fangs erupt from the screaming mouth, glistening with strings of saliva. Wiry hair spreads like a mold. Throwing back its head, it howls; the night and the hunt and the scent of fear given one terrible voice. The man is gone. There is only the beast.

While typified by the ubiquitous werewolf, in truth there are several varieties of lycanthrope, each of which transform into a different beast. Whether their transformation is voluntary and controlled, or a painful ordeal linked to the lunar cycle, depends on the character of the lycanthrope. Over the years, many a scholar has attempted to lead the charge in renaming the creatures 'therianthropes' to properly reflect their diverse forms (some of these scholars were, reportedly, non-werewolf lycanthropes themselves), but each has been ignored or shouted down.

Different types of lycanthrope, as a rule, mistrust if not outright despise one another. While rival groups are generally separated by preferences in territory or prey, conflicts can break out where they overlap. A shifting hierarchy exists between lycanthropes which, for centuries, has been topped by the numerous and ruthless werewolf. While enmities run deep between groups, different lycanthropes have been known to join together in times of extreme threat to their species as a whole. In such times, packs meet on neutral ground, and ancient tenets forbid the harming of fellow lycanthropes, tenets even the most bloodthirsty or vengeful werewolf would never think to break. The most common enemy faced in this way is the vampire, for whom all lycanthropes share an ingrained hatred.

Further fracturing lycanthropes is the ideological schism between those that embrace the condition, allowing the beast to bleed into their own personality, and so allowing them to control their physical change, and those that resist it, preventing the beast from affecting their personality, but releasing any level of control over the change that comes upon them at the time of the full moon. Embracers tend to feel some level of rivalry towards each other, and jostle to be top of the pecking order, while viewing suppressors as prissy fools missing out on the opportunities afforded to them.

Suppressors often view each other with distrust and caution, always questioning whether their fellows are taking as much care as they possibly could to control themselves, and view embracers as mindless brutes.

In its humanoid form, a lycanthrope might bear no sign of its condition. Suppressors may appear a little sickly and sleep-deprived around the time of the full moon, but otherwise resemble any other member of their race. Embracers tend to undergo some level of physical change to reflect the bestial nature which they have allowed to blend into their own life. Excessive body hair or claw-like nails are classic signs, but more obvious can be yellow, slitted, or otherwise bestial eyes, which reflect light in the dark.

By all accounts, transformation is an agonizingly painful process, as bones and muscle warp under the skin, growing or shrinking to the proportions of the beast. With practice, embracers can accelerate the process, in some cases shifting form entirely over the course of a single bound. For suppressors, however, the change is a thing to be dreaded each month, with their resistance only drawing out the experience and heightening the pain.

Lycanthropes carry a fearsome reputation, understandably tinged with a considerable level of paranoia. Much of the folklore surrounding them centers around discovering hidden lycanthropes, and can quickly fuel outbreaks of hysteria in superstitious areas where one is suspected. In such times, it is best to go clean-shaven, for even the most mildly hirsute individual may find themselves under close scrutiny (dwarves, in particular, suffer during these times, due to their social taboos concerning beard-cutting). Some traveling 'wolf-finders' may indeed be motivated by altruism, and may even know a handful of helpful rituals to seek out and aid accursed creatures, but many more are shameless charlatans or woefully misguided. A common practice is cutting the accused with a steel blade, with it being widespread knowledge that lycanthropes are immune to common metals. However, not only does this give no indication of the type of lycanthrope discovered (though, in times of panic, any and all are branded as evil as the basest of them), it is easy to misdirect – swindlers might use blunted or retractable blades to cast suspicion upon an expedient target – or misunderstand, with some using silvered blades and expecting to see a pelt beneath the skin to betray the existence of a lycanthrope.

ORIGIN

Some scholars theorize that the origin of the lycanthrope lies with their most hated enemy, the vampires. It is thought that, millennia ago, vampires experimented with imbuing some of their human 'livestock' with some measure of their own shapechanging power. Whether by oversight or design, these experiments were able to spread their condition in the same manner as their master – the bite. This goes some way to explain why the most numerous form of lycanthrope is the werewolf (the wolf being a common vampiric form), as well as their hatred of vampires. Whether lycanthropes escaped, and later diverged into different forms, or the vampires originally created them in the forms we see today, is unknown.

Another proposed origin is the natural magic of druids, fey, or other such creatures. More capricious spirits are famed for unorthodox punishments against those who disrespect nature or transgress her laws, and it is possible that on one or more occasions, rather than stopping at punishing a single transgressor, an entire bloodline may have been cursed. Good lycanthropes do tend to feel a pull towards protecting the balance of the natural world, so it is possible we can look to nature's more traditional guardians for their beginnings.

As well as spreading through bites, the condition can also be inherited. While the offspring of two lycanthropes will almost certainly be one too, lycanthropy becomes diluted through generations of breeding with non-lycanthropes. While the child of a lycanthrope and a non-lycanthrope may retain most, if not all, of their bestial powers, their offspring may only be able to transform into less and less monstrous transitional forms and, after a few more generations, have only a slight predilection for rare meat as a mark of their legacy. Conversely, those with a lycanthrope far back in their ancestry may develop the condition seemingly from nowhere; their grandmother's grandmother's dalliance with a hairy stranger having been long forgotten. With no guidance from others of their kind, these lycanthropes often prove to be the most dangerous and unpredictable.

All lycanthropes share a deep taboo against breeding in animal form, but there are rare exceptions. The vast majority of such offspring will not come to term and, of those, few will survive to adulthood. Those that do, resemble a lycanthrope in beast form; an unusually intelligent, but otherwise unremarkable, animal. Very rarely, however, the offspring inherit a kind of reverse lycanthropy, allowing them to change temporarily into a humanoid form, though retaining the intellect and character of a beast.

Environment

Lycanthropes may be found within any humanoid society and, depending on the exact form of the affliction, may have little impact on the group as a whole. Good-natured lycanthropes, for example, will go out of their way to remove themselves to the wilderness, or arrange to be physically restrained, when the change comes upon them. On the other hand, many brutal murders or apparent attacks by wild beasts can be traced back to evil, or simply uncontrolled, lycanthropes. The vast majority of lycanthropes keep their condition secret due to the social stigma, uninformed myths, and often well-deserved fear and suspicion from the general populace.

Conversely, within shamanistic societies, lycanthropes can attain positions of respect, even reverence. It is not unheard of to see tribes formed around lycanthropes acting as a spiritual advisor or even chieftain. Whether a lycanthrope uses their position to act for the good of the group, utilizing their powers in its defense, or perverts their course, demanding sacrifices to their appetites, depends on the individual in question. Regardless of their intentions, lycanthropes in these communities often choose not to infect those around them, whether due to a fear of losing their privileged position, a moral opposition to spreading their affliction, or a simple unwillingness to have to bother with any competition.

More commonly, lycanthropes band together with others of their kind both separate from greater civilization and secretly within it. Within society, lycanthropes may only meet in bestial form, and otherwise remain strangers, or may be closely linked (perhaps under the guise of mercenaries, thieves, or other professions which might explain their generally rougher appearance and demeanor). Outside of society, groups of lycanthropes exist more like animals or particularly savage bandits. Lycanthropes expelled from such a group, or left alone and unused to solitude, may spend the rest of their lives in beast form among their kin. Unusually aggressive wolf packs, or the sudden appearance of man-eating panthers, can often be traced back to such suddenly isolated lycanthropes taking over a local animal population.

Roleplaying Notes

While both engagers and suppressors constantly feel the call of their animalistic nature, the difference lies in whether they pay heed to it. When not in beast form, a suppressor may seem nervous, or strained, and appear quite sickly. They tend to be withdrawn from society, hoping to keep themselves away from any potentially stressful situations. Truly controlling the condition takes time and effort, so a suppressor is unlikely to simply lose their grip and transform unexpectedly, but most are unwilling to take the risk.

Engagers are generally more instinctive, and may appear simple or brutish at a glance, but they combine this with a predatory cunning. They tend to see themselves as superior to non-lycanthropes for embracing, rather than denying, the beast which they believe lurks within every civilized soul. Their willing acceptance of their condition allows some elements of their animalistic character to affect their humanoid character and mannerisms, as well as their appearance, though a wary lycanthrope goes to pains to keep these in check.

Beyond this, lycanthropes are as variable as any other folk. Whether they view their condition as a blessing or a curse depends greatly on the society in which they find themselves.

Combat Tactics

Should combat ensue, lycanthropes fight fearlessly, knowing that weapons coated with silver (and its attendant significance to the moon and its powers) are costly and rare. Good lycanthropes might make use of their relative invulnerability to attempt to de-escalate a conflict at little risk to themselves; evil lycanthropes fight mercilessly and savagely, using all the advantages afforded to them. Those wishing to spread their condition rarely kill outright, unless ravenously hungry, preferring to leave their victims weakened and infected before moving on.

Lycanthrope Encounters

d8	CR	Encounter
1	5	**Noblefeather Murder:** 5 Wereravens
2	7	**Nightprowler Pact:** 4 Werebats, 1 Werepanther
3	10	**Moonhunter Pack:** 3 Werewolf Maulers, 1 Dire Werewolf
4	12	**Moonlight Guard:** 3 Werebear Protectors, 2 Wereravens
5	17	**Dreamwarden Concord:** 1 Werebear Devotee, 4 Werebear Protectors, 3 Wereravens
6	18	**Beastblood Covenant:** 4 Werewolf Maulers, 2 Dire Werewolves, 1 Alpha Werewolf, 1 Werepanther, 1 Werebat

Suppressing Lycanthropy

The statistics presented in this chapter represent lycanthropes that embrace their bestial heritage. A lycanthrope that rejects the beast within is subject to slightly different rules. The following changes apply to a Suppressing Lycanthrope:

- The lycanthrope can be of any alignment.

- The lycanthrope cannot choose to change its shape. Instead, it involuntarily transforms on each night of the full moon. Instead of using its action to do so, the lycanthrope becomes incapacitated for 1d10 rounds, as an agonizing and slow transformation takes place. At dawn, the lycanthrope reverts to humanoid form, becoming incapacitated for 1d10 rounds as before. Once the lycanthrope has fully reverted, it cannot remember any of the events that transpired while it was in hybrid or beast form.

- Whether the lycanthrope transforms into hybrid or beast form depends on the form the lycanthrope that infected it was in when it transferred the curse. The suppressing lycanthrope takes on that same form.

- While transformed, the suppressing lycanthrope has the usual alignment for its type, but reverts to its normal alignment when reverting to humanoid form.

WEREBAT
Medium humanoid (human, shapechanger), neutral evil

Armor Class 13
Hit Points 58 (13d8)
Speed 30 ft. (fly 60 ft. in hybrid or bat form)

STR	DEX	CON	INT	WIS	CHA
14 (+2)	19 (+4)	11 (+0)	10 (+0)	14 (+2)	11 (+0)

Skills Perception +4
Damage Immunities bludgeoning, piercing, and slashing from nonmagical attacks that aren't silvered
Senses blindsight 60 ft. in hybrid or bat form, passive Perception 14
Languages Common, plus up to one other language (can't speak in bat form)
Challenge 3 (700 XP)

Shapechanger. The werebat can use its action to polymorph into a bat-humanoid hybrid, or into a Large giant bat, or back into its true form, which is humanoid. Its statistics, other than its size, are the same in each form. Any equipment it is wearing or carrying isn't transformed. It reverts to its true form if it dies.

Echolocation. The werebat can't use its blindsight while deafened.

Keen Hearing. The werebat has advantage on Wisdom (Perception) checks that rely on hearing.

ACTIONS

Multiattack (Humanoid or Hybrid Form Only). The werebat makes two attacks: one with its bite, and one with its dagger or claws.

Bite (Hybrid or Bat Form Only). *Melee Weapon Attack:* +6 to hit, reach 5 ft., one target. *Hit:* 7 (1d6 + 4) piercing damage. If the target is a humanoid, it must succeed on a DC 10 Constitution saving throw, or be cursed with werebat lycanthropy.

Claws (Hybrid Form Only). *Melee Weapon Attack:* +6 to hit, reach 5 ft., one target. *Hit:* 6 (1d4 + 4) slashing damage.

Dagger (Humanoid Form Only). *Melee or Ranged Weapon Attack:* +6 to hit, reach 5 ft. or range 30/60 ft., one target. *Hit:* 6 (1d4 + 4) piercing damage.

Screech (Hybrid or Bat Form Only; Recharges 5-6). The werebat emits a high-pitched cry. Each creature in a 15-foot cone must make a DC 12 Constitution saving throw. A creature takes 7 (2d6) thunder damage on a failed save, or half as much damage on a successful one.

Werebats retain a position close to the bottom of the lycanthrope pecking order, potentially due to the obvious comparisons to vampiric transformation (a stigma which werewolves manage to avoid, seemingly through physical intimidation alone). Amongst other lycanthropes, werebats tend towards resentful sycophancy though, when left to their own devices, their ability to fly can fill them with a feeling of superiority over lesser 'walkers'.

Werebear Protector

Medium humanoid (human, shapechanger), neutral good

Armor Class 13 (shield) in humanoid form, 14 (natural armor, shield) in hybrid form, or 12 (natural armor) in bear form
Hit Points 150 (20d8 + 60)
Speed 30 ft. (40 ft., climb 30 ft. in hybrid or bear form)

STR	DEX	CON	INT	WIS	CHA
20 (+5)	12 (+1)	17 (+3)	11 (+0)	14 (+2)	12 (+1)

Skills Athletics +8, Perception +8
Damage Immunities bludgeoning, piercing, and slashing from nonmagical attacks that aren't silvered
Senses passive Perception 18
Languages Common, plus up to one other language (can't speak in bear form)
Challenge 7 (2,900 XP)

Shapechanger. The werebear can use its action to polymorph into a Large bear-humanoid hybrid, or into a Large bear, or back into its true form, which is humanoid. Its statistics, other than its size and armor class, are the same in each form. Any equipment it is wearing or carrying isn't transformed. It reverts to its true form if it dies.

Defender. While the werebear is wielding a shield, allies within 5 feet of the werebear, that aren't wielding a shield, gain a +2 bonus to their armor class.

Keen Smell. The werebear has advantage on Wisdom (Perception) checks that rely on smell.

Mighty Grip (Hybrid Form Only). The werebear can ignore the Two-Handed trait of weapons made for Medium creatures.

Sentinel. If the werebear hits a creature with an opportunity attack, that creature's speed is reduced to 0 for the rest of its turn.

Actions

Multiattack. The werebear makes two attacks with its claws, or two with its halberd.

Bite (Hybrid or Bear Form Only). *Melee Weapon Attack:* +8 to hit, reach 5 ft., one target. *Hit:* 13 (2d8 + 4) piercing damage. If the target is a humanoid, it must succeed on a DC 14 Constitution saving throw, or be cursed with werebear lycanthropy.

Claws (Hybrid Form Only). *Melee Weapon Attack:* +8 to hit, reach 5 ft., one target. *Hit:* 14 (2d8 + 5) slashing damage.

Halberd (Humanoid or Hybrid Form Only). *Melee Weapon Attack:* +8 to hit, reach 10 ft., one target. *Hit:* 10 (1d10 + 5) slashing damage.

Hells' Hunters played an integral role in putting down the lycanthropes at this time. Tieflings' physical characteristics are belligerently robust, being passed on from parent to child regardless of any other genealogy, and it was believed that this made them highly resistant to, if not immune from, the bestial curse: "Twixt devil and dog, bet on the devil", said the old wisdom. Cadres of tiefling hunters set upon the lycanthropes with flame and silver but, come the war's end, all mention of them was scoured from official records.

-Quinlan Castiir, 'Forgotten History, Forgotten Lives'

Werebear Devotee
Medium humanoid (human, shapechanger), lawful good

Armor Class 11 in humanoid form, 12 (natural armor) in hybrid form or bear form
Hit Points 221 (26d8 + 104)
Speed 30 ft. (40 ft., climb 30 ft. in hybrid or bear form)

STR	DEX	CON	INT	WIS	CHA
20 (+5)	12 (+1)	19 (+4)	11 (+0)	12 (+1)	14 (+2)

Skills Athletics +9, Perception +9, Religion +4
Damage Immunities bludgeoning, piercing, and slashing from nonmagical attacks that aren't silvered
Senses passive Perception 19
Languages Common, plus up to one other language (can't speak in bear form)
Challenge 10 (5,900 XP)

Shapechanger. The werebear can use its action to polymorph into a Large bear-humanoid hybrid, or into a Large bear, or back into its true form, which is humanoid. Its statistics, other than its size and armor class, are the same in each form. Any equipment it is wearing or carrying isn't transformed. It reverts to its true form if it dies.

Healing Hands. The werebear has a pool of healing power that allows it to restore up to 60 hit points. As an action, the werebear can touch a creature and draw any number of points from its healing power, restoring that many hit points to the creature. The werebear's pool of healing power replenishes once it finishes a long rest.

Keen Smell. The werebear has advantage on Wisdom (Perception) checks that rely on smell.

Actions

Multiattack. The werebear makes two attacks with its claws or with its longsword.

Bite (Hybrid or Bear Form Only). *Melee Weapon Attack:* +9 to hit, reach 5 ft., one target. *Hit:* 13 (2d8 + 4) piercing damage, plus 4 (1d8) radiant damage. If the target is a humanoid, it must succeed on a DC 16 Constitution saving throw, or be cursed with werebear lycanthropy.

Claws (Hybrid Form Only). *Melee Weapon Attack:* +9 to hit, reach 5 ft., one target. *Hit:* 14 (2d8 + 5) slashing damage, plus 4 (1d8) radiant damage.

Longsword (Humanoid or Hybrid Form Only). *Melee Weapon Attack:* +9 to hit, reach 5 ft., one target. *Hit:* 9 (1d8 + 5) slashing damage, or 10 (1d10 + 5) slashing damage, if wielded in two hands, plus 4 (1d8) radiant damage.

Large Longsword (Hybrid Form Only). *Melee Weapon Attack:* +9 to hit, reach 5 ft., one target. *Hit:* 14 (2d8 + 5) slashing damage, or 16 (2d10 + 5) slashing damage, if wielded in two hands, plus 4 (1d8) radiant damage.

I call us here to meet, brothers and sisters of the skin.
By tooth and claw, by fur and feather and flesh,
By our bond of blood, and the great Moon Mother.
There are no foes but the foes of the pack.

-traditional oath beginning a meeting of lycanthrope clans

WEREPANTHER

Medium humanoid (human, shapechanger), chaotic neutral

Armor Class 13
Hit Points 49 (9d8 + 9)
Speed 30 ft. (50 ft., climb 40 ft. in hybrid or panther form)

STR	DEX	CON	INT	WIS	CHA
14 (+2)	17 (+3)	12 (+1)	11 (+0)	15 (+2)	10 (+0)

Skills Perception +4, Stealth +7
Damage Immunities bludgeoning, piercing, and slashing from nonmagical attacks that aren't silvered
Senses darkvision 60 ft., passive Perception 14
Languages Common, plus up to one other language (can't speak in panther form)
Challenge 3 (700 XP)

Shapechanger. The werepanther can use its action to polymorph into a panther-humanoid hybrid, or into a panther, or back into its true form, which is humanoid. Its statistics are the same in each form. Any equipment it is wearing or carrying isn't transformed. It reverts to its true form if it dies.

Keen Smell. The werepanther has advantage on Wisdom (Perception) checks that rely on smell.

Pounce (Hybrid or Panther Form Only). If the werepanther moves at least 15 feet straight toward a creature, and then hits it with a claws attack, the target must succeed on a DC 12 Strength saving throw, or be knocked prone. If the target is prone, the werepanther can make a bite attack against it as a bonus action.

ACTIONS

Multiattack (Humanoid or Hybrid Form Only). The werepanther makes two attacks with its shortswords or with its claws.

Bite (Hybrid or Panther Form Only). *Melee Weapon Attack:* +5 to hit, reach 5 ft., one target. *Hit:* 6 (1d6 + 3) piercing damage. If the target is a humanoid, it must succeed on a DC 11 Constitution saving throw, or be cursed with werepanther lycanthropy.

Claws (Hybrid or Panther Form Only). *Melee Weapon Attack:* +5 to hit, reach 5 ft., one target. *Hit:* 5 (1d4 + 3) slashing damage.

Shortswords (Humanoid or Hybrid Form Only). *Melee Weapon Attack:* +4 to hit, reach 5 ft., one target. *Hit:* 6 (1d6 + 3) piercing damage.

Werepanthers tend towards the life of a lone hunter, with a haughty pride in their self-sufficiency, and a vicious streak bordering on sadistic, barely contained below the surface. Would-be allies would do well to avoid wounding a werepanther's ego, for their loyalty is no sure thing, save to themselves.

Wereraven

Medium humanoid (human, shapechanger), lawful good

Armor Class 13
Hit Points 31 (7d8)
Speed 30 ft. (fly 50 ft. in hybrid or raven form)

STR	DEX	CON	INT	WIS	CHA
11 (+0)	17 (+3)	11 (+0)	14 (+2)	16 (+3)	13 (+1)

Skills Perception +5
Damage Immunities bludgeoning, piercing, and slashing from nonmagical attacks that aren't silvered
Senses passive Perception 15
Languages Common, plus up to one other language
Challenge 2 (450 XP)

Shapechanger. The wereraven can use its action to polymorph into a raven-humanoid hybrid, or into a Small raven, or back into its true form, which is humanoid. Its statistics, other than its size, are the same in each form. Any equipment it is wearing or carrying isn't transformed. It reverts to its true form if it dies. ·

Flyby. The wereraven doesn't provoke opportunity attacks when it flies out of an enemy's reach.

Mimicry. The wereraven can mimic simple sounds it has heard, such as whispering, screams of pain, or the cries of a wild animal. A creature that hears the sounds can identify them as imitations with a successful DC 13 Wisdom (Insight) check.

Plunging Attack. If the wereraven is flying, and dives at least 30 feet straight toward a creature and then hits it with a talons attack, the target must succeed on a DC 10 Dexterity saving throw, or become blinded for 1 minute. Any effect that restores hit points also removes this blindness.

Actions

Multiattack (Humanoid or Hybrid Form Only). The wereraven makes two weapon attacks.

Beak (Hybrid or Raven Form Only). *Melee Weapon Attack:* +5 to hit, reach 5 ft., one target. *Hit:* 5 (1d4 + 3) piercing damage. If the target is a humanoid, it must succeed on a DC 10 Constitution saving throw, or be cursed with wereraven lycanthropy.

Talons (Hybrid or Raven Form Only). *Melee Weapon Attack:* +5 to hit, reach 5 ft., one target. *Hit:* 5 (1d4 + 3) piercing damage.

Rapier (Humanoid or Hybrid Form Only). *Melee Weapon Attack:* +5 to hit, reach 5 ft., one target. *Hit:* 7 (1d8 + 3) piercing damage.

A rarity for taking on the form of a bird rather than a mammal, the transformation into a **wereraven** is particularly unpleasant, due to the differences in anatomy, and rarely undertaken lightly. Wereravens tend to be curious souls, eager and quick to learn, though wary of outsiders until they have proven themselves trustworthy.

To this humble scholar, it seems that lycanthropy is little different to the druidic craft of beastshaping. I propose that, should the alterations to the original spells be discovered, it would be no great effort to recreate its effects, though perhaps with animals easier to manage. Were-chameleons perhaps. I was always fond of chameleons.

—Druth, itinerant druid

Werewolf Mauler

Medium humanoid (human, shapechanger), chaotic evil

Armor Class 12 in humanoid form or 13 (natural armor) in hybrid or wolf form
Hit Points 65 (10d8 + 20)
Speed 30 ft. (40 ft. in wolf form)

STR	DEX	CON	INT	WIS	CHA
16 (+3)	14 (+2)	15 (+2)	9 (-1)	13 (+1)	10 (+0)

Skills Perception +5, Stealth +4
Damage Immunities bludgeoning, piercing, and slashing from nonmagical attacks that aren't silvered
Senses passive Perception 15
Languages Common, plus up to one other language (can't speak in wolf form)
Challenge 4 (1,100 XP)

Shapechanger. The werewolf can use its action to polymorph into a wolf-humanoid hybrid, or into a wolf, or back into its true form, which is humanoid. Its statistics, other than its armor class, are the same in each form. Any equipment it is wearing or carrying isn't transformed. It reverts to its true form if it dies. ·

Flying Pounce (Hybrid Form Only). If the werewolf leaps at least 15 feet directly towards a creature, and then hits it with a claw attack, the target takes an additional 9 (2d8) damage and must succeed on a DC 13 Strength saving throw, or be knocked prone.

Keen Hearing and Smell. The werewolf has advantage on Wisdom (Perception) checks that rely on hearing or smell.

Standing Leap (Hybrid or Wolf Form Only). The werewolf's long jump is up to 30 feet, and its high jump is up to 15 feet, with or without a running start.

Actions

Multiattack (Humanoid or Hybrid Form Only). The werewolf makes three attacks: one with its bite, and two with its claws or unarmed strike.

Bite (Hybrid or Wolf Form Only). *Melee Weapon Attack:* +5 to hit, reach 5 ft., one target. *Hit:* 7 (1d8 + 3) piercing damage. If the target is a humanoid, it must succeed on a DC 12 Constitution saving throw, or be cursed with werewolf lycanthropy.

Claws (Hybrid Form Only). *Melee Weapon Attack:* +5 to hit, reach 5 ft., one target. *Hit:* 8 (2d4 + 3) slashing damage.

Unarmed Strike (Humanoid Form Only). *Melee Weapon Attack:* +4 to hit, reach 5 ft., one target. *Hit:* 5 (1d4 + 3) bludgeoning damage.

Dire Werewolf

Medium humanoid (human, shapechanger), chaotic evil

Armor Class 11 in humanoid form or 14 (natural armor) in hybrid or dire wolf form
Hit Points 150 (20d8 + 60)
Speed 30 ft. (50 ft. in dire wolf form)

STR	DEX	CON	INT	WIS	CHA
19 (+4)	12 (+1)	17 (+3)	9 (-1)	11 (+0)	8 (-1)

Skills Perception +6, Stealth +4
Damage Immunities bludgeoning, piercing, and slashing from nonmagical attacks that aren't silvered
Senses passive Perception 16
Languages Common, plus up to one other language (can't speak in wolf form)
Challenge 7 (2,900 XP)

Shapechanger. The werewolf can use its action to polymorph into a Large wolf-humanoid hybrid, or into a Large dire wolf, or back into its true form, which is humanoid. Its statistics, other than its size and armor class, are the same in each form. Any equipment it is wearing or carrying isn't transformed. It reverts to its true form if it dies.

Keen Hearing and Smell. The werewolf has advantage on Wisdom (Perception) checks that rely on hearing or smell.

Actions

Multiattack (Humanoid or Hybrid Form Only). The werewolf makes two attacks, only one of which can be a bite.

Bite (Hybrid or Dire Wolf Form Only). *Melee Weapon Attack:* +7 to hit, reach 5 ft., one target. *Hit:* 13 (2d8 + 4) piercing damage. If the target is a humanoid, it must succeed on a DC 14 Constitution saving throw, or be cursed with dire werewolf lycanthropy.

Claws (Hybrid Form Only). *Melee Weapon Attack:* +7 to hit, reach 5 ft., one target. *Hit:* 11 (3d4 + 4) slashing damage.

Greatsword (Humanoid or Hybrid Form Only). *Melee Weapon Attack:* +7 to hit, reach 5 ft., one target. *Hit:* 11 (2d6 + 4) slashing damage.

"I didn't know he was no wolf 'til we quarreled. Tried to stick a knife in his guts and the blade broke off. Reported it to the constable, and we made him dance a jig. Let the bugger try to howl with a rope 'round his neck."

—Jants, tanner

Alpha Werewolf

Medium humanoid (human, shapechanger), chaotic evil

Armor Class 12 in humanoid form or 15 (natural armor) in hybrid or wolf form
Hit Points 180 (24d8 + 72)
Speed 30 ft. (40 ft. in wolf form)

STR	DEX	CON	INT	WIS	CHA
17 (+3)	14 (+2)	16 (+3)	11 (+0)	14 (+2)	10 (+0)

Skills Perception +12, Stealth +7
Damage Immunities bludgeoning, piercing, and slashing from nonmagical attacks that aren't silvered
Senses passive Perception 22
Languages Common, plus up to one other language (can't speak in wolf form)
Challenge 13 (10,000 XP)

Shapechanger. The werewolf can use its action to polymorph into a wolf-humanoid hybrid, or into a wolf, or back into its true form, which is humanoid. Its statistics, other than its armor class, are the same in each form. Any equipment it is wearing or carrying isn't transformed. It reverts to its true form if it dies.

Keen Hearing and Smell. The werewolf has advantage on Wisdom (Perception) checks that rely on hearing or smell.

Legendary Resistance (2/Day). If the werewolf fails a saving throw, it can choose to succeed instead.

Pack Leader. The alpha werewolf has advantage on an attack roll against a creature if at least one of the werewolf's allies is within 5 feet of the creature and the ally isn't incapacitated. Likewise, each of the alpha werewolf's allies has advantage on an attack roll against a creature if the alpha werewolf is within 5 feet of the creature and isn't incapacitated.

Actions

Multiattack (Humanoid or Hybrid Form Only). The werewolf makes four attacks: one with its bite, and three with its claws or longsword.

Bite (Hybrid or Wolf Form Only). *Melee Weapon Attack:* +8 to hit, reach 5 ft., one target. *Hit:* 8 (1d10 + 3) piercing damage. If the target is a humanoid, it must succeed on a DC 16 Constitution saving throw, or be cursed with werewolf lycanthropy.

Claws (Hybrid Form Only). *Melee Weapon Attack:* +8 to hit, reach 5 ft., one target. *Hit:* 8 (2d4 + 3) slashing damage.

Longsword (Humanoid Form Only). *Melee Weapon Attack:* +8 to hit, reach 5 ft., one creature. *Hit:* 7 (1d8 + 3) slashing damage, or 8 (1d10 + 3) slashing damage, if wielded in two hands.

Legendary Actions

The alpha werewolf can take 3 legendary actions, choosing from the options below. Only one legendary action option can be used at a time and only at the end of another creature's turn. The werewolf regains spent legendary actions at the start of its turn.

Slash. The werewolf makes one attack with its claws or longsword.

Transform. The werewolf uses its Shapechanger ability.

Pack Maneuver (Costs 2 Actions). The alpha werewolf, or an ally within 30 feet that can see and hear it, moves up to half its speed without provoking opportunity attacks.

"They walk among us, children! These beasts with the faces of men, abominations who commit atrocities by the light of the moon and brazenly mingle with the pure-hearted come day-break.
"But brother!" I hear you cry. "If a man has no memory of his deeds, and repents his actions, surely he must be forgiven!"
I say to you that, were it truly repentant, it would cast itself from a cliff and seek forgiveness from the rocks below! There is no penance but death for these devils. There is no refuge to be found but in our driving them out.
Know this, children, be it neighbor, friend, or brother, the heart of a monster beats ever in their chest."

-Father Grimaldis, 3rd Sermon of the Moon

THE LYCANTHROPE ARCHETYPE

Any Small or Medium humanoid can become a lycanthrope, either born as such or afflicted by the curse of lycanthropy from another lycanthrope's bite. In either case, the following changes apply:

- **Type.** The lycanthrope gains the shapechanger subtype.
- **Damage Immunity.** The lycanthrope becomes immune to bludgeoning, piercing, and slashing damage from nonmagical attacks that aren't silvered.
- **Shapechange.** As an action, the lycanthrope can polymorph into a beast-humanoid hybrid, or into a beast, or back into its true form, which is humanoid. Its statistics are the same in each form, although some species gain natural armor, or are sizes other than Medium in their hybrid or beast form. Any equipment it is wearing or carrying isn't transformed. It reverts to its true form if it dies. The lycanthrope does not have hands in beast form, cannot use weapons or items, and can't wear armor designed for its humanoid form in beast form.

  If the lycanthrope is a natural born lycanthrope, or has embraced its curse, it can use this ability at will. If it has been afflicted with the curse of lycanthropy, it automatically transforms into either hybrid or beast form during nights of the full moon. It loses control over its body as the beast within takes over. When the sun rises, it reverts to its true form, retaining no memory of the transformation.

- **Lycanthrope Species.** The lycanthrope has a specific species of beast that it transforms into. It inherits this species from its lycanthrope parents or the lycanthrope that transferred the curse of lycanthropy to it. Depending on its species, the lycanthrope gains different abilities.

  - *Werebat (giant bat):* Dexterity 19; Bite (1d6 piercing, plus curse of lycanthropy); Claws (1d4 slashing, hybrid form only); speed fly 60 ft.; blindsight 60 ft., Echolocation, Keen Hearing (all forms); Large bat form
  - *Werebear (bear):* Strength 19; Bite (2d10 piercing, plus curse of lycanthropy), Claws (2d8 slashing); natural armor 11; speed 40 ft., climb 30 ft.; Keen Smell (all forms); Large hybrid and bear forms
  - *Wereboar (boar):* Strength 17; Tusks (2d6 slashing, plus curse of lycanthropy); natural armor 11; speed 40 ft. (boar form only); Charge; Relentless (all forms)
  - *Werepanther (panther):* Dexterity 17; Bite (1d6 piercing, plus curse of lycanthropy), Claws (1d4 slashing); speed 50 ft., climb 40 ft.; darkvision 60 ft. (all forms); Keen Smell (all forms); Pounce
  - *Wererat (giant rat):* Dexterity 15; Bite (1d4 piercing, plus curse of lycanthropy); Keen Smell (all forms); Small rat form
  - *Wereraven (raven):* Dexterity 17; Beak (1d4 piercing, plus curse of lycanthropy), Talons (1d4 slashing); speed fly 50 ft.; Mimicry (all forms); Small raven form
  - *Weretiger (tiger):* Strength 17; Bite (1d10 piercing, plus curse of lycanthropy), Claws (1d8 slashing); speed 40 ft.; darkvision 60 ft. (all forms); Keen Hearing and Smell (all forms); Pounce; Large tiger form
  - *Werewolf (wolf):* Strength 15; Bite (1d8 piercing, plus curse of lycanthropy), Claws (2d4 slashing, hybrid form only); natural armor 11; speed 40 ft.; Keen Hearing and Smell (all forms)
  - *Dire Werewolf (dire wolf):* Strength 19; Bite (2d8 piercing, plus curse of lycanthropy), Claws (3d4 slashing, hybrid form only); natural armor 13; speed 40 ft.; Keen Hearing and Smell (all forms); Large hybrid and wolf forms

- With the exception of Strength and Dexterity scores, these abilities apply only in hybrid and beast form, unless otherwise noted. How exactly each ability affects the lycanthrope and functions is explained below.

- **Ability Scores.** The lycanthrope gains the Strength or Dexterity score of its species, unless its natural ability score is already higher.

- **Natural Weapons.** The lycanthrope gains the natural weapons of its species, along with proficiency with these weapons. These are melee weapons, dealing the listed amount and type of damage. The lycanthrope can choose whether to use Strength or Dexterity for attack and damage rolls. A natural attack that inflicts the curse of lycanthropy requires a humanoid target to make a Constitution saving throw (DC 8 + lycanthrope's proficiency bonus + lycanthrope's Constitution modifier), or be afflicted with the lycanthrope's type of lycanthropy.

- **Natural Armor.** If the lycanthrope's species has natural armor, its armor class becomes the listed value + the lycanthrope's Dexterity modifier, while it is not wearing armor.

- **Speed.** The lycanthrope gains the listed speed, unless it already has a natural speed of the same type that is higher.

- **Senses.** The lycanthrope gains its species' special senses, unless it already has the same sense with equal or greater range. If the lycanthrope's species has the Keen Sight, Smell, or Hearing ability, it has advantage on Wisdom (Perception) checks that rely on those senses. If the lycanthrope's species has the Echolocation ability, it can't use its blindsight while deafened, unless it has blindsight naturally without the Echolocation ability.

- **Size.** If the lycanthrope has a hybrid and/or beast form that is a size other than Medium, it becomes that size when assuming that form. This doesn't alter the creature's Hit Dice.

- **Special Attacks and Defenses.** Some lycanthrope species have additional special abilities that function as follows:

  - *Charge.* If the lycanthrope moves at least 15 feet straight toward a target, and then hits it with its tusks on the same turn, the target takes an extra 7 (2d6) slashing damage. If the target is a creature, it must succeed on a Strength saving throw (DC 8 + the lycanthrope's proficiency bonus + the lycanthrope's Strength modifier), or be knocked prone.
  - *Pounce.* If the lycanthrope moves at least 15 feet straight toward a creature, and then hits it with a claw attack on the same turn, the target must succeed on a Strength saving throw (DC 8 + the lycanthrope's proficiency bonus + the lycanthrope's Strength modifier), or be knocked prone. If the target is prone, the lycanthrope can make a bite attack against it as a bonus action.
  - *Relentless.* If the lycanthrope takes an amount of damage equal to its total number of Hit Dice + its Constitution modifier or less that would reduce it to 0 hit points, it is reduced to 1 hit point instead.

A lycanthrope can be cured of its affliction with a *remove curse* spell, while a natural born lycanthrope can only be cured by a *wish* spell.

The proceedings had been going on for some time, and the hangover made each dragging minute more painful than the last (trying to keep up with Thaddeus, still sore about the lich, the previous night had been a dreadful mistake). First, a shared oath recited by all present, sworn before moon-mothers, moon-maids, moon-calves and all manner of sundry lunar entities. I noted that, though Thaddeus did not join in the oath, he did mouth along respectfully. After that, it seemed the parties were content with grumbling to each other about centuries-old grudges until I was forced to wonder when the matter we, or rather Thaddeus, had been called to adjudicate would come into it. As I began to wonder if there would be time to surreptitiously close my eyes, the voices I had barely been paying attention to became more heated.

Markus, the largest of the forest clan, and therefore their leader, was as grizzled as he was wiry. His face was nearly as scarred as Thaddeus', though Thaddeus' face seemed to be made up of little *but* scars. I was keen to stay as far from him as possible for, though Thaddeus had assured me that all present would be bound by ancient and sacred rites of hospitality, a certain wolfish aspect never left Markus' eyes; a coiled spring of violence and hunger waiting for the slightest hint of an exposed throat. I had met (and subsequently avoided) men like him before though, to my knowledge, none of them could express their feral attributes in quite so definitive a fashion.

Beshka was a different matter entirely. Leader of the mountain clan, she was easily as broad as she was tall, helped along by the layers of thick furs she cocooned herself in. Her face was marked by decades of matronly smiles, and set by freezing wind until it resembled an old walnut. She spoke in a deep, croaking whisper one had to strain to hear.

"My people's oaths are as stone, Markus," she whispered now. "Your lands are forbidden to us, and we respect this. As deeply, I am sure, as you respect our borders. Perhaps your people were simply lost."

Markus growled deep in the back of his throat. He was clearly not a man to suffer even the mildest barb. Beshka's eyes flashed wickedly, seeing she had hit a nerve. Perhaps she was not the grandmotherly figure I had first taken her for.

"You presume upon my patience, She-Bear," he rasped, spitting out each word. "None of my kin have ventured within your borders. Perhaps you are going senile in your advancing years, as well as soft." This earned a howl of approval from the forest clan, and snarls from the mountain folk.

"You deny it, when tracks left by your brethren were seen not a moon's turn gone, a full mile beyond your borders?"

"There are many feet in the forest, our little brothers' too: or would you have us leash them as the townsmen do? We have only your word that those prints are ours. You see spirits and shadows, ghosts and ghoulies in the night - blame and hunt *them*, but do not shame my kin."

"You disgrace yourself with these lies, pup."

"We'll get nowhere trading insults," Thaddeus attempted to interject, managing to turn a couple of heads, but not Beshka's, nor Markus'. "If there is any-"

"By tooth and claw," snarled Markus, "I will rip out your tongue if you do not cease these baseless accusations."

"A challenge?" Beshka turned to Thaddeus. "I accept."

I looked to Thaddeus with some shock. He seemed unperturbed, as though he were expecting this outcome from the start.

"Terms," Thaddeus grunted, getting to his feet. "Markus?"

"Rights to the foothills. You barely come down from the mountains anyway, it's not like you need them."

Thaddeus turned to Beshka, who nodded, and replied, "I want nothing from you, Markus, but an apology, and your oath on bended knee before all assembled here that you will never set foot in our lands again."

Markus took a moment to contemplate this, but he nodded nonetheless. Thaddeus raised a hand to the assembled crowd. "A challenge has been issued and terms accepted. The truth shall be decided by battle." He stepped aside and muttered, "As it always is."

The two fighters began to circle one another, pacing a rough ring, neither seeming entirely willing to make the first move. Eventually, inevitably, it was Markus, charging across to the wizened, fur-clad woman. He dove bodily forwards, arms outstretched, but it was a pair of paws which hit the ground at a sprint. Mid jump, his human form had simply melted away, as smoothly and quickly as an expert swimmer diving into a still lake. Now, an enormous, ravening wolf closed the distance, a rangy, snapping creature, marked by battle, fur thinning around its numerous scars. It bore down on Beshka, who calmly raised a hand and, with that same melting smoothness, the largest bear I had ever seen brought its paw down on Markus.

The wolf dodged to the side and lunged at the bear's throat, who gave a terrible, earth shaking roar as she thrashed about to dislodge him. Eventually, he was forced off and, with a casual swat, thrown aside, clear across the ring.

"Weak, and alone, little dog," Beshka growled, a deep rumbling echo of her previous whisper.

So it went, speed against strength. Whenever she made space for herself, Beshka would allow herself another jibe, which only inflamed Markus to become more and more reckless. The tactic seemed simple, yet Markus fell for it every time.

Eventually, bleeding and bruised, Markus was thrown aside for the last time. Hemmed in on one side by the crowd of roaring mountain folk, whose aspects seemed to grow only more ursine as the fight progressed, he was cornered.

"No more room to run, Markus." Beshka was bleeding too, her raspy breathing heavy through her torn and tattered muzzle.

At that, the fight seemed to momentarily go out of the wolf. For a second, the growling, hackle-bristling beast was replaced by a wide-eyed, whipped cur, who had run out of options. That moment was all Beshka needed. Before he could recover, he was pinned to the floor by the enormous bear, who gave a bloody, spittle-laced roar a bare inch from the wolf's face. The fight was won.

"Victory goes to the mountain clan," said Thaddeus, trying to sound official, but mostly sounding like Thaddeus. "By the oaths you have made, this shall be the end of it."

Markus had no choice but to concede. In his human form, as rent and ragged as the wolf had been, he knelt, apologised, and swore, though he did so through bared teeth.

"Enjoy it while you can, She-Bear," he spat. "If we can't have your lands, maybe we won't guard them for you next time something worse comes around."

"Your envy is uglier than your scars, Markus," croaked the little woman as she waddled away. "Let us try not to meet again for a while, yes?"

Markus watched her leave with a rebellious sneer, but then turned to Thaddeus, who had been watching him intently for signs of trouble.

"Thaddeus," Markus growled with what was almost humility, "there *is* something else out there. My people know the night, and the night has turned against us. Something stinks. There's death on the wind. The pack needs to keep moving but, if the old bear won't have us on her lands, we shall soon run out of directions to run."

He seemed to fear that his openness was beginning to border on weakness, and his tone hardened.

"So if you don't want wolves in the streets of the nearest town, you'll see to it. My people are hunters, Thaddeus, and we're hungry. Find out what's going on, and end it." He stalked off without another word, howl, bark, or otherwise.

"If they're such good hunters," I asked Thaddeus, "why can't they deal with whatever it is themselves?"

Thaddeus grunted, eyes fixed on the retreating Markus, and I wondered if he was thinking the same thing.

MONGRELFOLK

The figure lopes down a dingy alleyway in a forgotten part of town, wrapped all about in a large and unshapely garment to disguise its large and unshapely form. A call and response is tapped out by its footsteps on the cobblestones - thud, clack, thud, clack, thud, clack - the pattern of sound and the ungainly asymmetry of its shoulders, rising and falling with each stride, describe the inequality of the feet beneath. It stops briefly as it approaches a doorway, turning its head almost full circle to survey the quiet street with too many eyes, and lets out a quiet grunt, a mixture of relief at its successful concealment, and despair at the iniquity of its existence.

The magical arts, despite what their practitioners may claim, are as unpredictable and dangerous as they are useful. A relative few well-worn combinations of words and gestures exist, deemed safe and reliable by specialists. Beyond these, however, is a great unknown, a tempting and tempestuous gulf of knowledge. Tentative sorties into the unknown can be profitable, but also hold the potential to go devastatingly wrong, as the unfortunate mongrelfolk demonstrate.

Horribly deformed by extreme arcane disturbances, mongrelfolk combine an assortment of humanoid and animal features, seemingly distributed at random. One might display insectoid claws and reptilian spines jutting from a human form, while another might appear ordinary were it not for the dangling hound's ears framing its face; both the specifics and severity of mutations vary wildly.

These mutations take a toll on the unfortunate creature's body, and it is common for their lifespan to be rather shorter than might otherwise be expected, depending on the specifics. It is rare for mutations to be as immediately fatal as, say, jaws unable process the kind of food a mismatched digestive system needs, but ongoing strains, such as large body parts paired with a small heart ill-equipped to support them, are quite common.

As a rule, mongrelfolk are sterile, their physiology too radically altered to produce children. However, in very rare cases where two individuals' mutations are similar or minor, reproduction is technically possible (though the irregular allocation of genetic traits makes it unlikely that any offspring will physically resemble their parents). Even in these rare cases, mongrelfolk often choose not to reproduce, given that any offspring might not survive their mutations, and will likely live as second-class citizens if they do.

Groups of mongrelfolk tend to be fractious, without a common culture and lacking the generational stability to develop one. Sometimes the eldest or wisest hold court, but it is just as common for the strongest to seize power and hold onto it as long as they can. Within larger groups, mongrelfolk might gather together with those most physically similar to themselves for convenience and companionship – those who are forced to eat the same unusual diet, for example. These in-groups often arrange into their own hierarchy, the exact nature of which is dependent on the outlook of the larger collective. For many mongrelfolk, those closest in appearance to 'normal' humanoids reign at the top of the pecking order. However, where the feeling is more angry and resentful, the more twisted and grotesque individuals may declare themselves as the furthest from the hated civilized folk, and the closest to a new form of life: stronger, more adaptable, and better than that which came before.

The overriding factor in the lives of almost all mongrelfolk is the reaction of the general populace to their very existence. Mongrelfolk are universally reviled, with superstition running rampant about their origins and nature. It is commonly held as unquestioned fact that mongrelfolk (or their parents) must have done something to deserve their fate, and have been cursed by the gods for some misdeed, or to mark their evil nature. It is also not uncommon for there to be some confusion with lycanthropy, which only serves to heighten people's fear and paranoia towards the condition. In truth, there is nothing in a mongrelfolk's nature to make them intrinsically evil, but the pariah status thrust upon them can sometimes force them that way, and understandably so.

ORIGIN

Mongrelfolk are created spontaneously in areas of extreme magical disturbance, where experimental spells have gone awry, or at sites of devastating arcane bombardments. In cases of teleportation, or plane-shifting magic, the unfortunate inhabitants of the affected area can be transformed almost instantaneously. For others, a painful and drawn out process of change takes place, as their bodies are warped over time by the lingering magical energy.

Where uncontrolled magic is allowed to seep into an environment, for example around the stronghold of a particularly experimental mage, there may be sporadic outbreaks of mongrelism. Without a single, powerful magical event, it is rare for adults to transform, but infants may be born with mongrelfolk traits on occasion. These individuals, who appear unpredictably and seemingly from nowhere, are the most maligned, and are almost always taken for a bad omen, or a curse from the gods for lack of piety.

On a smaller scale, it is not unknown for inexpert practitioners to accidently mutate themselves with a botched teleportation. These mutations tend to be minor, and from a single source; for example, a wizard may arrive at their destination bearing whiskers after accidently including a wayward rat in their teleportation circle.

ENVIRONMENT

Mongrelfolk settlements, such as they are, are places of necessity and seclusion, rather than comfort; communes of cast-offs with few commonalities other than their shared affliction.

Many such settlements develop, grow, and merge as needs dictate, often fizzling out completely after a few 'generations' have come and gone. On occasion, especially in areas where mongrels are born relatively commonly, powerful individuals might set up more permanent communes with the intent (or, at least, guise) of charity,

giving them a place to live in peace and safety in an isolated area, or less-trafficked part of town. Whether these communes exist primarily for the wellbeing of the mongrelfolk, or to spare the townspeople the unpleasant reminder of their existence, is another matter. All too often, this arrangement starts well, but quickly degenerates with any significant increase in the mongrelfolk population, as the commune becomes overcrowded, filthy and, eventually, ignored save for the occasional meager shipment of food and supplies.

Possibly the best life a mongrel can hope for is a nomadic one, and a group of mongrelfolk small enough to travel quietly, while large enough to defend themselves, can do fairly well. Some trade or undertake menial labor to pay their way, others lean on the superstition surrounding them to sell magical services such as charms and hexes (some of which may even work), and a few earn their pennies cavorting for the amusement of a jeering crowd. However they make a living, theirs is a life of continually anticipating (or fleeing from) the latest mob.

ROLEPLAYING MONGRELFOLK

The universal despisement of mongrelfolk does far more to shape their characters than anything in their nature. Most are simply resigned to their fate, and attempt to make the best of it, but tend towards the morose or cynical, as a result. Some take a more extreme view, riling against their stigma, and showing nothing but contempt for those who would cast them out, or else grow desperate for approval they will never gain, becoming sycophantic and fawning towards any 'normal' who will give them the time of day.

Popular superstition may paint mongrelfolk as sub-human, and little more than animals, but the truth is, while a mongrelfolk might take on a few more bestial aspects to their character, these are usually in the form of minor, unconscious physical ticks, such as preening, scratching, or sniffing for danger.

COMBAT TACTICS

Mongrelfolk approach combat in as many different ways as any other group of people. It is rare for a group to have much in the way of tactics, or even proper weaponry, as such practices are generally not encouraged by any authorities. An additional complication to developing cohesion in a group of mongrelfolk is that little can be assumed about the physical abilities of those in the group - fighting beside a large, tentacle-armed creature is a very different prospect to supporting a spring-legged, hopping one.

If a mongrelfolk's personality is subsumed by their bestial side, they may be consumed by animal fury in combat, and be difficult to reign in once blood is spilled. On the other hand, such a mongrelfolk might be markedly less violent than they otherwise would be; their feral instincts of self-preservation overriding any foolish human ideals of courage or glory.

MONGRELFOLK ENCOUNTERS

d4	CR	Encounter
1	1	**Hidden Outcasts:** 4 Mongrelfolk, 2 Mongrelfolk Mites
2	2	**Distrustful Community:** 2 Mongrelfolk Thugs, 6 Mongrelfolk, 3 Mongrelfolk Mites
3	4	**Reclusive Enclave:** 2 Mongrelfolk Warriors, 4 Mongrelfolk Thugs, 6 Mongrelfolk, 3 Mongrelfolk Mites
4	6	**Isolationist Gang:** 2 Mongrelfolk Brutes, 4 Mongrelfolk Warriors, 5 Mongrelfolk Thugs

MONGRELFOLK MITE

Small humanoid (mongrelfolk), any alignment

Armor Class 11
Hit Points 13 (3d6 + 3)
Speed 20 ft.

STR	DEX	CON	INT	WIS	CHA
10 (+0)	12 (+1)	12 (+1)	10 (+0)	10 (+0)	9 (-1)

Skills Deception +3, Perception +2
Senses passive Perception 12
Languages Common
Challenge 1/8 (25 XP)

Prominent Deformities. The mite has up to 4 features from the mongrelfolk deformity table (p.79), determined randomly by rolling a d4 and d20 each, or chosen by the GM.

ACTIONS

Bite. *Melee Weapon Attack:* +3 to hit, reach 5 ft., one creature. *Hit:* 3 (1d4 + 1) piercing damage.

Claw. *Melee Weapon Attack:* +3 to hit, reach 5 ft., one creature. *Hit:* 3 (1d4 + 1) slashing damage.

Dagger. *Melee or Ranged Weapon Attack:* +3 to hit, reach 5 ft. or range 20/60 ft., one creature. *Hit:* 3 (1d4 + 1) piercing damage.

MONGRELFOLK

Medium humanoid (mongrelfolk), any alignment

Armor Class 11 (natural armor)
Hit Points 19 (3d8 + 6)
Speed 20 ft.

STR	DEX	CON	INT	WIS	CHA
12 (+1)	9 (-1)	14 (+2)	9 (-1)	10 (+0)	7 (-2)

Skills Deception +2, Perception +2
Senses passive Perception 12
Languages Common
Challenge 1/4 (50 XP)

Prominent Deformities. The mongrelfolk has up to 4 features from the mongrelfolk deformity table (p.79), determined randomly by rolling a d4 and d20 each, or chosen by the GM.

ACTIONS

Multiattack. The mongrelfolk makes two attacks: one with its bite, and one with its claw or dagger.

Bite. *Melee Weapon Attack:* +3 to hit, reach 5 ft., one creature. *Hit:* 3 (1d4 + 1) piercing damage.

Claw. *Melee Weapon Attack:* +3 to hit, reach 5 ft., one creature. *Hit:* 3 (1d4 + 1) slashing damage.

Dagger. *Melee or Ranged Weapon Attack:* +3 to hit, reach 5 ft. or range 20/60 ft., one creature. *Hit:* 3 (1d4 + 1) piercing damage.

"A failed experiment can teach you far more than a successful one. I think of it as a new form of life. I am not better, or worse, than I was before. I am simply...different."

-Bromish Tidwael, wizard, known to locals as 'The Bird-Man of the Belfry'

MONGRELFOLK THUG

Medium humanoid (mongrelfolk), any alignment

Armor Class 12 (natural armor)
Hit Points 32 (5d8 + 10)
Speed 20 ft.

STR	DEX	CON	INT	WIS	CHA
14 (+2)	10 (+0)	15 (+2)	9 (-1)	10 (+0)	7 (-2)

Skills Athletics +4, Deception +2, Perception +2
Senses passive Perception 12
Languages Common
Challenge 1/2 (100 XP)

Prominent Deformities. The thug has up to 4 features from the mongrelfolk deformity table (p.79), determined randomly by rolling a d4 and d20 each, or chosen by the GM.

ACTIONS

Multiattack. The thug makes three attacks: one with its bite, one with its claw, and one with its spear. If it is wielding a shield, it can only attack once with its claw or spear.

Bite. *Melee Weapon Attack:* +4 to hit, reach 5 ft., one creature *Hit:* 4 (1d4 + 2) piercing damage.

Claw. *Melee Weapon Attack:* +4 to hit, reach 5 ft., one creature. *Hit:* 4 (1d4 + 2) slashing damage.

Spear. *Melee or Ranged Weapon Attack:* +4 to hit, reach 5 ft. or range 20/60 ft., one creature. *Hit:* 5 (1d6 + 2) piercing damage.

MONGRELFOLK WARRIOR

Medium humanoid (mongrelfolk), any alignment

Armor Class 14 (natural armor, shield)
Hit Points 45 (6d8 + 18)
Speed 20 ft.

STR	DEX	CON	INT	WIS	CHA
14 (+2)	10 (+0)	16 (+3)	9 (-1)	10 (+0)	7 (-2)

Skills Athletics +4, Deception +2, Perception +2
Senses passive Perception 12
Languages Common
Challenge 1 (200 XP)

Prominent Deformities. The warrior has up to 4 features from the mongrelfolk deformity table (p.79), determined randomly by rolling a d4 and d20 each, or chosen by the GM. Mongrelfolk warriors tend to have more actively beneficial deformities than their common kin. Instead of a d20, roll a d10 and add +10 to the result for the first two features generated.

ACTIONS

Multiattack. The warrior makes three attacks: one with its bite, one with its claw, and one with its spear. If it is wielding a shield, it can only attack once with its claw or spear.

Bite. *Melee Weapon Attack:* +4 to hit, reach 5 ft., one creature. *Hit:* 4 (1d4 + 2) piercing damage.

Claw. *Melee Weapon Attack:* +4 to hit, reach 5 ft., one creature. *Hit:* 4 (1d4 + 2) slashing damage.

Spear. *Melee or Ranged Weapon Attack:* +4 to hit, reach 5 ft. or range 20/60 ft., one creature. *Hit:* 5 (1d6 + 2) piercing damage.

Mongrelfolk Brute

Large humanoid (mongrelfolk), any alignment

Armor Class 14 (natural armor)
Hit Points 68 (8d10 + 24)
Speed 30 ft.

STR	DEX	CON	INT	WIS	CHA
18 (+4)	10 (+0)	17 (+3)	7 (-2)	10 (+0)	6 (-2)

Skills Athletics +6, Deception +2, Perception +2
Senses passive Perception 12
Languages Common
Challenge 3 (700 XP)

Prominent Deformities. The brute has up to 4 features from the mongrelfolk deformity table (p.79), determined randomly by rolling a d4 and d20 each, or chosen by the GM. Mongrelfolk brutes tend to have more powerful deformities than their common kin. Instead of a d20, roll a d10 and add +10 to the result for the first two features generated.

For deformities that mention damage dice, double the number of dice the mongrelfolk brute rolls. For example, a brute with a crablike pincer arm (result 16) rolls 2d8 damage for damage with its claw.

Actions

Multiattack. The brute makes three attacks: one with its bite, one with its claw, and one with its handaxe.

Bite. *Melee Weapon Attack:* +6 to hit, reach 5 ft., one creature. *Hit:* 9 (2d4 + 4) piercing damage.

Claw. *Melee Weapon Attack:* +6 to hit, reach 5 ft., one creature. *Hit:* 9 (2d4 + 4) slashing damage.

Handaxe. *Melee or Ranged Weapon Attack:* +6 to hit, reach 5 ft. or range 20/60 ft., one creature. *Hit:* 11 (2d6 + 4) piercing damage.

Unfortunate victims of extreme mutations, even by mongrelfolk standards, **brutes** typically pay for their increased physical power with a marked decrease in higher brain functions.

Mongrelfolk Deformities

When randomly determining a feature for a mongrelfolk, roll a d4 and a d20. The d4 determines which part of the body is affected, and the d20 determines the exact effect. If you just want to generate purely cosmetic traits, simply roll a d10 instead of a d20. To only generate traits with mechanical effects, add +10 to the result of the d10.

When rolling for features randomly, it is possible that you will roll the exact same feature twice; if you do, the feature applies twice, if possible. Numeric bonuses stack with themselves. For example, if you roll result 2 for legs twice, both legs end in hooves. A mongrelfolk can't have more than two of the same feature with a mechanical effect.

If two features are mutually exclusive, or you roll more than two of the same feature with a mechanical effect, reroll the feature you generated last until you get a feature that does not conflict with any other. It is up to you to decide whether to reconcile two features with each other, or find them to be mutually exclusive.

D20 \ D4	1. Head	2. Torso	3. Arms	4. Legs
1	Vertical pupils	Shaggy fur along the neck and shoulders	Humanoid hands in an unusual configuration, such as outward facing palms or zygodactylous fingers (two back and two front facing, like a parrot).	Vestigial extra leg
2	A patch of quills	Strongly hunched back	Vestigial animal limb protruding from one forearm, in addition to the humanoid hand	Hooves
3	Insectoid mandibles	Protruding spinal ridge	Bird-like talon for a hand	Shaggy fur covering one lower leg
4	A single crooked antler or horn	Dorsal fin	Large paw and shaggy fur along one forearm	One lizard-like foot
5	A set of vestigial antennae	Vestigial insect legs, extending from the torso	One arm has an additional elbow joint	One leg, covered in thin chitinous exoskeleton with an insectoid foot
6	Elongated, flexible neck	White, hairless albino skin	Large feathers growing from one forearm	A reduced number of large, fleshy toes
7	Split lower jaw	Bloated pot belly	Humanoid, non-functioning non-arm tissue (such as teeth, ears or digits) grow out of the upper arm and shoulder	Blunt, shovel-like claws
8	Needle-like teeth	Fur-covered tail	One hand's fingers are miniature tentacles	Knees bend backwards
9	Tentacle pseudopods surrounding the mouth	Disproportionately long torso	Fleshy membrane connects wrist to torso	One leg ends in two feet
10	Lipless mouth with exposed teeth and gums.	Newborn-sized limbs protrude from the chest	One hand is unusually heavy with thick fingers fused together like a mitten	Splayed, grasping toes
11	**Single cyclopean eye.** The mongrelfolk has disadvantage on attack rolls against targets 30 feet or farther away. This feature has no effect if the mongrelfolk also has additional, or compound, eyes.	**Open lesions.** The mongrelfolk has disadvantage on saving throws against diseases, being poisoned, and effects that deal necrotic or poison damage.	**Crooked arm.** The mongrelfolk has disadvantage on attack rolls made with its affected arm.	**Withered leg.** If the mongrelfolk takes a Dash action, it must succeed on a DC 10 Dexterity (Acrobatics) check, or fall prone at the end of its movement. If the mongrelfolk has this deformity twice, its speed is reduced by 5 feet.
12	**Prehensile tongue.** The mongrelfolk can pick up objects and attempt to grapple Tiny creatures using its tongue instead of a free hand. The tongue can grasp or grapple targets up to 10 feet away. Its Strength score, for the purpose of lifting and dragging loads, is 4.	**Scaly tail.** The mongrelfolk has advantage on Dexterity checks and saving throws made to resist being knocked prone.	**Oversized arm.** The mongrelfolk can ignore the two-handed property of a weapon it wields in its oversized hand. When rolling for damage for the claw of the oversized hand, the mongrelfolk rolls the damage dice one additional time and adds it to the total.	**Exceptionally muscular legs.** The mongrelfolk's walking speed increases by 10 feet.

D20 \ D4	1. Head	2. Torso	3. Arms	4. Legs
13	**Additional/compound eyes.** The mongrelfolk has advantage on Wisdom (Perception) checks that rely on sight. Additionally, it gains a +2 bonus to ranged attack rolls.	**Tough hide.** The mongrelfolk's armor class increases by 1.	**Third arm.** The mongrelfolk can wield items in two hands and still have a hand free to make a claw attack.	**Sensitive leg follicles.** The mongrelfolk has tremorsense out to a range of 30 feet.
14	**Muzzled face.** The mongrelfolk has advantage on Wisdom (Perception) checks that rely on hearing or smell. Its bite attack deals 1d6 damage, rather than 1d4.	**Bone spikes.** While the mongrelfolk is grappled, it can use a bonus action to deal 2d6 piercing damage to the grappler.	**Elongated Arm.** The mongrelfolk's reach increases by 5 feet for melee attacks made with the elongated arm.	**Digitigrade legs.** The mongrelfolk's long jump is up to 20 feet and its high jump is up to 10 feet, without a running start.
15	**Additional head.** The mongrelfolk has advantage on Wisdom (Perception) checks, and on saving throws against being blinded, charmed, deafened, frightened, stunned, or knocked unconscious.	**Pseudopod tentacles.** When the mongrelfolk makes a weapon attack against a creature, it can attempt to grapple it as a bonus action (escape DC = 10 + the mongrelfolk's Strength modifier).	**Tentacle.** Instead of a claw attack, the mongrelfolk makes a tentacle attack that functions the same way, except that it deals bludgeoning damage and the target is grappled on a hit (escape DC = 10 + the mongrelfolk's Strength modifier). Until the grapple ends, the mongrelfolk can't attack another target with its tentacle.	**Additional leg.** The mongrelfolk has advantage on Strength checks and saving throws to resist being moved or knocked prone. If the mongrelfolk has this feature twice, its walking speed increases by 5 feet.
16	**Gills.** The mongrelfolk can breathe in both air and water.	**Exceptionally muscular frame.** The mongrelfolk has advantage on Strength and Constitution saving throws.	**Pincer.** The mongrelfolk's claw attack with this arm deals 1d8 bludgeoning damage, instead of 1d4 slashing damage.	**Webbed toes.** The mongrelfolk has a swim speed equal to half its walking speed.
17	**Reflective eyes.** The mongrelfolk has darkvision out to a range of 60 feet.	**Wings.** The mongrelfolk has a flying speed of 40 feet.	**Abnormally long fingers.** The mongrelfolk has advantage on Dexterity (Sleight of Hand) checks and Dexterity checks using thieves tools.	**Snaking lower body.** The mongrelfolk gains a constrict attack. It can choose to make one constrict attack in place of both its bite and claw. The attack functions the same way as a claw attack, except that it deals 2d4 bludgeoning damage rather than 1d4 slashing damage, and the target is grappled on a hit (escape DC = 10 + the mongrelfolk's Strength modifier). Until the grapple ends, the target is restrained, and the mongrelfolk can't constrict another target.

D20 \ D4	1. Head	2. Torso	3. Arms	4. Legs
18	**Venomous fangs.** The mongrelfolk's bite attack deals an extra 1d4 poison damage. Additionally, as an action, or as part of its multiattack in place of its bite, the mongrelfolk can force a creature within 10 feet of it to make a Dexterity saving throw (DC = 10 + the mongrelfolk's Constitution modifier). On a failed save, the target takes 1d4 poison damage.	**Stinger.** The mongrelfolk can choose to make a stinger attack in place of either a claw or bite attack. The stinger functions identically to the mongrelfolk's bite, except that it deals 1d6 poison damage in addition to the regular damage.	**Climbing pads.** The mongrelfolk gains a climb speed equal to half its walking speed. If the mongrelfolk has the same feature on its legs, it can climb difficult surfaces, including upside down on ceilings.	**Climbing pads.** The mongrelfolk gains a climb speed equal to half its walking speed. If the mongrelfolk has the same feature on its arms, it can climb difficult surfaces, including upside down on ceilings.
19	**Flexible Vocal Organs.** The mongrelfolk can mimic any sound it has heard, including voices. A creature that hears the sound can tell they are imitations with a successful DC 12 Wisdom (Insight) check.	**Embedded maw.** When the mongrelfolk makes a bite attack against a creature it is grappling, or is grappled by, it can choose to have the bite deal 2d8 damage, rather than 1d4.	**Electrostatic hand.** The mongrelfolk can innately cast the *shocking grasp* cantrip. Its spellcasting ability for this is Wisdom.	**Padded feet.** As long as the mongrelfolk is not wearing footwear, it has advantage on Dexterity (Stealth) checks made to move silently.
20	**Bat ears.** The mongrelfolk has advantage on Wisdom (Perception) checks based on hearing and has blindsight out to a range of 30 feet. It can't use its blindsight while deafened.	**Rubbery hide.** The mongrelfolk regains 3 hit points at the start of each of its turns. If the mongrelfolk takes acid or fire damage, this trait doesn't function at the start of its next turn.	**Charred hand.** The mongrelfolk can innately cast the *produce flame* cantrip. Its spellcasting ability for this is Wisdom.	**Dragon-like legs.** The mongrelfolk has resistance against damage of the type associated with the scale color. 1-2: Black, Acid 3-4: Blue, Lightning 5-6: Green, Poison 7-8: Red, Fire 9-10: White, Cold

Item 24b – Persons/places of note

Lord Matthew Pitson Convalescent Estate for The Afflicted (referred to locally as the 'Mutt Pit') - Residents of the immediate surrounding suburbs have reported to council members their concerns that the rate of deterioration in the, so called, 'Mutt Pit' is starting to have an adverse effect on their house prices and personal safety. Despite multiple warnings, and threats of legal action, The Afflicted are leaving the boundary of their generously gifted convalescent estate to visit neighbouring wells, as theirs has, reportedly, been poisoned (city watch report, attached, is unable to confirm the validity of these claims. Poisoning recorded as 'accidental vandalism'). Local reports also suggest that Afflicted are eating their stillborn young.

Recommendations:

-Send sanitation officer and engineer, under guard, to purify the well, so the poor creatures do not have to trouble themselves leaving the safety of the estate.

-One extra scoop of millet and two additional jugs of ale in next month's food delivery wagon.

-taken from the minutes of Poznica bi-monthly city council meeting

Our contact's name was Cicatrix, though he went mostly by the charming moniker of 'Scab'. His place of residence was a back room of The Odds and Ends, a less than savoury establishment found in the city of Usenrog. To be more accurate, it was a less than savory establishment found in the sprawling mongrelfolk colony that clung to the side of Usenrog like a tumorous growth, a shared dumping ground for all the detritus the city would rather forget about.

We picked our way through streets awash with what I sincerely hoped was mud, and the lead-gray sky grew dimmer and dimmer as upper levels crowded and leaned in over the thoroughfare. The few sullen inhabitants we passed went hooded and cloaked, though whether this was against the rain or out of habit, I did not know. Most were quick to turn away, but I felt their eyes upon me as soon as they left my sight; the very shadows themselves seemed watchful, as if they knew I did not belong. Here and there, I glimpsed a mismatched face within the cowl. Thaddeus had warned me not to stare, but I found it difficult to heed his advice.

At a landmark I originally took for a pile of rags discarded on a street corner, Thaddeus gestured towards a barely-visible sign, creaking in the shadow of the eaves, and we made our way towards The Odds and Ends. It was only as I made to skirt the pile of rags that I realised it was, in fact, yet another misshapen figure, holding its ragged and patched cloak close about itself. The stub of a beak protruded from its hood. It was motionless, heeding neither our presence nor, seemingly, the downpour, but simply staring, listless and alone, the very picture of misery.

The interior scarcely served to improve the impression. True to its name, The Odds and Ends seemed to have been constructed from parts that other taverns had previously used and discarded; the younger sibling of all the taverns in the city proper, forced to wear their ill-fitting cast-offs. Sidling gingerly around mismatched crates, barrels and other items posing as furniture, we approached the bar and asked after our contact.

The barman, a man whose vastness dominated the bar, pinned though he was behind it, wrinkled his porcine nose at the mention of Scab's name, and gestured with a grunt towards a door in the back wall, which swung loosely in an aperture too large for it. Within, behind a table set with three (mismatched) tankards, sat our 'man'.

The thing I found immediately disconcerting about Scab was his eyes. His left was dark and beady, set deep in a morass of loose, drooping flesh which looked as if it had, at some point, been set too close to a flame and begun to melt. His right, however, protruded in a chameleonic cone of flesh. Both made darting passage across the room almost constantly, though not in synchrony. He parted his fleshy lips with a wet, bulbous tongue.

"Thad! Always a pleasure, never a chore. Do have a seat."

I noted that one of his eyes never left me, even as the other crinkled in a smile at Thaddeus. I introduced myself to the floor, not quite able to bring myself to meet them.

"Have a drink, the both of you. It's swill, but we all make do with what we've got, eh?"

"I'll skip the pleasantries, if it's all the same," said Thaddeus who, I noted, had no trouble meeting whichever eye was pointed at him. "Heard some rumors from the hill clans. Seems something's happening up that way, and I don't like the smell of it. Got anything you can tell me?"

"Oh yeah, yeah, I got lots I can tell you," Scab rasped. "I can tell you the sad tale of the captain who came home from the war to find his lady wife great with another man's child. I can tell you of the mucky scheme to fix the next bout at the rat pit. I could muse at length about our recent, inclement weather..."

"Let's start with something relevant."

"Relevant? Oh yeah, I can do relevant. 'Course the more... ah... relevant the information, the more..." He trailed off expectantly, staring pointedly at the spot on the table in front of him.

Thaddeus slid across a few pieces of silver, with a look that suggested that if silver would not serve, he would be happy to try again with steel. Scab declined to press his luck further, but pocketed the coins with a sycophantic smile.

"I can only tell you what I've heard. Some down here, they get by on what they're handed, and don't look for much more, but some, they got families, or they got pride, or they just want a bit more coin in their purse, they go looking for work topside." He gestured roughly towards the direction of the city proper. "Not strictly legal, but we work hard and we work cheap, and we ain't exactly gonna blab about it down the tavern.

"Now, it seems there's been a lot of work lately, excavation, buried treasure or some such, up in the hills. Seems quite a few of us lot have been hired over the last couple of months, and most of 'em haven't come back. Now, that's not the most unusual thing in the world; most of the time, we're hired because no one's gonna raise a stink topside if we end up counting worms. No, what makes it unusual is the story those who do come back have to tell."

He offered to take us to one of these unfortunates (for a price, of course), and we found ourselves trudging through the streets once more. I thought our initial jaunt had been bad but, as it transpired, the colony presented its best face to new visitors, and it was only downhill from there. As we walked, Scab whistled cheerfully, and had the unnerving habit of attempting to make eye contact with his swiveling, protruding eye without turning his head to the pair of us following along behind. Perhaps he should have been watching his feet, as he definitely tracked something nasty along with him for a few streets. He and Thaddeus scarcely seemed to mind the mire, or the smell which has since burnt its way into my mind, where I fear it will remain forever.

At a row of shacks, crude tenements clinging to the larger shacks of the more well-to-do, Scab gestured for us to stop. He entered one of the squat buildings and poked out his head a few moments later, inviting us to join him. Within was a firepit ringed by broken bits of brick, a pallet bed, and precious little else. Lying on the bed was a figure, muttering to itself. A twitching antenna was visible from behind, sprouting from its forehead, along with the scaled, bald tail of a rat, poking through a judicious hole in tattered breeches.

"Tell us what happened in the hills, Mullock," Scab said, gently but firmly, as one might to a sick child who must do something unpleasant for their own good.

"Doeszzzn't want," buzzed the reply, "go 'way." There was a definite clacking noise around the consonants I would describe as 'mandibular', and I became aware that I very much didn't want Mullock to turn around.

"It's important," intoned Thaddeus. "We want to stop it happening to anyone else."

"Didn't find no gold. All lies," sobbed Mullock. "Szzzoldiersz take Mullock away. Rotting and withered. Take him to the mountainsz. Take him into the mountainsz. Mullock is alone now, but he waszzzn't then. They took others too. Took them to the chamber, and did things to them, cut them and drew them and wrapped them all up, and they waszzzn't them when they got back up. Mullock tried to run, but they catched him. Draff fought them off, but they took him and they...they cut hiszzz heart out. Mullock ran. He ran and he left them all behind."

Thaddeus thanked him, placed a few coins beside the pallet, and motioned for us to leave.

"Cut out hearts? Chambers in the mountains? Some kind of death cult?" I asked, as soon as we emerged onto the street, wanting to appear the shrewd investigator.

"Worse, I think. The wrappings, the removal of the organs, victims getting back up. Death cult of a sort, I suppose – an ancient one. Royally endorsed. Thank you Scab, this has all been very useful."

"'Course," our informer said, stalking away. "We gotta look out for each other, ain't we?" He glanced behind a final time with his unnerving eye. "Lot of very strange folk around these days..."

Mummies

The thing that had been a king once inches a bandaged claw over the edge of its gilded sarcophagus. The richly carved walls show a figure of grace and dignity, but the creature now drawing itself up to full height has none of these qualities. Withered skin clings parchment-like to bones, barely concealed by the rotting, soiled bandages, woven with amulets and charms of protection for a restful afterlife. The lipless mouth gapes wide with a forlorn moan, a rattling breath from another world, and the sands swirl around it in protest.

Preparation of the dead, even involved and intricate preparation, is fairly common practice. The lengths the creators of mummies go to are unusual, but fairly widespread, though the fruits of their labor are only truly successful and long-lasting in very dry environments conducive to their preservation; primarily deserts and arid mountains. Priests and underlings work for months to leech all moisture from the body, remove and preserve separately the important organs, cleanse the dried corpse with sacred oils and resins, and finally inter the mummy in its tomb. The intent is to ensure the deceased has a worthy vessel to inhabit in the next life, but many of the rituals are, knowingly or unknowingly, perverted to instead create monstrosities.

One of the most infamous aspects of mummies is the terrible curse they bestow upon those who disturb their rest. It is undeniable that a mummy's touch can transfer a necrotic sickness which causes the victim to waste away over the course of a few days and, if we believe the tales, collapse into a pile of dust. Stories also tell of the 'mummy's curse'. Supposedly, those who disturb a mummy's tomb will be cursed with a rash of terrible misfortune (though many argue that some folk just have bad luck). Darker still, if the curse does exist, the tales mention not only the ruin and death of the original offenders, but also that of their acquaintances and loved ones. Rumors mention everything from further ill-luck, nightmare-plagued sleep and financial woes, to maiming and even death. All of these distressing details are accompanied by an overlying dark sense of humor, as the events that befall the victims often relate ironically to their discovery and invasion of the mummy's abode or events from the mummy's life. To make matters worse (should anyone be foolish enough to tempt fate, even after knowing all of this), the curse may be invoked by simple contact with stolen artefacts.

ORIGIN

Undead mummies are created when the lengthy embalming and burial rites practised by mummy-creating cultures are subtly altered. In some cases, agents from demonic cults have a hand in warping individual rites, in others, the sacred instructional texts have unknown infernal origins which had been assumed divine. A few, however, undertake the dark rituals knowingly; cultures of demon-worshippers, and those who believe the souls of the dead must suffer in order to be cleansed. Whatever the reasons for the corruption of the process, the deceased's spirit is condemned to a plane of torment and suffering, instead of passing on to the next world with all the grandeur it deserves.

The last stage of the rite of mummification is the interring of the body in its tomb and creating a magical seal. This seal protects the preserved body from any attempts to raise it by forces unintended by the ritual-casters. The seal may be a physical object, such as a tablet designed to break upon the opening of the tomb, or may be a curse triggered by the removal of objects from the tomb, speaking the mummy's name, or approaching the sarcophagus without the proper ceremony. Whatever the case, as soon as the seal is broken, the mummy is possessed and animates. Often, the spirit which inhabits the body is the original soul, driven mad by what could have been millennia of suffering in a hellish death plane. Other times, the spirit is demonic in nature; that of whichever foul creature consumed the original. In either case, the mummy, now consumed with rage, will seek out those who desecrated its resting place and destroy them.

Part of the mummification process is the removal of several key organs for their separate preservation, often in ornately decorated jars. For the most powerful mummies, these fulfil a similar function to a lich's phylactery, ensuring the mummy cannot be truly destroyed while the heart remains intact, although they do not require a phylactery's regular sacrifice of mortal souls to maintain, nor any input or consent from the mummy to create – indeed, many mummies seem positively enraged at their inability to die.

ENVIRONMENT

Two main factors inform the details of a mummy's tomb; the creation of a mummy is a lengthy, expensive process reserved for the very wealthy, and the desire to create a mummy is generally indicative of a culture which places great emphasis on the deceased's experiences in the afterlife.

A tomb is usually extensive, with multiple chambers serving to house grave goods; one might contain favorite weapons and serve as a display of martial might, another might contain statues of the gods to show their piety, and so on. The wealth within is a tempting target for raiders, so many tombs are unassuming from the outside; a would-be tomb robber stumbling into such a place might be unaware of its significance until they see the glint of gold and, perhaps, hear the scrape of the sarcophagus opening. A few, though, stand as monuments to the wealth and greatness of the interred; towering pyramids, or sprawling necropolises, fortified against those with plunder on their minds.

As well as their wealth, mummies are usually buried with objects it is believed they will need in the next life. Galleys and chariots to provide them transport, preserved food and jars of wine to sustain them, and figurines of servants to attend to their needs. Richer mummies may be buried with those who served them in life, with their tomb filled with the mummified corpses of their servants, spouses, and favored pets. It is unclear how willing these individuals are to sacrifice themselves to serve another after death, yet they line the dusty halls regardless.

When a mummy animates, it has complete control of the contents of its tomb and, unwilling though they may have been, these lesser mummies will animate to serve it. As well as these, some powerful mummies can animate their grave goods, sending animated statues against desecrators, from painted wooden servants, to towering gods of granite.

A mummy's tomb will generally contain multiple traps; some, within the tomb proper, might activate to prevent an intruder escaping back the way they came, while others may be seen as almost altruistic in nature, attempting to ward off the curious before they can reach and break the seal.

ROLEPLAYING MUMMIES

The mummy around whom the ritual is centered (not to be confused with the lesser mummies of a pet or servant) is not a mindless undead like a zombie or skeleton, but neither is it fully in control of its faculties. Rage clouds all other emotions, rage at those who disturb their rest, and rage against their very existence and the afterlife denied to them. Some, with more control of their personality, might hold less fury for those who treat them in a manner they feel appropriate to their station, worshiping them as the mix of god and monarch they were in life. Such individuals, rather than simply seeking revenge on the living, may aim to re-establish their old holdings anew, with the help of both living and undead thralls.

COMBAT TACTICS

Mummies possess much of the same intelligence they did in life, so a cunning warrior will fight just as cleverly, and a student of magic will cast spells just as efficiently. Conversely, the entombed servants are less skilled, yet compelled to fight regardless at their master's call.

The mummy's ire will always be focussed upon the individual who broke the seal of its tomb, followed by their companions, once they are disposed of. Should the perpetrators flee, the mummy will pursue them, and may extend its vengeance to include their families or, most extremely, anyone who comes into contact with them.

Lesser mummies will sacrifice themselves without thought in the defense of their master. However, while said master will fight mercilessly against those who have wronged them, they are unlikely to destroy themselves in the attempt, preferring to retreat to a place of safety and plan another attack.

MUMMY ENCOUNTERS

d12	CR	Encounter
1	4	**The Convicted Killers:** 2 Mummified Murderers
2	6	**The Hall Sentinels:** 3 Mummy Soldiers, 2 Tomb Hounds
3	8	**The King's Pets:** 4 Tomb Hounds, 2 Mummified Baboons, 2 Tarikhodiles, 1 Mummified Bull
4	11	**The False Grave:** 1 Mummy Acolyte False Mummy, 2 Mummified Murderer False Mummies, 4 Mummy Soldier False Mummies
5	12	**The Court Regiment:** 2 Praetorians, 8 Mummy Soldiers
6	13	**The Hidden Hand:** 1 Executioner Confidant, 2 Royal Assassins, 2 Mummified Murderers

d12	CR	Encounter
7	14	**The High Priest's Throng:** 1 Exalted Hierophant, 2 Court Priests, 4 Praetorians
8	18	**The Sacred Familiar:** 1 Bast Cat, 2 Court Priests, 6 Praetorians, 4 Ushabti
9	20	**The General's Coterie:** 1 Chosen Champion, 6 Praetorians, 8 Mummy Soldiers, 2 Royal Assassins
10	21	**The Riddle Room:** 1 Tarikhosphinx, 4 Praetorians, 2 Divine Tomb Guardians
11	23	**The Treasure Chamber:** 1 Executioner Confidant, 6 Divine Tomb Guardians, 8 Ushabti, 2 Miniature Infantry Regiments, 2 Miniature Chariots
12	25	**The Pharaoh's Tomb:** 1 Anointed King, 2 Court Priests, 6 Praetorians, 3 Royal Assassins, 2 Divine Tomb Guardians

MUMMY ROT

The exact symptoms of the cursed diseases referred to collectively as 'mummy rot' differ depending on the nature of the mummy that passed on the disease. In its most infamous form, mummy rot gradually turns the body to dust or sand. What begins as a seemingly innocuous cough soon becomes more serious as handfuls of coarse sand are hacked up from deteriorating lungs. Other varients might have the victim gradually disolve into tar, clay, peat, or even a mass of writhing beetles.

A creature cursed with mummy rot target can't regain hit points, and its hit point maximum decreases by 7 (2d6) for every 24 hours that elapse. If the curse reduces the target's hit point maximum to 0, the target dies, and its body turns to dust. The curse lasts until removed by the *remove curse* spell, or other magic.

MUMMY SOLDIER

Medium undead, lawful evil

Armor Class 15 (scale mail, shield)
Hit Points 45 (7d8 + 14)
Speed 20 ft.

STR	DEX	CON	INT	WIS	CHA
16 (+3)	9 (-1)	14 (+2)	7 (-2)	10 (+0)	11 (+0)

Skills Perception +2
Damage Vulnerabilities fire
Damage Resistances bludgeoning, piercing, and slashing from nonmagical attacks
Damage Immunities necrotic, poison
Condition Immunities charmed, exhaustion, frightened, paralyzed, poisoned
Senses darkvision 60 ft., passive Perception 12
Languages the languages it knew in life
Challenge 3 (700 XP)

ACTIONS

Multiattack. The soldier can use its Dreadful Glare and makes one attack with its Cursed Khopesh.

Cursed Khopesh. *Melee Weapon Attack:* +5 to hit, reach 5 ft., one creature. *Hit:* 6 (1d6 + 3) slashing damage, plus 7 (2d6) necrotic damage. If the target is a creature, it must succeed on a DC 12 Constitution saving throw, or be cursed with mummy rot (p.86).

Dreadful Glare. The soldier targets one creature it can see within 60 feet of it. If the target can see the soldier, it must succeed on a DC 10 Wisdom saving throw against this magic, or become frightened until the end of the soldier's next turn. If the target fails the saving throw by 5 or more, it is also paralyzed for the same duration. A target that succeeds on the saving throw is immune to the Dreadful Glare of all mummies with a challenge rating of 3 or less for the next 24 hours.

PRAETORIAN

Medium undead, lawful evil

Armor Class 15 (scale mail, shield)
Hit Points 75 (10d8 + 30)
Speed 20 ft.

STR	DEX	CON	INT	WIS	CHA
18 (+4)	9 (-1)	16 (+3)	8 (-1)	10 (+0)	11 (+0)

Skills Perception +3
Damage Vulnerabilities fire
Damage Resistances bludgeoning, piercing, and slashing from nonmagical attacks
Damage Immunities necrotic, poison
Condition Immunities charmed, exhaustion, frightened, paralyzed, poisoned
Senses darkvision 60 ft., passive Perception 13
Languages the languages it knew in life
Challenge 5 (1,800 XP)

Harrying Shield. While the praetorian has a shield equipped, the area within 5 feet of it is considered difficult terrain.

Indomitable (1/Day). The praetorian can reroll a failed save. It must use the new roll.

ACTIONS

Multiattack. The praetorian can use its Dreadful Glare and makes two attacks with its Cursed Khopesh.

Cursed Khopesh. *Melee Weapon Attack:* +7 to hit, reach 5 ft., one creature. *Hit:* 7 (1d6 + 4) slashing damage, plus 7 (2d6) necrotic damage. If the target is a creature, it must succeed on a DC 14 Constitution saving throw, or be cursed with mummy rot (p.86).

Dreadful Glare. The praetorian targets one creature it can see within 60 feet of it. If the target can see the praetorian, it must succeed on a DC 11 Wisdom saving throw against this magic, or become frightened until the end of the praetorian's next turn. If the target fails the saving throw by 5 or more, it is also paralyzed for the same duration. A target that succeeds on the saving throw is immune to the Dreadful Glare of all mummies with a challenge rating of 5 or less for the next 24 hours.

Chosen Champion

Medium undead, lawful evil

Armor Class 16 (half-plate, shield)
Hit Points 136 (16d8 + 64)
Speed 20 ft.

STR	DEX	CON	INT	WIS	CHA
18 (+4)	9 (-1)	18 (+4)	8 (-1)	10 (+0)	13 (+1)

Skills Perception +4
Damage Vulnerabilities fire
Damage Resistances bludgeoning, piercing, and slashing from nonmagical attacks
Damage Immunities necrotic, poison
Condition Immunities charmed, exhaustion, frightened, paralyzed, poisoned
Senses darkvision 60 ft., passive Perception 14
Languages the languages it knew in life
Challenge 10 (5,900 XP)

Harrying Shield. While the champion has a shield equipped, the area within 5 feet of it is considered difficult terrain.

Indomitable (2/Day). The champion can reroll a failed save. It must use the new roll.

Actions

Multiattack. The champion can use its Dreadful Glare and makes two attacks with its Cursed Khopesh.

Cursed Khopesh. *Melee Weapon Attack:* +8 to hit, reach 5 ft., one creature. *Hit:* 7 (1d6 + 4) slashing damage, plus 14 (4d6) necrotic damage. If the target is a creature, it must succeed on a DC 16 Constitution saving throw, or be cursed with mummy rot (p.86).

Dreadful Glare. The champion targets one creature it can see within 60 feet of it. If the target can see the champion, it must succeed on a DC 13 Wisdom saving throw against this magic, or become frightened until the end of the champion's next turn. If the target fails the saving throw by 5 or more, it is also paralyzed for the same duration. A target that succeeds on the saving throw is immune to the Dreadful Glare of all mummies with a challenge rating of 10 or less for the next 24 hours.

Legendary Actions

The champion can take 3 legendary actions, choosing from the options below. Only one legendary action option can be used at a time, and only at the end of another creature's turn. The champion regains spent legendary actions at the start of its turn.

Dreadful Glare. The champion uses its Dreadful Glare.

Shield Formation. The champion moves up to its speed. It must end this movement within 5 feet of either its master or closest ally, or it can't use this action.

Attack (Costs 2 Actions). The champion makes one attack with its Cursed Khopesh.

Some underlings are of such fanatical loyalty that, at the point of their master's death, they will gladly give their lives in order to continue their service and become a **chosen champion**. The death of a monarch or nobleman can be followed by a wave of death, as their household guard and soldiers give their lives to fill their tomb with protectors.

Cursed Weapons

The weapons wielded by mummies carry their rotting curse. The necrotic damage effect and mummy rot curse remain attached to the weapon, even if the mummy drops it or dies, and another wielder can make use of them. When a creature that is not a mummy starts its turn holding or touching the weapon, it takes 10 (3d6) necrotic damage, and must make a save against the mummy rot curse.

The curse can be removed from the weapon using the *remove curse* spell or other magic, turning the weapon into a mundane version of itself.

MUMMIFIED MURDERER

Medium undead, lawful evil

Armor Class 13 (natural armor)
Hit Points 38 (7d8 + 7)
Speed 30 ft.

STR	DEX	CON	INT	WIS	CHA
11 (+0)	13 (+1)	13 (+1)	10 (+0)	10 (+0)	11 (+0)

Skills Stealth +5
Damage Vulnerabilities fire
Damage Resistances bludgeoning, piercing, and slashing from nonmagical attacks
Damage Immunities necrotic, poison
Condition Immunities charmed, exhaustion, frightened, paralyzed, poisoned
Senses darkvision 60 ft., passive Perception 10
Languages the languages it knew in life
Challenge 3 (700 XP)

Quiet of the Grave. While in areas of dim light or darkness, the murderer can take the Hide action as a bonus action.

Sneak Attack (1/Turn). The murderer deals an extra 10 (3d6) damage when it hits a target with a weapon attack, and has advantage on the attack roll, or when the target is within 5 feet of an ally of the murderer that isn't incapacitated, and the murderer doesn't have disadvantage on the attack roll.

ACTIONS

Multiattack. The murderer can use its Dreadful Glare and makes one attack with its Cursed Knife.

Cursed Knife. *Melee Weapon Attack:* +3 to hit, reach 5 ft., one creature. *Hit:* 3 (1d4 + 1) piercing damage, plus 7 (2d6) necrotic damage. If the target is a creature, it must succeed on a DC 11 Constitution saving throw, or be cursed with mummy rot (p.86).

Dreadful Glare. The murderer targets one creature it can see within 60 feet of it. If the target can see the murderer, it must succeed on a DC 10 Wisdom saving throw against this magic, or become frightened until the end of the murderer's next turn. If the target fails the saving throw by 5 or more, it is also paralyzed for the same duration. A target that succeeds on the saving throw is immune to the Dreadful Glare of all mummies with a challenge rating of 3 or less for the next 24 hours.

ROYAL ASSASSIN

Medium undead, lawful evil

Armor Class 14 (natural armor)
Hit Points 58 (9d8 + 18)
Speed 30 ft.

STR	DEX	CON	INT	WIS	CHA
11 (+0)	15 (+2)	15 (+2)	10 (+0)	10 (+0)	13 (+1)

Skills Stealth +8
Damage Vulnerabilities fire
Damage Resistances bludgeoning, piercing, and slashing from nonmagical attacks
Damage Immunities necrotic, poison
Condition Immunities charmed, exhaustion, frightened, paralyzed, poisoned
Senses darkvision 60 ft., passive Perception 10
Languages the languages it knew in life
Challenge 5 (1,800 XP)

Quiet of the Grave. While in areas of dim light or darkness, the assassin can take the Hide action as a bonus action.

Sneak Attack (1/Turn). The assassin deals an extra 21 (6d6) damage when it hits a target with a weapon attack, and has advantage on the attack roll, or when the target is within 5 feet of an ally of the assassin that isn't incapacitated, and the assassin doesn't have disadvantage on the attack roll.

ACTIONS

Multiattack. The assassin can use its Dreadful Glare and makes one attack with its Cursed Knife. If it has two knives drawn, as a bonus action, the assassin can make an additional attack with the second Cursed Knife.

Cursed Knife. *Melee Weapon Attack:* +5 to hit, reach 5 ft., one creature. *Hit:* 4 (1d4 + 2) piercing damage, plus 7 (2d6) necrotic damage. If the target is a creature, it must succeed on a DC 13 Constitution saving throw, or be cursed with mummy rot (p.86).

Dreadful Glare. The assassin targets one creature it can see within 60 feet of it. If the target can see the assassin, it must succeed on a DC 12 Wisdom saving throw against this magic, or become frightened until the end of the assassin's next turn. If the target fails the saving throw by 5 or more, it is also paralyzed for the same duration. A target that succeeds on the saving throw is immune to the Dreadful Glare of all mummies with a challenge rating of 5 or less for the next 24 hours.

Executioner Confidant

Medium undead, lawful evil

Armor Class 16 (natural armor)
Hit Points 91 (14d8 + 28)
Speed 30 ft.

STR	DEX	CON	INT	WIS	CHA
11 (+0)	17 (+3)	15 (+2)	10 (+0)	10 (+0)	15 (+2)

Skills Stealth +11
Damage Vulnerabilities fire
Damage Resistances bludgeoning, piercing, and slashing from nonmagical attacks
Damage Immunities necrotic, poison
Condition Immunities charmed, exhaustion, frightened, paralyzed, poisoned
Senses darkvision 60 ft., passive Perception 10
Languages the languages it knew in life
Challenge 10 (5,900 XP)

Quiet of the Grave. While in areas of dim light or darkness, the confidant can take the Hide action as a bonus action.

Sneak Attack (1/Turn). The confidant deals an extra 28 (8d6) damage when it hits a target with a weapon attack, and has advantage on the attack roll, or when the target is within 5 feet of an ally of the confidant that isn't incapacitated, and the confidant doesn't have disadvantage on the attack roll.

Actions

Multiattack. The confidant can use its Dreadful Glare and makes one attack with its Cursed Knife. If it has two knives drawn, as a bonus action, the confidant can make an additional attack with the second cursed knife.

Cursed Knife. *Melee Weapon Attack:* +7 to hit, reach 5 ft., one creature. *Hit:* 4 (1d4 + 2) piercing damage, plus 14 (4d6) necrotic damage. If the target is a creature, it must succeed on a DC 14 Constitution saving throw, or be cursed with mummy rot (p.86).

Dreadful Glare. The confidant targets one creature it can see within 60 feet of it. If the target can see the confidant, it must succeed on a DC 14 Wisdom saving throw against this magic, or become frightened until the end of the confidant's next turn. If the target fails the saving throw by 5 or more, it is also paralyzed for the same duration. A target that succeeds on the saving throw is immune to the Dreadful Glare of all mummies with a challenge rating of 5 or less for the next 24 hours.

Legendary Actions

The confidant can take 3 legendary actions, choosing from the options below. Only one legendary action option can be used at a time, and only at the end of another creature's turn. The confidant regains spent legendary actions at the start of its turn.

Disappear. The confidant moves up to 15 feet and can take the Hide action.

Dreadful Glare. The confidant uses its Dreadful Glare.

Attack (Costs 2 Actions). The confidant makes one attack with its Cursed Knife.

Criminals who dared to raise a hand to their rightful masters, would-be **murderers**, are often interred as punishment - having undergone at least the preliminary stages of mummification while still alive - and forced to serve more faithfully after death.

Mummy Acolyte

Medium undead, lawful evil

Armor Class 11 (natural armor)
Hit Points 39 (6d8 + 12)
Speed 20 ft.

STR	DEX	CON	INT	WIS	CHA
11 (+0)	9 (-1)	14 (+2)	8 (-1)	16 (+3)	11 (+0)

Skills Arcana +1, Religion +3
Damage Vulnerabilities fire
Damage Resistances bludgeoning, piercing, and slashing from nonmagical attacks
Damage Immunities necrotic, poison
Condition Immunities charmed, exhaustion, frightened, paralyzed, poisoned
Senses darkvision 60 ft., passive Perception 12
Languages the languages it knew in life
Challenge 3 (700 XP)

Spellcasting. The acolyte is a 6th level spellcaster. Its spellcasting ability is Wisdom (spell save DC 13, +5 to hit with spell attacks). The acolyte has the following cleric spells prepared:

Cantrips: *sacred flame, thaumaturgy*

1st level (4 slots): *command, guiding bolt, shield of faith*

2nd level (3 slots): *hold person, spiritual weapon*

3rd level (3 slots): *dispel magic*

Actions

Multiattack. The acolyte can use its Dreadful Glare and makes one attack with its Cursed Touch.

Cursed Touch. *Melee Weapon Attack:* +2 to hit, reach 5 ft., one creature. *Hit:* 10 (3d6) necrotic damage. If the target is a creature, it must succeed on a DC 12 Constitution saving throw, or be cursed with mummy rot (p.86).

Dreadful Glare. The acolyte targets one creature it can see within 60 feet of it. If the target can see the acolyte, it must succeed on a DC 10 Wisdom saving throw against this magic, or become frightened until the end of the acolyte's next turn. If the target fails the saving throw by 5 or more, it is also paralyzed for the same duration. A target that succeeds on the saving throw is immune to the Dreadful Glare of all mummies with a challenge rating of 3 or less for the next 24 hours.

The body was embalmed seated, wrapped in bandages of woven hair and clay. The heart was placed in the cupped hands, the liver burnt as an offering. The other organs were eaten at the mourning feast. I declined the offer of a kidney, in favor of stewed roots.

—Derek Marney, 'Amongst the Hairy Folk'

COURT PRIEST

Medium undead, lawful evil

Armor Class 12 (natural armor)
Hit Points 75 (8d8 + 24)
Speed 20 ft.

STR	DEX	CON	INT	WIS	CHA
13 (+1)	9 (-1)	16 (+3)	8 (-1)	17 (+3)	13 (+1)

Skills Arcana +2, Religion +5
Damage Vulnerabilities fire
Damage Resistances bludgeoning, piercing, and slashing from nonmagical attacks
Damage Immunities necrotic, poison
Condition Immunities charmed, exhaustion, frightened, paralyzed, poisoned
Senses darkvision 60 ft., passive Perception 13
Languages the languages it knew in life
Challenge 5 (1,800 XP)

Spellcasting. The priest is an 8th level spellcaster. Its spellcasting ability is Wisdom (spell save DC 14, +7 to hit with spell attacks). The priest has the following cleric spells prepared:

Cantrips: *sacred flame, thaumaturgy*

1st level (4 slots): *command, guiding bolt, shield of faith*

2nd level (3 slots): *hold person, silence, spiritual weapon*

3rd level (3 slots): *animate dead, dispel magic*

4th level (2 slots): *divination*

ACTIONS

Multiattack. The priest can use its Dreadful Glare. It then makes an attack with its Cursed Touch or casts a spell with a casting time of an action.

Cursed Touch. *Melee Weapon Attack:* +4 to hit, reach 5 ft., one creature. *Hit:* 14 (4d6) necrotic damage. If the target is a creature, it must succeed on a DC 14 Constitution saving throw, or be cursed with mummy rot (p.86).

Dreadful Glare. The priest targets one creature it can see within 60 feet of it. If the target can see the priest, it must succeed on a DC 12 Wisdom saving throw against this magic, or become frightened until the end of the priest's next turn. If the target fails the saving throw by 5 or more, it is also paralyzed for the same duration. A target that succeeds on the saving throw is immune to the Dreadful Glare of all mummies with a challenge rating of 5 or less for the next 24 hours.

EXALTED HIEROPHANT
Medium undead, lawful evil

Armor Class 13 (natural armor)
Hit Points 97 (13d8 + 39)
Speed 20 ft.

STR	DEX	CON	INT	WIS	CHA
15 (+2)	9 (-1)	16 (+3)	8 (-1)	18 (+4)	15 (+2)

Skills Arcana +3, Religion +7
Damage Vulnerabilities fire
Damage Resistances bludgeoning, piercing, and slashing from nonmagical attacks
Damage Immunities necrotic, poison
Condition Immunities charmed, exhaustion, frightened, paralyzed, poisoned
Senses darkvision 60 ft., passive Perception 14
Languages the languages it knew in life
Challenge 10 (5,900 XP)

Spellcasting. The hierophant is a 11th level spellcaster. Its spellcasting ability is Wisdom (spell save DC 16, +8 to hit with spell attacks). The hierophant has the following cleric spells prepared:

Cantrips: *sacred flame, thaumaturgy*

1st level (4 slots): *command, guiding bolt, shield of faith*

2nd level (3 slots): *hold person, silence, spiritual weapon*

3rd level (3 slots): *animate dead, dispel magic*

4th level (3 slots): *divination, guardian of faith*

5th level (2 slot): *contagion*

6th level (1 slot): *create undead*

ACTIONS

Multiattack. The hierophant can use its Dreadful Glare. It then makes an attack with its Cursed Touch or casts a spell with a casting time of an action.

Cursed Touch. *Melee Weapon Attack:* +6 to hit, reach 5 ft., one creature. *Hit:* 21 (6d6) necrotic damage. If the target is a creature, it must succeed on a DC 15 Constitution saving throw, or be cursed with mummy rot (p.86).

Dreadful Glare. The hierophant targets one creature it can see within 60 feet of it. If the target can see the hierophant, it must succeed on a DC 14 Wisdom saving throw against this magic, or become frightened until the end of the hierophant's next turn. If the target fails the saving throw by 5 or more, it is also paralyzed for the same duration. A target that succeeds on the saving throw is immune to the Dreadful Glare of all mummies with a challenge rating of 10 or less for the next 24 hours.

LEGENDARY ACTIONS

The hierophant can take 3 legendary actions, choosing from the options below. Only one legendary action option can be used at a time, and only at the end of another creature's turn. The hierophant regains spent legendary actions at the start of its turn.

Cantrip. The hierophant casts a cantrip.

Dreadful Glare. The hierophant uses its Dreadful Glare.

Cast A Spell (Costs 3 Actions). The hierophant casts a spell from its list of prepared spells, using a spell slot as normal.

Court priests commonly owe their position to backstabbing their way into favor and, with their master gone, a quick ritual death and eternal preservation might be a kinder fate than what their rivals would have in store for them.

"I thank that mosquito every day. Had I not been laid up with firebrow, I would have been Head Translator on Varcanon's expedition. No, instead, I was left at home while my friends and colleagues were destroyed. As it was, my replacement died before she could leave the tomb, coughing up sand and chunks of lung, moments after deciphering the runic sequence required to open the burial chamber. Knowing what happened to poor Varcanon himself in the end, I wonder if she was the lucky one..."

Ansel Greer, linguist

Anointed King

Medium undead, lawful evil

Armor Class 16 (breastplate)
Hit Points 187 (22d8 + 88)
Speed 20 ft.

STR	DEX	CON	INT	WIS	CHA
19 (+4)	15 (+2)	18 (+4)	16 (+3)	20 (+5)	19 (+4)

Skills History +10, Religion +10
Damage Immunities necrotic, poison; bludgeoning, piercing, and slashing from nonmagical attacks
Condition Immunities charmed, exhaustion, frightened, paralyzed, poisoned
Senses darkvision 60 ft., passive Perception 15
Languages the languages it knew in life
Challenge 23 (50,000 XP)

Legendary Resistance (3/Day). If the anointed king fails a saving throw, it can choose to succeed instead.

Magic Resistance. The anointed king has advantage on saving throws against spells and other magical effects.

Rejuvenation. A destroyed anointed king gains a new body in 24 hours, if its heart is intact, regaining all its hit points and becoming active again. The new body appears within 5 feet of the anointed king's heart.

Spellcasting. The anointed king is an 18th level spellcaster. Its spellcasting ability is Wisdom (spell save DC 20, +12 to hit with spell attacks). The anointed king has the following cleric spells prepared:

Cantrips: *resistance, sacred flame, thaumaturgy*

1st level (4 slots): *command, inflict wounds, shield of faith*

2nd level (3 slots): *hold person, silence, spiritual weapon*

3rd level (3 slots): *animate dead, dispel magic*

4th level (3 slots): *divination, guardian of faith*

5th level (3 slots): *contagion, insect plague*

6th level (1 slot): *create undead, harm*

7th level (1 slot): *divine word*

8th level (1 slot): *control weather*

9th level (1 slot): *gate*

Turn Resistance. The anointed king has advantage on saving throws against any effect that turns undead.

Actions

Multiattack. The anointed king can use its Dreadful Glare. It then makes two attacks with its Cursed Fist or casts a spell with a casting time of an action.

Cursed Fist. *Melee Weapon Attack:* +11 to hit, reach 5 ft., one creature. *Hit:* 11 (2d6 + 4) bludgeoning damage, plus 21 (6d6) necrotic damage. If the target is a creature, it must succeed on a DC 19 Constitution saving throw, or be cursed with the pharaoh's curse. The cursed target can't regain hit points, and its hit point maximum decreases by 14 (4d6) for every 24 hours that elapse. If the curse reduces the target's hit point maximum to 0, the target dies, and its body turns to dust. The curse lasts until removed by the *remove curse* spell, or other magic. If the target is also cursed with mummy rot, the pharaoh's curse replaces the effects of mummy rot.

Dreadful Glare. The anointed king targets one creature it can see within 60 feet of it. If the target can see the anointed king, it must succeed on a DC 18 Wisdom saving throw against this magic, or become frightened until the end of the anointed king's next turn. If the target fails the saving throw by 5 or more, it is also paralyzed for the same duration. A target that succeeds on the saving throw is immune to the Dreadful Glare of all mummies with a challenge rating of 23 or less for the next 24 hours.

Legendary Actions

The anointed king can take 3 legendary actions, choosing from the options below. Only one legendary action option can be used at a time, and only at the end of another creature's turn. The anointed king regains spent legendary actions at the start of its turn.

Attack. The anointed king makes one attack with its cursed fist or uses its Dreadful Glare.

Baleful Proclamation (Costs 2 Actions). The anointed king utters a proclamation of its divine right. Creatures, other than undead, within 30 feet of the anointed king, that can hear this magical utterance must succeed on a DC 19 Charisma saving throw, or be frightened until the end of the anointed king's next turn.

Divine Bolster (Costs 2 Actions). The anointed king commands its followers to redouble their efforts. Allies within 30 feet of the anointed king, that can hear it, regain 9 (2d8) hit points.

Swarming Advance (Costs 2 Actions). The anointed king's form dissolves into a mass of scarabs which surge forward in a line that is 10 feet wide and up to 40 feet long. Each creature in the area must succeed on a DC 19 Dexterity saving throw, taking 18 (4d8) piercing damage on a failed save, or half as much damage on a successful one. The anointed king then reconstitutes from the scarabs at the opposite end of the line.

IT IS TO YOU WHO READ THIS THAT I SPEAK, UNWORTHY INVADER
YOU STEP FOOT IN THE RESTING-HOUSE OF A GOD
TAKE YOU SO MUCH AS ONE PEBBLE FROM THIS PLACE,
AND YOU SHALL RUE IT
YOU SHALL KNOW NO PEACE, NO JOY,
UNTIL THE TRANSGRESSION IS REDRESSED
YOUR NAME FORGOTTEN AND ACCURSED
YOUR LINE TURNED FALLOW, BARREN,
AND DRY AS THE DESERT SANDS
THESE ARE THE WORDS OF THE KING,
WROUGHT BY THE HAND OF HIS SERVANT

-INSCRIPTION FOUND INSIDE THE BURIAL COMPLEX OF AN UNKNOWN MONARCH

Mummified Baboon
Small undead, lawful evil

Armor Class 12 (natural armor)
Hit Points 13 (3d6 + 3)
Speed 30 ft.

STR	DEX	CON	INT	WIS	CHA
10 (+0)	13 (+1)	12 (+1)	3 (-4)	12 (+1)	4 (-3)

Damage Vulnerabilities fire
Damage Resistances bludgeoning, piercing, and slashing from nonmagical attacks
Damage Immunities necrotic, poison
Condition Immunities charmed, exhaustion, frightened, paralyzed, poisoned
Senses darkvision 60 ft., passive Perception 11
Languages —
Challenge 1/4 (50 XP)

Cursed Fangs. If the anointed baboon has advantage on an attack roll it makes with its bite against a creature and hits, the target must succeed on a DC 11 Constitution saving throw, or be cursed with mummy rot (p.86).

Pack Tactics. The anointed baboon has advantage on an attack roll against a creature if at least one of the baboon's allies is within 5 feet of the creature, and the ally isn't incapacitated.

Actions

Bite. *Melee Weapon Attack:* +3 to hit, reach 5 ft., one creature. *Hit:* 3 (1d4 + 1) piercing damage, plus 3 (1d6) necrotic damage.

Tomb Hound
Medium undead, lawful evil

Armor Class 13 (natural armor)
Hit Points 26 (4d8 + 8)
Speed 30 ft.

STR	DEX	CON	INT	WIS	CHA
14 (+2)	14 (+2)	14 (+2)	2 (-4)	10 (+0)	4 (-3)

Skills Perception +2
Damage Vulnerabilities fire
Damage Resistances bludgeoning, piercing, and slashing from nonmagical attacks
Damage Immunities necrotic, poison
Condition Immunities charmed, exhaustion, frightened, paralyzed, poisoned
Senses darkvision 60 ft., passive Perception 12
Languages —
Challenge 1 (200 XP)

Cursed Fangs. If the tomb hound has advantage on an attack roll it makes with its bite against a creature and hits, the target must succeed on a DC 12 Constitution saving throw, or be cursed with mummy rot (p.86).

Keen Hearing and Smell. The tomb hound has advantage on Wisdom (Perception) checks that rely on hearing or smell.

Actions

Bite. *Melee Weapon Attack:* +5 to hit, reach 5 ft., one creature. *Hit:* 5 (1d6 + 2) piercing damage, plus 7 (2d6) necrotic damage. If the target is a creature, it must succeed on a DC 12 Strength saving throw, or be knocked prone.

SWARM OF CURSED SNAKES

Medium swarm of Tiny undead, lawful evil

Armor Class 14 (natural armor)
Hit Points 44 (8d8 + 8)
Speed 30 ft.

STR	DEX	CON	INT	WIS	CHA
8 (-1)	16 (+3)	13 (+1)	1 (-5)	10 (+0)	1 (-5)

Saving Throws Con +2
Damage Resistances bludgeoning, piercing, poison, slashing
Damage Immunities necrotic, poison
Condition Immunities charmed, frightened, paralyzed, petrified, poisoned, prone, restrained, stunned
Senses blindsight 10 ft., darkvision 30 ft., passive Perception 10
Languages —
Challenge 2 (450 XP)

Swarm. The swarm can occupy another creature's space, and vice versa, and the swarm can move through any opening large enough for a Tiny snake. The swarm can't regain hit points or gain temporary hit points.

ACTIONS

Bites. *Melee Weapon Attack:* +5 to hit, reach 0 ft., one target in the swarm's space. *Hit:* 7 (2d6) piercing damage, plus 7 (2d6) necrotic damage, or 3 (1d6) piercing damage plus 3 (1d6) necrotic damage, if the swarm has half of its hit points or fewer. If the target is a creature, it must succeed on a DC 12 Constitution saving throw (or 8, if the swarm has half of its hit points or fewer), or be cursed with mummy rot (p.86).

WHY DID IT HAVE TO BE SNAKES?

Sometimes, in order to deter and punish would-be grave robbers, swarms of snakes are interred in a package of bandages made to look like a mummified body. These false mummies are still animated by the mummy's curse, and act much in the way mummies normally would, although their movements tend to be more staggered and erratic.

A false mummy can be any humanoid mummy of challenge rating 5 or lower. The statistics of a false mummy are unchanged, except that the mummy does not speak any languages and can't cast spells. Additionally, if the mummy is reduced to 0 hit points, a swarm of cursed snakes exits the body into the mummy's space or a space within 5 feet of the mummy. The swarm acts on the mummy's initiative.

"You've heard the stories; they seal 'em in there with mountains of gold. Golden masks, golden furniture, golden bleedin' chamber pots. You afraid of a few corpses?"

-Gaunts, tomb robber (deceased)

Tarikhodile

Large undead, lawful evil

Armor Class 14 (natural armor)
Hit Points 45 (6d10 + 12)
Speed 15 ft., burrow 30 ft.

STR	DEX	CON	INT	WIS	CHA
18 (+4)	10 (+0)	14 (+2)	2 (-4)	10 (+0)	4 (-3)

Skills Stealth +2
Damage Vulnerabilities fire
Damage Resistances bludgeoning, piercing, and slashing from nonmagical attacks
Damage Immunities necrotic, poison
Condition Immunities charmed, exhaustion, frightened, paralyzed, poisoned
Senses darkvision 60 ft., tremorsense 30 ft., passive Perception 12
Languages —
Challenge 3 (700 XP)

Cursed Fangs. If the tarikhodile has advantage on an attack roll it makes with its bite against a creature and hits, the target must succeed on a DC 12 Constitution saving throw, or be cursed with mummy rot (p.86).

Sand Swimmer. The tarikhodile can use its burrow speed only in loose ground, such as sand and soft earth.

Actions

Bite. *Melee Weapon Attack:* +6 to hit, reach 5 ft., one creature. *Hit:* 9 (1d10 + 4) piercing damage, plus 10 (3d6) necrotic damage and the target is grappled (escape DC 14). Until this grapple ends, the target is restrained and the tarikhodile can't bite another target.

Bast Cat

Tiny undead, lawful evil

Armor Class 15 (natural armor)
Hit Points 90 (20d4 + 40)
Speed 30 ft., climb 30 ft.

STR	DEX	CON	INT	WIS	CHA
2 (-4)	18 (+4)	14 (+2)	9 (-1)	14 (+2)	19 (+4)

Skills Perception +5, Stealth +7
Damage Vulnerabilities fire
Damage Resistances bludgeoning, piercing, and slashing from nonmagical attacks
Damage Immunities necrotic, poison
Condition Immunities charmed, exhaustion, frightened, paralyzed, poisoned
Senses darkvision 120 ft., passive Perception 15
Languages Common, Sphinx
Challenge 6 (2,300 XP)

Innate Spellcasting. The bast cat's innate spellcasting ability is Charisma (spell save DC 15, +7 to hit with spell attacks). It can innately cast the following spells, requiring no material components:

At will: *guidance, inflict wounds, light, shield of faith, thaumaturgy*

1/Day each: *antilife shell, bestow curse, hold person*

Spellclaw. When the bast cat casts a spell that requires a melee spell attack, it can make an attack with its Cursed Claws in place of that attack. If the claw attack hits, the spell's effect applies, in addition to the claw's effects.

Actions

Multiattack. The bast cat can use its Dreadful Glare and makes one attack with its Cursed Claws.

Cursed Claws. *Melee Weapon Attack:* +7 to hit, reach 5 ft., one creature. *Hit:* 1 slashing damage, plus 14 (4d6) necrotic damage. If the target is a creature, it must succeed on a DC 13 Constitution saving throw, or be cursed with mummy rot (p.86).

Dreadful Glare. The bast cat targets one creature it can see within 60 feet of it. If the target can see the bast cat, it must succeed on a DC 15 Wisdom saving throw against this magic, or become frightened until the end of the bast cat's next turn. If the target fails the saving throw by 5 or more, it is also paralyzed for the same duration. A target that succeeds on the saving throw is immune to the Dreadful Glare of all mummies with a challenge rating of 6 or less for the next 24 hours.

Mummified Bull

Large undead, neutral evil

Armor Class 11 (natural armor)
Hit Points 85 (10d10 + 30)
Speed 30 ft.

STR	DEX	CON	INT	WIS	CHA
19 (+4)	7 (-2)	16 (+3)	1 (-5)	6 (-2)	11 (+0)

Saving Throws Wis +1
Damage Vulnerabilities fire
Damage Resistances bludgeoning, piercing, and slashing from nonmagical attacks
Damage Immunities necrotic, poison
Condition Immunities charmed, exhaustion, frightened, paralyzed, poisoned
Senses darkvision 60 ft., passive Perception 8
Languages —
Challenge 6 (2,300 XP)

Cursed Horns. If the mummified bull has advantage on a gore attack against a creature and hits, the target must succeed on a DC 14 Constitution saving throw, or be cursed with mummy rot (p.86).

Dreadful Charge. If the mummified bull moves at least 15 feet straight toward a target, then hits the same target with a gore attack on the same turn, the target takes an extra 11 (2d10) piercing damage, and the target must succeed on a DC 15 Strength saving throw, or be knocked prone. Additionally, the target has disadvantage on saving throws against being frightened until the end of their next turn.

Actions

Gore. *Melee Weapon Attack:* +7 to hit, reach 5 ft., one target. *Hit:* 11 (2d6 + 4) piercing damage, plus 10 (3d6) necrotic damage.

A mummy's tomb is typically festooned with treasures, of both material and sentimental value to the interred. The burial chamber of the child queen Suranna was filled with her mummified pets; dogs, cats, hundreds of birds, and dozens of more exotic beasts. A sweet image, one might think; a girl who could not bear to be parted from her beloved companions. It soon turns sour, of course, when one imagines the executor of the will systematically throttling the poor creatures after the queen's death.

—Finthareal Ellanwe, 'Whispers from the Grave'

TARIKHOSPHINX

Large undead, lawful evil

Armor Class 17 (natural armor)
Hit Points 189 (18d10 + 90)
Speed 30 ft., fly 40 ft.

STR	DEX	CON	INT	WIS	CHA
20 (+5)	10 (+0)	20 (+5)	19 (+4)	18 (+4)	19 (+4)

Skills Arcana +9, Perception +9, Religion +9
Damage Vulnerabilities fire
Damage Immunities psychic, necrotic, poison; bludgeoning, piercing, and slashing from nonmagical attacks
Condition Immunities charmed, exhaustion, frightened, paralyzed, poisoned
Senses truesight 120 ft., passive Perception 19
Languages Common, Sphinx
Challenge 16 (15,000 XP)

Inscrutable. The tarikhosphinx is immune to any effect that would sense its emotions or read its thoughts, as well as any divination spell that it refuses. Wisdom (Insight) checks made to ascertain the tarikhosphinx's intentions or sincerity have disadvantage.

Magic Weapons. The tarikhosphinx's weapon attacks are magical.

Rejuvenation. A destroyed tarikhosphinx gains a new body in 24 hours, if its heart is intact, regaining all its hit points and becoming active again. The new body appears within 5 feet of the tarikhosphinx's heart.

Cleric Spellcasting (Androsphinx Only). If the tarikhosphinx was an androsphinx in life, it is an 11th level spellcaster. Its spellcasting ability is Wisdom (spell save DC 18, +10 to hit with spell attacks). It requires no material components to cast its spells. The tarikhosphinx has the following cleric spells prepared:

Cantrips (at will): *guidance, sacred flame, thaumaturgy*

1st level (4 slots): *command, detect evil and good, detect magic*

2nd level (3 slots): *hold person, silence, zone of truth*

3rd level (3 slots): *animate dead, dispel magic, tongues*

4th level (3 slots): *banishment, freedom of movement*

5th level (2 slot): *insect plague*

6th level (1 slot): *create undead*

Wizard Spellcasting (Gynosphinx Only). If the tarikhosphinx was a gynosphinx in life, it is an 11th level spellcaster. Its spellcasting ability is Intelligence (spell save DC 18, +10 to hit with spell attacks). It requires no material components to cast its spells. The tarikhosphinx has the following cleric spells prepared:

Cantrips (at will): *mage hand, minor illusion, prestidigitation*

1st level (4 slots): *detect magic, identify, shield*

2nd level (3 slots): *darkness, locate object, suggestion*

3rd level (3 slots): *animate dead, bestow curse, dispel magic, tongues*

4th level (3 slots): *banishment, greater invisibility*

5th level (2 slot): *legend lore*

6th level (1 slot): *create undead*

ACTIONS

Multiattack. The tarikhosphinx can use its Dreadful Glare. It then makes two attacks with its Cursed Claws.

Cursed Claws. *Melee Weapon Attack:* +11 to hit, reach 5 ft., one creature. *Hit:* 14 (2d8 + 5) piercing damage, plus 14 (4d6) necrotic damage. If the target is a creature, it must succeed on a DC 19 Constitution saving throw, or be cursed with mummy rot (p.86).

Dreadful Glare. The tarikhosphinx targets one creature it can see within 60 feet of it. If the target can see the tarikhosphinx, it must succeed on a DC 18 Wisdom saving throw against this magic, or become frightened until the end of the tarikhosphinx's next turn. If the target fails the saving throw by 5 or more, it is also paralyzed for the same duration. A target that succeeds on the saving throw is immune to the Dreadful Glare of all mummies with a challenge rating of 16 or less for the next 24 hours.

Scarab Squall (Recharge 5-6). The tarikhosphinx exhales a swarm of undead scarabs, which rend the flesh of creatures in a 40 foot cone and then quickly die as the fleeting necrotic energy that animates them subsides. Creatures in the area must make a DC 19 Dexterity saving throw, taking 42 (12d6) piercing damage on a failed save, or half as much damage on a successful one.

LEGENDARY ACTIONS

The tarikhosphinx can take 3 legendary actions, choosing from the options below. Only one legendary action option can be used at a time, and only at the end of another creature's turn. The tarikhosphinx regains spent legendary actions at the start of its turn.

Cantrip. The tarikhosphinx casts a cantrip.

Teleport (Costs 2 Actions). The tarikhosphinx magically teleports, along with any equipment it is wearing or carrying, up to 120 feet to an unoccupied space it can see.

Cast a Spell (Costs 3 Actions). The tarikhosphinx casts a spell from its list of prepared spells, using a spell slot as normal.

The **tarikhosphinx** is one of the most powerful tomb guardians, and a rare one, a sphinx in life being no easy thing to overpower, subdue, and embalm. After death, its loyalties lie with the mummy lord whom it guards, rather than the gods. While it may still set challenges and ask riddles, as it did as a bold androsphinx or wily gynosphinx in life, this habit is more for its own amusement. Whatever it was in life, a tarikhosphinx will rarely honor deals or promises made on the grounds of a challenge or riddle contest.

"Four legs in the morning, two at midday, and three at sunset, this much is known. But what of midnight? What of the next day? Or the next? What of the eternity of tomorrows beyond?"

—The Tarikhosphinx of Khnatum

Our search led us to the foothills of the nearby mountains. If I thought our going had been rough so far, I was woefully mistaken; the added verticality and gradually thinning air increased my struggle ten-fold, to say nothing of the increasing sharpness of the rocks beneath one's bedroll. Some, no doubt, would find the dry mountain air therapeutic, and to them I say, they are very welcome to it. My only comfort was coming across a large gold piece some traveler must have dropped on their passage. Having no way of reuniting it with its owner, I pocketed it. I saw no reason to tell Thaddeus.

The entrance to the tomb itself was rather underwhelming: a simple, rectangular hole in the rockface, basic and even clumsily carved (though far be it from me to criticise royal lodgings; perhaps its residents simply have a more acquired eye). It was certainly devoid of the self-aggrandising statues and frescos I had been expecting, but Thaddeus assured me the interior would be more to my liking. Perhaps this made a certain amount of sense; after all, if one was hoping to take all of one's opulent worldly goods off to paradise, it would hardly do to blatantly advertise where they were being stored to any passing tomb robber (or, as the case may be, any would-be regicidist). That and, I suppose, it would be rather gauche.

As we passed the threshold, Thaddeus pointed at the corners, where long strands of cobweb dangled, broken. We were clearly not the only ones to pass through this doorway recently.

Within, we were certainly not left wanting for carvings. The outer suite of chambers seemed to be something of a gallery, dedicated almost entirely to one crowned figure. Whether he be partaking in such various and charming activities as overseeing the execution of hundreds of prisoners (hearts extracted), partaking in the ritual letting of his own blood (via the insertion of a barbed string through a piercing in the tongue, it would seem), or flaying his enemies (exquisitely-carved detail in every furrow of pain and fear etched in their faces), the figure always loomed largest, with the sun itself shining from his crown. Doubtless, the pictograms carved around the figures could shed even more light on the matter, but neither of us could even begin to interpret them.

The images grew larger and bloodier as we progressed until, eventually, we came upon a chamber dominated by a single carving; the king, standing triumphant upon a mountain of skulls, surrounding a doorway into the depths of the tomb.

Thaddeus pointed to a collection of symbols above the lintel. "Reckon that says 'Do Not Enter'," he remarked, entering.

"You recognise those runes?" I asked.

"No," he replied, stooping down. "But I know a tomb seal when I see one."

"Isn't it sealed for a reason? Shouldn't we leave well enough alone?"

Thaddeus held up a jagged chunk of stone for my inspection. It seemed to be part of a disk, which perhaps would have been the size of a large dinner plate when whole.

"'Leaving well enough alone' was taken off the table a long time ago, looks like. The king would have been reanimated when this thing was broken. Could have been years ago. No doubt he had a couple of his household guard holed up in here with him as well. No telling how many of those woke up when he did. Keep your eyes open."

At this point, I was grabbed from behind.

Thaddeus' reactions were far better than mine, and he brought his sword down on the offending arm, before turning his attention to its owner. The shambling figure, wound about with bandages, bundled reeds, and clay-like mud, lashed at him clumsily. It was a one-sided affair, and soon my assailant lay unmoving on the dusty floor.

"Well, no matter how many of his guard came back with him, that's one less."

"I wouldn't be so sure," said Thaddeus grimly, as he strode towards the body. "Look at this."

I thought I was about to receive an impromptu lesson on the proper classification of mummies but, as I looked down, where Thaddeus' parted the bandages with the point of his sword, I saw what he was getting at. The bandages were in a suspiciously fresh state, and the flesh beneath, treated and leathery as it was, was clearly not centuries old. Not only that, but the flesh was mottled, with strange patches of hair here, and scales there. It was the skin of a mongrel.

"Looks like we're in the right place. Scab earned his silver. Let's keep going."

On we went, through the doorway and into the tomb proper. We passed through a chamber of stone slabs, each carved with grim figures of death and ritual. A rusty, metallic smell hung heavy in the still air, from the crust of old, brown blood which coated the stone.

"This must have been the room Mullock talked about. No wonder he was addled. How many do you think were... prepared?"

"Hard to say."

We didn't have far to travel before coming across another chamber, betrayed by the echoing emptiness in the darkness to our left. Peeking inside, our torches barely illuminated the cavernous space - it was easily the size of all our previously explored rooms combined. Looming large in the flickering light were more images of the king's splendor; the fertile lands of his people, his hunting exploits. Here and there, a glint of gold, or a flash of gemstone glittered on the floor, scattered as if carelessly dropped. On a hunch, I removed the coin from my pocket and compared it. Sure enough, the stern countenance was one and the same. These scant treasures were not all though, as we took a few steps inside, and our circles of light spread outwards...

"I'd be happy to take a guess now."

Bodies. Hundreds of them, haphazardly piled around the room, and all bandaged like our earlier assailant. We froze, but none showed any sign of movement.

"So many. Why so many? Any why leave them dormant? There's enough here to make a small army."

"Not happy with a small army, I suppose. Waiting for a big one. Whatever they've got in mind can't be good. A lot of troops, and it's something important too, or the gold would still be here."

"The gold?" I asked.

"Mummies are as gold-sick as dragons. This was the main treasure hoard, and it's been cleared out. Sloppily too - grave robbers wouldn't leave so much behind. Simply put, for whatever reason, he-" Thaddeus pointed to the gilded figure on the wall, "-needs these bodies more than he loves his gold."

"All that gold just dumped somewhere though..."

"Yeah, it would draw all sorts of people to the mountains," Thaddeus said grimly, gesturing to the stacks of bandaged corpses. We didn't say much more after that.

In the next chamber, we came upon the king, resting. It was a far smaller space than the great vault, something like a private audience chamber. At the top of a raised dais was a throne, at the center of a rune-etched sunburst. On the throne was the king. The years had not been kind to him. Far from the strapping warrior of the carvings, the creature slumped on the throne was a shrunken and shriveled creature. Were it not for the shining crown on its brow, it would have been unrecognizable. At our intrusion, it began to stir.

"There'll be a heart somewhere," Thaddeus hissed at me out of the corner of his mouth. "In a jar, or a chest. Need you to find it. Get it to me. I'll buy some time."

This was all the instruction I could expect from Thaddeus, who was already striding to the foot of the throne. With some resignation, I dropped to the floor in the hope that the king had not seen me (and, if he had, that perhaps this would be taken as a sign of prostration). As I crawled behind a gilded litter, scrabbling through the dust in search of whatever receptacle the creature had stashed its heart, there was a terrible screech as (I assumed) battle was joined. A collection of alcoves across the chamber looked promising and I scurried towards them, doing my best to ignore the shadows of the combatants dancing in the light of Thaddeus' discarded torch.

An ornate urn contained nothing but more gold coins (possibly more than I had ever seen in one place, though unremarkable in the setting). There seemed to be nothing else there beyond a few brightly painted wooden figurines.

"Any luck?" Thaddeus thudded into my vision, and the wall, with some force. I assume he had been thrown there. I shook my head, eyes wide, and he heaved himself to his feet to re-join the fight. The jars in the next alcove contained honey and oil (I could not vouch for their freshness). Daring to glance over my shoulder, I saw, beyond the melee, a collection of clay pots, uncharacteristically prominent for such unadorned vessels. Ducking down once more, I scurried and rolled my way over to them.

I immediately regretted my incautious approach as I gleefully plunged my hand into the first jar and removed it with a fistful of withered lung. Not only was this deeply unpleasant, but it seemed too much for His Highness to ignore. Throwing Thaddeus aside once more, it now turned its attention to me. In a panic, I scooped up the remaining three pots in my arms and ran blindly. Almost immediately, one of the jars slipped from my increasingly sweaty grip to shatter at my feet, and my pursuer stepped over the mummified liver without breaking stride. What my plan was, I did not know but, at the point that I backed into a corner and resorted to flinging a jar into the face of the implacable mummy king, I knew it was not a good one. It cast aside its own desiccated stomach with contempt.

"Thaddeus," I called out, in a wavering little voice. "I think I found it. Help."

I threw the last jar high, and hoped. For a moment, the three figures in the tomb paused to watch it arc through the air. At last, it cast its contents at Thaddeus' feet: a shrivelled puck of muscle, the dried husk of the mummy's heart.

Thaddeus scooped it up, brandishing the withered heart high in triumph, before holding the point of his dagger above it.

"I beg an audience, Your Radiance," he growled.

The crowned figure stiffened and was still, poised and glaring at Thaddeus. It's cobwebbed eye sockets were difficult to read, but it appeared to be weighing its options.

"Something more is going on here. An insurgence? A war? Reclaiming your lost kingdom? Tell me."

The figure said nothing. Thaddeus began to put pressure on the dagger, working the point into the outer layers of dried muscle. The king spasmed. If it had lungs, I know it would have gasped for breath. Then it did something I did not expect; it laughed.

It was an awful noise, rattling, wheezing and dry. A spiteful exhalation from another world. It took a few trudging steps towards Thaddeus, still laughing. As it drew nearer, I could smell the dry decay of the grave-stink belching out of its lipless mouth, and made a point to hold my breath.

"I'm warning you," yelled Thaddeus, knuckles white on the dagger's hilt.

Like a striking snake, the mummy lashed out a hand, grasping not the heart, not the dagger, but Thaddeus' fist and, with dreadful inevitability, plunged it down. Thaddeus grimaced as the point pierced the heart, and his palm beneath.

Cracks appeared in the mummy's papery skin, which began to slough away in dry flakes. It dissipated like dust in the wind, leaving until last the skull, still grinning with its final joke, which was gone before it hit the floor.

As exhilarating as the past few moments had been, I must admit I felt disheartened.

"Our one good lead turned to dust, and we still don't know anything!" I exclaimed. "What do we do now?"

"On the contrary," said Thaddeus, already binding his hand with a somewhat-clean piece of cloth. "Now we know a great deal. When it was alive, that creature was revered as a god, and death only confirmed its suspicions. The question is, what would a god be that loyal to?"

My torch began to gutter, and the shadows danced around us in the silence of the now empty crypt. I suspected that whatever the answer to his question, it was not a pleasant one.

Revenants

The corpse walks as if following an invisible thread, with the purpose of one walking so familiar a path that sight is unnecessary. It barely slows for ditch, hill, or stream. Almost absent-mindedly, its hand moves to its throat, where the knife left its ragged work. Its face is a hardened mask of patient fury, unmoving as flint, save for its mouth as it works to sound out the name, again and again, clench-jawed and hoarse, the same name. The sky darkens, the color of an old wound, and the corpse shows no sign of relenting.

Revenants are engines of vengeance, potentially denying themselves their afterlife in order to avenge themselves upon those responsible for their own unjust deaths. Upon their resurrection, they have just one year to enact their revenge, with the afterlife awaiting them upon their success, and obliteration should they fail.

In overall appearance, revenants resemble zombies, being animated corpses (though typically of a fresher vintage), but it is unlikely even a casual observer would confuse the two. Even from a distance, the purposeful stride of a revenant could not be more different from the twitching shamble of a zombie and, up close, there is no mistaking the grim, determined focus in its eyes. To begin with, a revenant will inhabit its original body but, should that be destroyed, its spirit can inhabit any other corpse, provided it can find one fast enough. Original body or no, the dread gaze of a revenant is unmistakable, especially to its target, who will always recognize the identity of the hateful spirit within. A revenant's regenerative abilities (a combination of magical healing and sheer tenacity) makes it able to shrug off most mundane damage, and even reverses some of the process of decay, should it inhabit an older corpse (though they still appear clearly dead).

Origin

Revenants are birthed by betrayal and fueled by revenge. Unlike the many and varied goals a ghost might need to see completed, or the self-serving ambitions of a wight, a revenant has only one clear and simple goal; the deaths of all those involved in their unjust murder. Nothing will stay their hand in this; should their body be destroyed, their spirit shall simply find another to inhabit, should their target run or hide, they innately know their location and distance.

Dead bodies they may be, but they are not mindless, nor are they restricted by the same rules as often govern the undead. Divine powers do not especially affect them, as their resurrection is not due to the meddling of gods, but a result of the greater powers of balance and justice in the cosmos, to which even they must bend. Some personal choice must also be involved, somewhat similar to the creation of a wight, for not every victim of betrayal becomes a revenant.

The existence of a revenant is one of desperation. While the drive for revenge is a powerful stimulant, it must always be tinged with the knowledge of what awaits them should they fail. No peace awaits a failed revenant, no crossing over to reunite with loved ones and muse upon their shortcomings, only oblivion, nothingness. The obliteration of a failed revenant's soul is a powerful act by the unknowable and pitiless forces of cosmic balance, forces above even the gods. This process can go awry, with the trauma and bitterness of revenge denied, twisting the shattered remnants to collapse into a wraith. This depends upon the character of the revenant, as well as the nature of its failure; should a particularly bloodthirsty revenant be on the verge of its revenge, only for it to be snatched away at the last moment, those powerful feelings of rage are more likely to disrupt and warp the soul's destruction.

Should a revenant's target die without the revenant's involvement, most will be satisfied and pass on to peace, or move on to their next target. For some, those with a selfish streak, or who had a particularly personal relationship with their betrayer, their target's death alone is not enough – they must be the one to strike the killing blow. Such a revenant might rail against this further injustice strongly enough to break their covenant, and take their anger out on the living in general. These wight-like failed revenants might even begin their vendetta by seeking out and destroying the killers of their original target.

Environment

Revenants tend to be transitory by nature, with their location determined by their target rather than any preference on their part. With no need for food, drink, or even air, the promise of revenge is all they need for sustenance. For the most part, a revenant will travel by the most direct route towards its target though, being intelligent, they are willing to make exceptions. For example, revenants avoid centers of civilization (unless their target is located within), for convenience more than any other reason; the more people there are around, the more things there are to get in their way, and those of a religious bent tend to not take too kindly to wandering undead. While revenants' regenerative abilities and resistance to many effects used to destroy the undead (being resurrected by greater forces than those channeled by the pious), such distractions are still unworthy of their time.

Roleplaying Revenants

Revenants are not senseless; while they are driven solely by their need for revenge, they can be reasoned with, up to a point. A revenant might enlist the help of others, either allies they knew in life or other capable folk looking to right injustices. While they retain much of their former personality, revenants are colder, seeing former interests and attachments as, if not worthless, severely diminished in importance compared to their vengeance. Their knowledge of their target's location constantly plays on their mind like an involuntarily repeating song, making it impossible to put aside, even for a moment.

Revenants can be conversed with, especially if someone can give them information they need, though they will not stop for idle chit-chat. As long as it does not hinder them from their purpose, some even seem happy (or as close to happy as they can be) for some company though, should they ever be forced to choose between the pursuit of their target and the welfare of their companions, even the most amiable revenant will choose the former every time.

Combat Tactics

Most revenants will avoid combat (along with all other activities) unless it furthers their agenda, and are unlikely to be goaded towards violence with their cold and dulled emotions. Once noble or good-natured revenants might go so far as attempting to persuade potential combatants to stand down and save their own lives, though others will simply try to get the violence over with as quickly as possible. Revenants are able to shrug off most attacks and, given that they can inhabit a new body the next day, most are fearless in combat unless they are in a good position to strike at their target in their current form and location (advantages they would be unwilling to part with for the sake of a pointless brawl).

The manner in which a revenant seeks to kill their target depends greatly on their relationship and the magnitude of their betrayal, as well as the revenant's personality in life. A more pragmatic revenant might be happy to simply kill the target in their sleep, satisfied enough that the deed was done. Others, of a more honor-bound or emotional bent, might deeply feel the need for their target to know it was they who sent them to their doom, for their face to be the last thing the target sees. Those who lived a life of violence, or whose deaths were particularly traumatic, might not be satisfied unless the target's death is some parallel of their own, such as burning down the house of one who burnt them at the stake, or ensuring the family of the target witness their killing, if the same was true for the revenant.

Revenant Seeker

Medium undead, neutral

Armor Class 13 (leather armor)
Hit Points 90 (12d8 + 36)
Speed 30 ft.

STR	DEX	CON	INT	WIS	CHA
16 (+3)	14 (+2)	17 (+3)	12 (+1)	15 (+2)	16 (+3)

Saving Throws Con +5, Wis +4, Cha +5
Skills Athletics +5, Insight +4, Perception +4
Damage Resistances necrotic, psychic
Damage Immunities poison
Condition Immunities charmed, exhaustion, frightened, paralyzed, poisoned, stunned
Senses darkvision 60 ft., passive perception 15
Languages the languages it knew in life
Challenge 4 (1,100 XP)

Deadly Attacks. The seeker rolls its weapon damage dice an additional time and adds the result to the damage total. This bonus is already included in its attacks.

Regeneration. The seeker regains 10 hit points at the start of its turn. If the seeker takes fire or radiant damage, this trait doesn't function at the start of the seeker's next turn.

Turn Immunity. The seeker is immune to effects that turn undead.

Vengeance Seeker. The seeker knows the distance and direction of any creature against which it seeks revenge, even if the creature and the revenant are on different planes of existence. If the creature being tracked by the seeker dies, the seeker knows and loses its Regeneration ability.

Without Rest. When the seeker is killed, it reanimates with its full hit points after 24 hours. If the seeker's body has lost body parts, its body regenerates from the head, and any lost body parts are restored when it reanimates. If the seeker's head is destroyed, its soul seeks a new body. After 24 hours, the soul inhabits and animates the nearest humanoid corpse on the same plane of existence and regains all its hit points. While the soul is bodiless, a *wish* spell can be used to force the soul to go to the afterlife and not return.

Actions

Multiattack. The seeker makes two melee attacks.

Dagger. *Melee or Ranged Weapon Attack:* +5 to hit, reach 5 ft. or range 30/60 ft., one target. *Hit:* 8 (2d4 + 3) piercing damage. If the target is a creature that the seeker seeks vengeance against, it deals an additional 7 (3d4) piercing damage.

Fist. *Melee Weapon Attack:* +5 to hit, reach 5 ft., one target. *Hit:* 8 (2d4 + 3) bludgeoning damage. If the target is a creature that the seeker seeks vengeance against, it deals an additional 7 (3d4) bludgeoning damage.

Grab. *Melee Weapon Attack:* +5 to hit, reach 5 ft., one Medium or smaller creature. *Hit:* The creature is grappled (escape DC 13). Until this grapple ends, the seeker can't grab another target, but it can make a fist attack against the grappled creature, as a bonus action. If the seeker seeks vengeance against the target, this attack automatically hits.

CAPTAIN: *Forget now this grisly case, and mark me well*
Cease enmity for Kane. Pursue him not.
If you do not this warning well attend
I shall, with all my power, strike you down.
And, without insignia or sword,
A guard you'll be no more; you have my word.
EXIT
THEMIO: *And so Kane's victims lie silent in their graves,*
while their killer walks free. Would that they could speak.
ADRESTIO: *And if dead tongues could wag, what wouldst thou ask?*
THEMIO: *You did startle me, so deathly quiet was your step.*
You know of Kane, my grave fellow?
ADRESTIO: *He shall be a corpse ere long.*
THEMIO: *You look half a corpse yourself, what know'st thee?*
ADRESTIO: *This much alone: t'was him who murdered me.*

-Warrick Brandishpole, 'The Unlike Pair', Act I Scene V

TENACIOUS REVENANT
Medium undead, neutral

Armor Class 15 (studded leather)
Hit Points 153 (18d8 + 72)
Speed 30 ft.

STR	DEX	CON	INT	WIS	CHA
18 (+4)	16 (+3)	19 (+4)	15 (+2)	17 (+3)	18 (+4)

Saving Throws Str +7, Con +6, Wis +6, Cha +7
Skills Athletics +7, Insight +6, Perception +6
Damage Resistances necrotic, psychic
Damage Immunities poison
Condition Immunities charmed, exhaustion, frightened, paralyzed, poisoned, stunned
Senses darkvision 60 ft., passive perception 16
Languages the languages it knew in life
Challenge 8 (3,900 XP)

Deadly Attacks. The revenant rolls its weapon damage dice an additional time and adds the result to the damage total. This bonus is already included in its attacks.

Regeneration. The revenant regains 20 hit points at the start of its turn. If the revenant takes fire or radiant damage, this trait doesn't function at the start of the revenant's next turn.

Turn Immunity. The revenant is immune to effects that turn undead.

Vengeance Seeker. The revenant knows the distance and direction of any creature against which it seeks revenge, even if the creature and the revenant are on different planes of existence. If the creature being tracked by the revenant dies, the revenant knows and loses its Without Rest and Regeneration abilities.

Without Rest. When the revenant is killed, it reanimates with its full hit points after 24 hours. If the revenant's body has lost body parts, its body regenerates from the head, and any lost body parts are restored when it reanimates. If the revenant's head is destroyed, its soul seeks a new body. After 24 hours, the soul inhabits and animates the nearest humanoid corpse on the same plane of existence and regains all its hit points. While the soul is bodiless, a *wish* spell can be used to force the soul to go to the afterlife and not return.

ACTIONS

Multiattack. The revenant makes two attacks.

Longsword. *Melee Weapon Attack:* +7 to hit, reach 5 ft., one target. *Hit:* 12 (2d8 + 3) slashing damage. If the target is a creature that the revenant is seeking vengeance against, it deals an additional 13 (3d8) slashing damage.

Fist. *Melee Weapon Attack:* +7 to hit, reach 5 ft., one target. *Hit:* 10 (2d6 + 3) bludgeoning damage. If the target is a creature that the revenant seeks vengeance against, it deals an additional 10 (3d6) bludgeoning damage.

Grab. *Melee Weapon Attack:* +7 to hit, reach 5 ft., one Medium or smaller creature. *Hit:* The creature is grappled (escape DC 15). Until this grapple ends, the revenant can't grab another target, but it can make a fist attack against the grappled creature, as a bonus action. If the revenant seeks vengeance against the target, this attack automatically hits.

Relentless Harrier
Medium undead, neutral

Armor Class 16 (studded leather)
Hit Points 228 (24d8 + 120)
Speed 30 ft.

STR	DEX	CON	INT	WIS	CHA
20 (+5)	18 (+4)	20 (+5)	15 (+2)	18 (+4)	19 (+4)

Saving Throws Str +10, Con +10, Wis +9, Cha +9
Skills Athletics +10, Insight +9, Perception +9
Damage Resistances necrotic, psychic
Damage Immunities poison
Condition Immunities charmed, exhaustion, frightened, paralyzed, poisoned, stunned
Senses darkvision 60 ft., passive perception 19
Languages the languages it knew in life
Challenge 16 (15,000 XP)

Deadly Attacks. The harrier rolls its weapon damage dice an additional time and adds the result to the damage total. This bonus is already included in its attacks.

Legendary Resistance (3/Day). When the harrier fails a saving throw, it can choose to succeed instead.

Regeneration. The harrier regains 30 hit points at the start of its turn. If the harrier takes fire or radiant damage, this trait doesn't function at the start of the harrier's next turn.

Turn Immunity. The harrier is immune to effects that turn undead.

Vengeance Seeker. The harrier knows the distance and direction of any creature against which it seeks revenge, even if the creature and the harrier are on different planes of existence. If the creature being tracked by the harrier dies, the harrier knows and loses its Without Rest and Regeneration abilities.

Without Rest. When the harrier is killed, it reanimates with its full hit points after 24 hours. If the harrier's body has lost body parts, its body regenerates from the head and any lost body parts are restored when it reanimates. If the harrier's head is destroyed, its soul seeks a new body. After 24 hours, the soul inhabits and animates the nearest humanoid corpse on the same plane of existence and regains all its hit points. While the soul is bodiless, a *wish* spell can be used to force the soul to go to the afterlife and not return.

"Justice? Justice lies rotting in the ground with my husband. You look upon the face of vengeance."

-Kinrama shathaan, revenant

Actions

Multiattack. The harrier makes three attacks.

Longsword. *Melee Weapon Attack:* +10 to hit, reach 5 ft., one target. *Hit:* 14 (2d8 + 5) slashing damage. If the target is a creature that the harrier seeks vengeance against, it deals an additional 18 (4d8) slashing damage.

Longbow. *Melee Weapon Attack:* +9 to hit, range 120/600 ft., one target. *Hit:* 13 (2d8 + 4) piercing damage. If the target is a creature that the harrier seeks vengeance against, it deals an additional 18 (4d8) piercing damage

Fist. *Melee Weapon Attack:* +10 to hit, reach 5 ft., one target. *Hit:* 10 (2d6 + 3) bludgeoning damage. If the target is a creature that the harrier is seeking vengeance against, it deals an additional 14 (4d6) bludgeoning damage.

Grab. *Melee Weapon Attack:* +10 to hit, reach 5 ft., one Medium or smaller creature. *Hit:* The creature is grappled (escape DC 18). Until this grapple ends, the harrier can't grab another target, but it can make a fist attack against the grappled creature, as a bonus action. If the harrier seeks vengeance against the target, this attack automatically hits.

Legendary Actions

The harrier can take 3 legendary actions, choosing from the options below. Only one legendary action option can be used at a time, and only at the end of another creature's turn. The harrier regains spent legendary actions at the start of its turn.

Attack. The harrier makes a weapon attack. This attack does not deal additional damage against the target of the harrier's vengeance.

Eyes of the Avenger. Until the end of its next turn, the harrier can see creatures it seeks vengeance against as if it had truesight with a range of 120 feet.

Relentless Advance. The harrier moves up to its speed directly toward a creature it seeks revenge against. It can attempt to move through another creature's space. If it does, the creature must succeed on a DC 17 Strength saving throw, or be pushed 5 feet out of the harrier's path and knocked prone. If the creature succeeds on its saving throw, or can't be pushed out of the harrier's path, the harrier can't pass and must end its movement within 5 feet of that creature.

Failed Revenant

Medium undead, chaotic evil

Armor Class 13 (leather)
Hit Points 153 (18d8 + 72)
Speed 30 ft.

STR	DEX	CON	INT	WIS	CHA
20 (+5)	15 (+2)	19 (+4)	15 (+2)	17 (+3)	18 (+4)

Saving Throws Str +7, Con +7, Wis +6, Cha +7
Skills Insight +6, Perception +6
Damage Resistances necrotic, psychic
Damage Immunities poison
Condition Immunities charmed, exhaustion, frightened, paralyzed, poisoned, stunned
Senses darkvision 60 ft., passive perception 16
Languages the languages it knew in life
Challenge 8 (3,900 XP)

Deadly Attacks. The failed revenant rolls its weapon damage dice an additional time and adds the result to the damage total. This bonus is already included in its attacks.

Deathly Rage. At the start of each of its turns, a failed revenant can choose to gain advantage on all melee weapon attacks. If it does so, attacks against the failed revenant have advantage until the start of its next turn.

Regeneration. The failed revenant regains 10 hit points at the start of its turn. If the failed revenant takes fire or radiant damage, this trait doesn't function at the start of the failed revenant's next turn. The failed revenant's body is destroyed only if it starts its turn with 0 hit points and doesn't regenerate.

Turn Resistance. The failed revenant has advantage on saving throws against any effect that turns undead.

Actions

Multiattack. The failed revenant makes two attacks.

Greataxe. *Melee Weapon Attack:* +8 to hit, reach 5 ft., one target. *Hit:* 37 (5d12 + 5) slashing damage.

Fist. *Melee Weapon Attack:* +8 to hit, reach 5 ft., one target. *Hit:* 22 (5d6 + 5) bludgeoning damage.

Grab. *Melee Weapon Attack:* +8 to hit, reach 5 ft., one Medium or smaller creature. *Hit:* The creature is grappled (escape DC 15). Until this grapple ends, the failed revenant can't grab another target, but it can make a fist attack against the grappled creature, as a bonus action.

"Boss thought the old fort was a safe bet, so we holed up there and kept a lookout. Sure enough, Bernill stomps up the path, bold as you like, skin all flaking off from lying in the river. "Give him up," he shouts, "and the rest of you won't be harmed." Well, we stuck him full of arrows as he made for the gate, and that was the end of that.

Next day, and up comes another corpse. "Give him up, and the rest of you won't be harmed." This one damn near touches the gate before we bring him down.

Well, come day ten, we was out of arrows."

—Qorrik, bandit, account of a revenant attack

The stew was fair-to-middling, which was better than it would have been if Thaddeus had cooked it (I use such revolutionary methods as 'herbs' and 'making sure the meat is cooked all the way through'). Our campsite, hemmed in by firs on one side, and bordered by a mirror-still lake on the other, was positively picturesque, despite the chill in the air.

As I turned back from the view of the water, I was astounded to find a third had joined us around the fire, sat on a wooden stump, having made apparently silent passage across the carpet of pine needles. The only other person I had known to move quite so stealthily was Thaddeus himself and, indeed, the stranger seemed known to him, as he barely reacted upon looking up from his bowl to find them there.

"Erm," I said, quite taken aback and forgetting myself. "Good evening, friend, you're welcome to share the fire. We've little food, but–"

"He's not hungry," said Thaddeus, simply. "Right, Abner?"

"No, not hungry," replied, presumably, Abner. His wheezing voice made him sound like he was about to break into a hacking cough at any moment.

"Been a while. Not seen you since..."

"Since the necromancer in Belengrad."

"That's right, saving my hide from that last curse," said Thaddeus, pulling down his shirt to point vaguely at one of the network of scars which covered his chest. I'm not sure I could have told you, if pushed, which it was. "That one almost had my name on it. Still owe you for that."

"Oh?" I piped in. "You're a hunter too?"

"Was. In a previous life, yeah," said Abner. "If we're showing off scars, Thaddeus..." He unfastened his cloak, revealing a deep gash across his neck. I am no healer, but even I could tell that this was not the kind of injury one would typically walk away with to boast of later. This was more the kind of injury one would suffer from very briefly, but very definitively, and then suffer no more. It was, in a word, mortal.

"I *was* wondering," said Thaddeus, through a mouthful of stew. "Didn't want to mention it."

I sputtered incoherently. Now the wound had been revealed, I could see the sunken cast of Abner's features in the glow of the fire, and his graying, bloodless skin (having presumably bid farewell to said blood shortly after having made acquaintance with the knife). If I had not expected a third to join us for dinner, I had certainly not expected that third to be a corpse.

"I'm here to call in that favor, Thaddeus. The last favor anyone will ever do me."

"Who was it?" asked Thaddeus after a pause.

"Ludwik. He's gone over."

"What?" I asked. "He's undead too?"

Both looked at me as if I had said something blunderingly offensive.

"No, he's still alive, for now. He's working with the enemy though. The dead. Struck a deal, or something, must be. Not really all that interested outside of putting a knife in him, to be honest." There was an unnerving, cold hunger in his eyes though, I suppose, if I had been killed, I would be somewhat upset about it myself.

"The three of us used to work together," explained Thaddeus (as Abner contented himself with twisting chunks of bark from his stump with the point of his knife). "So what do you need from me? You should know where he is, right?"

"Yeah, I can find him," muttered Abner, tapping at his temple. "Reckon he'll have someone - some*thing* - with him, though. Bodyguard. I can take him one-on-one, but I can't risk him getting away. Need you to clear the field for me. Monster hunter stuff, you know."

Thaddeus nodded, though I wasn't entirely sure Abner was prepared to take no for an answer, judging by the large pile of bark chips which now littered the ground around his feet.

After a restless sleep (I was fairly certain Abner had just sat slowly demolishing his seat all night), we broke camp and prepared to move at first light. Having traveled with Thaddeus for some time, I thought myself used to a fairly unforgiving pace, but the revenant was an even harder taskmaster. It was not helped by the fact that Abner appeared to be moving in more or less a straight line, regardless of terrain; he seemed unperturbed, but the hills and ditches we took head on slowed our progress, to his great annoyance. He seemed to take any request for a break as a personal slight and, while he would occasionally acquiesce, he was clearly impatient to get going again as soon as we stopped.

After a few days of rough going (with minimal time allowed for sleep, naturally), I sensed we were closing in on our quarry. Abner seemed even more on edge, pacing like a caged panther at every slowdown. He, at least, had energy to burn, even as we (or, at least, I) began to flag. As we crested a ridge, Abner gestured for silence, and for us to get down. Crawling to the cover of a gorse thicket, we caught the first glimpse of the infamous Ludwik.

He was, truth be told, something of a disappointment. The palpable hatred felt towards him by Abner, who grew only more frightful the closer we came to our goal, had made him monstrous in my mind; surely some terror from a campfire story made flesh: a scheming, wicked villain. What I saw was a man, perhaps a little greasy from too long on the road, true, but a man nonetheless.

Abner bared his teeth when he saw him, in a silent hiss of fury. Thaddeus grimaced as well, though I suspected this was in response to Ludwik's companion, who now came into view.

'Cold' was my first thought. It was a cold, withered, hateful creature. It may have walked on two legs, and been clad in leather armor, but it was no person. Its brow was furrowed in a perpetual scowl overhanging its dead, black eyes. It seemed dissatisfied with its company, its surroundings, even with the presence of sun, overcast though it was.

"Wight," whispered Thaddeus. "Free-willed undead with a bitter hatred of the living. Usually drag themselves back on account of some selfish obsession."

I raised my eyebrows and nodded towards our companion, who was still staring at Ludwik. Thaddeus shook his head, though I thought I saw the hint of a rueful smile.

"Now," hissed Abner. "You go, I'll follow."

Thaddeus sprang from cover, sword drawn. The wight was taken on the back foot, and barely had time to react. It gave an unearthly shriek as the blade arced down towards it, dodging aside to turn an assuredly deadly blow into a glancing one. In response, it darted out a hand and grasped Thaddeus by the wrist. His skin steamed, as though branded. Gritting his teeth, Thaddeus threw the contents of a flask into the creature's face. From where I remained hidden, it looked to be nothing more than water, but the wight recoiled as though blistered by acid. Already on the backfoot, this stumble was all the opening Thaddeus needed to strike a finishing blow.

"Thaddeus?" Ludwik cried, in disbelief. "But that... No!" He turned to flee, and found Abner waiting for him. Realising he was trapped, he sank to his knees. "Please. The rising is inevitable. It is inevitable! Please, believe me. If we submit, our minds can be spared. Abner couldn't see, but you–" Ludwik's pleas not only fell on deaf ears, but were cut brutally short. With a terrible, rasping gurgle, he sank to the ground, clutching at his throat, at the gushing wound, twin to the one he had dealt Abner.

Dropping the bloody knife, Abner looked, for the first time since he had entered our camp, at peace.

"What did he mean, 'inevitable'?" Thaddeus asked.

"It doesn't matter," Abner replied, distantly. "It's done now."

His eyes lost their focus almost in an instant, and I knew that he was gone. He toppled backwards, just a corpse now, bereft of spirit, his final smile still etched on his face.

"No," said Thaddeus, taking one last look at his erstwhile allies, before bending to collect the first branch for their shared pyre. "I don't think it is."

SHADOWS

Nothing but the slightest movement betrays it, a shifting of black within black, shadow within shadow. With no change to the light or surrounds, the shadow spreads, a silently seeping, oily pool. In a smooth motion, limbs billow out like ink in water, grasping and clutching. It rises, a towering column of void, its predatory focus unmistakable even in its featureless, shapeless form. Like smoke on the wind, it is gone as soon as it appeared, and all is shadows once more.

Consummate ambush predators, shadows are attracted to goodness, to those whose darkest desires are suppressed most deeply, for the brighter the light, the darker the shadow it creates. By killing a virtuous individual, a shadow is able to separate those parts of their character consigned to the darkness, unleashing them upon the world as a new shadow. Only the most depraved are truly safe from a shadow's interest, though the more a person gives in to their darker side, the weaker a shadow they will create, and so the less likely they are to be attacked.

Fear of shadows has mixed and mingled with the primal fear of the dark felt by nearly every culture. Those wishing to mask their fear with logic might point to shadows as a justification, for any area of darkness might mask a killer waiting to strike. Regardless, they stand as undead proof of that which the fearful already know; that night and shadow are a world in which the living are not welcome.

Origin

The theory goes that shadows came into being as the result of a botched experiment. Some well-meaning soul, through ritual, bargain, or alchemy, attempted to portion off those instincts, desires, and hungers which were most abhorrent to them. Rather than disappearing, as they no doubt hoped, this darker remnant of their soul lingered. Without any remnant of good nature limiting it, the shadow's growth was unconstrained, gaining strength as its originator weakened.

Shadows are simply unleashed darkness, without ambition or purpose beyond their animalistic drives to feed and reproduce, and intelligence not far exceeding that of a simple beast. However, their supernatural powers make them particularly effective and sinister hunters, able to slip through areas of darkness with stealth beyond any ambush predator and sap the strength of their victims, siphoning away the drive of their darker nature, before making their attack.

For a shadow, attacking the living is primarily a means of reproduction, for when a shadow kills, another shadow will arise from the victim's corpse. Shadows feel no kinship to the ones who spawn them, nor to the corpse from which they emerge. However, should said corpse return to life for whatever reason, it is likely its shadow will seek it out, whether through malice or curiosity it is difficult to say. Whatever the shadow's inscrutable motivation, should it find its 'parent', the result is usually fatal. Infamously, those who were killed by a shadow and return cast no shadow themselves. Rare as they are, such individuals have historically been maligned and ostracized as harbingers of bad luck; after all, someone so obviously marked as a target by a supernatural foe is not someone most want to be around.

Environment

Shadows share the same hunger for the living as other undead but, being so well suited for stealth, they are able to exist where others cannot. Were they capable of the emotion, other undead would surely be envious of shadows' rich choice of hunting grounds. While they are still found in the typical crypts and lichyards, they are commonly drawn to more populous areas, where both prey and hiding places are plentiful. There may be many watchful eyes in the city, but there will always be a dark alley somewhere with some good-natured soul who has found themselves, despite their better judgement, quite alone.

Additionally, shadows have no tell-tale signs which might betray them; no foul odor surrounds them, no footprints betray their passing, no noises, changes of temperature, or any other sign of the undead. Beyond the subtle shifting of darkness within darkness which escapes the notice of all but the keenest of observers, a shadow is utterly hidden.

Roleplaying Shadows

Shadows have no remnant of personality from their 'parent', nor much in the way of individuality, behaving far more like predatory animals than intelligent beings. They are solitary by nature, as it is easier to remain hidden, though they may gather where hiding places are plentiful and swarm prey together. Shadows are intelligent enough to be tamed and trained for specific tasks by any individual evil enough to be of little interest as prey (not to mention, to be willing to employ shadows). Tamed shadows may be sent after a particular target, assassins able to sneak into any area with ease.

Combat Tactics

Shadows are, of course, far more dangerous in areas of darkness which allow them to ambush their prey unseen, as well as quickly melt away to regain the advantage in the confusion. However, they are not constrained to dark areas, and a clever shadow will know how to slip between areas of darkness, using moving, mundane shadows to mask its own movements, even during bright sunshine, though it will use these skills only to watch and stalk, waiting for darkness to cover all before launching an attack. Shadows show marked preference to attacking those of greatest virtue, those good-hearted souls who will create the strongest shadows upon their deaths.

While supernatural, shadows have the instincts of ambush predators, and are secure in their ability to disappear, should the fight turn against them. Most often, they will retreat just a fraction, and then continue stalking, unseen, hoping to strike at their prey again before it can recover its strength.

Shadow Encounters

d4	CR	Encounter
1	4	**Lingering Imprint:** 3 Silhouette Shadows
2	7	**Trailing Afterimage:** 1 Treacherous Shadow, 4 Silhouette Shadows
3	11	**Lurking Gloom:** 3 Treacherous Shadows, 5 Silhouette Shadows
4	14	**Suffocating Darkness:** Consuming Darkness, 4 Treacherous Shadows

Silhouette Shadow
Medium undead, chaotic evil

Armor Class 12
Hit Points 36 (8d8)
Speed 30 ft.

STR	DEX	CON	INT	WIS	CHA
5 (-3)	15 (+2)	11 (+0)	6 (-2)	13 (+1)	7 (-2)

Skills Stealth +6
Damage Vulnerabilities radiant
Damage Resistances acid, cold, fire, lightning, thunder; bludgeoning, piercing, and slashing from nonmagical attacks
Damage Immunities necrotic, poison
Condition Immunities exhaustion, frightened, grappled, paralyzed, petrified, poisoned, prone, restrained
Senses darkvision 60 ft., passive Perception 11
Languages —
Challenge 2 (450 XP)

Amorphous. The silhouette can move through a space as narrow as 1 inch wide, without squeezing.

Shadow Silhouette. While unobserved, the silhouette can attempt to hide without being obscured, so long as it remains motionless. When it does so, it resembles an ordinary shadow, even if there is no object to cast it nearby.

Shadow Camouflage. While fully within a natural shadow, or an area of dim light or darkness, the silhouette is invisible.

Sunlight Weakness. While in sunlight, the silhouette has disadvantage on attack rolls, ability checks, and saving throws.

Actions

Strength Drain. *Melee Weapon Attack:* +4 to hit, reach 5 ft., one creature. *Hit:* 12 (3d6 + 3) necrotic damage, and the target's Strength score is reduced by 1d4. The target dies if this reduces its Strength to 0. Otherwise, the reduction lasts until the target finishes a short or long rest.

If a non-evil humanoid dies from this attack, a new silhouette shadow rises from the corpse 1d4 hours later.

"I take back my wish!" cried the boy. "It's so lonely without it! I just want my shadow back!"

"Granted," whispered the voice from the darkness.

-Willum Jacobs, 'The Boy Without A Shadow' (from 'The Candlelight's Companion')

TREACHEROUS SHADOW
Medium undead, chaotic evil

Armor Class 14
Hit Points 65 (10d8 + 20)
Speed 40 ft.

STR	DEX	CON	INT	WIS	CHA
7 (-2)	18 (+4)	15 (+2)	10 (+0)	13 (+1)	7 (-2)

Skills Stealth +10
Damage Vulnerabilities radiant
Damage Resistances acid, cold, fire, lightning, thunder; bludgeoning, piercing, and slashing from nonmagical attacks
Damage Immunities necrotic, poison
Condition Immunities exhaustion, frightened, grappled, paralyzed, petrified, poisoned, prone, restrained
Senses darkvision 60 ft., passive Perception 11
Languages —
Challenge 5 (1,800 XP)

Amorphous. The treacherous shadow can move through a space as narrow as 1 inch wide, without squeezing.

Shadow Camouflage. While fully within a natural shadow, or an area of dim light or darkness, the treacherous shadow is invisible.

Sneak Attack (1/Turn). The treacherous shadow deals an extra 21 (6d6) damage when it hits a target with a weapon attack and has advantage on the attack roll, or when the target is within 5 feet of an ally of the shadow that isn't incapacitated, and the shadow doesn't have disadvantage on the attack roll.

Sunlight Weakness. While in sunlight, the treacherous shadow has disadvantage on attack rolls, ability checks, and saving throws.

ACTIONS

Strength Drain. *Melee Weapon Attack:* +7 to hit, reach 5 ft., one creature. *Hit:* 18 (4d6 + 4) necrotic damage, and the target's Strength score is reduced by 1d4. The target dies if this reduces its Strength to 0. Otherwise, the reduction lasts until the target finishes a short or long rest.

If a non-evil humanoid dies from this attack, a new treacherous shadow rises from the corpse 1d4 hours later.

Two shadows, run.
No shadow, pray.

-words of wisdom

Umbral Betrayal (1/Day). The treacherous shadow possesses a mundane shadow it can see, within 60 feet, that is cast by a humanoid who is unaware of the shadow's presence. The treacherous shadow disappears into the possessed shadow. The target is unaware of the possession and carries the treacherous shadow around as its own shadow, which can choose to mimic the target's movements.

While the treacherous shadow is possessing a creature's shadow, the shadow takes only half damage dealt to it, and the creature whose shadow is possessed takes the other half.

The possession lasts until the target drops to 0 hit points, the treacherous shadow ends it using a bonus action, or the treacherous shadow is turned or forced out by an effect like a *dispel evil and good* spell. When the possession ends, the treacherous shadow reappears in an unoccupied space within 5 feet of the target.

Particularly clever shadows can overwhelm and possess the shadows of living creatures, without their notice. These **treacherous shadows** might use this ability to stalk prey for days, waiting for an opportune moment to strike, to flee danger unseen by their enemies, or simply to quickly close a gap to spring an attack. These shadows are prized as assassins by those able to control them.

CONSUMING DARKNESS

Medium undead, chaotic evil

Armor Class 15
Hit Points 127 (15d8 + 60)
Speed 40 ft.

STR	DEX	CON	INT	WIS	CHA
11 (+0)	20 (+5)	18 (+4)	14 (+2)	15 (+2)	7 (-2)

Skills Stealth +13
Damage Vulnerabilities radiant
Damage Resistances acid, cold, fire, lightning, thunder; bludgeoning, piercing, and slashing from nonmagical attacks
Damage Immunities necrotic, poison
Condition Immunities exhaustion, frightened, grappled, paralyzed, petrified, poisoned, prone, restrained
Senses darkvision 90 ft., passive Perception 12
Languages —
Challenge 9 (5,000 XP)

Amorphous. The consuming darkness can move through a space as narrow as 1 inch wide, without squeezing.

Shadow Camouflage. While fully within a natural shadow, or an area of dim light or darkness, the consuming darkness is invisible.

Spreading Shadows (Recharge 5-6). As a bonus action, the consuming darkness emits magical darkness in a 30-foot radius. The darkness spreads around corners. A creature that starts its turn within this darkness takes 7 (2d6) necrotic damage. Darkvision can't see through this darkness, and nonmagical light can't illuminate it. If any of the darkness' area overlaps with an area of light created by a spell of 2nd level or lower, the spell that created the light is dispelled.

The darkness lasts for as long as the consuming darkness maintains concentration, up to 10 minutes (as though it were concentrating on a spell). While it is concentrating on the effect, it can't roll to recharge its use of the ability.

Sunlight Weakness. While in sunlight, the consuming darkness has disadvantage on attack rolls, ability checks, and saving throws.

True Darkvision. The consuming darkness' vision isn't impeded by magical darkness.

ACTIONS

Multiattack. The consuming darkness makes three Strength Drain attacks. It can't hit the same creature more than once in a turn.

Strength Drain. *Melee Weapon Attack:* +9 to hit, reach 5 ft., one creature. *Hit:* 19 (4d6 + 5) necrotic damage, and the target's Strength score is reduced by 1d4. The target dies if this reduces its Strength to 0. Otherwise, the reduction lasts until the target finishes a short or long rest.

If a non-evil humanoid dies from this attack, a new consuming darkness rises from the corpse 1d4 hours later.

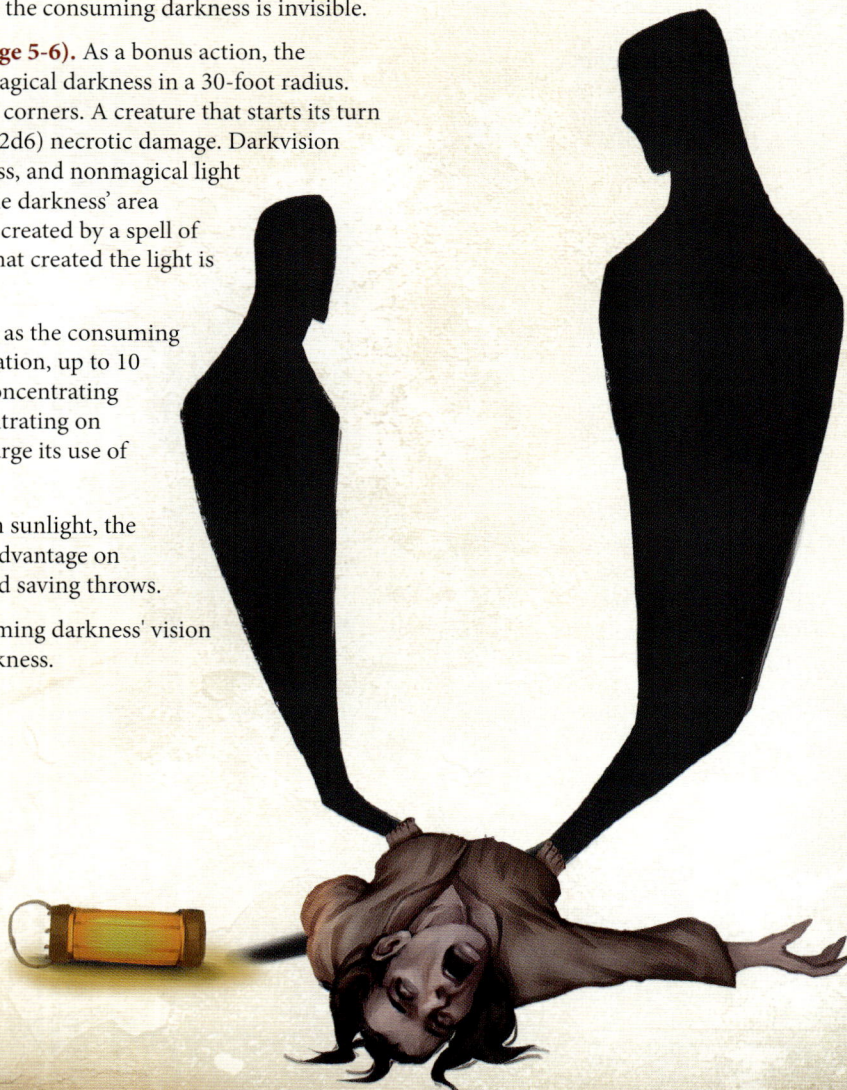

The timing had to be exact which, it had to be said, was complicated by the fact I did not altogether trust the town clock. Even if the bells had been reliable, however, I would have found it difficult to do anything other than stare through the thin curtains, waiting, and watching the skyline.

Thaddeus snoozed in the corner. His apparent ability to sleep anywhere seemed to be an adaptation to his equal ability to go without sleep for days at a time. Lacking both of these attributes, I was given the task of waking him as soon as the market place began to empty.

The sheer number of candles made the room sweltering, and I dared not open the window even a crack for fear of extinguishing any, not to mention the fear of what might creep in. Thaddeus was adamant they be attended to during his rest. The light wouldn't keep them out, he explained, pre-empting my question, but they don't like to attack if they can't hide first.

"So there's really nothing stopping them attacking us at any time?" I asked.

"Not a thing," he replied, helpfully.

It was around this time that all thoughts of rest left my mind.

Thaddeus had been on edge for a few days. He was twitchy, his head snapping around at the slightest noise, and he was even less interested in conversation than usual. Most tellingly, he insisted on seeking accommodation at night. Granted, his standard of accommodation was somewhat less than I would have liked but four solid walls are an undeniable improvement on a cloak propped up on sticks, regardless of how much the plaster is flaking. When I asked him the reason for his strange behaviour, he simply replied, "Being followed. Thought we'd shaken them. We haven't."

His appropriately dark response of, "Shadows", in response to my blank look, scarcely served to alleviate my concerns.

"Need to trap them, lure them in. Can't let them know we've seen them until it's time."

Thus, we found ourselves in the bustling city of Norvosk; replete with twisting alleyways and overhanging buildings, it was, simply put, a shadow's playground. If we wanted to make ourselves look like easy targets for an ambush, there could be few better places. Our plan was to lure our pursuers to the marketplace just as the last few stallholders left and, for a few minutes, we would have our arena; an open space, devoid of innocent bystanders and, as important, devoid of hiding places for our umbral assailants. Of course, the sun would be lowering all the time, lengthening the shadows, shifting the balance away from us, and heralding the oncoming night. Thaddeus, it seems, thrives on this kind of knife's-edge planning in exactly the way I do not.

As it transpired, he sprang awake with eerie precision just as I turned from the window to rouse him. I suspect he gave me the job as a courtesy, to make me feel included. Taking the time only to buckle his swordbelt, he strode to the door and turned to me with a look one might use to hurry along a partner who is delaying one's excursion to the market which, I guess, I was. When I signalled my readiness, he threw back the door, and we were running. Down the creaking corridor, through the front door, and out into the street, past alleyways transformed into gaping chasms of dancing darkness in my mind. Here and there, we passed stragglers from the market, eyeing us suspiciously with the shadows of giants in the lowering sun. I fancied I saw one of these shadows turn to watch us go, even as its purported owner walked the other way, though it may have been a trick of the light.

After far more running than I, as a rule, would be entirely comfortable with, we burst into the marketplace, the cobblestones now a brilliant, gleaming orange. Happy to have a moment to catch my breath, I cast my eyes about, examining the terrain as I imagined a seasoned fighter should.

Only now did I catch a glimpse of the force that had been pursuing us. It was not a shadow formed by the absence of light, but active darkness; a difference I would have thought arbitrary, had I not seen it myself, but a most arresting one when seen in person. It bled through the shade like ink in water.

"There," said Thaddeus, gesturing the other way. "See it? By the broken cart." I looked and saw nothing and, in so doing, lost sight of the shadow I had seen.

"But Tha-" I began, but was cut off.

"Now, there," he said, pointing to the well in the centre of the marketplace. "Move! Flush it out of hiding!"

He directed me from place to place, following along behind, describing with his experienced eyes the exact position of the shadow at all times, which remained entirely obscured to me. It occured to me that this may have been the most I had heard Thaddeus speak at one time. Clearly, this foe had him rattled, which was to say nothing of my condition. Now and then, a cool breeze gusted against me and, each time, I could have sworn it was a spectral hand reaching to grab at me.

The sun was very low now, and I was beginning to lose hope, when Thaddeus drove us towards a crooked market stall, its owner having seemingly given it up for a bad job part way through taking it down. The menacing glance Thaddeus threw in my direction was meant for the shadow, I knew, but I could not suppress the chill I felt as he bore down on me.

"Why do you hunt us?" he called out to the empty darkness.

"It was contracted," came the hissing whisper. So soft was the voice, and so echoing the market square, I could not place it. It could have come from anywhere. Thaddeus' hand went to his sword hilt.

"Who sent you?" He drew his sword and held it ready. I could see my own wide-eyed face in the silvered surface.

"You cannot see the blade. How can you comprehend the hand that wields it?" whispered the reply. There was a hunger to it. I sensed that it was closing in for the strike.

"Oh, I see you," growled Thaddeus and, quick as lightning, he thrust his sword towards me.

Time seemed to slow. The blade hissed through the air towards my left ear, even as the darkness seemed to loom larger behind Thaddeus himself. I began to cry out, though whether in fear, or an attempt at a warning, I would never find out. In a fluid motion, the sword pivoted its arc, sparking against the cobblestones as it swung down, and around. Wheeling about, Thaddeus stabbed into the encroaching blackness, and found resistance. A smoldering outline began to describe itself, like parchment thrown on a fire. For the merest second, the featureless shape of a man could be seen, clawing at the blade embedded in its chest, and then was gone.

Thaddeus held out a hand to help me to my feet, his eyes darting as he assured himself that there were no other assailants lurking about. The marketplace was empty, grey and cold. Darkness had fallen at last.

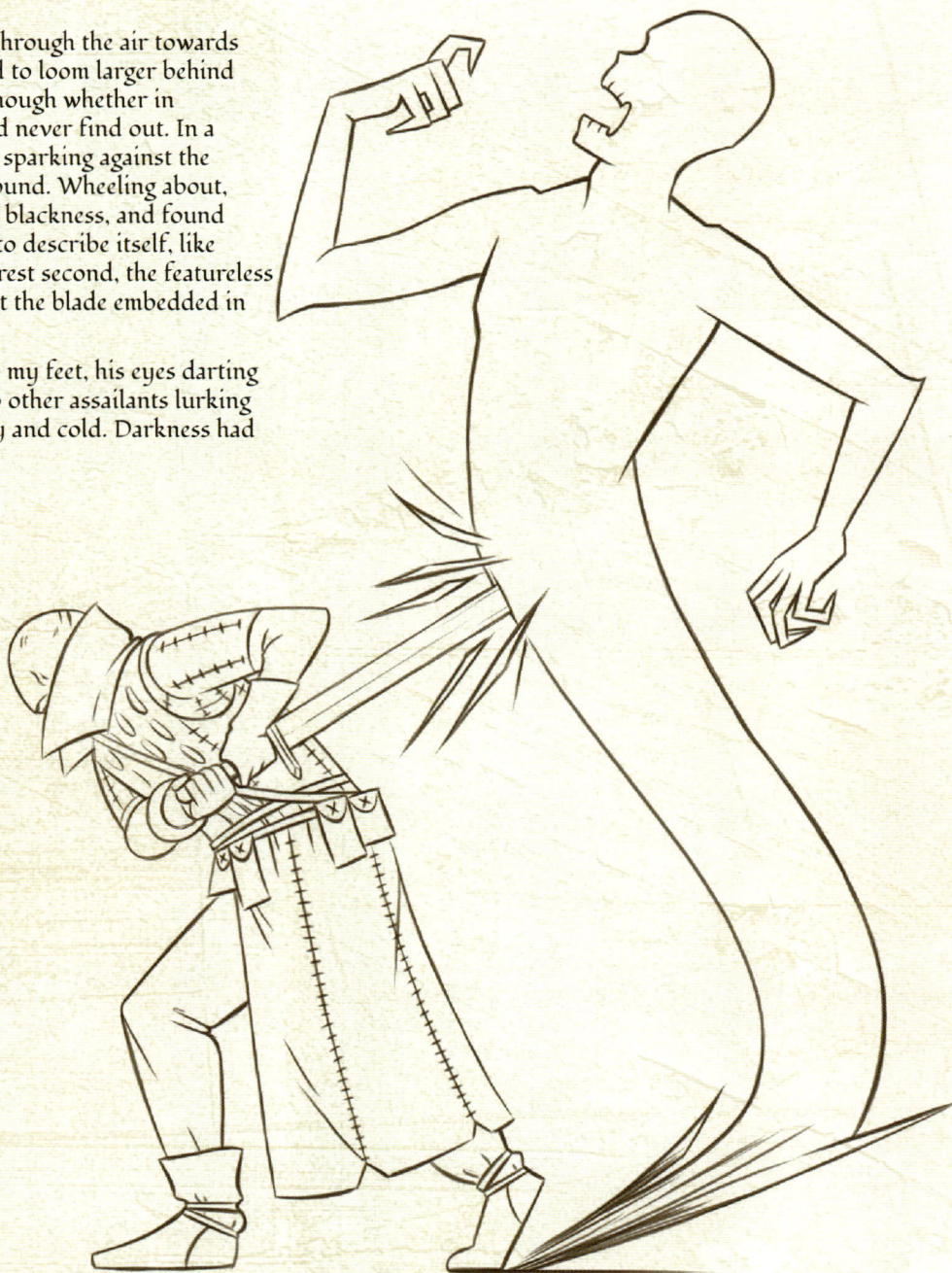

SKELETONS

The disjointed pile of dusty bones begins to twitch and shudder. Ball snaps into socket, hinges devoid of flesh flex and test their limits. Each vertebra clicks into place as the thing rises until, with a final crack, the skull finds its mounting. Jaw hanging limply, it lets out a creaking chuckle from long-disappeared lungs, and wrenches the rust-bitten remnants of a sword from its empty ribcage.

The rattle of bone on bone, the clack of untethered jaws: these are the rhythm and the metronome of the undead hordes. Ensorcelled remains, animated beyond their time, stand to attend a new master, caring not whoever it may be, for they are legion, a mass of the mindless. They wait, infesting the warrens of the destitute, the cellars of ancient places, and bowels of the world - a ready army for those with the stomach and the will.

Skeletons are among the most commonly encountered undead, being simple to create and able to reliably carry out instructions (many free-willed undead will seek to carry out their own agendas, while mindless ones can be easily distracted by living flesh)

While a skeleton does not require flesh in order to move, being animated entirely magically, a *lack* of flesh is not a requirement. Though certainly not the norm, and requiring unorthodox magics, even the recently dead can have their skeletons animated, heaving their soft tissues along with them until they eventually rot and slough away, revealing the walking bones beneath. The tell-tale sign of a skeleton is the dim, glowing light within the eye sockets, betraying the magic which knits the bones together.

ORIGIN

Skeletons are, in essence, specialised magical automata. The spells required to create them resemble those used to animate objects more than those that raise the dead. The difference lies in the fact that magically animated skeletons use the residual energies left in the bones to power the spell, putting their creation firmly in the camp of necromancy.

The spells animating the skeleton replace the tendons and muscles needed in order to move, so centuries-old bones have just as much mobility as those still knitted together with gristle. While perhaps more robust than living tissue, the effect is not indestructible and, should the skeleton sustain enough damage, the forces holding the bones together will cease doing so.

Though usually the case for simplicity's sake, the bones do not strictly need to be from the same individual or species. 'Bone memory', while a somewhat muddy and esoteric field of magical theory, suggests that some imprint of reflexes and practised actions remains dormant in the bones after death, meaning the bones of a soldier will be marginally more suited to martial work, for example. This is another reason necromancers typically raise the skeleton of an individual, though the disparate bones of those with similar life experiences will create a cohesive whole as well.

If the necromancer can imagine it, and coax the magic to animate them in a plausible way, skeletal colossi can be created from an amalgam of different parts. However, such creations are rare; the movements necessary to cause a humanoid form to walk and fight come without thought to the average spellcaster, but working out how to move a pile of mismatched bones without it tripping over its own feet requires an expert's understanding of the craft.

Lastly, skeletons may also spontaneously arise in areas of necromantic energy and, having no master, will instinctively seek to destroy any living creature which comes into their vicinity. These skeletons are likely the ones found in ancient crypts and otherwise-uninhabited locales.

Environment

Skeletons, having no real mind or free will of their own, have little effect on their environment, and have no preference of location beyond their master's orders. Until animated, they are simply bones like any other and will be found wherever they have fallen or been interred.

The ideal use for a group of skeletons is as a source of free, dependable labor, so they are often employed towards dangerous, repetitive, or time-consuming work. Such skeletons might dig for minerals necessary for a ritual, construct dark temples, or simply act as undead pack animals.

Roleplaying Skeletons

Skeletons have little initiative of their own and will follow whatever instruction they were last given by their master to the letter. Their lack of flexibility in their thinking can easily be exploited, and the experienced necromancer knows better than to allow for any room for interpretation in their orders.

Without specific instruction, 'bone memory' takes over, and a skeleton will pantomime common actions from its life. If a skeleton is made up of the bones of many different individuals, these actions can be difficult to interpret as each bone attempts to drive its own movement.

Combat Tactics

Skeletons exist to serve, and so will fight with no heed to their own safety, and will attack relentlessly to destroy the living. Their reliance on orders, however, can be something of a hindrance if they are required to do more than this. Even simple teamwork and cooperation to defend their allies and strike in a coordinated fashion is beyond the ability of a skeleton acting without instruction.

For this reason, the manner in which a skeleton fights can tell the enemy a great deal about their master. Skeletons who attack wildly were likely raised for non-combat purposes, or perhaps by an unskilled tactician (or were stationed in an area their master did not expect to be attacked). Should a group of skeletons adopt formations and defend themselves tactically, they are likely under the control of one with at least some level of martial strategy.

Skeleton Encounters

CR 1/2-7

d8	CR	Encounter
1	1/2	**Clattering Skirmish:** 1 Skeleton Warrior, 1 Skeleton Infantry, 1 Skeleton Archer
2	1	**Bone Cohort:** 4 Skeleton Warriors, 2 Skeleton Archers
3	2	**Dried Regiment:** 10 Skeleton Infantry
4	3	**Deathless Hunt:** 4 Skeleton Archers, 1 Skeleton Marksman, 6 Skeletal Dogs
5	4	**Osseous Formation:** 1 Skeleton Pikeneer, 8 Skeleton Infantry, 6 Skeleton Archers
6	5	**Rattling Horde:** 5 Skeletal Dogs, 6 Skeleton Infantry, 4 Skeleton Archers, 2 Skeleton Soldiers, 2 Skeletal Riding Horses
7	6	**Skeletal Infantry:** 4 Skeleton Pikeneers, 2 Skeleton Soldiers
8	7	**Marrow Riders:** 6 Skeletal Riding Horses, 4 Skeleton Soldiers, 2 Skeleton Marksmen

CR 9-21

d6	CR	Encounter
1	9	**Ivory Spearhead:** 2 Skelephants, 7 Skeleton Warriors, 1 Skeleton Soldier, 7 Skeleton Infantry, 1 Skeleton Pikeneer
2	11	**Dusty Elite:** 1 Skeleton Veteran, 8 Skeleton Pikeneers, 4 Skeleton Marksmen
3	13	**Thrashskull Shocktroop:** 1 Skeleton Sharpshooter, 8 Skeleton Soldiers, 1 Skelephant, 1 Skeletal Minotaur Warrior
4	14	**Big-Boned Unit:** 1 Bone Horror, 1 Skeletal Minotaur Warrior, 1 Skeletal Hill Giant, 1 Skelephant
5	17	**Smashing Bones:** 1 Skeletal Minotaur Warlord, 2 Bone Horrors, 1 Skeleton Veteran
6	21	**Titanic Boneyard:** 1 Skeletal Wartitan, 2 Bone Horrors

SKELETON WARRIOR
Medium undead, lawful evil

Armor Class 15 (chain shirt scraps, shield)
Hit Points 9 (2d8)
Speed 30 ft.

STR	DEX	CON	INT	WIS	CHA
9 (-1)	15 (+2)	10 (+0)	6 (-2)	8 (-1)	4 (-3)

Damage Vulnerabilities bludgeoning, radiant
Damage Immunities poison, necrotic
Condition Immunities exhaustion, poisoned
Senses darkvision 60 ft., passive perception 9
Languages understands the languages it knew in life, but can't speak
Challenge 1/4 (50 XP)

Skeletal Appearance. While the warrior is lying still, it is indistinguishable from a mundane skeletal corpse. It can still be detected by a *detect evil and good* spell, or similar magic.

ACTIONS

Scimitar. *Melee Weapon Attack:* +4 to hit, reach 5 ft., one target. *Hit:* 5 (1d6 + 2) slashing damage.

SKELETON SOLDIER
Medium undead, lawful evil

Armor Class 15 (chain shirt scraps, shield)
Hit Points 36 (8d8)
Speed 30 ft.

STR	DEX	CON	INT	WIS	CHA
10 (+0)	16 (+3)	11 (+0)	6 (-2)	8 (-1)	4 (-3)

Damage Vulnerabilities bludgeoning, radiant
Damage Immunities poison, necrotic
Condition Immunities exhaustion, poisoned
Senses darkvision 60 ft., passive perception 9
Languages understands the languages it knew in life, but can't speak
Challenge 2 (450 XP)

Skeletal Appearance. While the soldier is lying still, it is indistinguishable from a mundane skeletal corpse. It can still be detected by a *detect evil and good* spell, or similar magic.

ACTIONS

Multiattack. The soldier makes two weapon attacks.

Scimitar. *Melee Weapon Attack:* +5 to hit, reach 5 ft., one target. *Hit:* 6 (1d6 + 3) slashing damage.

Take some time to walk around and truly focus on your movements. Of course, walking is a trivial and automatic task, but imagine trying to explain it to a being which has no concept of movement (for soon you will have to, and in the limited time of the casting); the sheer amount of interdependent parts may seem daunting. However, note the simplicity of each individual task: the rotation of the hip joint, the flexing of the ankle, the balance provided by the swinging arms, and do not allow yourself to be intimidated.

-Nestovir Dres, 'The Necromancer's Pocketbook'

SKELETON VETERAN
Medium undead, lawful evil

Armor Class 16 (rusted chain shirt, shield)
Hit Points 88 (16d8 + 16)
Speed 30 ft.

STR	DEX	CON	INT	WIS	CHA
12 (+1)	17 (+3)	12 (+1)	6 (-2)	8 (-1)	4 (-3)

Damage Vulnerabilities radiant
Damage Resistances piercing and slashing damage from nonmagical attacks
Damage Immunities poison, necrotic
Condition Immunities exhaustion,poisoned
Senses darkvision 60 ft., passive perception 9
Languages understands the languages it knew in life, but can't speak
Challenge 5 (1,800 XP)

Legendary Durability (3/Day). If the veteran fails a saving throw, it can choose to reroll the saving throw.

Skeletal Appearance. While the veteran is lying still, it is indistinguishable from a mundane skeletal corpse. It can still be detected by a *detect evil and good* spell, or similar magic.

ACTIONS

Multiattack. The veteran makes two scimitar attacks and uses its Shield Bash.

Scimitar. *Melee Weapon Attack:* +6 to hit, reach 5 ft., one target. *Hit:* 6 (1d6 + 3) slashing damage.

Shield Bash. *Melee Weapon Attack:* +4 to hit, reach 5 ft., one target. *Hit:* 3 (1d4 + 1) bludgeoning damage and the target must succeed on a DC 12 Strength saving throw, or be knocked prone.

REACTIONS

Osseous Counter. When the veteran is hit by a melee weapon attack, it can attempt to catch the weapon in between its bones. The attacker must succeed on a DC 14 Dexterity saving throw, or its weapon becomes stuck. While the weapon is stuck, the creature wielding it is grappled by the veteran. The creature can end the grapple by dropping the weapon. A creature can use its action to attempt to retrieve a weapon stuck this way by succeeding on a DC 14 Strength check. If the veteran willingly offers the weapon, or is incapacitated, no check is necessary to retrieve the weapon.

LEGENDARY ACTIONS

The veteran can take 3 legendary actions, choosing from the options below. Only one legendary action option can be used at a time, and only at the end of another creature's turn. The veteran regains spent legendary actions at the start of its turn.

Attack. The veteran makes a scimitar attack.

Whirling Leap (Costs 2 Actions). The veteran moves up to 30 feet in a straight line without provoking opportunity attacks and ignoring nonmagical difficult terrain. During this movement, it can make a single scimitar attack against each enemy that enters its reach. The veteran can't use this action while grappling another creature.

SKELETON INFANTRY

Medium undead, lawful evil

Armor Class 13 (chain shirt scraps)
Hit Points 9 (2d8)
Speed 30 ft.

STR	DEX	CON	INT	WIS	CHA
13 (+1)	14 (+2)	11 (+0)	6 (-2)	8 (-1)	4 (-3)

Damage Vulnerabilities bludgeoning, radiant
Damage Immunities poison, necrotic
Condition Immunities exhaustion, poisoned
Senses darkvision 60 ft., passive perception 9
Languages understands the languages it knew in life, but can't speak
Challenge 1/4 (50 XP)

Skeletal Appearance. While the infantry is lying still, it is indistinguishable from a mundane skeletal corpse. It can still be detected by a *detect evil and good* spell, or similar magic.

ACTIONS

Pike. *Melee Weapon Attack:* +3 to hit, reach 10 ft., one target. *Hit:* 6 (1d10 + 1) piercing damage.

REACTIONS

Brace Pike. When a creature enters its reach, the infantry can make a pike attack against it.

SKELETON PIKENEER

Medium undead, lawful evil

Armor Class 14 (rusted chain shirt)
Hit Points 44 (8d8 + 8)
Speed 30 ft.

STR	DEX	CON	INT	WIS	CHA
14 (+2)	14 (+2)	12 (+1)	6 (-2)	8 (-1)	4 (-3)

Damage Vulnerabilities bludgeoning, radiant
Damage Immunities poison, necrotic
Condition Immunities poisoned
Senses darkvision 60 ft., passive perception 9
Languages understands the languages it knew in life, but can't speak
Challenge 2 (450 XP)

Skeletal Appearance. While the pikeneer is lying still, it is indistinguishable from a mundane skeletal corpse. It can still be detected by a *detect evil and good* spell, or similar magic.

ACTIONS

Multiattack. The pikeneer makes two weapon attacks.

Pike. *Melee Weapon Attack:* +4 to hit, reach 10 ft., one target. *Hit:* 7 (1d10 + 2) piercing damage.

REACTIONS

Brace Pike. When a creature enters its reach, the pikeneer can make a pike attack against it.

A skeleton once complained that he'd been attacked by my dog.
I told him he didn't have a leg to stand on.

-popular joke

SKELETON PIKEMASTER

Medium undead, lawful evil

Armor Class 15 (rusted chain shirt)
Hit Points 97 (15d8 + 30)
Speed 30 ft.

STR	DEX	CON	INT	WIS	CHA
16 (+3)	15 (+2)	14 (+2)	6 (-2)	8 (-1)	4 (-3)

Damage Vulnerabilities radiant
Damage Resistances piercing and slashing damage from nonmagical attacks
Damage Immunities poison, necrotic
Condition Immunities exhaustion, poisoned
Senses darkvision 60 ft., passive perception 9
Languages understands the languages it knew in life, but can't speak
Challenge 5 (1,800 XP)

Legendary Durability (3/Day). If the pikemaster fails a saving throw, it can choose to reroll the saving throw.

Skeletal Appearance. While the pikemaster is lying still, it is indistinguishable from a mundane skeletal corpse. It can still be detected by a *detect evil and good* spell, or similar magic.

Osseous Phalanx. As a bonus action, the pikemaster can push its pike through the ribcage of another willing skeleton. The impaled skeleton takes no damage, but is considered grappled by the pikemaster until either skeleton ends the condition on its turn as part of its movement. Until this grapple ends, as long as the impaled skeleton is not destroyed, the pikemaster has three-quarters cover.

ACTIONS

Multiattack. The pikemaster makes two weapon attacks.

Pike. *Melee Weapon Attack:* +6 to hit, reach 10 ft., one target. *Hit:* 8 (1d10 + 3) piercing damage.

REACTIONS

Brace Pike. When a creature enters its reach, the pikemaster can make a pike attack against it.

LEGENDARY ACTIONS

The pikemaster can take 3 legendary actions, choosing from the options below. Only one legendary action option can be used at a time, and only at the end of another creature's turn. The pikemaster regains spent legendary actions at the start of its turn.

Attack. The pikemaster makes a pike attack.

Impaling Vault (Costs 2 Actions). The pikemaster makes a pike attack against a target within its reach. It then moves to an unoccupied space it can see within 10 feet of the target, without provoking opportunity attacks, and can make a pike attack against another target within its reach. The pikemaster can't use this action while grappling another creature.

As the ranks passed me by, I noticed, right at the back of our column, a team of various young attendants and serving persons from our camp, flanked by four burly-looking chaps in full plate. The group was unarmored and unarmed, save for mallets I recognised as being the kind to hammer in tent pegs. They waited for the column to clear a section of tunnel and would then, as one, descend on each fallen skeleton that had been dispatched there, working quickly and methodically to turn the pile of bones to dust. I wondered at the usefulness of such a task force until, out of a side-passage, came a boney figure wielding a long pike. Seeing itself outnumbered, the skeleton proceeded to skewer the ribcage of one of its fallen comrades and hold the body up in front of itself like a long, pavise shield. When I saw how well it could protect itself against two of the plate-clad protectors, my doubts about the benefits of the hammer team were vanquished.

-Second Lieutenant Ida Grey, Howling Hippogriffs regiment

SKELETON ARCHER
Medium undead, lawful evil

Armor Class 12
Hit Points 9 (2d8)
Speed 30 ft.

STR	DEX	CON	INT	WIS	CHA
9 (-1)	15 (+2)	10 (+0)	6 (-2)	10 (+0)	4 (-3)

Damage Vulnerabilities bludgeoning, radiant
Damage Immunities poison, necrotic
Condition Immunities exhaustion, poisoned
Senses darkvision 60 ft., passive perception 10
Languages understands the languages it knew in life, but can't speak
Challenge 1/4 (50 XP)

Skeletal Appearance. While the archer is lying still, it is indistinguishable from a mundane skeletal corpse. It can still be detected by a *detect evil and good* spell, or similar magic.

ACTIONS

Dagger. *Melee Weapon Attack:* +4 to hit, reach 5 ft., one target. *Hit:* 4 (1d4 + 2) slashing damage.

Longbow. *Ranged Weapon Attack:* +4 to hit, range 120/600 ft., one target. *Hit:* 6 (1d8 + 2) piercing damage.

SKELETON MARKSMAN
Medium undead, lawful evil

Armor Class 14 (leather)
Hit Points 40 (9d8)
Speed 30 ft.

STR	DEX	CON	INT	WIS	CHA
9 (-1)	16 (+3)	10 (+0)	6 (-2)	11 (+0)	4 (-3)

Skills Perception +2
Damage Vulnerabilities bludgeoning, radiant
Damage Immunities poison, necrotic
Condition Immunities exhaustion, poisoned
Senses darkvision 60 ft., passive perception 12
Languages understands the languages it knew in life, but can't speak
Challenge 2 (450 XP)

Skeletal Appearance. While the marksman is lying still, it is indistinguishable from a mundane skeletal corpse. It can still be detected by a *detect evil and good* spell, or similar magic.

ACTIONS

Multiattack. The marksman makes two dagger or longbow attacks.

Dagger. *Melee Weapon Attack:* +5 to hit, reach 5 ft, one target. *Hit:* 5 (1d4 + 3) slashing damage.

Longbow. *Ranged Weapon Attack:* +5 to hit, range 120/600 ft., one target. *Hit:* 7 (1d8 + 3) piercing damage.

"Hvaral wanted to show off, so he wagered that his skeleton could outshoot any of us. Sure enough, he told it to aim where we aimed and, more often than not, it was splitting our arrows down the middle with its own. Move the target between shots though and, if it didn't get new instructions, it wasn't even hitting the board; it still aimed at the empty space the target was when we shot at it. Maybe Hvaral didn't quite have the knack of it, or maybe skeletons are just that thick."

-Amory Figg, game warden

Skeleton Sharpshooter

Medium undead, lawful evil

Armor Class 14 (leather)
Hit Points 80 (18d8)
Speed 30 ft.

STR	DEX	CON	INT	WIS	CHA
9 (-1)	17 (+3)	10 (+0)	6 (-2)	12 (+1)	4 (-3)

Skills Perception +4
Damage Vulnerabilities radiant
Damage Resistances piercing and slashing damage from nonmagical attacks
Damage Immunities poison, necrotic
Condition Immunities exhaustion, poisoned
Senses darkvision 60 ft., passive perception 14
Languages understands the languages it knew in life, but can't speak
Challenge 5 (1,800 XP)

Legendary Durability (3/Day). If the sharpshooter fails a saving throw, it can choose to reroll the saving throw.

Skeletal Appearance. While the sharpshooter is lying still, it is indistinguishable from a mundane skeletal corpse. It can still be detected by a *detect evil and good* spell, or similar magic.

Osseous Sniper. Other skeletal creatures (animated or otherwise) never provide cover against the sharpshooter's ranged attacks.

Actions

Multiattack. The sharpshooter makes two weapon attacks.

Dagger. *Melee Weapon Attack:* +6 to hit, reach 5 ft., one target. *Hit:* 5 (1d4 + 3) slashing damage.

Longbow. *Ranged Weapon Attack:* +6 to hit, range 120/600 ft., one target. *Hit:* 7 (1d8 + 3) piercing damage.

Legendary Actions

The sharpshooter can take 3 legendary actions, choosing from the options below. Only one legendary action option can be used at a time, and only at the end of another creature's turn. The sharpshooter regains spent legendary actions at the start of its turn.

Attack. The sharpshooter makes a longbow attack.

Covered Retreat (Costs 2 Actions). The sharpshooter makes a longbow attack against up to two creatures within 10 feet of it. It doesn't suffer disadvantage on these attacks if it is within 5 feet of a hostile creature. It can then move up to its speed without provoking opportunity attacks from the targets of these attacks.

"What is the lot of the mortal but to strive, sometimes fruitlessly, for meaning and purpose? Given a clear and achievable task, a mortal is contented. We must, I think, imagine the skeleton happy. Perhaps this is why they grin so."

-Aticus Greenmoss, minstrel

SKELETAL HILL GIANT
Huge undead, lawful evil

Armor Class 14 (natural armor)
Hit Points 95 (10d12 + 30)
Speed 40 ft.

STR	DEX	CON	INT	WIS	CHA
21 (+5)	10 (+0)	17 (+3)	5 (-3)	7 (-2)	4 (-3)

Damage Vulnerabilities radiant
Damage Immunities poison, necrotic
Condition Immunities exhaustion, poisoned
Senses darkvision 60 ft., passive perception 8
Languages understands Giant, but can't speak
Challenge 5 (1,800 XP)

Skeletal Appearance. While the skeletal hill giant is lying still, it is indistinguishable from a mundane skeletal corpse. It can still be detected by a *detect evil and good* spell, or similar magic.

ACTIONS

Multiattack. The skeletal hill giant makes two greatclub attacks.

Greatclub. *Melee Weapon Attack:* +8 to hit, reach 5 ft., one target. *Hit:* 18 (3d8 + 5) bludgeoning damage.

Rock. *Ranged Weapon Attack:* +8 to hit, range 60/180 ft., one target. *Hit:* 21 (3d10 + 5) bludgeoning damage.

SKELETAL MINOTAUR WARRIOR
Large undead, lawful evil

Armor Class 14 (rusted breastplate)
Hit Points 136 (16d10 + 48)
Speed 40 ft.

STR	DEX	CON	INT	WIS	CHA
19 (+4)	10 (+0)	17 (+3)	6 (-2)	8 (-1)	4 (-3)

Damage Vulnerabilities bludgeoning, radiant
Damage Immunities poison, necrotic
Condition Immunities exhaustion, poisoned
Senses darkvision 60 ft., passive perception 9
Languages understands Abyssal, but can't speak
Challenge 7 (2,900 XP)

Skeletal Appearance. While the skeletal minotaur is lying still, it is indistinguishable from a mundane skeletal corpse. It can still be detected by a *detect evil and good* spell, or similar magic.

Charge. If the skeletal minotaur moves at least 10 feet straight toward a target, and then hits it with a gore attack on the same turn, the target takes an extra 9 (2d8) piercing damage. If the target is a creature, it must succeed on a DC 14 Strength saving throw, or be pushed up to 10 feet away and knocked prone.

ACTIONS

Multiattack. The skeletal minotaur makes one greataxe attack, and one gore attack.

Greataxe. *Melee Weapon Attack:* +7 to hit, reach 5 ft., one target. *Hit:* 17 (2d12 + 4) slashing damage.

Gore. *Melee Weapon Attack:* +7 to hit, reach 5 ft., one target. *Hit:* 13 (2d8 + 4) piercing damage.

By this point, we were all hungry for a scrap and, when the corpses started up the hill, we thought we were going to have an easy time of it. Not to blow our own trumpets, but we were clearly a seasoned lot of warriors; who on earth thought some zombies would cut it? Well, we started making bets and throwing stones, as you do. It wasn't until Gormer knocked one of their heads clean off and it kept coming that we noticed the weapons in their hands.

"Blimey. Skeletons," says I. "Some bugger's raised them with their skins on."

-Mercer Dale, 'Tales From A Soldier of Fortune'

Skeletal Minotaur Warlord

Large undead, lawful evil

Armor Class 15 (rusted half-plate)
Hit Points 209 (22d10 + 88)
Speed 40 ft.

STR	DEX	CON	INT	WIS	CHA
21 (+5)	10 (+0)	19 (+4)	6 (-2)	8 (-1)	4 (-3)

Damage Vulnerabilities radiant
Damage Resistances piercing and slashing damage from nonmagical attacks
Damage Immunities poison, necrotic
Condition Immunities exhaustion, poisoned
Senses darkvision 60 ft., passive perception 9
Languages understands Abyssal, but can't speak
Challenge 10 (5,900 XP)

Charge. If the skeletal minotaur moves at least 10 feet straight toward a target, and then hits it with a gore attack on the same turn, the target takes an extra 9 (2d8) piercing damage. If the target is a creature, it must succeed on a DC 15 Strength saving throw, or be pushed up to 10 feet away and knocked prone.

Skeletal Appearance. While the skeletal minotaur is lying still, it is indistinguishable from a mundane skeletal corpse. It can still be detected by a *detect evil and good* spell, or similar magic.

Actions

Multiattack. The skeletal minotaur makes one greataxe attack, and one gore attack. It can make a hoof attack in place of its greataxe attack.

Greataxe. *Melee Weapon Attack:* +9 to hit, reach 5 ft., one target. *Hit:* 17 (2d12 + 5) slashing damage.

Gore. *Melee Weapon Attack:* +9 to hit, reach 5 ft., one target. *Hit:* 13 (2d8 + 5) piercing damage.

Hoof. *Melee Weapon Attack:* +9 to hit, reach 5 ft., one target. *Hit:* 10 (1d10 + 5) bludgeoning damage, or 16 (2d10 + 5) bludgeoning damage, if the target is prone.

Legendary Actions

The skeletal minotaur can take 3 legendary actions, choosing from the options below. Only one legendary action option can be used at a time, and only at the end of another creature's turn. The skeletal minotaur regains spent legendary actions at the start of its turn.

Kick. The skeletal minotaur makes a hoof attack.

Charge (Costs 2 Actions). The skeletal minotaur moves up to its speed in a straight line toward a creature, and makes a gore attack against that creature.

The magical properties of dragon body parts are well-documented, useful in everything from tinctures to cure heart conditions to element-resistant textiles. To many cults, however, a dragon's bones are powerful enough to be worthy of worship themselves.

To raise those bones to soar overhead once more is a dream shared by many of that ilk, and one which they all too often come to regret.

-Wulfgang Boor, 'WYRM CULTS: Dragon Worshippers, Their Beliefs and Habits'

SKELETAL DRAGON
Gargantuan undead, lawful evil

Armor Class 18 (natural armor)
Hit Points 310 (20d20 + 100)
Speed 40 ft., fly 40 ft.

STR	DEX	CON	INT	WIS	CHA
23 (+6)	12 (+1)	20 (+5)	6 (-2)	8 (-1)	4 (-3)

Damage Vulnerabilities radiant
Damage Resistances piercing and slashing damage from nonmagical attacks
Damage Immunities poison, necrotic
Condition Immunities exhaustion, poisoned
Senses darkvision 60 ft., passive perception 9
Languages understands Draconic and Common, but can t speak
Challenge 17 (18,000 XP)

Legendary Durability (3/Day). If the skeletal dragon fails a saving throw, it can choose to reroll the saving throw.

Poor Flyer. The dragon's skeletal wings can't hold it aloft for long. If it starts its turn flying, it must end its turn on the ground or fall prone.

Residual Element. The skeletal dragon has a faded connection to the elemental energy it possessed during life. The damage type of the skeleton's breath weapon is acid, cold, fire, lightning, or poison, depending on the damage type it had in life. Additionally, the dragon has resistance to damage of the same type.

Skeletal Appearance. While the skeletal dragon is lying still, it is indistinguishable from a mundane skeletal corpse. It can still be detected by a *detect evil and good* spell, or similar magic.

ACTIONS

Multiattack. The skeletal dragon makes two attacks with its claws, and one attack with its bite.

Claw. *Melee Weapon Attack:* +12 to hit, reach 5 ft., one target. *Hit:* 13 (2d6 + 6) slashing damage.

Bite. *Melee Weapon Attack:* +12 to hit, reach 10 ft., one target. *Hit:* 17 (2d10 + 6) piercing damage.

Tail. *Melee Weapon Attack:* +12 to hit, reach 15 ft., one target. *Hit:* 15 (2d8 + 6) bludgeoning damage.

Residual Breath (Recharge 5-6). The skeletal dragon exhales a faded version of its breath weapon energy in a 40 foot cone. Creatures in that area must make a DC 19 Constitution saving throw, taking 42 (12d6) damage on a failed save, or half as much damage on a successful one.

LEGENDARY ACTIONS

The skeletal dragon can take 3 legendary actions, choosing from the options below. Only one legendary action option can be used at a time, and only at the end of another creature's turn. The skeletal dragon regains spent legendary actions at the start of its turn.

Tail. The skeletal dragon makes a tail attack.

Wing Attack (Costs 2 Actions). The skeletal dragon beats its wings. Each creature within 15 feet of the skeletal dragon must succeed on a DC 20 Dexterity saving throw, or take 13 (2d6 + 6) bludgeoning damage and be knocked prone. The skeletal dragon can then fly up to half its flying speed.

The innate magical nature and sheer power of **dragons** make them wilful and unpredictable necromantic subjects. A necromancer of supreme ability may be able to bend an undead dragon to their will, but it is just as common for the beast to retain some level of autonomy.

Skeletal Riding Horse

Large undead, lawful evil

Armor Class 12
Hit Points 22 (3d10 + 6)
Speed 60 ft.

STR	DEX	CON	INT	WIS	CHA
16 (+3)	14 (+2)	14 (+2)	2 (-4)	8 (-1)	4 (-3)

Damage Vulnerabilities bludgeoning, radiant
Damage Immunities poison, necrotic
Condition Immunities exhaustion, poisoned
Senses darkvision 60 ft., passive perception 9
Languages —
Challenge 1/2 (100 XP)

Skeletal Appearance. While the skeletal horse is lying still, it is indistinguishable from a mundane skeletal corpse. It can still be detected by a *detect evil and good* spell, or similar magic.

Actions

Hooves. *Melee Weapon Attack:* +5 to hit, reach 5 ft., one target. *Hit:* 8 (2d4 + 3) bludgeoning damage.

Skeletal horses are reliable and fearless mounts, though a heavily-padded saddle is recommended for a living rider.

Skeletal Dog

Medium undead, lawful evil

Armor Class 13
Hit Points 7 (2d8 - 2)
Speed 60 ft.

STR	DEX	CON	INT	WIS	CHA
12 (+1)	16 (+3)	9 (-1)	2 (-4)	10 (+0)	4 (-3)

Damage Vulnerabilities bludgeoning, radiant
Damage Immunities poison, necrotic
Condition Immunities exhaustion, poisoned
Senses darkvision 60 ft., passive perception 9
Languages —
Challenge 1/4 (50 XP)

Skeletal Appearance. While the skeletal dog is lying still, it is indistinguishable from a mundane skeletal corpse. It can still be detected by a *detect evil and good* spell, or similar magic.

Actions

Bite. *Melee Weapon Attack:* +5 to hit, reach 5 ft., one target. *Hit:* 6 (1d6 + 3) piercing damage.

SKELEPHANT
Huge undead, lawful evil

Armor Class 13 (natural armor)
Hit Points 67 (9d12 + 9)
Speed 40 ft.

STR	DEX	CON	INT	WIS	CHA
22 (+6)	10 (+0)	13 (+1)	2 (-4)	8 (-1)	4 (-3)

Damage Vulnerabilities radiant
Damage Immunities poison, necrotic
Condition Immunities exhaustion, poisoned
Senses darkvision 60 ft., passive perception 9
Languages —
Challenge 5 (1,800 XP)

Rib Carrier. A Medium or smaller ally of the skelephant, that is also a skeleton, can use 10 feet of its movement to enter the skelephant's space and crawl into its ribcage. The skelephant can carry up to 8 Medium or smaller skeletons in its ribcage. A skeleton can leave the skelephant's ribcage by using 5 feet of movement. When it does, it exits prone in an unoccupied space within 5 feet of the skelephant.

Creatures in the skelephant's ribcage have half cover against attacks from outside the skelephant. Attacks that would have advantage when targeting the skelephant, also have advantage when targeting any creature in the skelephant's ribcage.

Skeletal Appearance. While the skelephant is lying still, it is indistinguishable from a mundane skeletal corpse. It can still be detected by a *detect evil and good* spell, or similar magic.

Trampling Charge. If the skelephant moves at least 20 feet straight toward a target, and then hits it with a gore attack on the same turn, the target must succeed on a DC 16 Strength saving throw, or be knocked prone. If the target is prone, the skelephant can then make one stomp attack against it as a bonus action.

ACTIONS

Gore. *Melee Weapon Attack:* +9 to hit, reach 5 ft., one target. *Hit:* 19 (3d8 + 6) piercing damage.

Stomp. *Melee Weapon Attack:* +9 to hit, reach 5 ft., one prone creature. *Hit:* 22 (3d10 + 6) bludgeoning damage.

SKELEPHANT BARDING

Some skelephants are clad in armored barding to protect both them and the skeletons hidden inside. Barding grants the skelephant an Armor Class of 16. Additionally, it grants creatures in its ribcage total cover against attacks from outside the skelephant. Creatures must expend an additional 5 feet of movement to climb into, and out of, the skelephant's ribcage.

"Ladies and gentlemen, children of all ages, tonight you will behold wonders beyond imagination, experience excitement without compare - you shall howl with laughter, and shriek with terror. Now, slacken your jaws with appal and astonishment, and cast your eyes with horror and disbelief, to the center ring to welcome Xalahira, mistress of death, and her amazing skeletal orchestra!"

-Adolphus Gildinelli, traveling showman

Bone Horror
Huge undead, lawful evil

Armor Class 15 (natural armor)
Hit Points 157 (15d12 + 60)
Speed 35 ft.

STR	DEX	CON	INT	WIS	CHA
24 (+7)	8 (-1)	18 (+4)	2 (-4)	8 (-1)	4 (-3)

Damage Vulnerabilities radiant
Damage Resistances piercing and slashing damage from nonmagical attacks
Damage Immunities poison, necrotic
Condition Immunities exhaustion, poisoned
Senses darkvision 60 ft., passive perception 9
Languages —
Challenge 10 (5,900 XP)

Collapse. The bone horror can use a bonus action to collapse into a pile of bones, becoming indistinguishable from a mundane bone pile. Doing so ends any grappled or restrained conditions affecting it, or that the bone horror has imposed on another creature. It can still be detected by a *detect evil and good* spell, or similar magic. While in this state, the bone horror's speed is 0 and it cannot benefit from any bonuses to its speed. It can't take any actions or reactions, other than reassembling itself.

As an action, a collapsed bone horror can reassemble itself. If it does, it can use a bonus action to make a single weapon attack on the same turn. The bone horror cannot reassemble itself on the same turn it collapsed, or vice versa.

Actions

Multiattack. The bone horror makes three weapon attacks; it can't use the same attack twice with the same action. However, if it attacks once with its claws, it can make a second claws attack as a bonus action.

Bite. *Melee Weapon Attack:* +11 to hit, reach 10 ft., one target. *Hit:* 18 (2d10 + 7) piercing damage, and the target is grappled (escape DC 17). Until this grapple ends, the target is restrained and the bone horror can't bite another target.

Claws. *Melee Weapon Attack:* +11 to hit, reach 10 ft., one target. *Hit:* 12 (1d10 + 7) slashing damage

Gore. *Melee Weapon Attack:* +11 to hit, reach 10 ft., one target. *Hit:* 25 (4d8 + 7) piercing damage.

Slam. *Melee Weapon Attack:* +11 to hit, reach 10 ft., one creature. *Hit:* 23 (3d10 + 7) bludgeoning damage, and the target must succeed on a DC 19 Strength saving throw, or be knocked prone.

Lash. *Melee Weapon Attack:* +11 to hit, reach 20 ft., one prone creature. *Hit:* 24 (5d6 + 7) slashing damage.

Shard Volley. *Ranged Weapon Attack:* +11 to hit, range 40/80 ft., one target. *Hit:* 23 (3d10 + 7) piercing damage.

Shard Explosion. The bone horror makes a single Shard Volley attack against each creature within 15 feet.

A somewhat crude necromantic experiment, the **bone horror** is nonetheless effective, and an efficient use of incomplete remains, if a necromancer is sufficiently skilled to articulate and animate them. Consisting as they do of a multitude of disparate parts, no two bone horrors are exactly alike, though all excel at crude butchery.

Having familiarized yourself with the intuitive movements of humanoid and simple beast, the true (and, I hope, enjoyable) challenge begins. The skilled necromancer can, in time, animate almost any collective of bones they have at their disposal. It helps to begin with a more modest creation, the locomotion of which you are able to act out yourself (it may be best to do this in private, or amongst supportive companions).

– Nestovir Dres, 'The Necromancer's Pocketbook'

SKELETAL WARTITAN
Huge undead, lawful evil

Armor Class 19 (natural armor) or 21 with shield
Hit Points 275 (22d12 + 132)
Speed 30 ft.

STR	DEX	CON	INT	WIS	CHA
26 (+8)	18 (+4)	22 (+6)	4 (-3)	12 (+1)	4 (-3)

Damage Vulnerabilities radiant
Damage Resistances piercing and slashing damage from nonmagical attacks
Damage Immunities poison, necrotic
Condition Immunities exhaustion, poisoned
Senses darkvision 60 ft., passive perception 11
Languages —
Challenge 20 (25,000 XP)

Bone Weaponry. As a bonus action, the wartitan can form its limbs into a weapon of its choice that are sized for itself. This can be a single two-handed weapon, two one-handed weapons, or a one-handed weapon and shield. The below weapons are examples. Keep in mind that huge weapons have three times the damage dice of Medium sized weapons of the same type.

Whenever the wartitan makes a ranged attack with its bone weaponry, its current and maximum hit points are reduced by 7 (2d6). The wartitan can use its Strength in place of its Dexterity modifier for attack and damage rolls with ranged bone weaponry.

Collapse. The wartitan can use a bonus action to collapse into a pile of bones, becoming indistinguishable from a mundane bone pile. Doing so ends any grappled or restrained conditions affecting it, or that the wartitan has imposed on another creature. It can still be detected by a *detect evil and good* spell, or similar magic. While in this state, the wartitan's speed is 0 and it cannot benefit from any bonuses to its speed. It can't take any actions or reactions, other than reassembling itself.

As an action, a collapsed wartitan can reassemble itself. If it does, it can use a bonus action to make a single weapon attack on the same turn. The wartitan cannot reassemble itself on the same turn it collapsed, or vice versa.

Legendary Resistance (2/Day). If the wartitan fails a saving throw, it can choose to succeed instead.

Siege Monster. The wartitan deals double damage to objects and structures.

ACTIONS

Multiattack. The wartitan makes three attacks with its bone weaponry. If it is wielding a pair of one-handed bone weapons, it makes three attacks with one weapon and one additional attack with the other weapon.

Unarmed Strike. *Melee Weapon Attack:* +14 to hit, reach 10 ft., one target. *Hit:* 15 (3d4 + 8) bludgeoning damage.

Bone Pike. *Melee Weapon Attack:* +14 to hit, reach 15 ft., one target. *Hit:* 24 (3d10 + 8) piercing damage.

Bone Longsword. *Melee Weapon Attack:* +14 to hit, reach 10 ft., one target. *Hit:* 21 (3d8 + 8) slashing damage, or 24 (3d10 + 8) slashing damage, if wielded in two hands.

Bone Maul. *Melee Weapon Attack:* +14 to hit, reach 10 ft., one target. *Hit:* 29 (6d6 + 8) bludgeoning damage.

Bone Longbow. *Ranged Weapon Attack:* +14 to hit, range 150/600 ft., one target. *Hit:* 21 (3d8 + 8) piercing damage.

LEGENDARY ACTIONS

The wartitan can take 3 legendary actions, choosing from the options below. Only one legendary action option can be used at a time, and only at the end of another creature's turn. The wartitan regains spent legendary actions at the start of its turn

Surge. The wartitan becomes a roiling mass of bones. It moves up to half its speed and, during this movement, can pass through the spaces of other creatures.

Kick. The wartitan makes one unarmed strike.

Change Weapon. The wartitan reforms its bone weaponry as per its Bone Weaponry ability.

Only a true master of the necromantic arts has the power and vision to create a **skeletal wartitan**. A refinement of the cruder bone horror, a wartitan is massive enough that its weaponry itself is made of animated bone, reshaping and adapting to suit the situation.

"I saw it, clear as you like: not a scrap of skin on, and walking about without a care in the world. I was making my way down the main channel of the south sewer (she's draining clear as a bell now, you'll be pleased to hear), so I reckon it must have wandered in from the bankside graveyard. Now, we get all sorts down in the tunnels, I could tell you some stories, but skellingbones; that's a new one."

I had mentioned to Thaddeus, in passing, once or twice, that I was less than enthused at the amount of peril I had endured and rest I had missed and, of those rare nights of sleep, the proportion spent on hard earth, rather than a mattress. Thaddeus, unmoved by my perfectly legitimate concerns, had snapped back that featherbeds and cotton sheets are paid for with silver. I, with patience and politeness bordering on saintly, put in that most people are paid for their labor, and that our recent exploits remained unremunerated ones. Lacking an argument, or with no mind to provide one, he stomped up to the innkeeper, asking him to put the word out that a monster hunter was in residence and searching for paid work.

We had soon established a contract with a nobleman whose family mausoleum had been disturbed. While none of the grave goods had been taken, as one would expect from simple tomb robbers, the (he paused and gulped dramatically) *bodies* were nowhere to be seen. With our down payment in hand, we had begun interviewing the locals.

"Hold on," I said, looking up from my notes. "Bankside graveyard? Why aren't the graves dug outside the city walls?"

"City planners thought it was safer to keep them accessible. Entrances are guarded day and night, and they're far enough underground that they don't foul the waters. There's miles of tunnels under the city, might as well put them to use. Higher-ups said it was practical. I reckon it was laziness. Budget cuts," she concluded, darkly.

Thaddeus nodded, knowingly.

Our interviews with the guards confirmed the story. None that we spoke to had spotted anyone attempting to enter the tunnels, save for sewerage workers and crypt keepers. This was echoed again and again as we circuited the guards posted at each entrance. It seemed we had hit upon a dead end, until we came upon a more secluded entryway. The guard stationed there gave no response to our greeting, their full-face helm giving no hint of thought or emotion. As we drew closer, they held out their halberd to block the doorway, but still said nothing.

"Alright," I said, as we took a step back, and they returned their weapon to an upright position. "We don't mean to trouble you. We just have a few questions about some goings-on in the tunnels. May we approach?"

They gave no response, but lowered the halberd again as we took a step forward. Thaddeus grunted, and motioned for us to retreat once more (the guard, again, raised their halberd). There was a clang as he let his swordbelt fall to the floor, along with his crossbow and sundry daggers. Before I could question this strange development, he stalked forward, displaying his open, empty hands. The strange guard gave no response as he drew closer. Once within striking distance, Thaddeus darted out a hand, and flipped up the guard's visor, revealing their face or, rather, lack of one. Staring forward, upright and unmoving, were the yellowed bones of a grinning skull peeking through flaking, gray flesh.

"Thought so," grimaced Thaddeus. "Instructed to not let anyone pass if they're armed. Would be too suspicious if it blocked entry to workers. People would start asking questions."

"Why isn't it... trying to eat our brains, or what have you?" I asked, having taken several steps back at the reveal of the corpse, quite quickly.

"Not a job for a zombie. Not that a zombie would be particularly interested in our brains, either. No, skeleton. Undead automaton. Smart enough to follow instructions to the letter, dumb enough to not understand why. Not wholly fleshless yet, but that makes no difference. Chuck me my sword?"

I did so (it seemed weapons *sans* wielders were permitted to pass), and Thaddeus quickly dispatched the boney foe. Once it had collapsed, and I had assured myself that it wasn't about to spring up again, I followed Thaddeus into the tunnels.

The mausoleum was not hard to find (clearly, one's connections in life correlate with the convenience of one's burial site), and it was exactly as our employer had described. Every tomb was empty, as if his long-deceased relatives had simply got up and walked away. Which, of course, they had.

The mystery of what had happened to the bodies having been solved for us left us the larger questions of why and who, and we resigned ourselves to a search of the tunnels. Our informant told no lie: there were miles of them, and every foot of them looked the same to me. I started to think we were just traversing a never-ending loop until, down one unremarkable tunnel, Thaddeus raised a hand for silence and I heard a faint, but distinct, clacking sound. To pull a simile from the ether, it sounded like the small bones of a foot striking a stone surface. He motioned for us to continue moving, but he moved more carefully now and, at every fork and intersection, listened intently and followed the route where the sound resonated loudest.

We arrived in the largest chamber we had come across so far; a large, unremarkable, dirt-packed crypt. Crudely-cut alcoves, barely bigger than the bodies that had recently vacated them, lined the walls. Those interred within these humble tombs were the lucky ones, however; the loose earth of the chamber floor told of a jumble of even less distinguished resting places. Across the tomb, back currently turned to us, a figure bent over a wrapped form, faintly glowing with a pale green light, its hand resting on a glowing, golden orb. A band of skeletons, some merely coated in dirt, others in ragged patches of decomposing flesh, scrabbled in the ground, evidently unearthing more allies.

Thaddeus sighed wearily, walked forward, and the figure turned to him. The Maid of Sorrows looked, to put it politely, a little the worse for wear (and she was no oil painting to begin with). Clearly, a phylactery-less life was not agreeing with her. Rents in her papery skin exposed the bone beneath, lit by flares of whatever magical energy was sustaining her.

"Thaddeus." She sounded tired. "I assumed I would see you before too long." The light within her pulsed, and her skeletal cohort began to edge forwards.

"No phylactery. This goes badly for you, and you don't get another try. Tell them to stand down. Tell me what you know, and..." Thaddeus' jaw clenched so hard I feared his teeth would shatter. "Tell me, and I'll... let you go."

Had she eyes, I am certain she would have rolled them. Nevertheless, with a dismissive flick of her wrist, the skeletons dissolved with some force, their constituent bones clattering a surprising distance into a pile across the chamber.

"What is The Shrouded One?" Thaddeus asked, kicking aside a rib that had bounced across the floor to rest at his feet.

"Powerful. And very interested in you, Thaddeus." She seemed unstable, her hand movements erratic. "It seems that It wished very much to *remain* shrouded. It wants you dead, badly. The shadow failed, obviously; I did think that it would take more than that to kill you, and considered mentioning it, but The Shrouded One does not brook dissension."

"So you're its lackey now?"

"I'll admit it's not ideal, but you left me with little choice. I cannot best it and, thanks to you, I cannot survive as a free agent. Thus, I must submit. The rising is inevitable."

She swept her hands up and, too late, we realised what she had done. As the last of the discarded bones clacked into place, a horrible osseous amalgam, the rough shape of a man, rose up some ten feet tall. With a roar, it slammed down a fist the size of a ribcage in the spot Thaddeus would have been, had he not darted behind the cover of a brick pillar.

The creature swung again, connecting with the pillar, and causing the whole chamber to shake.

"Get him!" the lich shrieked. "Kill him!"

The colossus strove to obey, swinging blindly as Thaddeus backed away. For a time, he tried to parry, but his sword looked little more than a toothpick against the veritable wall of fleshless bone. He fled and, for a moment, I was dismayed. Quickly though, I saw his plan, and was dismayed for entirely different reasons. Thaddeus had positioned himself near to another pillar and, like a bullfighter, was goading the skeletal horror to charge. With no more nuanced instructions telling it otherwise, it did so. Thaddeus threw himself to the side, and I braced for impact. Too late, the lich attempted to call a halt, but she was quickly cut off in the thunderous crash that followed.

Rubble rained down from the ceiling. For what felt like minutes we were engulfed in a dark world of dust and brick. I was unscathed, having stayed at the fringes, but Thaddeus sported some nasty cuts and bruises from his escape (at least, I thought they looked nasty; he probably barely registered them).

Once we had assured ourselves that the avalanche had stopped, we set to the task of combing through the rubble. There was no shortage of bone fragments, both from the slain colossus and, perhaps, from further levels of tombs above us.

"Found her." Thaddeus' face was impassive.

"Is she-?"

"For good, this time," he replied, replacing the stones which had covered her.

Something caught my eye; a faint glow which, as I scrabbled through the wreckage, revealed itself to be the lich's orb, still faintly glowing. For reasons I did not fully understand, I stowed it in my pack. I opened my mouth to tell Thaddeus but, as I turned towards him, I saw but a fleeting impression of his back rounding the corner out of the chamber. I hurried after him, following the echoes of his leaden, heavy footsteps as they reverberated through tunnels now silent as the grave.

SPECTERS

oiling fog pours forward, glowing from within with crackling lightning, like a distant storm. A figure coalesces, a figure of swirling mist, barely containing the tumultuous, churning light. Dancing strands seep out from it, lashing and cracking at random. The form is difficult to determine, shifting and morphing as it is, but its face is clear to see: a skull, twisted and hateful, flicking in an instant from a malignant snarl to a howl of anguish.

One must pity the specter: a writhing miasma of bitterness, confusion, dismay and hate that so unjustly exists, but exist it does. To be severed from the mortal ties of one's life while still in the midst of living does not bear thought, for dwelling upon such can drive even the most stalwart to madness. The myriad flavors of life, the common things relied upon day after day, create an unseen cocoon of comforting familiarity. But, should this snug refuge be rent asunder, the soul within unceremoniously set adrift, pity that soul, and any who chance to meet it.

Specters differ from ghosts in that the latter are true spirits of the dead, imprints of once-living souls and reflective, at least in part, of those individuals. A specter, by contrast, is formed when a being's soul is ripped from them while they still live. Without a natural death, there is no chance for the soul to pass on as it should, leaving only a hateful and malignant creature. Stripped of all personhood and character, desperately hungry for the life it can never return to, specters are murderously envious of any who still cling to it. The sun itself, a symbol and giver of life, is hateful to a specter, enraging even as it weakens them.

Specters are formed of unstable soul essence, and that instability is reflected in their appearance. A specter is of roughly humanoid shape, made up of crackling, dancing energy, like a rioting thundercloud given form. The strands of energy which flare away from it react negatively with any living soul they come across, attempting to latch on and draw back any fragments they can seize upon, draining life from the victim in a vain attempt to possess it for themselves.

Were they not so dangerous, specters would be pitiable creatures. Almost universally, specters became so unwittingly and unwillingly. No redemption, rest, or hope for salvation awaits them, and no ambition or hope drives them. All a specter can do is bring down as many living creatures as it can before it is snuffed from existence.

The most dire mistake one can make when encountering a specter is to assume that, like a ghost, it can be put to rest should its business be completed, for it has no business but to extinguish life, and no rest but oblivion.

ORIGIN

Specters are created when powerful dark magic, or an evil entity, separates an unwilling living soul from their body. This act disrupts the natural order, warping the soul into an unstable and crude approximation of an undead spirit. Wraiths commonly create specters to serve them and demoralize their living enemies. Specters might also be created as byproducts of particularly foul rituals, such as one to summon an extraplanar entity into a living, but empty, 'vessel'.

ENVIRONMENT

Specters are attracted to strong emotions, both positive and negative, though they swarm towards misery like flies to dead flesh. They gather together in areas suffused with these feelings, such as graveyards and old battlefields. Drinking in these emotions is only a reminder that such things are denied to them, and so increases their hatred.

The superstition goes that catching even a glimpse of a specter is an omen of one's imminent (and probably miserable) death. This is not true in and of itself, but can often prove a self-fulfilling prophecy; the presence of a specter is likely to warp emotions towards negativity, and begin a downward spiral into despair and apathy, which can prove deadly in its own right, to say nothing of the deadly attentions of the specter itself.

ROLEPLAYING SPECTERS

Specters are sentient and free-willed, but focused enough to be somewhat predictable in their behavior. Above all, they crave what is forever barred to them – life; specters will kill the living for no reason other than to jealously deprive others of what they cannot have. While they are devoid of their original personalities, specters as a whole tend to fall into two camps, dependent on how they choose to hunt their victims. Some thrive on the quantity of death they can accomplish, traveling far and wide and killing at will to rid as many beings of life as possible. Others seem to prefer the 'quality' of suffering they can inflict on the world, stalking an individual, or a small group, and taking their time to ensure their target spirals as far into despair as they can, before granting them the mercy of death.

COMBAT TACTICS

Most specters prefer to engage in hit-and-run tactics, wearing down their foe over a series of attacks before utilizing their incorporeal nature to retreat to safety. In combat, a specter will remain mobile as much as possible, flitting from point to point and trusting that its very presence is as damaging to its victims' souls as a direct attack.

Many specters, particularly those who prefer quality over quantity in the misery and death they bring about, will flee a fight if the odds turn against them. It is, however, common to see them fight until their own destruction, attacking mercilessly and fearlessly. Given the torment of their very existence, it is easy to interpret this not only as ferocity, but also a longing to end their own misery.

SPECTER ENCOUNTERS

d6	CR	Encounter
1	4	**Wayward Souls:** 6 Traversing Specters
2	7	**Spectral Infestation:** 2 Deadly Specters, 4 Traversing Specters
3	11	**Deathly Omen:** 1 Spectral Raven, 2 Deadly Specters, 5 Traversing Specters
4	15	**Foreboding Triad:** 1 Spectral Horror, 1 Spectral Raven, 1 Deadly Specter
5	19	**Doom's Entourage:** 1 Spectral Horror, 2 Spectral Ravens, 4 Deadly Specters
6	21	**Life-Eater's Hoard:** 1 Spectral Dragon, 1 Spectral Horror, 8 Deadly Specters

"So when I come to, there's some hooded fella standing over me, and he's chanting. I'm not one for languages, but it sounds like nothing good. I try to look around me, 'cause I'm tied to this slab you know, and I see the bodies of the last poor sods who was in here, all shriveled and that, like old leather. My new friend notices and he says, "the others did not survive the extraction, but you are of hardier stock. You shall make a fine vessel."

Now, I don't like the sound of that one bit, and then I sees over his shoulder in the middle of the room is this statue. Nasty great leering thing it is. And as I look at it, its eyes begin to glow, and I feel this... tug inside me, like someone's trying to yank something out of me. My mind goes all fuzzy, like I'm losing who I am, like all I am is that feeling. You'll think I'm daft, but I swear I saw myself, from above as it were; my own body on the slab, and I HATED it. I hated that body like I've never hated anything in my life. Well, then I hear a crash as the door gets kicked in, and that jerks me back to earth. Let me tell you, I've never been so pleased to see a guardsman in all my life!"

-Hallard, Jackdaws gang member

TRAVERSING SPECTER

Medium undead, chaotic evil

Armor Class 12
Hit Points 18 (4d8)
Speed 0 ft., fly 40 ft. (hover)

STR	DEX	CON	INT	WIS	CHA
1 (-5)	15 (+2)	10 (+0)	10 (+0)	10 (+0)	14 (+2)

Damage Vulnerabilities radiant
Damage Resistances acid, cold, fire, lightning, thunder; bludgeoning, piercing, and slashing damage from nonmagical attacks
Damage Immunities necrotic, poison
Condition Immunities charmed, exhaustion, grappled, paralyzed, petrified, poisoned, prone, restrained, unconscious
Senses darkvision 60 ft., passive perception 10
Languages the languages it knew in life
Challenge 1 (200 XP)

Draining Form (1/Turn). If the specter moves through another creature's space on its turn, it can force that creature to make a DC 12 Constitution saving throw. On a failed save, the creature takes 10 (3d6) necrotic damage, and its hit point maximum is reduced by an amount equal to the damage. On a successful save, the creature takes half as much damage, and its hit point maximum isn't reduced. This reduction lasts until the creature finishes a long rest. The target dies if this effect reduces its hit point maximum to 0. The specter can't use its Draining Form and Life Drain against the same target on the same turn.

Incorporeal Movement. The specter can move through other creatures and objects as if they were difficult terrain. It takes 5 (1d10) force damage if it ends its turn inside an object.

Sunlight Sensitivity. While in sunlight, the specter has disadvantage on attack rolls, as well as Wisdom (Perception) checks that rely on sight.

ACTIONS

Life Drain. *Melee Weapon Attack:* +4 to hit, reach 5 ft., one creature. *Hit:* 7 (2d6) necrotic damage, and the target must succeed on a DC 12 Constitution saving throw, or its hit point maximum is reduced by an amount equal to the damage taken. This reduction lasts until the creature finishes a long rest. The target dies if this effect reduces its hit point maximum to 0.

DEADLY SPECTER

Medium undead, chaotic evil

Armor Class 13
Hit Points 55 (10d8 + 10)
Speed 0 ft., fly 40 ft. (hover)

STR	DEX	CON	INT	WIS	CHA
1 (-5)	16 (+3)	12 (+1)	10 (+0)	10 (+0)	16 (+3)

Damage Vulnerabilities radiant
Damage Resistances acid, cold, fire, lightning, thunder; bludgeoning, piercing, and slashing damage from nonmagical attacks
Damage Immunities necrotic, poison
Condition Immunities charmed, exhaustion, grappled, paralyzed, petrified, poisoned, prone, restrained, unconscious
Senses darkvision 60 ft., passive perception 10
Languages the languages it knew in life
Challenge 4 (1,100 XP)

Draining Form (2/Turn). If the specter moves through another creature's space on its turn, it can force that creature to make a DC 13 Constitution saving throw. On a failed save, the creature takes 14 (4d6) necrotic damage, and its hit point maximum is reduced by an amount equal to the damage. On a successful save, the creature takes half as much damage, and its hit point maximum isn't reduced. This reduction lasts until the creature finishes a long rest. The target dies if this effect reduces its hit point maximum to 0. The specter can't use its Draining Form and Life Drain against the same target on the same turn, and can't use its Draining Form on the same creature more than once per turn.

Incorporeal Movement. The specter can move through other creatures and objects as if they were difficult terrain. It takes 5 (1d10) force damage if it ends its turn inside an object.

Sunlight Sensitivity. While in sunlight, the specter has disadvantage on attack rolls, as well as Wisdom (Perception) checks that rely on sight.

ACTIONS

Life Drain. *Melee Weapon Attack:* +5 to hit, reach 5 ft., one creature. *Hit:* 10 (3d6) necrotic damage, and the target must succeed on a DC 13 Constitution saving throw, or its hit point maximum is reduced by an amount equal to the damage taken. This reduction lasts until the creature finishes a long rest. The target dies if this effect reduces its hit point maximum to 0.

SPECTRAL HORROR

Medium undead, chaotic evil

Armor Class 13
Hit Points 132 (24d8 + 24)
Speed 0 ft., fly 40 ft. (hover)

STR	DEX	CON	INT	WIS	CHA
1 (-5)	16 (+3)	12 (+1)	10 (+0)	10 (+0)	13 (+4)

Skills Perception +4
Damage Vulnerabilities radiant
Damage Resistances acid, cold, fire, lightning, thunder; bludgeoning, piercing, and slashing damage from nonmagical attacks
Damage Immunities necrotic, poison
Condition Immunities charmed, exhaustion, grappled, paralyzed, petrified, poisoned, prone, restrained, unconscious
Senses darkvision 60 ft., passive perception 14
Languages the languages it knew in life
Challenge 12 (8,400 XP)

Draining Form (3/Turn). If the horror moves through another creature's space on its turn, it can force that creature to make a DC 16 Constitution saving throw. On a failed save, the creature takes 21 (6d6) necrotic damage, and its hit point maximum is reduced by an amount equal to the damage. On a successful save, the creature takes half as much damage, and its hit point maximum isn't reduced. This reduction lasts until the creature finishes a long rest. The target dies if this effect reduces its hit point maximum to 0. The horror can't use its Draining Form and Life Drain against the same target on the same turn, and can't use its Draining Form on the same creature more than once per turn.

Incorporeal Movement. The horror can move through other creatures and objects as if they were difficult terrain. It takes 5 (1d10) force damage if it ends its turn inside an object.

Legendary Resistance (1/Day). When the horror fails a saving throw, it can choose to succeed instead.

Sunlight Sensitivity. While in sunlight, the horror has disadvantage on attack rolls, as well as Wisdom (Perception) checks that rely on sight.

ACTIONS

Life Drain. *Melee Weapon Attack:* +7 to hit, reach 5 ft., one creature. *Hit:* 14 (4d6) necrotic damage, and the target must succeed on a DC 16 Constitution saving throw, or its hit point maximum is reduced by an amount equal to the damage taken. This reduction lasts until the creature finishes a long rest. The target dies if this effect reduces its hit point maximum to 0.

LEGENDARY ACTIONS

The horror can take 3 legendary actions, choosing from the options below. Only one legendary action option can be used at a time, and only at the end of another creature's turn. The horror regains spent legendary actions at the start of its turn.

Detect. The horror makes a Wisdom (Perception) check.

Life Drain. The horror uses its Life Drain.

Spectral Pervasion (Costs 2 Actions). The specter horror moves up to its fly speed without provoking opportunity attacks from any creatures whose space it passes through. During this movement, it can target one creature with its Draining Form.

SPECTRAL RAVEN

Small undead, chaotic evil

Armor Class 14
Hit Points 98 (28d6)
Speed 0 ft., fly 60 ft. (hover)

STR	DEX	CON	INT	WIS	CHA
5 (-3)	19 (+4)	10 (+0)	6 (-2)	15 (+2)	16 (+3)

Damage Vulnerabilities radiant
Damage Resistances acid, cold, fire, lightning, thunder; bludgeoning, piercing, and slashing damage from nonmagical attacks
Damage Immunities necrotic, poison
Condition Immunities charmed, exhaustion, grappled, paralyzed, petrified, poisoned, prone, restrained, unconscious
Senses darkvision 60 ft., passive perception 12
Languages understands all languages, but can't speak
Challenge 9 (5,000 XP)

Draining Form (4/Turn). If the spectral raven moves through another creature's space on its turn, it can force that creature to make a DC 15 Constitution saving throw. On a failed save, the creature takes 14 (4d6) necrotic damage, and its hit point maximum is reduced by an amount equal to the damage. On a successful save, the creature takes half as much damage, and its hit point maximum isn't reduced. This reduction lasts until the creature finishes a long rest. The target dies if this effect reduces its hit point maximum to 0. The spectral raven can't use its Draining Form and Life Drain against the same target on the same turn, and can't use its Draining Form on the same creature more than once per turn.

Incorporeal Movement. The spectral raven can move through other creatures and objects as if they were difficult terrain. It takes 5 (1d10) force damage if it ends its turn inside an object.

Looming Presence. If the spectral raven doesn't move or take any actions on its turn, creatures other than undead, within 60 feet of the raven who are aware of it, must succeed on a DC 15 Charisma saving throw against this magic, or be charmed by the raven for 1 minute. While charmed in this manner, a creature is stunned, falls prone, and can't stand. At the end of each of its turns, a creature can repeat the saving throw, ending the effect on itself on a success.

Sunlight Sensitivity. While in sunlight, the spectral raven has disadvantage on attack rolls, as well as Wisdom (Perception) checks that rely on sight.

ACTIONS

Life Drain. *Melee Weapon Attack:* +8 to hit, reach 5 ft., one creature. *Hit:* 7 (2d6) necrotic damage, and the target must succeed on a DC 15 Constitution saving throw, or its hit point maximum is reduced by an amount equal to the damage taken. This reduction lasts until the creature finishes a long rest. The target dies if this effect reduces its hit point maximum to 0.

Death's Echo (Recharge 4-6). The spectral raven emits a soul-chilling cry, inducing unnatural despair. Creatures, other than undead, within 60 feet of the raven that can hear it, must succeed on a DC 15 Charisma saving throw against this magic, or be frightened for 1 minute. At the end of each of its turns, a creature can repeat the saving throw, ending the effect on itself on a success.

The **spectral raven** is an enigma, as it is seemingly not the soul of a once-mortal creature. Its cry induces supernatural terror but, perhaps worse, the very presence of the raven is enough to drive living creatures to paroxysms of grief and apathy from which they may never recover. Scholars speculate that the phenomenon is formed of stray astral essence corrupted by the same magical disturbances which form more common specters, or else a collective of rent souls somewhat akin to a wraith. Whatever the case, the raven is silent on the matter.

> "It is only in this final piece, we perhaps begin to understand the artist's mind. At this point, towards the end of her life, Lenyra began to confide in the few friends she had of the disturbing dreams which had haunted her for months. When asked for clarification, she would say no more than, "The Raven, The Raven."
>
> Popular myth states that, with the final brushstroke committing her tormentor to canvas, Lenyra died on the spot, and was found with an expression of contentment and peace unknown to her in life. Romantic as the idea may be, reports from the time instead note 'a face of exquisite terror'. An unhappy end, it would seem, to a short, unhappy life."
>
> –Zhanhara Tilvayne, art curator, on Xhan Lenyra's 'Raven'

SPECTRAL DRAGON
Huge undead, chaotic evil

Armor Class 15
Hit Points 212 (25d12 + 50)
Speed 0 ft., fly 60 ft. (hover)

STR	DEX	CON	INT	WIS	CHA
10 (+0)	20 (+5)	14 (+2)	16 (+3)	14 (+2)	22 (+6)

Skills Perception +7
Damage Vulnerabilities radiant
Damage Resistances acid, cold, fire, lightning, thunder; bludgeoning, piercing, and slashing damage from nonmagical attacks
Damage Immunities necrotic, poison
Condition Immunities charmed, exhaustion, grappled, paralyzed, petrified, poisoned, prone, restrained, unconscious
Senses darkvision 120 ft., blindsight 60 ft., passive perception 17
Languages Common, Draconic
Challenge 16 (15,000 XP)

Draining Form (3/Turn). If the spectral dragon moves through another creature's space on its turn, it can force that creature to make a DC 19 Constitution saving throw. On a failure, the creature takes 28 (8d6) necrotic damage, and its hit point maximum is reduced by an amount equal to the damage. On a successful save, the creature takes half as much damage, and its hit point maximum isn't reduced. This reduction lasts until the creature finishes a long rest. The target dies if this effect reduces its hit point maximum to 0. The spectral dragon can't use its Draining Form and Life Drain against the same target on the same turn, and can't use its Draining Form on the same creature more than once per turn.

Incorporeal Movement. The spectral dragon can move through other creatures and objects as if they were difficult terrain. It takes 5 (1d10) force damage if it ends its turn inside an object.

Legendary Resistance (3/Day). When the spectral dragon fails a saving throw, it can choose to succeed instead.

Sunlight Sensitivity. While in sunlight, the spectral dragon has disadvantage on attack rolls, as well as Wisdom (Perception) checks that rely on sight.

ACTIONS

Multiattack. The spectral dragon makes one attack with its Life Drain, and two attacks with its Blood-Chilling Claws.

Life Drain. *Melee Weapon Attack:* +10 to hit, reach 10 ft., one creature. *Hit:* 21 (6d6) necrotic damage, and the target must succeed on a DC 19 Constitution saving throw, or its hit point maximum is reduced by an amount equal to the damage taken. This reduction lasts until the creature finishes a long rest. The target dies if this effect reduces its hit point maximum to 0.

Blood-Chilling Claws. *Melee Weapon Attack:* +10 to hit, reach 5 ft., one creature. *Hit:* 14 (4d6) cold damage.

Spectral Whip. *Melee Weapon Attack:* +10 to hit, reach 15 ft., one creature. *Hit:* 17 (5d6) psychic damage.

Life-Stealing Breath (Recharge 5-6). The spectral dragon inhales the life force of creatures in a 60-foot cone. Creatures in the area must make a DC 19 Constitution saving throw, taking 42 (12d6) necrotic damage and having their hit point maximum reduced by an amount equal to the damage taken, on a failed save. On a successful save, they take half as much damage, and their hit point maximum isn't reduced. This reduction to a creature's hit point maximum lasts until the creature finishes a long rest.

LEGENDARY ACTIONS

The spectral dragon can take 3 legendary actions, choosing from the options below. Only one legendary action option can be used at a time, and only at the end of another creature's turn. The spectral dragon regains spent legendary actions at the start of its turn.

Detect. The spectral dragon makes a Wisdom (Perception) check.

Spectral Whip. The spectral dragon uses its Spectral Whip.

Spectral Impact (Costs 2 Actions). The spectral dragon moves up to half its fly speed. If it ends this movement on the floor, or solid ground, it explodes in a psychic wave before reconstituting. Creatures within 10 feet of the exploding spectral dragon must succeed on a DC 19 Charisma saving throw, or take 14 (4d6) psychic damage and be knocked prone.

The sundered soul of a **dragon** is a horribly powerful force of chaos and woe, raised and set loose only by the most powerful undead, or the most insane necromancers. Spectral dragons are able to focus the lingering psychological effects common to all specters into a blasting wave of despair and torment.

Thaddeus was sullen; not simply his usual taciturn self, but moody. He had been out of sorts since our second encounter with The Maid of Sorrows. I was unsure if he was unsatisfied with his indirect involvement with her death, or simply missed the focus of a known central figure of hatred. Having a nemesis, it seemed, had its mental advantages for, without this focus, Thaddeus' mood deteriorated into (dare I say?) petulant impatience, and it was affecting our work.

We had offered to help with the recovery efforts having been, at least in part, responsible for the collapse of the crypt in the first place. The chamber in question had been the resting place of many of the poorer residents of the city and, with so many jumbled and broken bones amongst the rubble, identifying any individuals was an impossibility. Therefore, it was decided that all the remains would be hauled to the surface to be reconsecrated and reinterred as a collective. The locals of cheapside had decided that, now the bones had been touched by necromancy, a series of pyres would be prudent, with the cleansed ashes to be scattered outside the city walls. The decision may have come from a place of superstition and fear, but was sensible enough for even the local dwarven contingent to not argue for traditional burial.

The mood was sombre, but restrained. After all, the deceased had been deceased for some while; the time for mourning come and gone, sometimes generations before the living residents were even born. As the days wore on, however, the mood began to change. I brought it up to Thaddeus, but he quickly dismissed it.

"People get sad at funerals," he snapped. I did not press the issue, but suspected there was more to it. The residents were not simply sad at the deaths (or even reanimation) of their loved ones, but were becoming morose and introspective, dragging their feet more and more as they slumped towards each cremation service. The crowds began to thin, and I suspected that many had been unable to find the energy to leave their homes.

As the days wore on, the mystery of this strange mood began to matter less to me. In fact, I found it very difficult to care about anything very much, as if the apathy of the townsfolk was an infection. Particularly at night, as I lay sleepless in the back room of the nearest inn (the inkeep had enthusiastically refused payment in thanks for our 'service to the town' when we first arrived, though he could now barely muster a nod of greeting), my thoughts turned towards darkness. A bed had been put aside for Thaddeus in the same room, but he had yet to use it and, apparently, spent his nights wandering. It was at these times that fear began to take me. At first, I feared that Thaddeus would simply not return, but as the nights wore on, I found I cared less and less. In fact, I cared little about anything.

As much as mere weeks beforehand, I would have killed (or at least grievously wounded) for a proper bed, regular hot meals, and daily access to a bathtub, I quickly found myself numb to these comforts. My hair grew greasy; keeping up appearances seemed such an unimportant vanity. I found it difficult to grow enthused with any options at mealtimes, and simply ate whatever was put in front of me. It all tasted the same. I assumed that my pale forays into the adventuring life had taken their toll on me. I decided that I should give up on these ridiculous aspirations and that, at the next opportunity, I should tell Thaddeus I was going to make my way back home. That is, the next time I could muster the energy and wherewithal to leave bed. It seemed simpler to just lie in darkness.

"It's a specter!" a voice that belonged to Thaddeus announced, bursting into my room at an ungodly hour. Such was the stygian darkness that I didn't see the point of turning my head.

"Hmm?" I managed.

"A specter. Maybe a couple. Souls wrenched from their bodies while they were still alive. Makes them unstable, and they latch onto living souls, and feed on emotions. That's why everyone is so bloody gloomy around here." I could almost hear his inappropriate grin.

"They have just re-buried all their loved ones, Thaddeus. I think they might be permitted a few days of mourning. Leave them alone." I pulled the blanket over my head in a clear indication that the conversation was over, and that we should both be asleep. The blanket was, almost immediately, torn from my grasp and thrown to the other side of the modest room. The night was cold. As were my feet.

"It's a specter. I saw it. We can beat it, and you can write about it. No sense just lying here feeling sorry for yourself." I thought this was a little rich, considering his recent funk, but his argument (and, more immediately, his hand pulling me upright) was persuasive.

Thaddeus seemed positively manic at the prospect of confronting a phantasmal horror and, I admit, I felt myself buoyed by his enthusiasm, albeit gradually.

We crept through the darkened streets, and I began to feel that sense of hopelessness once more. After Thaddeus' revelation, however, it felt an artificial thing, clearly an outside force attempting to act on me. The trick having been revealed, I did not fall for it again. We halted at a corner and peered around it onto some sort of dumping ground. There, I caught my first sight of the specters.

They were gathered as though attending some fiendish ceremony, a trio of figures rising from a swirling morass of dark cloud. Purple light crackled and sparked within and around them. I found it difficult to look at them; something within me revolted at their presence far more than at the simple horror of a walking corpse. They were wrong things.

Before the specters was a corporeal figure, a ragged cloak thrown over their dark armor.

"You have done admirable work here, among the mortals," it said in a cold, thin voice.

A wight. Thaddeus was practically vibrating with glee.

"We play. We feed. We want not for a master." They spoke one after the other, their voices a hissing chorus.

"The Shrouded One does not seek your subordination, but your friendship. Feed as you will and, once your prey is drained and hollow and of no more amusement to you, give us the husks. In turn, we can direct you towards places steeped in suffering, and rife with despair."

The specters seemed to find this prospect intriguing; the crackling light within them burst with more frequency. They were not, it would seem, the type to keep their cards close to their chests.

"Not yet. There is life here still to siphon. It takes time to leech a soul."

"The Shrouded One is patient. You can have your fun."

"Once the fight is gone from them. Once all memory of joy is lost to them. Once hope is cleansed from them. Then we shall move on. Then we shall feed anew. Then we may go to your master."

Before they could deliberate further, Thaddeus, perhaps a little over-excited to have something he could hit, charged out like a madman, sword flashing in the moonlight. He descended on the wight in a fury; a flurry of savage blows it struggled to withstand, let alone counter.

"Help me!" it wheezed, shrinking before the onslaught.

"It is not ready," the specters cried in return. "There is no sport here. It reeks of hope."

"Curse you and be damned, shades!"

"You know nothing of damnation," the retreating voices howled on the night breeze, drowning out the wight's death rattle.

Come morning, the fugue seemed to have lifted. The locals were glum, but resumed business as normal, albeit at a slower pace. A night's relief from the specters' predation was, apparently, just what was needed for the healing to begin. As the final pyre was lit, it seemed to take the recent worries of the community with it, to dissipate, as smoke in the breeze. Perhaps they thought it part of the natural process of mourning; with the specters put to flight, we were certainly not going to be the ones to tell them otherwise.

We left quietly as the embers began to die. Thaddeus, invigorated with new purpose, was keen to seek out another contract.

Vampires

A cloud of bats flits in front of the thin slash of a moon. The squeaking mass of fur and leathern wings swirls together, tighter and tighter, manifesting into a lean, poised form. From the edge of the rooftop, it peers into the gloom of the street. Hunger flashes in its eyes and, for an instant, its perfect oil portrait of a face is twisted into a terrible, ravening thing before returning to civility with a twitch. A lone figure picks its way through the darkness below, glancing behind like a hunted beast. The creature grins, fangs glinting in the moonlight, and leaps.

For as long as there have been beings with blood in their veins, there have been vampires to drink it.

In common parlance, one can be transformed into a vampire; this is incorrect, though the difference is subtle. A person is killed by a vampire, and their vampiric essence enters the now dead body. While the dead person's memories and remnants of personality may be accessible, a vampire is not the person transformed - a vampire is a vampire, wearing their corpse. These vestiges left in the body become twisted by the vampire; the vampiric character tends towards obsession and possessiveness, so a lingering, unrequited love might become a predatory fixation (which, due to the vampire's enhanced lifespan, may transfer over generations of a family, or simply to physically similar victims).

Most vampires, especially older individuals who have lived out all of their violent fantasies in their youth, find some channel for their intensity of feeling. Some turn to arcane study, politics, or the arts, while others prefer a life of criminal empire-building, or remain content to simply hone their skills as a killer. Whatever it sets its mind to, a vampire has, potentially, millennia to practice, and can exceed any mortal master. As with personality remnants, their activities can quickly turn into all-consuming obsessions.

Most vampires take a different stance on immortality than liches; instead of distancing themselves from the living and seeing them as an annoyance, or an obstacle, vampires entwine their lives with that of their prey. While this is, in part at least, due to their need to regularly feed on living blood, there does also seem to be some need for social control and power in the vampire's psyche. A vampire might lurk behind the scenes of generations of local rulers, subtly nudging them towards their own ends.

It is true that vampires are forced to adhere to a great many odd and restrictive behaviors, and it is generally accepted that these are due to the abhorrence felt for them by the gods – as beings neither living nor dead, no god lays claim to the vampire and, though some worship a nameless, blood-drenched deity, most vampires claim to be above such concerns, entities unto themselves. Gods of the river burn them as they attempt to cross, gods of hearth and home forbid them access (save for those invited in under the ageless laws of hospitality) and, with the most vehement hatred of them all, the sun scorches them where it catches them in its gaze.

The same cannot be said of the folklore surrounding vampires. Perhaps more than any other accursed creature, they are the subject of innumerable superstitions amongst the unlearned. A stake of sharpened wood through the chest will incapacitate a vampire, it is true (as, it must be said, it would incapacitate most creatures), but the practice of planting a yew tree above an evil-doer's grave will do little to dissuade the dead from rising in any form (though, given the swiftness of a vampire's revival, a slow-growing tree seems singularly unsuited to that task). That a vampire can be distracted by casting grains of rice or salt on the ground can also be disregarded: some scholars theorize an individual vampire obsessed with the study of mathematics may indeed have stopped to count some accidentally-spilled grains at some point in the distant past or, perhaps, that some ignorant observer mistook some vampire-hunter's ritual circle as cast salt.

Origin

While vampirism is a virulent curse, true vampires remain rare. The predatory cunning of a vampire precludes it from spreading its 'gift' in an uncontrolled fashion, lest it draw attention to itself; far better to meticulously plan, enthralling only those necessary to get within striking distance of their target. Whether this progeny becomes a lesser vampire in their service, or is allowed to drink their sire's blood and become a fully-fledged independent, depends on the vampire in question. Many vampires prefer the unquestioned authority that comes of thralls and spawn, though some easily grow bored of being unchallenged and, trusting to their powers of persuasion or combat prowess, allow free-willed allies to flourish. These partnerships, though thankfully unusual, can be truly fearsome if they continue unchecked. One powerful vampire can, over time, bend an entire region to its thrall: two vampires, with decades or centuries of experience working in concert, does not bear thinking about.

While vampires can eat and drink, they do not need to, and common food is dull and flavorless to them. Those that do choose to partake typically only consume the richest and most indulgent meals, both to sample the greatest flavor (and therefore approach a level of taste they can appreciate), and to complement their taste for an indulgent lifestyle. Some take a perverse pleasure in taking food from the mouths of others, and eat to excess purely out of spite, knowing that someone, somewhere is eating less as a result.

The only sustenance required for a vampire to survive is blood. The blood of any living creature will serve, though each vampire has their own tastes, with those few vampires open to commenting likening it to one's taste in wine. Preference for particular races is common, though some vampire's tastes are more esoteric; refusing to drink anything but the blood of aged, magically-inclined elves for instance. The blood of animals is considered too crude for any but pariahs to consider drinking in anything less than the direst of emergencies, though it is commonly used by good vampires, as rare as they may be.

Without regular feeding, the vampire's physical form will devolve to reflect its nature, becoming more twisted and bestial over time, as its shapeshifting powers wane and its human and animal forms begin to bleed into one another. A hungry vampire tends to be the most dangerous; being unable to blend in amongst its prey, it has little to lose from killing at will, and everything to gain. A vampire's form will also alter with extreme age, with truly ancient vampires appearing truly monstrous (rather than the bestial melding of a hungry vampire). The disease's potency increases with age, as demonstrated by elder vampires' resilience and power, and it may be that this increased potency brings with it further physical mutations, which in turn require more effort from the vampire in question, should it wish to mask them. Many ancient vampires, it seems, are simply unwilling to make the effort, unless absolutely necessary.

Environment

The nature of a vampire's lair will depend entirely upon its relationship with society as a whole. Those that live secretly amongst their prey might settle for a relatively modest lifestyle, curbing their darker impulses for the ease with which they can access blood. The dwelling of such a vampire might be indistinguishable from that of a living being (save that there may be traces of the obsessive personality which comes part and parcel of their curse) or, more commonly, may hide a place of sanctuary in which the creature might indulge in its true nature. A hidden cellar might house a coffin (or, at least, a source of grave dirt for the vampire's rest) or restraints to keep a living food source close by.

Exposed vampires, or those without the wit or desire to attempt to blend in, may have no choice but to embrace their role as monsters in the night. Such individuals are unlikely to retreat to the wilderness, like many similar creatures, and may instead be forced into a parasitic existence in the backstreets, sewers, and slums. Vampires of this kind are the most likely to band together and to create full-fledged vampires to swell their ranks, as their scavenger lifestyle benefits from strength of numbers.

At the other end of the scale are those rare vampires who live openly in a position of power (which they will, almost universally, abuse): with a network of enthralled underlings to support them, they are free to shape their environment exactly to their liking. These demagogues will take residence in the grandest abode available, and may demand the construction of even more opulent or defensive dwellings. Depending on the vampire's personality, it may wish enthralled mortals to offer themselves as willing food sources, or might prefer to keep a stock of 'cattle'; imprisoned, enslaved, or enthralled people who exist only as a source of blood for the vampire or, in the best-case scenario, as favored pets. A secure vampire can afford to produce many underlings to help keep their position (though many, the more paranoid or power-hungry, do not), and an entire class of undead nobility can spring up, with commoners offering up their children as tribute for the hope of giving them a better 'life', or vampires selecting from their paramours.

Roleplaying Vampires

Vampires, when taken as a whole, are as many and varied as any group of peoples and, thus, each individual vampire will be an individual unto itself. However, there are three common elements that pervade the vampiric character.

Vampires are very powerful, and most of them are aware of this fact. Given this knowledge, a vampire is likely to be confident, or at least skeptical, of opposition, be it physical or mental. A young vampire may be full of vigor, so excited by the massive degree of ability it now possesses, and run the risk of becoming rash and unthoughtful.

A vampire's extremely protracted life (barring any run-ins with external influences precipitating the ending of their un-life) gives them, above almost anything, perspective. Wisdom comes from experience. Patience comes from practice in waiting. Boredom comes from the feeling of having seen or done everything worth seeing or doing. With this comes the common vampiric trait of obsession, and mastery of a particular subject or skill.

As mentioned, vampires are drawn to people, often the more the better. This means places such as towns and cities can be havens for them, especially if they are able to restrain themselves to allow for coexistence. Within these settings, vampires gravitate toward culture of many kinds. Sometimes appreciating, sometimes participating, but always seeing the value in the finer things. This does not always mean material possessions, or the typical indulgences or vices. It can also mean simply valuing, even in someone they may otherwise detest, the rarity and value of a truly stimulating conversation. As a vampire ages, their tastes are honed and refined; not only in matters of food, but in all aspects of life.

Lastly, after all else, at its most base, a vampire is ferocious. When all pretense is flung aside, niceties discarded, and any semblance of sophistication and poise is done away with, a vampire stands as a manifestation of bestial thirst and fury; an apex predator fully aware of its status, and with little to no regard for any beings that might be so foolish as to deny their will. Any who do so will be swept aside or, more likely, devoured.

Combat Tactics

Whether a vampire will participate in combat is purely dependent on their mood and perspective. If they don't take the opponent seriously, or have something better to do, they will often leave handling of those threats to underlings. If, however, the vampire *does* feel a need (or desire) to participate, they will hold nothing back.

A vampire in its full fury is a thing to behold. It will fight tooth and claw, employing flight or shapeshifting when advantageous. They will engage in melee combat and displays of magical power with equal prowess. A vampire is a natural ambusher, typically biding their time until the opportune moment, and then springing into horrific, unrelenting violence. Targets are chosen first based upon eliminating the potential for opponents to recover and, second, based on who seems like the easiest prey, then moving up the food chain.

In a familiar environment, and at the height of its power, it is not uncommon for vampires to play with their victims, as a cat with a mouse, allowing them a false sense of security before unleashing their full fury. Some enjoy this simply for the feeling of superiority, while others claim the increased level of fear adds a unique flavor to the blood.

Vampire Encounters

d8	CR	Encounter
1	12	**Low-blooded Gang:** 4 Vampire Fledglings
2	14	**Kinslayer Party:** 3 Dampyrs
3	18	**Bloodthrall Band:** 1 Dampyr, 4 Vampire Fledglings, 4 Vampire Spawn
4	19	**Shadow Flight:** 4 Vampire Nightstalkers
5	22	**Bloodseeker Pack:** 6 Vampire Packrunners
6	23	**Night Hunt:** 1 Vampire Noble, 2 Vampire Nightstalkers, 4 Vampire Packrunners
7	24	**Dark Wedding:** 2 Vampire Nobles, 3 Vampire Nightstalkers, 4 Vampire Fledglings, 6 Vampire Spawn
8	25	**Bloodtithe Ceremony:** 1 Vampire Ancient, 1 Vampire Noble, 2 Vampire Packrunners, 1 Vampire Nightstalker, 4 Vampire Fledglings, 6 Vampire Spawn

Vampire Fledgling
Medium undead (shapechanger), neutral evil

Armor Class 15 (natural armor)
Hit Points 91 (14d8 + 28)
Speed 30 ft.

STR	DEX	CON	INT	WIS	CHA
17 (+3)	16 (+3)	15 (+2)	14 (+2)	13 (+1)	15 (+2)

Saving Throws Dex +6, Wis +4
Skills Perception +4, Stealth +6
Damage Resistances necrotic; bludgeoning, piercing, and slashing from nonmagical attacks
Senses darkvision 120 ft., passive perception 14
Languages the languages it knew in life
Challenge 6 (2,300 XP)

Shapechanger. If the fledgling isn't in sunlight or running water, it can use its action to polymorph into a Medium cloud of mist. While in mist form, the fledgling can't take any actions, speak, or manipulate objects. It is weightless, has a flying speed of 20 feet, can hover, and can enter other creature's spaces and stop there. In addition, it can pass through any space that air can pass through, without squeezing, but cannot pass through water. It is immune to all nonmagical damage, other than radiant damage from sunlight.

Misty Escape. When the fledgling drops to 0 hit points while outside its resting place, it transforms into mist form instead of falling unconscious, provided that it isn't in sunlight or running water. If it can't transform, it is destroyed.

While it has 0 hit points in mist form, it can't revert to vampire form, and it must reach its resting place within 1 hour, or be destroyed. Once in its resting place, it reverts to its vampire form. It is then paralyzed until it regains at least 1 hit point. After spending 1 hour in its resting place with 0 hit points, it regains 1 hit point.

Regeneration. The fledgling regains 10 hit points at the start of its turn if it has at least 1 hit point, isn't in sunlight or running water, or a piercing weapon made of wood isn't embedded in its heart. If the fledgling takes radiant damage, or damage from holy water, this trait doesn't function at the start of the fledgling's next turn.

Spider Climb. The fledgling can climb difficult surfaces, including upside down on ceilings, without needing to make an ability check.

Vampire Weaknesses. The fledgling has the following flaws:

Forbiddance. The fledgling can't enter a residence without an invitation from one of the occupants.

Harmed by Running Water. The fledgling takes 20 acid damage when it ends its turn in running water.

Stake to the Heart. The fledgling is paralyzed if a piercing weapon made of wood is driven into its heart while it is incapacitated in its resting place. It remains paralyzed, and cannot regain hit points, until the stake is removed.

Sunlight Hypersensitivity. The fledgling takes 20 radiant damage when it starts its turn in sunlight. While in sunlight, it has disadvantage on attack rolls and ability checks.

Actions

Multiattack. The fledgling makes two melee attacks, one with its bite, and one with another weapon.

Unarmed Strike (Vampire Form Only). *Melee Weapon Attack:* +6 to hit, reach 5 ft., one target. *Hit:* 7 (1d8 + 3) bludgeoning damage. Instead of dealing damage, the fledgling can grapple the target (escape DC 13).

Bite (Vampire Form Only). *Melee Weapon Attack:* +6 to hit, reach 5 ft., one willing creature or a creature that is grappled by the fledgling or one of the fledgling's allies, incapacitated, or restrained. *Hit:* 6 (1d6 + 3) piercing damage, plus 7 (2d6) necrotic damage. The target's hit point maximum is reduced by a number equal to the necrotic damage taken, and the fledgling regains an equal number of hit points. This reduction lasts until the creature finishes a long rest. If the creature's hit point maximum is reduced to 0 by this effect, the creature dies. A humanoid slain this way, and then buried in the ground, rises the following night as a free-willed vampire spawn.

Fledglings are lesser vampires, near to the bottom of the social order, though still a formidable foe to those untrained in combating them.

DAMPYR
Medium undead (shapechanger), neutral

Armor Class 15 (natural armor)
Hit Points 105 (14d8 + 42)
Speed 30 ft.

STR	DEX	CON	INT	WIS	CHA
18 (+4)	17 (+3)	16 (+3)	15 (+2)	13 (+1)	16 (+3)

Saving Throws Dex +6, Con +6, Wis +4, Cha +6
Skills Perception +4, Stealth +6
Damage Resistances necrotic; bludgeoning, piercing, and slashing from nonmagical attacks
Senses darkvision 60 ft., passive perception 14
Languages the languages it knew in life
Challenge 8 (3,900 XP)

Shapechanger. If the dampyr isn't in sunlight or running water, it can use its action to polymorph into a Medium cloud of mist, or back into its true form. While in mist form, the dampyr can't take any actions, speak, or manipulate objects. It is weightless, has a flying speed of 20 feet, can hover, and can enter other creature's spaces and stop there. In addition, it can pass through any space that air can pass through, without squeezing, but cannot pass through water. It is immune to all nonmagical damage, other than radiant damage from sunlight.

Misty Escape. When the dampyr drops to 0 hit points while outside its resting place, it transforms into mist form instead of falling unconscious, provided that it isn't in sunlight or running water. If it can't transform, it is destroyed.

While it has 0 hit points in mist form, it can't revert to dampyr form, and it must reach its resting place within 1 hour, or be destroyed. Once in its resting place, it reverts to its dampyr form. It is then paralyzed until it regains at least 1 hit point. After spending 1 hour in its resting place with 0 hit points, it regains 1 hit point.

Regeneration. The dampyr regains 15 hit points at the start of its turn if it has at least 1 hit point, isn't in sunlight or running water, or a piercing weapon made of wood isn't embedded in its heart. If the dampyr takes radiant damage, or damage from holy water, this trait doesn't function at the start of the dampyr's next turn.

Dampyr Weaknesses. The dampyr has the following flaws:

Harmed by Running Water. The dampyr takes 20 acid damage when it ends its turn in running water.

Stake to the Heart. The dampyr is paralyzed if a piercing weapon made of wood is driven into its heart while it is incapacitated in its resting place. It remains paralyzed, and cannot regain hit points, until the stake is removed.

Spider Climb. The dampyr can climb difficult surfaces, including upside down on ceilings, without needing to make an ability check.

ACTIONS

Multiattack (Dampyr Form Only). The dampyr makes two melee attacks, only one of which can be a bite.

Unarmed Strike (Dampyr Form Only). *Melee Weapon Attack:* +7 to hit, reach 5 ft., one target. *Hit:* 8 (1d8 + 4) bludgeoning damage. Instead of dealing damage, the dampyr can grapple the target (escape DC 15).

Bite (Dampyr Form Only). *Melee Weapon Attack:* +7 to hit, reach 5 ft., one willing creature, or a creature that is grappled by the dampyr or one of the dampyr's allies, incapacitated, or restrained. *Hit:* 7 (1d6 + 4) piercing damage plus 10 (3d6) necrotic damage. The dampyr regains a number of hit points equal to the necrotic damage taken.

The origins of the **dampyr** remain something of a mystery. Possessing lessened versions of a vampire's strengths, along with fewer of their weaknesses (most markedly, they are unharmed by sunlight), they are clearly a fusion of mortal and undead, and it is theorized that they are born of women bitten while pregnant, though they are rare enough that proper studies have yet to take place. Without the inherent evil nature of a full vampire, dampyrs eke out an uneasy life on the fringes, mistrusted by the living and loathed by the dead. It is not uncommon for them to turn to a mercenary life, or even to make a living as itinerant monster hunters, seeking out and destroying their estranged kin.

VAMPIRE NIGHTSTALKER
Medium undead (shapechanger), neutral evil

Armor Class 17 (natural armor)
Hit Points 120 (16d8 + 48)
Speed 40 ft.

STR	DEX	CON	INT	WIS	CHA
18 (+4)	20 (+5)	16 (+3)	16 (+3)	18 (+4)	17 (+3)

Saving Throws Dex +9, Con +7, Cha +7
Skills Perception +8, Stealth +13
Damage Resistances necrotic; bludgeoning, piercing, and slashing from nonmagical attacks
Senses darkvision 120 ft. blindsight 60 ft., passive perception 14
Languages the languages it knew in life
Challenge 10 (5,900 XP)

Shapechanger. If the nightstalker isn't in sunlight or running water, it can use its action to polymorph into a Tiny Bat, a Medium cloud of mist, or back into its true form.

While in bat form, the nightstalker can't speak, its walking speed is 5 feet, and it has a flying speed of 40 feet. Its statistics, other than its size and speed, are unchanged. Anything it is wearing transforms with it, but nothing it is carrying does. It reverts to its true form if it dies.

While in mist form, the nightstalker can't take any actions, speak, or manipulate objects. It is weightless, has a flying speed of 20 feet, can hover, and can enter other creature's spaces and stop there. In addition, it can pass through any space that air can pass through, without squeezing, but cannot pass through water. It is immune to all nonmagical damage, other than radiant damage from sunlight.

Echolocation. The nightstalker can't use its blindsight while deafened.

Legendary Durability (1/Day). If the nightstalker fails a saving throw, it can choose to reroll the saving throw.

Misty Escape. When the nightstalker drops to 0 hit points while outside its resting place, it transforms into mist form instead of falling unconscious, provided that it isn't in sunlight or running water. If it can't transform, it is destroyed.

While it has 0 hit points in mist form, it can't revert to vampire form, and it must reach its resting place within 1 hour, or be destroyed. Once in its resting place, it reverts to its vampire form. It is then paralyzed until it regains at least 1 hit point. After spending 1 hour in its resting place with 0 hit points, it regains 1 hit point.

Regeneration. The nightstalker regains 15 hit points at the start of its turn if it has at least 1 hit point, isn't in sunlight or running water, or a piercing weapon made of wood isn't embedded in its heart. If the nightstalker takes radiant damage, or damage from holy water, this trait doesn't function at the start of the nightstalker's next turn.

Vampire Weaknesses. The nightstalker has the following flaws:

Forbiddance. The nightstalker can't enter a residence without an invitation from one of the occupants.

Harmed by Running Water. The nightstalker takes 20 acid damage when it ends its turn in running water.

Stake to the Heart. The nightstalker is paralyzed if a piercing weapon made of wood is driven into its heart while it is incapacitated in its resting place. It remains paralyzed, and cannot regain hit points, until the stake is removed.

Sunlight Hypersensitivity. The nightstalker takes 20 radiant damage when it starts its turn in sunlight. While in sunlight, it has disadvantage on attack rolls and ability checks.

Spider Climb. The nightstalker can climb difficult surfaces, including upside down on ceilings, without needing to make an ability check.

Stalker's Leap. The nightstalker's long jump is up to 40 feet, and its high jump is 20 feet, with or without a running start.

ACTIONS

Multiattack (Vampire Form Only). The nightstalker makes three attacks: one with its bite, and two with its claws.

Claws (Vampire Form Only). *Melee Weapon Attack:* +9 to hit, reach 5 ft., one target. *Hit:* 12 (2d8 + 3) slashing damage, and the target is grappled (escape DC 17).

Bite (Vampire or Bat Form Only). *Melee Weapon Attack:* +9 to hit, reach 5 ft., one willing creature, or a creature that is grappled by the nightstalker or one of the nightstalker's allies, incapacitated, or restrained. *Hit:* 6 (1d6 + 3) piercing damage, plus 10 (3d6) necrotic damage. The target's hit point maximum is reduced by a number equal to the necrotic damage taken, and the nightstalker regains an equal number of hit points. This reduction lasts until the creature finishes a long rest. If the creature's hit point maximum is reduced to 0 by this effect, the creature dies. A humanoid slain this way, and then buried in the ground, rises the following night as a vampire spawn under the nightstalker's control.

Invisibility (Vampire Form Only). The nightstalker turns invisible, provided it is not in sunlight or running water. The invisibility lasts until the nightstalker makes an attack, casts a spell, or until its concentration ends (as if concentrating on a spell). The nightstalker automatically loses its concentration if it takes radiant damage or damage from running or holy water.

Higher vampires have a great amount of control over the nature of the curse they pass onto their progeny, and seem able to guide their physiological development to suit their needs. **Nightstalkers** are even more well-adapted for silent ambushes than would be expected of a vampire, and are able to close distances from the shadows with unnatural, bounding leaps.

VAMPIRE FAMILIARS

Vampires can, through a ritual involving repeated use of their Charm ability and an exchange of blood, establish a psychic link with a humanoid, and turn it into a vampire familiar. Any living humanoid, with a challenge rating lower than the vampire's, can be turned into a vampire familiar. A vampire familiar gains the following changes:

- The familiar becomes permanently charmed by its master.

- While the familiar and its master are on the same plane of existence, the master can telepathically communicate with the familiar, although the familiar can only communicate general emotions to its master. Further, the master knows when the familiar becomes charmed by another creature.

Discovered the source of the blockage.
Something's made a nest down here. Looks like they've been here a while. Doesn't smell bad enough to be gnolls, and gnolls don't leave desiccated corpses piled in the water.
Probably three or four of them, by my reckoning.
Didn't stick around for a thorough survey. I'll be taking those days of leave you owe me, if it's all the same to you.

-Nigs, sewerage worker

VAMPIRE PACKRUNNER

Medium undead (shapechanger), lawful evil

Armor Class 16 (natural armor)
Hit Points 153 (18d8 + 72)
Speed 30 ft.

STR	DEX	CON	INT	WIS	CHA
20 (+5)	17 (+3)	18 (+4)	16 (+3)	20 (+5)	15 (+2)

Saving Throws Dex +7, Con +8, Cha +6
Skills Perception +13, Stealth +7, Survival +9
Damage Resistances necrotic; bludgeoning, piercing, and slashing from nonmagical attacks
Senses darkvision 120 ft., passive perception 23
Languages the languages it knew in life
Challenge 11 (7,200 XP)

Pack Tactics. The packrunner has advantage on an attack roll against a creature if at least one of the packrunner's allies is within 5 feet of the creature, and the ally isn't incapacitated.

Shapechanger. If the packrunner isn't in sunlight or running water, it can polymorph into a Medium wolf as a bonus action, or a Medium cloud of mist, or back into its true form as an action.

While in wolf form, the packrunner can't speak and its walking speed is 60 feet. Its statistics, other than its speed, are unchanged. Anything it is wearing transforms with it, but nothing it is carrying does. It reverts to its true form if it dies.

While in mist form, the packrunner can't take any actions, speak, or manipulate objects. It is weightless, has a flying speed of 20 feet, can hover, and can enter other creature's spaces and stop there. In addition, it can pass through any space that air can pass through, without squeezing, but cannot pass through water. It is immune to all nonmagical damage, other than radiant damage from sunlight.

Keen Hearing and Smell. The packrunner has advantage on Wisdom (Perception) checks that rely on hearing or smell.

Legendary Durability (1/Day). If the packrunner fails a saving throw, it can choose to reroll the saving throw.

Misty Escape. When the packrunner drops to 0 hit points while outside its resting place, it transforms into mist form instead of falling unconscious, provided that it isn't in sunlight or running water. If it can't transform, it is destroyed.

While it has 0 hit points in mist form, it can't revert to vampire form, and it must reach its resting place within 1 hour or be destroyed. Once in its resting place, it reverts to its vampire form. It is then paralyzed until it regains at least 1 hit point. After spending 1 hour in its resting place with 0 hit points, it regains 1 hit point.

Regeneration. The packrunner regains 15 hit points at the start of its turn if it has at least 1 hit point, isn't in sunlight or running water, or a piercing weapon made of wood isn't embedded in its heart. If the packrunner takes radiant damage, or damage from holy water, this trait doesn't function at the start of the packrunner's next turn.

Vampire Weaknesses. The packrunner has the following flaws:

Forbiddance. The packrunner can't enter a residence without an invitation from one of the occupants.

Harmed by Running Water. The packrunner takes 20 acid damage when it ends its turn in running water.

Stake to the Heart. The packrunner is paralyzed if a piercing weapon made of wood is driven into its heart while it is incapacitated in its resting place. It remains paralyzed, and cannot regain hit points, until the stake is removed.

Sunlight Hypersensitivity. The packrunner takes 20 radiant damage when it starts its turn in sunlight. While in sunlight, it has disadvantage on attack rolls and ability checks.

Spider Climb. The packrunner can climb difficult surfaces, including upside down on ceilings, without needing to make an ability check.

ACTIONS

Multiattack (Vampire Form Only). The packrunner makes two attacks, only one of which may be a bite attack.

Unarmed Strike (Vampire Form Only). *Melee Weapon Attack:* +9 to hit, reach 5 ft., one target. *Hit:* 7 (1d8 + 3) bludgeoning damage, and the target is grappled (escape DC 18).

Bite (Vampire or Wolf Form Only). *Melee Weapon Attack:* +9 to hit, reach 5 ft., one target in wolf form, or one willing creature or a creature that is grappled by the packrunner or one of the packrunner's allies, incapacitated, or restrained in vampire form. *Hit:* 6 (1d6 + 3) piercing damage, plus 10 (3d6) necrotic damage in vampire form, or 12 (2d8 + 3) piercing damage, plus 17 (5d6) necrotic damage in wolf form. The target's hit point maximum is reduced by a number equal to the necrotic damage taken, and the packrunner regains an equal number of hit points. This reduction lasts until the creature finishes a long rest. If the creature's hit point maximum is reduced to 0 by this effect, the creature dies. This reduction lasts until the creature finishes a long rest. If the creature's hit point maximum is reduced to 0 by this effect, the creature dies. A humanoid slain this way, and then buried in the ground, rises the following night as a vampire spawn under the packrunner's control.

Packrunners are selected (or, possibly, 'bred') for their ferocity and feral cunning and kept half-starved by higher vampires in order to increase their savagery. Individually, they are loyal bodyguards, but their true strength lies in sniffing out and destroying threats to their master, as a pack.

Subject notes

Subject was delivered as little more than a head with a handful of cervical vertebrae. Within two days, nerves had began to sprout, root-like from the stump, allowing precautionary restraints to be put in place. As soon as the eyes regrew, acid was applied to the distal nerves, with pupil dilation confirming that pain response was present and constant. Organ and muscle regeneration followed swiftly, along with the ability to speak. Wordless shrieking, to begin with, while the brain readjusted.

With its full body restored, it quickly became clear that the restraints were insufficient and would soon fail. Not willing to endanger the other experiments, the failsafe was put into effect; the curtains were removed, allowing sunlight to flood the south-facing chamber.

Blood and ash samples located in cabinet 3-C.

—Nimh, physician, personal notes

Vampire Noble

Medium undead (shapechanger), lawful evil

Armor Class 16 (natural armor)
Hit Points 204 (24d8 + 96)
Speed 30 ft.

STR	DEX	CON	INT	WIS	CHA
18 (+4)	18 (+4)	18 (+4)	16 (+3)	16 (+3)	18 (+4)

Saving Throws Dex +9, Con +9, Cha +9
Skills Perception +13, Stealth +9
Damage Resistances necrotic; bludgeoning, piercing, and slashing from nonmagical attacks
Senses darkvision 120 ft., passive perception 23
Languages the languages it knew in life
Challenge 15 (13,000 XP)

Shapechanger. If the noble isn't in sunlight or running water, it can use its action to polymorph into a Tiny bat, a Medium wolf, a Medium cloud of mist, or back into its true form.

While in bat form, the noble can't speak, its walking speed is 5 feet, and it has a flying speed of 40 feet. Its statistics, other than its size and speed, are unchanged. Anything it is wearing transforms with it, but nothing it is carrying does. It reverts to its true form if it dies.

While in wolf form, the noble can't speak and its walking speed is 40 feet. Its statistics, other than its speed, are unchanged. Anything it is wearing transforms with it, but nothing it is carrying does. It reverts to its true form if it dies.

While in mist form, the noble can't take any actions, speak, or manipulate objects. It is weightless, has a flying speed of 20 feet, can hover, and can enter other creature's spaces and stop there. In addition, it can pass through any space that air can pass through, without squeezing, but cannot pass through water. It is immune to all nonmagical damage, other than radiant damage from sunlight.

Legendary Resistance (3/Day). If the noble fails a saving throw, it can choose to succeed instead.

Misty Escape. When the noble drops to 0 hit points while outside its resting place, it transforms into mist form instead of falling unconscious, provided that it isn't in sunlight or running water. If it can't transform, it is destroyed.

While it has 0 hit points in mist form, it can't revert to vampire form, and it must reach its resting place within 1 hour, or be destroyed. Once in its resting place, it reverts to its vampire form. It is then paralyzed until it regains at least 1 hit point. After spending 1 hour in its resting place with 0 hit points, it regains 1 hit point.

Regeneration. The noble regains 25 hit points at the start of its turn if it has at least 1 hit point, isn't in sunlight or running water, or a piercing weapon made of wood isn't embedded in its heart. If the noble takes radiant damage, or damage from holy water, this trait doesn't function at the start of the noble's next turn.

Spider Climb. The noble can climb difficult surfaces, including upside down on ceilings, without needing to make an ability check.

Vampire Weaknesses. The noble has the following flaws:

Forbiddance. The noble can't enter a residence without an invitation from one of the occupants.

Harmed by Running Water. The noble takes 20 acid damage when it ends its turn in running water.

Stake to the Heart. The noble is paralyzed if a piercing weapon made of wood is driven into its heart while it is incapacitated in its resting place. It remains paralyzed, and cannot regain hit points, until the stake is removed.

Sunlight Hypersensitivity. The noble takes 20 radiant damage when it starts its turn in sunlight. While in sunlight, it has disadvantage on attack rolls and ability checks.

ACTIONS

Multiattack (Vampire Form Only). The noble makes two attacks, only one of which may be a bite attack.

Unarmed Strike (Vampire Form Only). *Melee Weapon Attack:* +9 to hit, reach 5 ft., one target. *Hit:* 8 (1d8 + 4) bludgeoning damage, and the target is grappled (escape DC 18).

Bite (Bat, Wolf or Vampire Form Only). *Melee Weapon Attack:* +9 to hit, reach 5 ft., one willing creature, or a creature that is grappled by the noble or one of the noble's allies, incapacitated, or restrained in bat or vampire form, or one target in wolf form. *Hit:* 7 (1d6 + 4) piercing damage, plus 14 (4d6) necrotic damage. The target's hit point maximum is reduced by a number equal to the necrotic damage taken, and the noble regains an equal number of hit points. This reduction lasts until the creature finishes a long rest. If the creature's hit point maximum is reduced to 0 by this effect, the creature dies. A humanoid slain this way, and then buried in the ground, rises the following night as a vampire spawn under the noble's control.

Charm. The noble targets one humanoid it can see within 30 feet of it. If the target can see the noble, the target must succeed on a DC 17 Wisdom saving throw against this magic, or be charmed by the noble. The charmed target regards the noble as a trusted friend to be heeded and protected.

Although the target isn't under the noble's control, it takes the noble's requests or actions in the most favorable way it can, and it is a willing target for the noble's bite attack.

Each time the noble, or the noble's allies, do anything harmful to the target, it can repeat the saving throw, ending the effect on itself on a success. Otherwise, the effect lasts 24 hours, or until the noble is destroyed, is on a different plane of existence than the target, or takes a bonus action to end the effect.

REACTIONS

Deflect Missile (Vampire Form Only). In response to being hit by a ranged weapon attack, the noble deflects the missile. The damage it takes from the attack is reduced by 2d10 + 4. If the damage is reduced to 0, the noble catches the missile, if it's small enough to hold in one hand and the noble has a hand free. If a missile the noble caught this way is nonmagical, the noble can then automatically break the missile, making it unusable.

LEGENDARY ACTIONS.

The noble can take 3 legendary actions, choosing from the options below. Only one legendary action option can be used at a time, and only at the end of another creature's turn. The noble regains spent legendary actions at the start of its turn.

Strike. The noble makes an unarmed strike.

Bite (Costs 2 Actions). The noble makes a bite attack.

Misty Shift (Costs 2 Actions). The noble changes into mist form, moves up to its flying speed, and then reverts to its true form.

Near to the top of the vampiric pecking order, **nobles** are among the most powerful undead an average person might have the misfortune to encounter.

When the conversation turns to her early history, Ilandrei's brilliant eyes flash with an aspect I did not expect to see; dare I say she looked vulnerable?

"I remember it clearly, of course," she relates. "Mortals do not remember their births, so it is difficult to relate the feeling of it. It hurt at first, the bite, but as the blood began to drain from me, it felt... I hesitate to say pleasurable, but there was a sense of acceptance, of inevitability. That I was being fed upon was simply a fact of my life. I was only dimly aware of him stopping to bite his hand and offer it to me but, when he did, the desire to feed was overwhelming. That was pleasurable. It was the taste of life itself. Every other time I've fed, I think, is just a pale imitation of that first time."

I ask about the vampire that turned her (her 'sire', she quickly informs me).

"We run into each other from time to time. If you live long enough, that tends to happen. We mostly move in different circles, however."

When asked if they are estranged, she chuckles. It is her power to make one feel at once a child and the most important person in the world.

"My dear, he is closer to me than you can imagine. You would not understand, perhaps, but a sire is your parent, your most intimate lover, and part of yourself, all together. We are never apart, truly."

I begin to change the subject, but Ilandrei comments that I might be more comfortable were I to remove my kerchief and undo a few of my shirt buttons. At this point, I terminate the interview and beat a hasty retreat into the sunlight.

—Vars Limri, 'Conversations With Monsters'

Ancient Vampire

Medium undead (shapechanger), lawful evil

Armor Class 17 (natural armor), or 19 in abomination form
Hit Points 285 (30d8 + 150)
Speed 30 ft.

STR	DEX	CON	INT	WIS	CHA
21 (+5)	20 (+5)	20 (+5)	19 (+4)	22 (+6)	21 (+5)

Saving Throws Str +12, Dex +12, Con +12, Cha +12
Skills Perception +13, Stealth +12
Damage Resistances necrotic; bludgeoning, piercing, and slashing from nonmagical attacks
Senses darkvision 120 ft., passive perception 23
Languages the languages it knew in life
Challenge 21 (33,000 XP)

Shapechanger. If the ancient isn't in sunlight, it can use its action to polymorph into a Tiny bat, a Medium wolf, a Medium cloud of mist, a Large abomination, or back into its true form.

While in bat form, the ancient can't speak, its walking speed is 5 feet, and it has a flying speed of 40 feet. Its statistics, other than its size and speed, are unchanged. Anything it is wearing transforms with it, but nothing it is carrying does. It reverts to its true form if it dies.

While in wolf form, the ancient can't speak and its walking speed is 40 feet. Its statistics, other than its speed, are unchanged. Anything it is wearing transforms with it, but nothing it is carrying does. It reverts to its true form if it dies.

While in mist form, the ancient can't take any actions, speak, or manipulate objects. It is weightless, has a flying speed of 20 feet, can hover, and can enter other creature's spaces and stop there. In addition, it can pass through any space that air can pass through, without squeezing, but cannot pass through water. It is immune to all nonmagical damage, other than radiant damage from sunlight.

While in abomination form, the ancient has advantage on Strength checks and saving throws, resistance to all damage types except fire, force, psychic, and radiant damage, as well as acid damage from holy water, and a fly speed of 40 feet. Anything it is wearing transforms with it, but nothing it is carrying does.

Legendary Resistance (3/Day). If the ancient fails a saving throw, it can choose to succeed instead.

Misty Escape. When the ancient drops to 0 hit points while outside its resting place, it transforms into mist form instead of falling unconscious, provided that it isn't in sunlight or running water. If it can't transform, it is destroyed.

While it has 0 hit points in mist form, it can't revert to vampire form, and it must reach its resting place within 1 hour, or be destroyed. Once in its resting place, it reverts to its vampire form. It is then paralyzed until it regains at least 1 hit point. After spending 1 hour in its resting place with 0 hit points, it regains 1 hit point.

Regeneration. The ancient regains 30 hit points at the start of its turn if it has at least 1 hit point, isn't in sunlight or running water or a piercing weapon made of wood isn't embedded in its heart. If the ancient takes radiant damage, or damage from holy water, this trait doesn't function at the start of the ancient's next turn.

Vampire Weaknesses. The ancient has the following flaws:

Stake to the Heart. The ancient is paralyzed if a piercing weapon made of wood is driven into its heart while it is incapacitated in its resting place. It remains paralyzed, and cannot regain hit points, until the stake is removed.

Sunlight Hypersensitivity. The ancient takes 20 radiant damage when it starts its turn in sunlight. While in sunlight, it has disadvantage on attack rolls and ability checks.

Spider Climb. The ancient can climb difficult surfaces, including upside down on ceilings, without needing to make an ability check.

Why fear most the vampire? Their savagery? Surely the werewolf is more savage, yet none pairs it with such wicked intelligence. Their magicks? The lich wields more power, but seldom takes an interest in mortal affairs. That they prey upon us? All manner of beasts will do so, given half the chance.

No, we fear the vampire for their spark of humanity. For the fear that, within our family, or our neighbors, or our lovers, lurks a sleeping monster waiting for release.

We fear the vampire within us all.

—Quynel Varvenos, 'VAMPYR'

ACTIONS

Multiattack (Vampire or Abomination Form Only). The ancient makes three attacks, only one of which can be a bite.

Unarmed Strike (Vampire Form Only). *Melee Weapon Attack:* +12 to hit, reach 5 ft., one target. *Hit:* 9 (1d8 + 5) bludgeoning damage. Instead of dealing damage, the ancient can choose to grapple the target (escape DC 20).

Bite (Bat, Wolf, Abomination or Vampire Form Only). *Melee Weapon Attack:* +12 to hit, reach 5 ft., one willing creature, or a creature that is grappled by the ancient or one of the ancient's allies, incapacitated, or restrained in bat or vampire form, or one target in abomination or wolf form. *Hit:* 8 (1d6 + 5) piercing damage, plus 14 (4d6) necrotic damage, or 14 (2d8 + 5) piercing damage, plus 21 (6d6) necrotic damage in abomination form. The target's hit point maximum is reduced by a number equal to the necrotic damage taken, and the ancient regains an equal number of hit points. This reduction lasts until the creature finishes a long rest. If the creature's hit point maximum is reduced to 0 by this effect, the creature dies. A humanoid slain this way, and then buried in the ground, rises the following night as a vampire spawn under the ancient's control.

Claws (Abomination Form Only). *Melee Weapon Attack:* +12 to hit, reach 10 ft., one target. *Hit:* 14 (2d8 + 5) slashing damage, and the target is grappled (escape DC 20).

Charm. The ancient targets one humanoid it can see within 30 feet of it. If the target can see the ancient, the target must succeed on a DC 18 Wisdom saving throw against this magic, or be charmed by the ancient. The charmed target regards the ancient as a trusted friend to be heeded and protected.

Although the target isn't under the ancient's control, it takes the ancient's requests or actions in the most favorable way it can, and it is a willing target for the ancient's bite attack.

Each time the ancient, or the ancient's allies, do anything harmful to the target, it can repeat the saving throw, ending the effect on itself on a success. Otherwise, the effect lasts 24 hours, or until the ancient is destroyed, is on a different plane of existence than the target, or takes a bonus action to end the effect.

Summon Pack (1/Night). The ancient magically calls 2d4 swarms of bats or rats, provided that the sun isn't up. While outdoors, the ancient can call 3d6 wolves instead. The called creatures arrive in 1d4 rounds, acting as allies of the ancient and obeying its spoken commands. The beasts remain for 1 hour, until the ancient dies, or until the ancient dismisses them as a bonus action.

REACTIONS

Deflect Missile (Vampire Form Only). In response to being hit by a ranged weapon attack, the ancient deflects the missile. The damage it takes from the attack is reduced by 3d10 + 5. If the damage is reduced to 0, the ancient catches the missile, if it's small enough to hold in one hand and the vampire has a hand free. If a missile the ancient caught this way is nonmagical, the ancient can then automatically break the missile, making it unusable.

LEGENDARY ACTIONS.

The ancient can take 3 legendary actions, choosing from the options below. Only one legendary action option can be used at a time, and only at the end of another creature's turn. The ancient regains spent legendary actions at the start of its turn.

Move. The ancient moves up to its speed, without provoking opportunity attacks.

Strike. The ancient makes an unarmed strike or claws attack.

Bite (Costs 2 Actions). The ancient makes a bite attack.

Change (Costs 2 Actions). The ancient uses its Shapechange ability.

A vampire simply does not attain the great age necessary to be counted as truly **ancient** without a frightening combination of intelligence, cunning, and deadly skill. While they can appear as normal, living beings, as all vampires can, many choose to embrace their monstrous nature, appearing as an unholy fusion of human, bat, and demonic other.

THE VAMPIRE ARCHETYPE

Any living humanoid can be turned into a vampire spawn by a full vampire's bite. A vampire spawn gains the following changes:

- The vampire gains resistance to necrotic damage and bludgeoning, piercing, and slashing damage from nonmagical attacks.

- The vampire's unarmed strikes deal 1d8 damage, and the vampire can choose to grapple the target instead of dealing damage (escape DC 8 + the vampire's proficiency bonus + the vampire's Strength modifier).

- The vampire gains darkvision with a range of 60 feet, if it doesn't already have darkvision with equal or greater range.

- **Regeneration.** The vampire regains 10 hit points at the start of its turn if it has at least 1 hit point, isn't in sunlight or running water, or a piercing weapon made of wood isn't embedded in its heart. If the vampire takes radiant damage, or damage from holy water, this trait doesn't function at the start of the vampire's next turn.

- **Spider Climb.** The vampire can climb difficult surfaces, including upside down on ceilings, without needing to make an ability check.

- **Vampire Weaknesses.** The vampire has the following flaws:

    - *Forbiddance.* The vampire can't enter a residence without an invitation from one of the occupants.

    - *Harmed by Running Water.* The vampire takes 20 acid damage when it ends its turn in running water.

    - *Stake to the Heart.* The vampire is paralyzed if a piercing weapon made of wood is driven into its heart while it is incapacitated in its resting place. It remains paralyzed, and cannot regain hit points, until the stake is removed.

    - *Sunlight Hypersensitivity.* The vampire takes 20 radiant damage when it starts its turn in sunlight. While in sunlight, it has disadvantage on attack rolls and ability checks.

- **Vampire Bite.** The vampire gains a bite melee attack that deals 1d6 piercing damage, plus 2d6 necrotic damage. It can only target willing creatures and creatures that are restrained or grappled by the vampire or one of the vampire's allies. The attack uses the vampire's Dexterity or Strength modifier, whichever is higher, for attack and damage rolls. Whenever the vampire deals necrotic damage with its bite, it regains a number of hit points equal to the necrotic damage dealt.

The vampire spawn can turn into a full vampire, if allowed to draw blood from its master. Once turned into a full vampire, the following changes apply, in addition to the above:

- **Shapechange.** The vampire gains the ability to polymorph into a Medium cloud of mist.
  While in mist form, the vampire can't take any actions, speak, or manipulate objects. It is weightless, has a flying speed of 20 feet, can hover, and can enter other creature's spaces and stop there. In addition, it can pass through any space that air can pass through, without squeezing, but cannot pass through water. It is immune to all nonmagical damage, other than radiant damage from sunlight.

- The vampire's darkvision extends to a range of 120 feet, unless it is already greater.

- **Misty Escape.** When the vampire drops to 0 hit points while outside its resting place, it transforms into mist form instead of falling unconscious, provided that it isn't in sunlight or running water. If it can't transform, it is destroyed.
  While it has 0 hit points in mist form, it can't revert to vampire form, and it must reach its resting place within 1 hour, or be destroyed. Once in its resting place, it reverts to its vampire form. It is then paralyzed until it regains at least 1 hit point. After spending 1 hour in its resting place with 0 hit points, it regains 1 hit point.

- **Vampiric Destruction.** The vampire can only be destroyed if it is reduced to 0 hit points by radiant damage from sunlight, acid damage from running or holy water, or decapitated while paralyzed by a wooden piercing weapon embedded in its heart. If not destroyed by these means, the vampire will begin regaining hit points as soon as the prerequisites are met.

As a vampire advances in age, its vampiric abilities develop further. Once a vampire leaves fledgling stage, and becomes its own master, it gains any or all of the following changes to its existing vampire abilities:

- **Shapechange.** In addition to a cloud of mist, the vampire can transform into a Tiny bat, or a Medium wolf.
  In bat form, the vampire can't speak or cast spells. Its walking speed is 5 feet and it has a fly speed of 40 ft. While in this form, the vampire can only use its vampire bite attack and abilities that do not depend on its humanoid form.
  In wolf form, the vampire can't speak or cast spells. Its walking speed is 40 feet. While in this form, the vampire can only use its vampire bite attack and abilities that do not depend on its humanoid form. The target of the bite doesn't have to be a creature, willing, grappled, or restrained.

- **Regeneration.** The vampire regains 15 or 20 hit points each turn, instead of 10.

- **Vampire Bite.** When the vampire's bite hits a creature, the target's hit point maximum is reduced by an amount equal to the necrotic damage taken. This reduction lasts until the creature finishes a long rest. If the creature's hit point maximum is reduced to 0 by this effect, the creature dies. A humanoid slain this way, and then buried in the ground, rises the following night as a vampire spawn under the vampire's control.

The night and the grave are cold as death,
But the blood, my dear, the blood.

-refrain from 'The Vampires' Lament',
popular song

The body lay in an almost peaceful pose, lying amongst the other discarded scraps in the alley, as if reclining on a featherbed. The neat pair of puncture wounds in the neck were almost poetic. The stomach-churning quantities of drying blood soaked into the victim's clothing were not. Whatever did this was severely lacking in table manners, though this was, arguably, not their most egregious fault.

It was the third such body we had discovered since the watch captain had enlisted our (or, rather, Thaddeus') services. The others bore additional, terrible injuries which made diagnosing their cause of death more difficult. This one though...

"It's a bloodsucker, alright. Thought as much. If we're lucky, we're dealing with some kind of lesser vampire. Might explain why the bodies aren't being raised. Could just be hungry."

"And if we're not lucky?" I ventured.

"Then it's something a lot worse, and killing for the fun of it."

"Nothing we can't handle though, right?"

Thaddeus grunted. I was not entirely filled with confidence.

As I cast my eyes about the scene, I caught sight of a figure watching us calmly. Rake-thin and tall, dark against the rising moon, it would have been enigmatic even if it weren't standing on a shingle roof overlooking the alleyway. I went to point out the curious sight to Thaddeus, only to find him already sprinting, vaulting up a stack of crates towards the rooftops himself. The figure sped away with inhuman alacrity, showing as little concern for their terrain as a sprinter would on a racetrack. I admit I was not enthused by the prospect, but began to climb the crates after Thaddeus, regardless.

And so we went; the weightless grace of the stranger ahead, flowing like mist through the night sky, pursued by Thaddeus, sturdy on his feet, making implacable progress. I followed. As we progressed on our night-time tour of the city, a fog rolled in to either side of us, yet our path ahead seemed clear. Within, I fancied I saw the rolling shadows of wolves running at our heels, like a shepherd's dogs.

Our destination, it would appear, was an attic room in a somewhat dilapidated district of the city. It was, at least, not somewhere I would expect to frequent at this time of night and leave without a handful of holes I didn't have before. Luckily, we were not on street level. The stranger darted in through a window. Thaddeus, hot on his heels, crashed through a boarded-up doorway, sword drawn. Being a few rooftops behind, I joined the ensuing battle part-way through, entering through the same doorway as Thaddeus with, I hoped, the impression that I might be of some use as back-up.

I am unsure whether my entrance was noted by either combatant. Thaddeus was fighting with a fury I had never seen before and, far from shrinking away, his opponent met him blow for blow, each swing dodged or parried by the stranger whose hands, I now saw, ended with wickedly sharp (and, evidently, very strong) claws. Buying space with a feint, Thaddeus deftly drew a vial from his jacket and flung it. It shattered against the wall as its intended target dissolved into mist and, in a flash, reappeared to strike from behind.

With effort, Thaddeus turned in time, managing to turn a deadly blow into a glancing one. The claws left a ragged rent in his jerkin and the shoulder beneath but, at least, did not remove his head. Thaddeus returned the blow, occupying one claw with his sword, while striking with a concealed dagger, drawing a thin crimson line across the pale flesh of the enemy's cheek. A single, red tear made slow progress towards the corner of his mouth. It seemed far from a fair exchange.

For the first time, now that their positions were reversed, the creature noticed me, and I shudder to recall the full intensity of his glare, brief though it was. I felt the immediate need to do something drastic in order to impress him, and began to look around to see if there was anything I could strike Thaddeus with. Before I got the chance, however, the creature took a step back with an easy smile, and held up his hands in a gesture of nonviolence. Thaddeus continued to circle, his sword point fixed towards his foe's throat.

"You are nearly as good as they say you are, Thaddeus." The creature's voice was silk. I wanted nothing more than to keep listening to it. Thaddeus, by contrast, was breathing heavily. "You've made quite the name for yourself, you know."

"For killing creatures like you."

"No," he chuckled. "I think not."

"You've killed people."

"I can assure you, the world is better off without them. The most recent ones, anyway. Dreadful people, truly. Besides, I had to get your attention."

"If you think words will save you-"

"It is not myself I am trying to save," he said softly, pointing upwards. Raising our eyes to the rafters we saw, clustering there, dozens of figures, passively observing the events below them. I was put in mind of bats huddling in the roof of a cave.

Thaddeus lowered the point of his sword. His assessment of the situation seemed to be the same as mine.

"What do you want?"

"I understand you are tracking something. Whatever great power is pulling the strings. The Shrouded One." He smirked, now assured of Thaddeus' full attention. "A wraith, and a particularly old and angry one. It has slumbered for centuries. The war awoke it, and the war will provide it soldiers. A united front of undeath which it will use to scour this world of life."

"You'll be fine then. Why are you telling me?"

"Because I want you to kill it, of course. I have no desire for the end of the world. No more than the wolf has a desire for the end of sheep. You'll find it north-west of here; the old war graves. It seems you put paid to some of its more wide-ranging plans and it has returned to basics, somewhat. You may leave now."

"What makes you think I won't be back for you?"

"Assuming you survive? You'll never see me again. I have no interest in you kicking down my door and embarrassing yourself. Me and mine will be gone from here as soon as you are. I shan't ask again."

We retreated to the rooftop and, in the light of the moon, a cloud of bats exploded from the chimney and windows behind us. Some were, doubtless, simple beasts, but I was sure that a good number of them were the very same undead horrors we had encountered inside.

"Look," I said, with forced cheer. "They're fleeing. Got them on the run."

Thaddeus sagged. I had never seen him so tired. He looked as though the encounter had aged him, though whether it was the battle he had just fought, or the knowledge of the one to come, I did not know.

WIGHTS

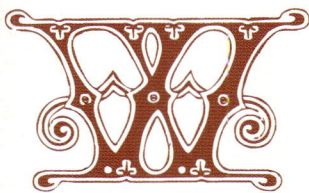

ith each step, the ground blackens; grass withers in the blighted rot spreading from its foot-fall. The air grows cold, as if the warmth of life itself grows unnerved and shrinks before its approach. Its downturned face, riven by deep crevasses of ancient flesh, is passionless save for the hint in the corner of its mouth of a sneer of contempt. The dark, black pits of its eyes, however, burn with undisguised hatred.

Clawing their way back from the dead through dark pacts, wights are beings trapped between life and undeath, and truly of neither world. Though they somewhat resemble withered corpses, their sunken features are not the result of natural decay, nor will they deteriorate further; a wight's visage forever marks it as the terrible creature it has become.

The unhappy existence of a wight is often the fate of those in morality tales who do not correct their ways of vanity and greed, forced to linger on forever regretful of their past deeds. In truth, wights lack the capacity for repentance; their emotions are cold, and their memories dimmed and faded. Clinging to their semblance of life is the only worthy goal.

ORIGIN

A wight rises when a soul consumed with unfulfilled ambition, revenge, or greed calls out as it screams towards the afterlife and is heard by some dark entity. Of course, there are many who feel such emotions upon death, but only the truly wicked or desperate are willing to pay the price asked of them to return to some form of life. For most, this is vanity, ambition, greed, and superiority – these are people who think simple death is beneath them and the world owes them an extension on life. Warlocks who swear their pacts to more sinister forces may be risen as wights if their benefactor deems them to have outstanding tasks. Very rarely do folk plan in advance to become a wight, but those few carry curse tablets upon their person if they suspect their death is at hand; thin sheets of lead carved with a plea to whatever will hear it, promising their soul in exchange for a chance to carry on in wight form.

A wight is returned to its body and given free will to act as it sees fit, provided it also aid the undead against the living at any given opportunity, and fulfil any other task its dark master may ask of it. While not compelled to do so (as this would deprive them of their free will), each wight is keenly aware that they are allowed to exist only at the whim of their master, and that failure to comply means destruction, or condemnation to mindless undead servitude.

ENVIRONMENT

Life itself rebels against the presence of a wight; grass blackens and rots at their feet, streams sour at their crossing, and beasts flee before them. These effects reverse in time but, should a wight remain in an area for a time, it is possible nothing shall ever grow there again.

The sun is nothing but a reminder of the life the wight once had, and it would avoid and despise the light even if it didn't cause it immense physical discomfort. This, as well as their ability, and ofttimes need, to raise the dead as their unthinking servants, drives them towards barrows and tombs as places of respite. Unless driven together by a higher power, as lieutenants in an undead army for example, wights tend to work alone, so infestations are rare (thankfully, as a lone wight and its minions is usually trouble enough).

ROLEPLAYING WIGHTS

Wights retain little of their former personality, and feel nothing towards former friends or allies. They keep their memories, compartmentalized as if those of another, so will recognize characters from their past, but feelings of companionship or love are dimmed. They retain knowledge of their associates in terms of skill set, usefulness, or expendability; sentiment is considered pointless when compared to the goal of their well-deserved eternal life. They can only mimic emotions and sentiment to prey upon gullible or naïve acquaintances, perhaps leaning on a once-trusted friend for some useful influence, or feigning outrage to be gifted a boon from a former ally. These are but illusion, however, and any who know a wight would do well to accept that the person they knew is dead and gone.

One familiar with ghosts might assume that a wight is released from undeath upon the fulfilment of their goal but, as the wight *has* no specific goal but to cling to life itself, the force that powers them lingers indefinitely. Devoid of personal ambitions, wights exist only to hinder the living, serve their patron, and extend their own existence, only growing in cold, patient anger as the memories of their former self fade. After enough time, most forget why they hang on to life but, remembering no other purpose, continue to do so at all costs.

COMBAT TACTICS

For a wight, self-preservation is key, given the price they paid to return to the land of the living, so they do not act rashly. They think nothing of using their underlings as arrow-fodder – what does it matter if their minions are expended, so long as they themselves survive?

Should a wight find itself outnumbered, it will focus its attacks on the individuals it deems the weakest in turn, raising them as undead allies as they fall and, in time, turning the numbers to its advantage.

Wights have the luxury of time on their side and, devoid of heated emotion, are content to wait and plan the eradication of any personal threats, be they individuals or entire settlements.

WIGHT ENCOUNTERS

d8	CR	Encounter
1	8	**Malicious Triad:** 1 Wight Tracker, 1 Wight Warrior, 1 Wight Malignant
2	11	**Murderous Bodyguard:** 1 Wight Champion, 2 Wight Malignants, 6 Human Zombies, 3 Dwarf Zombies
3	13	**Wicked Trinity:** 1 Wight Hunter, 1 Wight Champion, 1 Wight Despoiler
4	16	**Lifehunter Conclave:** 1 Slayer of the Living, 2 Wight Hunters, 3 Wight Trackers
5	17	**Butcher Squad:** 1 Insatiable Executioner, 2 Wight Champions, 3 Wight Warriors, 4 Human Zombies, 2 Dwarf Zombie
6	18	**Hatesworn Retinue:** 1 Oathsworn Annihilator, 2 Wight Despoilers, 2 Wight Trackers, 4 Wight Warriors
7	19	**Cursed Triumvirate:** 1 Slayer of the Living, 1 Insatiable Executioner, 1 Oathsworn Annihilator
8	20	**Frostlord's Company:** 1 Frost Wight, 1 Wight Despoiler, 1 Wight Champion, 1 Wight Hunter, 4 Wight Warriors, 10 Human Zombies, 6 Elf Zombies

WIGHT TRACKER
Medium undead, neutral evil

Armor Class 15 (leather)
Hit Points 60 (8d8 + 24)
Speed 30 ft.

STR	DEX	CON	INT	WIS	CHA
13 (+1)	18 (+4)	16 (+3)	10 (+0)	16 (+3)	15 (+2)

Skills Perception +5, Stealth +6, Survival +5
Damage Vulnerabilities radiant
Damage Resistances bludgeoning, piercing, and slashing from nonmagical attacks that aren't silvered
Damage Immunities poison, necrotic
Condition Immunities exhaustion, poisoned
Senses darkvision 60 ft., passive perception 15
Languages the languages it knew in life
Challenge 4 (1,100 XP)

Favored Prey. When a creature fails a saving throw against the tracker's Life Drain, the tracker can choose to make that creature its favored prey. The tracker gains a +2 bonus to weapon damage rolls against its favored prey. The creature remains the tracker's favored prey for 24 hours. This effect ends early if the creature dies, or the tracker chooses a new favored prey.

Life Hunter. The tracker has advantage on Wisdom (Survival) checks to track living creatures.

Spellcasting. The tracker is a 3rd level spellcaster. Its spellcasting ability is Wisdom (spell save DC 13, +5 to hit with spell attacks). The tracker has the following ranger spells prepared:

1st level (4 slots): *detect magic, hail of thorns, hunter's mark*

2nd level (2 slots): *pass without trace*

Sunlight Sensitivity. While in sunlight, the tracker has disadvantage on attack rolls, as well as on Wisdom (Perception) checks that rely on sight.

Turn Resistance. The tracker has advantage on saving throws against any effect that turns undead.

ACTIONS

Multiattack. The tracker makes a rapier attack and uses its Life Drain. If the tracker has a shortsword drawn, it can make a shortsword attack in place of its Life Drain.

Life Drain. *Melee Weapon Attack:* +6 to hit, reach 5 ft., one target. *Hit:* 5 (1d6 + 2) necrotic damage. The target must succeed on a DC 13 Constitution saving throw, or its hit point maximum is reduced by an amount equal to the damage taken. This reduction lasts until the target finishes a long rest. The target dies if this effect reduces its hit point maximum to 0.

A humanoid or beast slain by this attack rises 24 hours later as a zombie under the tracker's control, unless the creature is restored to life or its body is destroyed. The tracker can have no more than 12 zombies under its control at one time.

Rapier. *Melee Weapon Attack:* +6 to hit, reach 5 ft., one target. *Hit:* 8 (1d8 + 4) piercing damage.

Shortsword. *Melee Weapon Attack:* +6 to hit, reach 5 ft., one target. *Hit:* 7 (1d6 + 4) piercing damage.

Longbow. *Ranged Weapon Attack:* +6 to hit, range 150/600 ft., one target. *Hit:* 8 (1d8 + 4) piercing damage.

WIGHT HUNTER

Medium undead, neutral evil

Armor Class 16 (studded leather)
Hit Points 120 (16d8 + 48)
Speed 30 ft.

STR	DEX	CON	INT	WIS	CHA
13 (+1)	19 (+4)	16 (+3)	10 (+0)	16 (+3)	16 (+3)

Skills Perception +6, Stealth +7, Survival +6
Damage Vulnerabilities radiant
Damage Resistances bludgeoning, piercing, and slashing from nonmagical attacks that aren't silvered
Damage Immunities poison, necrotic
Condition Immunities exhaustion, poisoned
Senses darkvision 60 ft., passive perception 16
Languages the languages it knew in life
Challenge 7 (2,900 XP)

Favored Prey. When a creature fails a saving throw against the hunter's Life Drain, the hunter can choose to make that creature its favored prey. The hunter gains a +4 bonus to weapon damage rolls against its favored prey. The creature remains the hunter's favored prey for 24 hours. This effect ends early if the creature dies, or the hunter chooses a new favored prey.

Life Hunter. The hunter has advantage on Wisdom (Survival) checks to track living creatures.

Spellcasting. The hunter is a 5th level spellcaster. Its spellcasting ability is Wisdom (spell save DC 14, +6 to hit with spell attacks). The hunter has the following ranger spells prepared:

1st level (4 slots): *detect magic, hail of thorns, hunter's mark*

2nd level (3 slots): *pass without trace, spike growth*

3rd level (2 slots): *conjure barrage*

Sunlight Sensitivity. While in sunlight, the hunter has disadvantage on attack rolls, as well as on Wisdom (Perception) checks that rely on sight.

Turn Resistance. The hunter has advantage on saving throws against any effect that turns undead.

ACTIONS

Multiattack. The hunter makes two rapier attacks and uses its Life Drain, or makes two longbow attacks. If the hunter has a shortsword drawn, it can make a shortsword attack in place of its Life Drain.

Life Drain. *Melee Weapon Attack:* +7 to hit, reach 5 ft., one target. *Hit:* 10 (2d6 + 3) necrotic damage. The target must succeed on a DC 14 Constitution saving throw, or its hit point maximum is reduced by an amount equal to the damage taken. This reduction lasts until the target finishes a long rest. The target dies if this effect reduces its hit point maximum to 0.

A humanoid or beast slain by this attack rises 24 hours later as a zombie under the hunter's control, unless the creature is restored to life or its body is destroyed. The hunter can have no more than 25 zombies under its control at one time.

Rapier. *Melee Weapon Attack:* +7 to hit, reach 5 ft., one target. *Hit:* 8 (1d8 + 4) piercing damage.

Shortsword. *Melee Weapon Attack:* +7 to hit, reach 5 ft., one target. *Hit:* 7 (1d6 + 4) piercing damage.

Longbow. *Ranged Weapon Attack:* +7 to hit, range 150/600 ft., one target. *Hit:* 8 (1d8 + 4) piercing damage.

SLAYER OF THE LIVING

Medium undead, neutral evil

Armor Class 16 (studded leather)
Hit Points 165 (22d8 + 66)
Speed 30 ft.

STR	DEX	CON	INT	WIS	CHA
13 (+1)	20 (+5)	16 (+3)	10 (+0)	18 (+4)	18 (+4)

Skills Perception +8, Stealth +9, Survival +8
Damage Vulnerabilities radiant
Damage Resistances bludgeoning, piercing, and slashing from nonmagical attacks that aren't silvered
Damage Immunities poison, necrotic
Condition Immunities exhaustion, poisoned
Senses darkvision 60 ft., passive perception 18
Languages the languages it knew in life
Challenge 11 (7,200 XP)

Favored Prey. When a creature fails a saving throw against the slayer's Life Drain, the slayer can choose to make that creature its favored prey. The slayer gains a +4 bonus to weapon damage rolls against its favored prey. The creature remains the slayer's favored prey for 24 hours. This effect ends early if the creature dies, or the slayer chooses a new favored prey.

Life Hunter. The slayer has advantage on Wisdom (Survival) checks to track living creatures.

Spellcasting. The slayer is a 8th level spellcaster. Its spellcasting ability is Wisdom (spell save DC 16, +8 to hit with spell attacks). The slayer has the following ranger spells prepared:

1st level (4 slots): *detect magic, hail of thorns, hunter's mark*

2nd level (3 slots): *pass without trace, spike growth*

3rd level (3 slots): *conjure barrage, lightning arrow*

4th level (2 slots): *freedom of movement, stoneskin*

Sunlight Sensitivity. While in sunlight, the slayer has disadvantage on attack rolls, as well as on Wisdom (Perception) checks that rely on sight.

Turn Resistance. The slayer has advantage on saving throws against any effect that turns undead.

ACTIONS

Multiattack. The slayer makes two rapier attacks and uses its Life Drain, or makes two longbow attacks. If the slayer has a shortsword drawn, it can make a shortsword attack in place of its Life Drain.

Life Drain. *Melee Weapon Attack:* +9 to hit, reach 5 ft., one target. *Hit:* 14 (3d6 + 4) necrotic damage. The target must succeed on a DC 16 Constitution saving throw, or its hit point maximum is reduced by an amount equal to the damage taken. This reduction lasts until the target finishes a long rest. The target dies if this effect reduces its hit point maximum to 0.

A humanoid or beast slain by this attack rises 24 hours later as a zombie under the slayer's control, unless the creature is restored to life or its body is destroyed. There is no limit to the number of zombies the slayer can control.

Rapier. *Melee Weapon Attack:* +9 to hit, reach 5 ft., one target. *Hit:* 9 (1d8 + 5) piercing damage.

Shortsword. *Melee Weapon Attack:* +9 to hit, reach 5 ft., one target. *Hit:* 8 (1d6 + 5) piercing damage.

Longbow. *Ranged Weapon Attack:* +9 to hit, range 150/600 ft., one target. *Hit:* 9 (1d8 + 5) piercing damage.

LEGENDARY ACTIONS

The slayer can take 3 legendary actions, choosing from the options below. Only one legendary action option can be used at a time, and only at the end of another creature's turn. The slayer regains spent legendary actions at the start of its turn.

Command Zombie. One zombie, under the control of the slayer, makes a melee attack against a creature of the slayer's choice.

Life Drain. The slayer uses its Life Drain. On a hit, it can take a second legendary action to immediately cast *hunter's mark* or make the target its Favoured Prey.

Vanish. The slayer moves up to half its speed and can take the Hide action.

Cast a Spell (Costs 2 Actions). The slayer casts from its list of prepared spells, using a spell slot as normal.

> "Theirs is a cold and passionless hatred. I saw one skin a man alive once, and it didn't even frown. Gods, I would have preferred if it had laughea..."
>
> -Rhona, former soldier

WIGHT WARRIOR

Medium undead, neutral evil

Armor Class 16 (chain mail)
Hit Points 75 (10d8 + 30)
Speed 30 ft.

STR	DEX	CON	INT	WIS	CHA
16 (+3)	10 (+0)	17 (+3)	11 (+0)	11 (+0)	14 (+2)

Skills Athletics +5, Perception +2
Damage Vulnerabilities radiant
Damage Resistances bludgeoning, piercing, and slashing from nonmagical attacks that aren't silvered
Damage Immunities poison, necrotic
Condition Immunities exhaustion, poisoned
Senses darkvision 60 ft., passive perception 12
Languages the languages it knew in life
Challenge 4 (1,100 XP)

Second Wind (1/Day). As a bonus action, the warrior regains 10 hit points.

Sunlight Sensitivity. While in sunlight, the warrior has disadvantage on attack rolls, as well as on Wisdom (Perception) checks that rely on sight.

Turn Resistance. The warrior has advantage on saving throws against any effect that turns undead.

ACTIONS

Multiattack. The warrior makes two weapon attacks. It can use its Life Drain in place of one melee attack.

Life Drain. *Melee Weapon Attack:* +5 to hit, reach 5 ft., one target. *Hit:* 5 (1d6 + 2) necrotic damage, and the target is grappled (escape DC 13). Until this grapple ends, the warrior must use one hand to maintain the grapple, but can automatically hit the grappled creature with its Life Drain. The target must succeed on a DC 12 Constitution saving throw, or its hit point maximum is reduced by an amount equal to the damage taken. This reduction lasts until the target finishes a long rest. The target dies if this effect reduces its hit point maximum to 0.

A humanoid slain by this attack rises 24 hours later as a zombie under the warrior's control, unless the humanoid is restored to life or its body is destroyed. The warrior can have no more than 12 zombies under its control at one time.

Greatsword. *Melee Weapon Attack:* +5 to hit, reach 5 ft., one target. *Hit:* 10 (2d6 + 3) slashing damage.

Handaxe. *Melee or Ranged Weapon Attack:* +5 to hit, reach 5 ft. or range 30/60 ft., one target. *Hit:* 6 (1d6 + 3) slashing damage.

"I felt such fear before. I was afraid, and I didn't want to die. I am free of such weakness now. Now, I don't feel much of anything.
You will though."

— Urzkhan the Heartless, wight

WIGHT CHAMPION
Medium undead, neutral evil

Armor Class 17 (splint)
Hit Points 136 (16d8 + 64)
Speed 30 ft.

STR	DEX	CON	INT	WIS	CHA
17 (+3)	10 (+0)	18 (+4)	11 (+0)	11 (+0)	15 (+2)

Skills Athletics +6, Perception +3
Damage Vulnerabilities radiant
Damage Resistances bludgeoning, piercing, and slashing from nonmagical attacks that aren't silvered
Damage Immunities poison, necrotic
Condition Immunities exhaustion, poisoned
Senses darkvision 60 ft., passive perception 13
Languages the languages it knew in life
Challenge 8 (3,900 XP)

Indomitable (1/Day). The champion can reroll a failed save. It must use the new roll.

Second Wind (1/Day). As a bonus action, the champion regains 15 hit points.

Sunlight Sensitivity. While in sunlight, the champion has disadvantage on attack rolls, as well as on Wisdom (Perception) checks that rely on sight.

Turn Resistance. The champion has advantage on saving throws against any effect that turns undead.

ACTIONS

Multiattack. The champion makes three weapon attacks. It can use its Life Drain in place of one melee attack.

Life Drain. *Melee Weapon Attack:* +6 to hit, reach 5 ft., one target. *Hit:* 9 (2d6 + 2) necrotic damage, and the target is grappled (escape DC 14). Until this grapple ends, the champion must use one hand to maintain the grapple, but can automatically hit the grappled creature with its Life Drain. The target must succeed on a DC 13 Constitution saving throw, or its hit point maximum is reduced by an amount equal to the damage taken. This reduction lasts until the target finishes a long rest. The target dies if this effect reduces its hit point maximum to 0.

A humanoid slain by this attack rises 24 hours later as a zombie under the champion's control, unless the humanoid is restored to life or its body is destroyed. The champion can have no more than 25 zombies under its control at one time.

Greatsword. *Melee Weapon Attack:* +6 to hit, reach 5 ft., one target. *Hit:* 10 (2d6 + 3) slashing damage.

Handaxe. *Melee or Ranged Weapon Attack:* +6 to hit, reach 5 ft. or range 30/60 ft., one target. *Hit:* 6 (1d6 + 3) slashing damage.

We know well to hate and fear wights as they do, of course, hate and envy us that still breathe. First hand accounts of wights are rare, as they are loathe to suffer victims to live. But what drives someone, perhaps even someone who was once human, to be so cold, so pitiless, so vain and greedy that it cannot know peace, even in death? I put to you that a wight is a creature that we should not hate but pity and, in this book, I aim to explore their damaged psyche and dark motives while I ask – what is the wight side of the undeath debate?

-Glim Gilforth, foreword from 'The Wight Side'

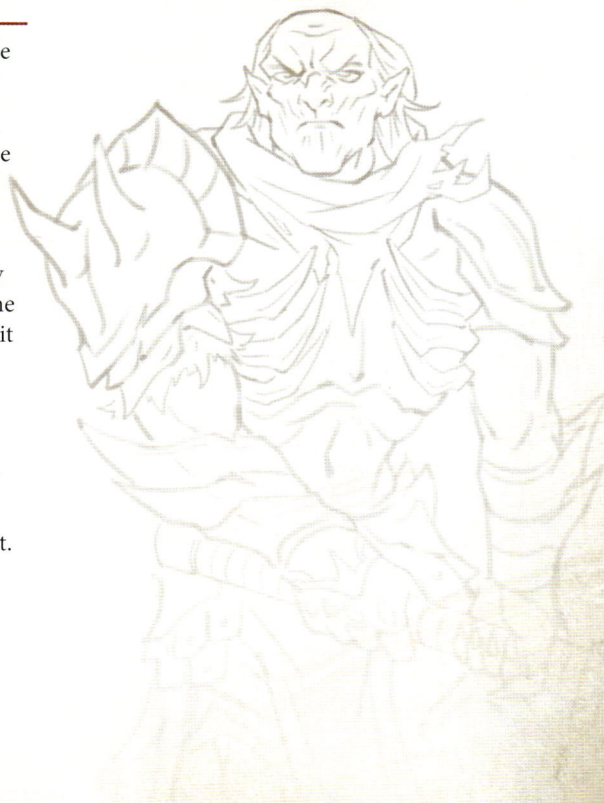

INSATIABLE EXECUTIONER

Medium undead, neutral evil

Armor Class 18 (plate)
Hit Points 187 (22d8 + 88)
Speed 30 ft.

STR	DEX	CON	INT	WIS	CHA
18 (+4)	10 (+0)	19 (+4)	11 (+0)	11 (+0)	16 (+3)

Skills Athletics +8, Perception +4
Damage Vulnerabilities radiant
Damage Resistances bludgeoning, piercing, and slashing from nonmagical attacks that aren't silvered
Damage Immunities poison, necrotic
Condition Immunities exhaustion, poisoned
Senses darkvision 60 ft., passive perception 10
Languages the languages it knew in life
Challenge 12 (8,400 XP)

Indomitable (2/Day). The executioner can reroll a failed save. It must use the new roll.

Second Wind (1/Day). As a bonus action, the executioner regains 20 hit points.

Sunlight Sensitivity. While in sunlight, the executioner has disadvantage on attack rolls, as well as on Wisdom (Perception) checks that rely on sight.

Turn Resistance. The executioner has advantage on saving throws against any effect that turns undead.

ACTIONS

Multiattack. The executioner makes four weapon attacks. It can use its Life Drain in place of one melee attack.

Life Drain. *Melee Weapon Attack:* +8 to hit, reach 5 ft., one target. *Hit:* 13 (3d6 + 3) necrotic damage, and the target is grappled (escape DC 16). Until this grapple ends, the executioner must use one hand to maintain the grapple, but can automatically hit the grappled creature with its Life Drain. The target must succeed on a DC 15 Constitution saving throw, or its hit point maximum is reduced by an amount equal to the damage taken. This reduction lasts until the target finishes a long rest. The target dies if this effect reduces its hit point maximum to 0.

A humanoid slain by this attack rises 24 hours later as a zombie under the executioner's control, unless the humanoid is restored to life or its body is destroyed. There is no limit to the number of zombies the executioner can control.

Greatsword. *Melee Weapon Attack:* +8 to hit, reach 5 ft., one target. *Hit:* 11 (2d6 + 4) slashing damage.

Handaxe. *Melee or Ranged Weapon Attack:* +8 to hit, reach 5 ft. or range 30/60 ft., one target. *Hit:* 7 (1d6 + 4) slashing damage.

LEGENDARY ACTIONS

The executioner can take 3 legendary actions, choosing from the options below. Only one legendary action option can be used at a time, and only at the end of another creature's turn. The executioner regains spent legendary actions at the start of its turn.

Attack. The executioner attacks with its greatsword or handaxe.

Breakthrough. The executioner moves up to its speed. It can move through the space of a single Large or smaller creature. If it does so, the creature must succeed on a DC 16 Strength saving throw, or be knocked prone and unable to make opportunity attacks against the executioner this turn.

Command Zombie. One zombie, under the control of the executioner, makes a melee attack against a creature of the executioner's choice.

Life Syphon (Costs 2 Actions). The executioner uses its Life Drain against a creature it is grappling. If the target fails its saving throw, the executioner regains a number of hit points equal to the damage dealt by the attack.

WIGHT MALIGNANT

Medium undead, neutral evil

Armor Class 16 (scale mail, shield)
Hit Points 58 (9d8 + 18)
Speed 30 ft.

STR	DEX	CON	INT	WIS	CHA
14 (+2)	10 (+0)	15 (+2)	10 (+0)	11 (+0)	17 (+3)

Skills Religion +3
Damage Vulnerabilities radiant
Damage Resistances bludgeoning, piercing, and slashing from nonmagical attacks that aren't silvered
Damage Immunities poison, necrotic
Condition Immunities exhaustion, poisoned
Senses darkvision 60 ft., passive perception 10
Languages the languages it knew in life
Challenge 5 (1,800 XP)

Draining Smite. When the malignant hits a creature with a melee weapon attack, the malignant can expend a spell slot to also hit the target with its Life Drain. If the malignant expends a spell slot of 2nd level or higher, its Life Drain deals 4 (1d8) extra damage for each level above 1st.

Spellcasting. The malignant is a 3rd level spellcaster. Its spellcasting ability is Charisma (spell save DC 13, +5 to hit with spell attacks). The malignant has the following paladin spells prepared:

1st level (4 slots): *command, detect magic, shield of faith, thunderous smite*

2nd level (2 slots): *find steed, magic weapon*

Sunlight Sensitivity. While in sunlight, the malignant has disadvantage on attack rolls, as well as on Wisdom (Perception) checks that rely on sight.

Turn Resistance. The malignant has advantage on saving throws against any effect that turns undead.

ACTIONS

Multiattack. The malignant makes two longsword attacks. If it is not wielding a shield, it can use its Life Drain in place of one melee attack.

Life Drain. *Melee Weapon Attack:* +5 to hit, reach 5 ft., one target. *Hit:* 6 (1d6 + 3) necrotic damage. The target must succeed on a DC 14 Constitution saving throw, or its hit point maximum is reduced by an amount equal to the necrotic damage taken. This reduction lasts until the target finishes a long rest. The target dies if this effect reduces its hit point maximum to 0.

A humanoid slain by this attack rises 24 hours later as a zombie under the malignant's control, unless the humanoid is restored to life or its body is destroyed. The malignant can have no more than 12 zombies under its control at one time.

Longsword. *Melee Weapon Attack:* +5 to hit, reach 5 ft., one target. *Hit:* 6 (1d8 + 2) slashing damage, or 7 (1d10 − 2) slashing damage, if used in two hands.

"I have never met a wight worth having a conversation with. Many people would kill for eternal life, and many have, so why waste your time being so damned gloomy?"

-Mihaelia Rhamonos, vampire

WIGHT DESPOILER

Medium undead, neutral evil

Armor Class 17 (half plate, shield)
Hit Points 112 (15d8 + 45)
Speed 30 ft.

STR	DEX	CON	INT	WIS	CHA
15 (+2)	10 (+0)	16 (+3)	10 (+0)	11 (+0)	18 (+4)

Skills Religion +3
Damage Vulnerabilities radiant
Damage Resistances bludgeoning, piercing, and slashing from nonmagical attacks that aren't silvered
Damage Immunities poison, necrotic
Condition Immunities exhaustion, poisoned
Senses darkvision 60 ft., passive perception 10
Languages the languages it knew in life
Challenge 7 (2,900 XP)

Draining Smite. When the despoiler hits a creature with a melee weapon attack, the despoiler can expend a spell slot to also hit the target with its Life Drain. If the despoiler expends a spell slot of 2nd level or higher, its Life Drain deals 4 (1d8) extra damage for each level above 1st.

Spellcasting. The despoiler is a 6th level spellcaster. Its spellcasting ability is Charisma (spell save DC 15, +7 to hit with spell attacks). The despoiler has the following paladin spells prepared:

1st level (4 slots): *command, detect magic, shield of faith, thunderous smite*

2nd level (3 slots): *find steed, magic weapon, zone of truth*

3rd level (3 slots): *dispel magic, elemental weapon, magic circle*

Sunlight Sensitivity. While in sunlight, the despoiler has disadvantage on attack rolls, as well as on Wisdom (Perception) checks that rely on sight.

Turn Resistance. The despoiler has advantage on saving throws against any effect that turns undead.

ACTIONS

Multiattack. The despoiler makes two longsword attacks. If it is not wielding a shield, it can use its Life Drain in place of one melee attack.

Life Drain. *Melee Weapon Attack:* +5 to hit, reach 5 ft., one target. *Hit:* 10 (2d6 + 4) necrotic damage. The target must succeed on a DC 15 Constitution saving throw, or its hit point maximum is reduced by an amount equal to the damage taken. This reduction lasts until the target finishes a long rest. The target dies if this effect reduces its hit point maximum to 0.

A humanoid slain by this attack rises 24 hours later as a zombie under the despoiler's control, unless the humanoid is restored to life or its body is destroyed. The despoiler can have no more than 25 zombies under its control at one time.

Longsword. *Melee Weapon Attack:* +5 to hit, reach 5 ft., one target. *Hit:* 6 (1d8 + 2) slashing damage, or 7 (1d10 + 2) slashing damage, if used in two hands.

Should I die without breath to curse, hear my words. I call upon you, o demon, whoever you are, to grant me once more my life. I shall pay any price, undertake any service, for the cold of the grave should not be mine and my deeds are not yet done.

-inscription on a lead curse tablet

Oathsworn Annihilator

Medium undead, neutral evil

Armor Class 20 (plate, shield)
Hit Points 157 (21d8 + 63)
Speed 30 ft.

STR	DEX	CON	INT	WIS	CHA
16 (+3)	10 (+0)	17 (+3)	10 (+0)	11 (+0)	19 (+4)

Skills Religion +4
Damage Vulnerabilities radiant
Damage Resistances bludgeoning, piercing, and slashing from nonmagical attacks that aren't silvered
Damage Immunities poison, necrotic
Condition Immunities exhaustion, poisoned
Senses darkvision 60 ft., passive perception 10
Languages the languages it knew in life
Challenge 12 (8,400 XP)

Draining Smite. When the annihilator hits a creature with a melee weapon attack, the annihilator can expend a spell slot to also hit the target with its Life Drain. If the annihilator expends a spell slot of 2nd level or higher, its Life Drain deals 4 (1d8) extra damage for each level above 1st.

Spellcasting. The annihilator is an 8th level spellcaster. Its spellcasting ability is Charisma (spell save DC 16, +8 to hit with spell attacks). The annihilator has the following paladin spells prepared:

1st level (4 slots): *command, detect magic, shield of faith, thunderous smite*

2nd level (3 slots): *find steed, magic weapon, zone of truth*

3rd level (3 slots): *dispel magic, elemental weapon, magic circle*

4th level (2 slots): *banishment, staggering smite*

Sunlight Sensitivity. While in sunlight, the annihilator has disadvantage on attack rolls, as well as on Wisdom (Perception) checks that rely on sight.

Turn Resistance. The annihilator has advantage on saving throws against any effect that turns undead.

Actions

Multiattack. The annihilator makes two longsword attacks. It can use its Life Drain in place of one melee attack.

Life Drain. *Melee Weapon Attack:* +7 to hit, reach 5 ft., one target. *Hit:* 14 (3d6 + 4) necrotic damage. The target must succeed on a DC 16 Constitution saving throw, or its hit point maximum is reduced by an amount equal to the damage taken. This reduction lasts until the target finishes a long rest. The target dies if this effect reduces its hit point maximum to 0.

A humanoid slain by this attack rises 24 hours later as a zombie under the annihilator's control, unless the humanoid is restored to life or its body is destroyed. There is no limit to the number of zombies the annihilator can control.

Longsword. *Melee Weapon Attack:* +7 to hit, reach 5 ft., one target. *Hit:* 7 (1d8 + 3) slashing damage, or 8 (1d10 + 3) slashing damage, if used in two hands.

Legendary Actions

The annihilator can take 3 legendary actions, choosing from the options below. Only one legendary action option can be used at a time, and only at the end of another creature's turn. The annihilator regains spent legendary actions at the start of its turn.

Attack. The annihilator makes one longsword attack. It can't use its Draining Smite with this attack.

Command Zombie. One zombie, under the control of the annihilator, makes a melee attack against a creature of the annihilator's choice.

Shield Up. The annihilator equips its shield if it is carrying, but not already wielding, it and gains an additional +2 bonus to its armor class until the start of its next turn.

Cleansing Touch (Costs 2 Actions). The annihilator ends one spell on itself or a willing creature it touches.

Frost Wight

Medium undead, neutral evil

Armor Class 17 (half-plate)
Hit Points 165 (22d8 + 66)
Speed 40 ft.

STR	DEX	CON	INT	WIS	CHA
19 (+4)	15 (+2)	16 (+3)	10 (+0)	12 (+1)	18 (+4)

Saving Throws Int +5, Wis +6
Skills Arcana +5, Perception +6
Damage Vulnerabilities radiant, fire
Damage Resistances bludgeoning, piercing, and slashing from nonmagical attacks that aren't silvered
Damage Immunities cold, poison, necrotic
Condition Immunities exhaustion, poisoned
Senses darkvision 60 ft., passive perception 16
Languages Common, Aquan, Abyssal
Challenge 16 (15,000 XP)

Frost Stride. Difficult terrain composed of ice or snow doesn't cost the frost wight extra moment, and, while on ice, it ignores any penalties or disadvantage to Strength and Dexterity checks or saving throws for being on a slippery surface.

Legendary Resistance (3/Day). When the frost wight fails a saving throw, it can choose to succeed instead.

Sunlight Sensitivity. While in sunlight, the frost wight has disadvantage on attack rolls, as well as on Wisdom (Perception) checks that rely on sight.

Turn Resistance. The frost wight has advantage on saving throws against any effect that turns undead.

Winter Sight. The frost wight can see clearly in areas obscured by falling snow, flurries, snow storms, and fog.

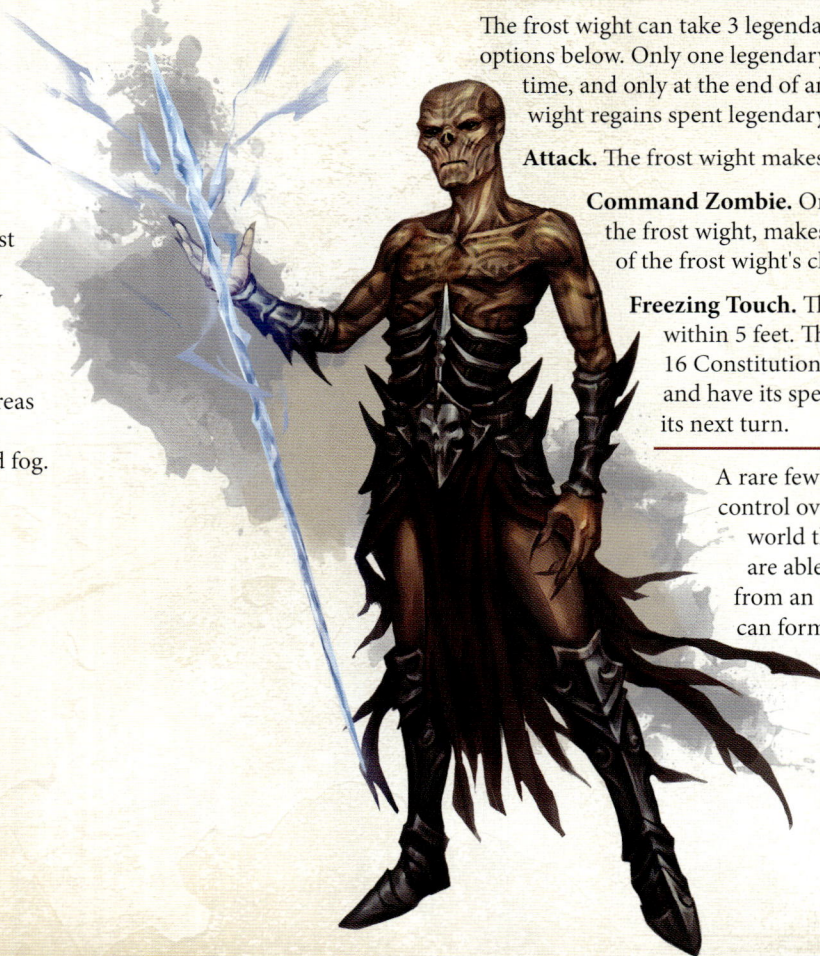

Actions

Multiattack. The frost wight makes two weapon attacks with its longsword or ice javelin. It can use its Draining Cold in place of one melee attack.

Draining Cold. *Melee Weapon Attack:* +9 to hit, reach 5 ft., one target. *Hit:* 17 (4d6 + 3) necrotic damage. The target must succeed on a DC 16 Constitution saving throw, or its hit point maximum is reduced by an amount equal to the damage taken. This reduction lasts until the target finishes a long rest. The target dies if this effect reduces its hit point maximum to 0.

A creature, other than an undead or construct, slain by this attack rises 24 hours later as a zombie under the frost wight's control, unless the creature is restored to life or its body is destroyed. There is no limit to the number of zombies the frost wight can control. Zombies created this way are immune to cold damage.

Longsword. *Melee Weapon Attack:* +9 to hit, reach 5 ft., one target. *Hit:* 7 (1d8 + 3) slashing damage, plus 14 (4d6) cold damage, or 8 (1d10 + 3) slashing damage plus 14 (4d6) cold damage, if used in two hands.

Ice Javelin. *Melee or Ranged Weapon Attack:* +9 to hit, reach 5 ft. or range 30/120 ft., one target. *Hit:* 7 (1d6 + 4) piercing damage, plus 13 (4d6) cold damage.

Legendary Actions

The frost wight can take 3 legendary actions, choosing from the options below. Only one legendary action option can be used at a time, and only at the end of another creature's turn. The frost wight regains spent legendary actions at the start of its turn.

Attack. The frost wight makes a longsword or ice javelin attack.

Command Zombie. One zombie, under the control of the frost wight, makes a melee attack against a creature of the frost wight's choice.

Freezing Touch. The frost wight touches a creature within 5 feet. The target must succeed on a DC 16 Constitution saving throw, or be incapacitated and have its speed reduced to 0 until the end of its next turn.

A rare few wights have a greater level of control over their sapping of life from the world than their kin. These **frost wights** are able to siphon away the warmth from an area with such precision that they can form weapons of ice from the frozen moisture of the air.

"Anything to report?" whispered Thaddeus, returning with a handful of blackberries. We had picked the immediate area clean, so he was having to travel further afield (and didn't trust me to do so, after I brought back yew berries by mistake).

"Nothing. Ox came to the entrance about half an hour ago, but went straight back. Seems like they're waiting for something, but it hasn't happened yet, whatever it is. Remind me not to come back as a wight. Their un-lives are incredibly dull."

This was our third day hidden in the bushes overlooking the wights' barrow. After our previous unpleasant encounters, Thaddeus had reasoned that The Shrouded One was sending out wights as emissaries to recruit allies and oversee its far-flung operations. Having no ties binding them to one particular location, and the flexibility of free will, wights made the perfect lieutenants, he told me. Thus armed with our hypothesis, we set out into the field to put it to the test or, more specifically, to find a wight. After what I suspect leant towards the shorter end of the usual timescale (having no frame of reference for the average amount of time it takes to find a wight), we came upon a path through the undergrowth of dying vegetation, a blackened and blighted trail that was sure to lead us to the creature we sought.

The track ended at the entrance to an ancient burial mound, the stone blocking the entrance having been thrown aside. Unwilling to blunder into a wight's lair blindly, Thaddeus suggested we watch and wait to see what information we could glean. It quickly became apparent that the barrow was home to two wights, neither of whom seemed entirely happy with the company, but both of whom, we quickly learned, were indeed there on the instruction of The Shrouded One. Not having been formally introduced, I gave them names, more to alleviate boredom than anything else.

"What weapon did Ox have? Anything we've not seen yet?" Thaddeus had been reluctant to start using my nicknames, but soon came round, with no other clear way to distinguish between them. Perhaps he was bored too.

"Nasty bit of ironmongery. Big, heavy chopper," I said, helpfully.

"Falchion. 'Big, heavy chopper' is a falchion. Probably got more gear stashed deeper in. Expecting trouble."

Such was the nature of what passed for conversation over the last few days. In fact, when a third wight came stalking up to the entrance, I was positively delighted to have another undead killing machine in close proximity as a welcome change of pace.

"Why does the master have us waiting here?" asked the wight I called Ox, of the newcomer. He had been the first to exit the barrow. The other, (older, female, and mean-looking; I'd named her Beldam), lingered in the doorway, as if weighing up whether the exchange would be worthy of her time.

"Heard Loach was sniffing around. The monster hunter."

"What's one mortal? All be dead soon. Isn't that the plan?"

"That mortal has killed two of The Hand. To allow the filth to keep breathing is an insult to the great one." I decided Coxcomb would be a suitable name for the newcomer.

Beldam gave a dry cough that might have been a snort of laughter.

"Something to say?"

"You are young. Your faith is endearing. Your fanaticism so... *lively.*"

Coxcomb stiffened. Clearly this was a grave insult.

"Stand down, boy. You keep going as long as I have, and all the doom-bringers start to blend together. The Shrouded One isn't the first, and I'll be damned again if he's the last."

"Blasphemy! The master shall scourge the filth of mortality from this world. His shall be an empire eternal!"

"Fine, fine. So where are we to go once the hunter's dealt with?"

"We're to bring the body to the grave at the site of the battle of burning hills. Last battle of the mortals' war. In a valley to the north. The master waits there. He's got plans for him."

If Thaddeus had any strong feelings about whatever plans the wraith might have for his corpse, he gave no indication as the trio retreated into the barrow. My burgeoning resentment at being overlooked had dissipated quickly, though.

"Ready?" asked Thaddeus, his eyes on the barrow.

I sputtered something which might have resembled "what?", if you were generous with your interpretation.

"Well, they're not going to stroll out while the sun's up. Got to take them now. Ambush them while they think they have the advantage."

"There's no *think* about it, Thaddeus," I said, quite surprising myself. "They outnumber us, they harbor an unnatural hatred of the living, and it's *dark*."

Thaddeus grunted.

"It seems unnecessary, anyway. We just found out where the wraith is. I say we head there and leave the wights be. Live and let... um... Well, you get the point."

"They called themselves 'The Hand'," growled Thaddeus. "How many fingers does a hand have?"

I resisted saying something pithy. Thaddeus raised his hand, fingers spread, lowered two of them with an air of significance, and pointed the remaining three towards the wights' hiding place. Two down, three to go.

"We get rid of them, the wraith loses its top lieutenants. No one to take up the mantle if we succeed in putting The Shrouded One down. And, if we fail, we've given the next poor bugger to try a head start."

Reluctant as I was, I could not deny the logic therein. Nevertheless, I couldn't allow us to storm in without calling upon any advantages we had. Without thinking, my hand went to my pack, where the lich's orb still resided. Through the trials, emotional and physical, of the last few days, it had slipped my mind to mention it. It still gave off a faint glow, which I was quick to throw a cloak over in fear of revealing our position.

"Can we use this? Maybe boost it or something? Blind them?"

I attempted to recall the strange, guttural phrase the lich had uttered. It was of no language I had ever heard, yet I managed a crude approximation. When I did so with my hand on the orb, it flared with light, which rapidly dissipated. By repeating the phrase, I was able to extend the blazing light, though it ceased the moment I did. Thaddeus relaxed the furrow that had appeared in his brow at the sight of his old enemy's weapon, and he nodded in assent of the plan, scant as it was.

The battlelines thus drawn, we stormed the barrow; myself behind, attempting to not tie my tongue in knots around the chanted phrase, Thaddeus ahead, sword at the ready. Despite the size of the hill, the chambers within were cramped. I am unversed in military tactics, but I would describe it as 'defensible', and I grew ever more glad that I did not allow Thaddeus to run in unaided. The light was a great comfort, as though I were armed with the sun, and life itself, against the dead.

Ox was the first. He rounded a corner ready to fight, filling the corridor with undead bulk. He reeled back from the light, as though in physical pain (I myself found it difficult to look directly at it; an effect I can only assume was heightened for these creatures of darkness). My own eyes cast downwards, I followed close at Thaddeus' heels, trying to make as little of a nuisance of myself as I could, while also thrusting the light as close to the wight's face as I could. Ox bellowed like his namesake as he attacked; blinded as he was, he swung wildly to compensate, an inefficient tactic in the limited space available. Thaddeus was not cowed, and struck at the openings which the sightless foe could not defend. Soon, he bellowed no more, and slumped against the tunnel wall. Three down, two to go.

Beldam came next. Not one to be drawn in as easily as her compatriot, she attempted to slay us from afar. The light threw off her aim, however, and the arrows skittered short, or whistled over our heads to break against the walls. It also masked Thaddeus' approach, and he sprung from it as an assassin would from shadow.

"You're not the first," she croaked, as she parried with her bow.

"But I will be the last," he replied, burying his sword in her chest. Four down, one to go.

Coxcomb was waiting for us. His eyes closed, he looked at peace.

"Loach. I would pity you, were I capable. I give thanks that the great one cleansed me of such weaknesses."

"Pity?"

"To be blind to salvation, when it is offered. To reject the chance to be freed from mortal frailty, from sin, from suffering. To turn your back on a world scoured of the injustices of life."

I felt something grab at my ankle, and a cold, searing pain. As I gasped, the light faltered, and the orb slipped from my grasp. I glanced down to see Beldam's face, frozen in a sneer as her last strength left her, and we were plunged into darkness.

"Blind to the hopelessness of your position," Coxcomb continued in the darkness, his voice echoing in the empty chamber. "Our numbers only grow with each village we pass, with each grave we uncover, with each man, woman, and child uplifted to the cause. The Shrouded One's mercy extends even to his most hated enemies, Thaddeus."

Thaddeus, I sensed, was listening intently. I fumbled on the ground in search of the orb and, to my horror, discovered only shattered fragments.

"Life is a disease," continued the voice from all around us. "A devouring, multiplying plague. The rising–"

"You talk too much," said Thaddeus. There was a swish and, a second later, a thud as something heavy and meaty fell to the ground.

"Five down." *An army to go.*

WILL-O'-WISPS

he light dances, faint, but made enticing by the surrounding gloom. The dark, scummed water glows green with its reflection. It dances, always so close, always out of reach, as if daring itself to be caught. The water grows deeper, the trees thicker. Another light appears, and another, bobbing, dancing, dazzling. Then, suddenly, darkness, no up or down, only the rising water. Voices whisper from the shadows all around, too quiet to make out, but gleeful, and hungry.

Lost in the darkness, the weary and wandering reach out, hearts open, for hope. Much to their surprise, out of the disorienting gloom bobs a faint light. The traveler smiles warmly, imagining themselves finally nearing warmth and rest. Little do they know that, as they follow that dancing guide, the only rest awaiting them will be that of the grave.

Seemingly innocuous, and perhaps even inviting, will-o'-wisps present themselves as drifting points of light in the darkness guiding lost travelers to safety. What little evidence there is suggests otherwise, for most who choose to follow those faint beacons are no more.

Will-o'-wisps appear infrequently in folklore and, where they do appear, the information about them is fairly accurate, consisting largely of the advice, "don't follow the lights". Some additional details are likely apocryphal, however, namely that the first will-o'-wisp formed when 'the wickedest man that e'er there was' was found to be too evil, even for the devils of the deepest hell, and was cast back to the material with only a glowing ember to light his way in the darkness. This original 'Will of the wisp' (or 'Jack of the lantern', depending on the storyteller) lured unwary travelers to their doom among the marshlands, it is true, but is likely a fictitious character, created long after the fact.

ORIGIN

Will-o'-wisps are formed where beings die miserably in areas suffused with magic, which interferes with the spirit passing on or becoming a ghost. Subtle variations of wisp exist, governed by the overriding emotion experienced by the dying soul, and each seeks to perpetuate that same emotion; fear, anguish, despair, or rage. Wisps feed on these emotions, growing stronger as they absorb them and, in so doing, draining the life from their prey. Particular strength and relish is gained from the dying breaths of those consumed by their chosen emotion.

Beings of pure emotion, will-o'-wisps have no vestige of their original personality left and exist only to spread their torment. Appearing as lights in the darkness, they lure unwary travelers astray, leading them towards hazards or dangerous creatures, or simply getting them so hopelessly lost that they will perish just as surely.

ENVIRONMENT

Will-o'-wisps linger in the magic-infused places that birthed them, areas upon which death and sadness lay thick and heavy as fog. Being generally unwilling to engage in combat with prey not physically or emotionally brought low, they make use of existing dangers to weaken their targets. Bogs and marshes are their most common habitat; confusing and repetitive terrain one could easily get lost in, and full of deep, sucking pools eager to ensnare and suffocate. Concealed cliff edges and pitfalls might also attract attendant wisps, especially those which are likely to fatally injure and cripple without killing outright, allowing an extended agony for the wisps to revel in.

Their method of luring with light requires some level of darkness in order to be effective. Some simply emerge at twilight and hunt through the night, but those who dwell in shadowed forests, caves, swamps, or areas of constant fog or mist, are able to work tirelessly throughout the day. Places of perpetual twilight therefore birth a large population of wisps, as twice the victims can be led astray and harvested.

ROLEPLAYING WILL-O'-WISPS

Wisps are intelligent and can speak, though they rarely do so, and rarer still do they truly converse. For the most part, they use short, simple phrases in order to lure and pacify with quiet, child-like voices; the juxtaposition of their innocent voices and depraved actions generally considered quite disturbing. Many remain silent until their true nature is made clear, using their voices only to mock and terrify their prey.

Wisps are unlikely to be reasoned with, with no real goal beyond feasting on whatever emotion drives them, though a few might be willing to allow victims to leave alive if there is good reason to believe a greater feast would come of it (for example, if said victim promised to direct unwary travelers towards the wisp's territory in future).

COMBAT TACTICS

While they often end up pursuing the same prey, will-o'-wisps do not truly work together. Groups mob together out of convenience and coincidence. When multiple wisps attempt to lure the same traveler, they are even more likely to become isolated and lost, and so all can share in the spoils. Once a target is at their mercy, all wisps in the area will be drawn to their suffering, and they will descend upon it in a feeding frenzy, all seeking to drink in as much anguish as possible, before spreading out again to watch for the next potential victim.

In a similar vein, wisps can often be found around the lairs of more powerful monsters (especially if natural hazards are less common in the area). The wisps lead prey towards the lair and weaken the victim while the monster dispatches it and feeds. Such a symbiotic relationship benefits both parties though, if enough wisps form in the area, they may end up overwhelming and devouring their erstwhile ally in a feeding frenzy.

WILL-O'-WISP ENCOUNTERS

d4	CR	Encounter
1	5	**Pale Fright:** 5 Ghostflames
2	6	**Glowing Desire:** 4 Wisps of Yearning
3	10	**Flickering Anxiety:** 1 Red Wisp, 4 Ghostflames
4	15	**Incandescent Deathwish:** 2 Red Wisps, 3 Wisps of Yearning, 6 Ghostflames

Oh come to the end of the road, my friend
And fear not the dark of the night.
We've a candle to guide you the way, my friend
And you'll soon have your own little light.

-from 'Candles of the Grave', popular song

GHOSTFLAME
Tiny undead, chaotic evil

Armor Class 18
Hit Points 25 (10d4)
Speed 0 ft., fly 40 ft. (hover)

STR	DEX	CON	INT	WIS	CHA
1 (-5)	26 (+8)	10 (+0)	11 (+0)	14 (+2)	13 (+1)

Damage Resistances acid, cold, lightning, necrotic, thunder; bludgeoning, piercing, and slashing from nonmagical attacks
Damage Immunities fire, poison
Condition Immunities exhaustion, grappled, paralyzed, poisoned, prone, restrained, unconscious
Senses darkvision 120 ft., passive Perception 12
Languages the languages it knew in life
Challenge 2 (450 XP)

Ephemeral. The ghostflame can't wear or carry anything.

Incorporeal Movement. The ghostflame can move through other creatures and objects as if they were difficult terrain. It takes 5 (1d10) force damage if it ends its turn inside an object.

Nightmare Drain. As a bonus action, the ghostflame can target one sleeping or unconscious creature it can see within 5 feet. The target must succeed on a DC 11 Wisdom saving throw against this magic, or experience horrific nightmares, taking 7 (2d6) psychic damage. Additionally, the ghostflame regains a number of hit points equal to the damage dealt. A sleeping creature doesn't wake up after taking damage from this ability.

Variable Illumination. The ghostflame sheds bright light in a radius of between 10 and 30 feet, and dim light in a radius of an equal number of feet. The ghostflame can change the radius as a bonus action.

ACTIONS

Ignite. *Melee Spell Attack:* +4 to hit, reach 5 ft., one creature. *Hit:* 4 (1d8) fire damage. If the target is a creature, it must succeed on a DC 12 Wisdom saving throw, or catch fire. While on fire, a creature takes 4 (1d8) fire damage at the start of each of its turns. At the end of each of its turns, a burning creature can repeat the saving throw, ending the effect on itself on a success. The fire is ghostly in nature and can't be extinguished by water or mundane means.

Invisibility. The ghostflame, and its light, magically turn invisible until the ghostflame attacks or uses its Nightmare Drain. The ghostflame must concentrate to maintain its invisibility, like concentrating on a spell.

Ghostflames form from the souls of those who died in intense fear. To propagate, they psychically attack the sleeping and unconscious, forcing them to experience terrible – and sometimes deadly – nightmares. While they prefer to attack only in dreams, they can summon ethereal flames to engulf conscious targets, should they have to.

WISP OF YEARNING

Tiny undead, chaotic evil

Armor Class 18
Hit Points 37 (15d4)
Speed 0 ft., fly 40 ft. (hover) ft.

STR	DEX	CON	INT	WIS	CHA
1 (-5)	26 (+8)	10 (+0)	13 (+1)	15 (+2)	21 (+5)

Damage Resistances acid, cold, fire, necrotic, thunder; bludgeoning, piercing, and slashing from nonmagical attacks
Damage Immunities lightning, poison
Condition Immunities exhaustion, grappled, paralyzed, poisoned, prone, restrained, unconscious
Senses darkvision 120 ft., passive Perception 9
Languages the languages it knew in life
Challenge 3 (700 XP)

Consume Desire. As a bonus action, the wisp can target a creature within 30 feet that has been charmed by the wisp. The target takes 7 (2d6) psychic damage, or 14 (4d6) psychic damage, if the target is within 5 feet of the wisp. The wisp regains a number of hit points equal to the damage dealt. While charmed, the target is unaware of this damage.

Ephemeral. The wisp can't wear or carry anything.

Incorporeal Movement. The wisp can move through other creatures and objects as if they were difficult terrain. It takes 5 (1d10) force damage if it ends its turn inside an object.

Variable Illumination. The wisp sheds bright light in a radius of between 10 and 30 feet, and dim light in a radius of an equal number of feet. The wisp can change the radius as a bonus action.

ACTIONS

Shock. *Melee Spell Attack:* +4 to hit, reach 5 ft., one creature. *Hit:* 7 (2d6) lightning damage.

Image of Desire. The wisp magically learns of a deep desire of a creature it can see within 40 feet. It creates an illusion around itself of a creature the target desires to be close to. For example, this can be a lost loved one, the subject of unrequited romantic feelings, or simply a creature that appears attractive and sexually desirable. The wisp's voice sounds appropriate to the illusion. The wisp must concentrate to maintain the illusion, like concentrating on a spell.

At the start of each of its turns, the target must succeed on a DC 16 Wisdom saving throw. On a failure, the creature is charmed by the wisp for as long as it maintains the illusion. While charmed, the creature must obey the wisp's requests, provided these requests don't put the creature in obvious danger, or require it to harm its allies.

Invisibility. The wisp, and its light, magically turn invisible until the wisp attacks or uses its Consume Desire. The wisp must concentrate to maintain its invisibility, like concentrating on a spell.

Wisps of yearning pulse gently with the rhythm of a calm heartbeat, aiming to put their prey at ease. They form from souls whose last thoughts were yearning for another, and lure in more victims by appearing as a vision of whoever they desire most, before feeding off their unfulfilled longing.

Lot 24
A daring and alternative lighting piece. Consisting of a captured wisp in a reinforced glass container, it is sure to be the talk of any gathering, combining unpredictable thrills with ethereal beauty.
Disclaimer. Do not position this item close to sleepers. Do not listen to the whispers. DO NOT OPEN THE JAR.

-listing from The New Silvercleft Auction House

RED WISP
Huge undead, chaotic evil

Armor Class 16
Hit Points 105 (14d12 + 14)
Speed 0 ft., fly 50 ft. (hover)

STR	DEX	CON	INT	WIS	CHA
8 (-1)	22 (+6)	12 (+1)	8 (-1)	15 (+2)	18 (+4)

Damage Resistances acid, cold, fire, necrotic, thunder; bludgeoning, piercing, and slashing from nonmagical attacks
Damage Immunities lightning, poison
Condition Immunities exhaustion, grappled, paralyzed, poisoned, prone, restrained, unconscious
Senses darkvision 120 ft., passive Perception 12
Languages the languages it knew in life
Challenge 9 (5,000 XP)

Ephemeral. The red wisp can't wear or carry anything.

Fear Leech. As a bonus action, the red wisp feeds on the fear of all creatures within 60 feet. Each frightened creature, within range, must succeed on a DC 15 Wisdom saving throw, or take 21 (6d6) psychic damage. Additionally, the red wisp regains 10 (3d6) hit points for each creature that fails its saving throw.

Incorporeal Movement. The red wisp can move through other creatures and objects as if they were difficult terrain. It takes 5 (1d10) force damage if it ends its turn inside an object.

Variable Illumination. The red wisp sheds bright light in a radius of between 30 and 60 feet, and dim light in a radius of an equal number of feet. The red wisp can change the radius as a bonus action.

ACTIONS

Shock. *Melee Spell Attack:* +8 to hit, reach 5 ft., one creature. *Hit:* 13 (3d8) lightning damage.

Lightning Strike (Recharge 5-6). The red wisp fires a red bolt of lightning in a 60-foot line that is 5 feet wide. Each creature in the area must make a DC 17 Dexterity saving throw, taking 27 (6d8) lightning damage on a failed save, or half as much damage on a successful one.

Invisibility. The red wisp, and its light, magically turn invisible until the red wisp attacks or uses its Lightning Strike. The red wisp must concentrate to maintain its invisibility, like concentrating on a spell.

Frightening Flash (While Invisible Only). The red wisp becomes visible for a moment, flashing with its eerie, red light. Creatures within the radius of the red wisp's bright light must succeed on a DC 15 Wisdom saving throw, or become frightened for 1 minute. At the end of each of its turns, a frightened creature can repeat the saving throw, ending the effect on itself on a success.

There is little subtle about **red wisps**. These enormous wisps are formed from souls who died consumed by frustration, fear, and rage, with their size and power making them more than able to extend these feelings to their victims.

WARNING – WISPS DWELL IN THIS AREA
DO NOT travel alone.
DO NOT lose sight of your companion.
DO NOT follow lights or unseen voices.
Trust only these signs to guide you.
Taking risks endangers your life and the lives of others after your death.

-sign on the border of Auld Claggie swampland

As we progressed north, the ground became progressively softer and wetter, and our travel slowed until we found ourselves on the outskirts of fully-fledged swampland. A tangle of briar and stunted trees, combined with the flatness of the land, made it next to impossible to tell how far the mire stretched before us. We made camp on the driest piece of land we could (a rocky outcrop, which was no more comfortable for its lack of moisture), as Thaddeus deliberated.

"Through's the most direct route. Could be all manner of foulness lurking in there, though. Could chart a path 'round, but it'll add who knows how long to the journey. What do you think?"

It was rare that Thaddeus asked my opinion on how to proceed; I suspected he was quietly impressed with my keeping a cool head before storming the barrow, though he gave no indication of it whatsoever. Wanting to continue this impression of unflappability in the face of danger, I voted we push through.

The next morning, we passed the treeline and into the swamp.

Almost immediately, the dense canopy of sickly boughs plunged us into cool, damp twilight. We struggled to keep our course; what little sun we could make out was so feeble, we could barely tell the time of day, let alone our bearing. Mist clung low to the sodden earth, obscuring all manner of snags and crannies, eager for an ankle to turn. Even on seemingly level ground, pockets of muck sucked at our boots and, on more than one occasion, I had to be pulled out by the armpits by Thaddeus. The hours stretched on in exhausting, wet, gray monotony under an unchanging, wet, gray sky.

We made camp on the first night, and Thaddeus had the idea of improvising hammocks to give us a brief respite from the damp. It seemed such an obvious course of action that it was a wonder we hadn't thought of it before. As I searched through my pack, I found cloaks and canvas already knotted together with ropes. While still marveling at this strange occurrence, I began preparing our meager dinner, and found we were short of ingredients; I estimated we had gone through three days of rations. I slept fitfully.

When I awoke, Thaddeus was gone.

It was darker than before, though I do not know if the sun was lower in the sky, or the sullen clouds were thicker. The thin mist had become a fog and, in the fog, I saw a light. My first thought was that Thaddeus had started off to scout a path, torch in hand, and I hurried to meet him. Hurry as I might, though, stumbling over the uneven ground all the while, the light seemed no closer. I called out to him, but there was no response. I thought it best to return to camp but, try as I might, I could not retrace my steps. I walked a few, wide circles, passing the same gnarled trees, and finally accepted that I was lost.

"We can help," whispered a soft voice in the fog. It was faint, childlike, almost shy. A faint light glimmered.

"Help me find Thaddeus?" I asked.

"Yes, Thaddeus. Thaddeus sent us. Follow." And, like a fool, I did.

What trail there was soon disappeared. The light danced over deep pools of muck, and I trudged after it. I fell, but the light was encouraging.

"Keep going," it whispered.

"Yes, keep going." It was joined by another timid whisper, and another bobbing light. "We'll lead you to Thaddeus."

And so it went. Sometimes the light I followed winked out, but there was always another to take its place, though they often seemed to switch direction. My attention split between keeping my feet and keeping the light (or lights) in view, I paid no heed to where I was going, and would not have been able to find my way back if I tried. I began to wonder if I would end my days wandering in the swamp. The ground sloped away, step by step, almost imperceptibly, until I found myself at the bottom of a hollow. I could see only deep pools of green-tinged water.

"Where are we going?" I called out to the lights. There were several of them now, buoys in the ocean of gray fog.

"Where are we going?" the mocking reply came. Another repeated it, and another, each growing in theatrical panic.

I stumbled backwards and tripped on something hard, lodged beneath the fetid water. Thinking I might be able to use whatever it was to defend myself, I reached into the muck and dredged it out. It was a human jawbone, dripping with algae.

"Failed as a writer," said a flickering, turquoise voice. "Thinks it's an adventurer now."

I got back to my feet, numbly. The water was up to my knees.

"Not so brave now it's all alone," said another, pale green. It was right; I had been in danger before, but it had always been obvious and immediate, and Thaddeus had been with me.

"It's giving up. They all give up. It's not special." The water was up to my navel. I could feel more bones beneath my feet. Dimly, I wondered how many had preceded me. Would I become a light as well? Would my legacy be to lead more bones to the pit?

"Not far now. You're almost there."

The water covered my chest, shockingly cold. It was soothing. Everything would be washed away.

Then the light brightened. It grew so bright I could hardly bear to look at it. Not tempting, but searing, and painful, filling and consuming all vision. There was nothing in the world but the light. It burnt away all the rest.

"Come with me." It was not an invitation, it was a command. With no other option, and driven half mad, I blindly followed once more. In time, we came to a clearing, lit not by the otherworldly glow of wisps, or the glare of my savior, but by the sun. The sight of it was almost as welcome to me as the sight of Thaddeus emerging from the treeline. Caked in mud and filth, he was a monstrous sight, but it was all I could do not to run and embrace him.

He eyed the glowing figure warily. It was roughly the shape of a man, though any more details were difficult to make out; it was like gazing at the sun.

"Your friend is safe, as you requested," it said, dispassionately.

"You alright?" Thaddeus turned his attention to me.

I told him what had happened, of my ordeal with the wisps. It transpired that he had been led astray as well, that the glowing figure had found him, and that he had sent it to seek me out, trusting that he would be able to find his own way to safety. I asked what the wisps had said to him.

"Nothing. Didn't say anything." He had a great many talents, but lying was not one of them, and he could not disguise the mud that coated him up to his shoulders. I couldn't help but wonder what hardships he had suffered, but my curiosity on the matter was quashed by my joy at our reunion, and the question of our new companion.

"What is it, Thaddeus?" I whispered.

"That," he said, distastefully, "is a wraith."

WRAITHS

he faltering candle flames gutter and die, as all light and life must, in the oppressive presence of the spirit. The darkness deepens, and heat seems sucked from the air, or is driven away, fleeing before it. The spirit at the center is darker still, not the mere absence of light, but an emanation of pressing blackness. The form of a face or, perhaps, a skull, can be glimpsed, as though shrouded in linen and, from within, the pinpoints of its shining eyes, a sickly gleam which illuminates nothing of the swirling cloud.

The wraith is one of the most powerful forms of incorporeal undead and, rightly, the most feared. The twisted remnants of anguished souls, wraiths harbor a burning hatred for the living, unmatched by even the most bitter of wights.

Wraiths possess only the barest hint of a humanoid form, appearing as swirling maelstroms of shadow (or perhaps light is simply made dimmer by their immediate presence), save for the baleful eyes peering from the gloom. Within the darkness, a figure can sometimes be glimpsed, draped in billowing, cloth-like smoke, resembling a burial shroud.

Wraiths are seldom spoken of by common folk, for the prickling feeling of fear that the mere mention of them evokes. Some more superstitious types believe that simply bringing up the name of such a spirit is an invitation to misfortune, or could even invoke an attack from a wraith upon the speaker. Wraiths are seen as an embodiment of all the misfortunes in the world, a relentless, spreading evil from which most can only cower and pray to escape notice. Rather than a foe to be fought, a wraith is viewed more like a hurricane; a terrible, implacable event to be endured or, preferably, fled from at the first sign.

ORIGIN

The most common variety of wraith forms when an individual who has pledged their soul to some dark pact dies. This may be a conscious choice on the part of the other entities involved, keeping the soul from death to act as an undead servant, or may be a simple by-product of the pact itself, if it is wicked enough that death itself spits back the soul in disgust, or as punishment. The existence of a wraith, while powerful, is clearly a miserable one.

Wraiths can also form in areas permeated by restless spirits. Where enough unhappy souls gather, they may be swept together, feeding off the growing negative energy, until they collapse in on themselves, concentrating their combined misery into a singular wraith. Similar wraiths can come into existence where multiple people died in a single, traumatic event, with wraiths of entire villages or armies coalescing after plague, slaughter or disaster.

Such wraiths might remember the occasional glimpse of the individuals that formed it but, on the whole, is a new entity, consumed only by its tormented existence and the need to spread pain and death. Very rarely, if a particularly good individual's soul went into the creation of a wraith, glimpses of this unparalleled goodness might, over time, build up like the abrasive grains of sand which eventually form a pearl (presumably, much to the consternation of the oyster). Eventually, these glimpses may build enough to force an epiphany, wherein the wraith's very nature is changed into a powerful force for good. Such 'bright wraiths' are semi-legendary, assumed by many to be a flight of fancy, a device invented to comfort children during winter nights, but multiple sources suggest such beings exist, dedicated to putting to rest their darker, and far more numerous, brethren.

Environment

Wraiths tend to remain in the area they were raised, though they have the ability to wander freely.

Much like the presence of an apex predator, such as a lion or manticore, indicates the health of an ecosystem, so the presence of a wraith suggests a booming presence of undead in their vicinity. The unstable necrotic energy inherent in a wraith's very existence seeps into the environment around it and grows in intensity if allowed to remain. Unconsecrated dead spontaneously rise, holy magic dims, and a sense of dread and despair pervades wherever they settle, leaching the positive emotions out of any living things nearby. Those living within a wraith's influence will feel lethargic, remembering past happiness dimly, and with great effort, as if it happened only in a distant story. Those who die in such an area (through unrelated means, driven to suicide, or simply weakening and fading away) are likely to rise as spirits themselves; specters under the wraith's control, or ghosts fuelled by their own deep unhappiness.

Bright wraiths do not suffuse an area with light or happiness, but will stem the tide of darkness brought on by a wraith and, given time, begin to reverse the effects. Common undead find the presence of a bright wraith abhorrent and will avoid areas where they reside, possibly seeking refuge closer to their darker kin. In this way, a bright wraith in the area can, unintentionally, force a grand confrontation between the living and the dead, gathering the region's undead around a single figurehead if it does not eliminate a wraith quickly.

Roleplaying Wraiths

Many undead are compelled to destroy the living where they come across them, but wraiths feel hatred beyond this. Anything with a beating heart is anathema to them and, rather than simply ending life where they find it, they seek to snuff out life on a grand scale. To a wraith, the world is not a tolerable place to exist unless all life has been scourged from it and, unlike many with such grandiose ambitions, wraiths often have the powers and numbers to put them into effect.

There can be no negotiating or reasoning with a wraith. They see themselves as commanders in a war against life itself. The only living being acceptable is one which submits itself, willing to turn against its fellows in order to survive, and even these shall have their souls ripped out to serve the wraith as specters at the smallest hint of displeasure.

Combat Tactics

A wraith will rarely be found without a surrounding contingent of lesser undead in its thrall. It has no compunctions about sacrificing its minions, knowing that it can easily replace them, and has the intelligence to utilize their abilities to the greatest effect.

Wraiths will attack without mercy, but see themselves as too important to their cause to risk their own destruction. A wraith will patiently wear down a foes' resolve and weaken them, before attacking in force when victory is all but assured. Should defeat seem inevitable, a wraith will sacrifice all in order to escape to safety; it has all the time in the world to build up its forces for another attack, time the living sorely lack.

Wraith Encounters

d4	CR	Encounter
1	8	**Transient Grudge:** 2 Hateful Wraiths, 4 Traversing Specters
2	11	**Shimmering Grace:** 1 Bright Wraith, 5 Bright Motes
3	14	**Persistent Enmity:** 1 Baleful Void, 3 Hateful Wraiths, 6 Traversing Specters
4	21	**Perpetual Animus:** Seething Oblivion, 2 Baleful Voids, 4 Hateful Wraiths, 8 Traversing Specters

Hateful Wraith
Medium undead, neutral evil

Armor Class 13
Hit Points 65 (10d8 + 20)
Speed 0 ft., fly 60 ft. (hover)

STR	DEX	CON	INT	WIS	CHA
5 (-3)	16 (+3)	15 (+2)	13 (+1)	14 (+2)	16 (+3)

Damage Vulnerabilities radiant
Damage Resistances acid, cold, fire, lightning, thunder; bludgeoning, piercing, and slashing damage from nonmagical attacks
Damage Immunities necrotic, poison
Condition Immunities charmed, exhaustion, grappled, paralyzed, petrified, poisoned, prone, restrained, unconscious
Senses darkvision 60 ft., passive perception 12
Languages the languages it knew in life
Challenge 5 (1,800 XP)

Incorporeal Movement. The hateful wraith can move through other creatures and objects as if they were difficult terrain. It takes 5 (1d10) force damage if it ends its turn inside an object.

Sunlight Sensitivity. While in sunlight, the hateful wraith has disadvantage on attack rolls, as well as Wisdom (Perception) checks that rely on sight.

Actions

Life Drain. *Melee Weapon Attack:* +6 to hit, reach 5 ft., one creature. *Hit:* 22 (5d8) necrotic damage, and the target must succeed on a DC 14 Constitution saving throw, or its hit point maximum is reduced by an amount equal to the damage taken. This reduction lasts until the creature finishes a long rest. The target dies if this effect reduces its hit point maximum to 0.

If a creature is slain by this attack, its spirit rises on the next turn as a traversing specter (p.138) in the space of its corpse, or in the nearest unoccupied space. The specter is under the hateful wraith's control. The hateful wraith can have no more than 7 specters under its control at a time.

"A dank pit of sorrow into which suffering has been packed tight until it spills over, inky black and hateful. Pressure and time turns peat into coal, and hate into wraiths."

-Castanor Greeve, medium

Baleful Void
Medium undead, neutral evil

Armor Class 14
Hit Points 195 (26d8 + 78)
Speed 0 ft., fly 60 ft. (hover)

STR	DEX	CON	INT	WIS	CHA
6 (-2)	18 (+4)	17 (+3)	14 (+2)	15 (+2)	18 (+4)

Damage Vulnerabilities radiant
Damage Resistances acid, cold, fire, lightning, thunder; bludgeoning, piercing, and slashing damage from nonmagical attacks
Damage Immunities necrotic, poison
Condition Immunities charmed, exhaustion, grappled, paralyzed, petrified, poisoned, prone, restrained, unconscious
Senses darkvision 60 ft., passive perception 12
Languages the languages it knew in life
Challenge 10 (5,900 XP)

Incorporeal Movement. The baleful void can move through other creatures and objects as if they were difficult terrain. It takes 5 (1d10) force damage if it ends its turn inside an object.

Specter Servants. The baleful void's Life Drain and Create Specter abilities can both create specters under the wraith's control. The baleful void can have no more than 11 total specters under its control at a time.

Sunlight Sensitivity. While in sunlight, the baleful void has disadvantage on attack rolls, as well as Wisdom (Perception) checks that rely on sight.

Actions

Life Drain. *Melee Weapon Attack:* +8 to hit, reach 5 ft., one creature. *Hit:* 36 (8d8) necrotic damage, and the target must succeed on a DC 16 Constitution saving throw, or its hit point maximum is reduced by an amount equal to the damage taken. This reduction lasts until the creature finishes a long rest. The target dies if this effect reduces its hit point maximum to 0.

If a creature is slain by this attack, its spirit rises on the next turn as a traversing specter (p.138) in the space of its corpse, or in the nearest unoccupied space. The specter is under the baleful void's control.

Create Specter. The baleful void targets a corpse within 10 feet of it that has been dead for no longer than an hour, and died violently. The target's spirit rises as a traversing specter in the space of its corpse, or in the nearest unoccupied space. The specter is under the baleful void's control.

"They were dead when we got there, the entire village. Didn't look like they managed to put up much of a fight. Death found them behind locked doors and huddled in their cellars. No blood. Just a look of terror. That and the cold. A couple of them had weapons in their hands, for all the good it did them. We're not an enemy to them, we're vermin."

-Barker, soldier, account of a wraith attack

SEETHING OBLIVION

Medium undead, neutral evil

Armor Class 15
Hit Points 246 (29d8 + 116)
Speed 0 ft., fly 60 ft. (hover)

STR	DEX	CON	INT	WIS	CHA
7 (-2)	20 (+5)	19 (+4)	14 (+2)	15 (+2)	20 (+5)

Damage Vulnerabilities radiant
Damage Resistances acid, cold, fire, lightning, thunder; bludgeoning, piercing, and slashing damage from nonmagical attacks
Damage Immunities necrotic, poison
Condition Immunities charmed, exhaustion, grappled, paralyzed, petrified, poisoned, prone, restrained, unconscious
Senses darkvision 60 ft., passive perception 12
Languages the languages it knew in life
Challenge 18 (20,000 XP)

Incorporeal Movement. The seething oblivion can move through other creatures and objects as if they were difficult terrain. It takes 5 (1d10) force damage if it ends its turn inside an object.

Legendary Resistance (3/Day). When the seething oblivion fails a saving throw, it can choose to succeed instead.

Specter Servants. The seething oblivion's Life Drain and Create Specter abilities can both create specters under the seething oblivion's control. The seething oblivion can have no more than 11 total specters under its control at a time.

Sunlight Sensitivity. While in sunlight, the seething oblivion has disadvantage on attack rolls, as well as Wisdom (Perception) checks that rely on sight.

ACTIONS

Life Drain. *Melee Weapon Attack:* +11 to hit, reach 5 ft., one creature. *Hit:* 54 (12d8) necrotic damage, and the target must succeed on a DC 19 Constitution saving throw, or its hit point maximum is reduced by an amount equal to the damage taken. This reduction lasts until the creature finishes a long rest. The target dies if this effect reduces its hit point maximum to 0.

If a creature is slain by this attack, its spirit rises on the next turn as a deadly specter (p.138) in the space of its corpse, or in the nearest unoccupied space. The specter is under the seething oblivion's control.

Necrotic Lash. *Melee Weapon Attack:* +11 to hit, reach 5 ft., one creature. *Hit:* 22 (5d8) necrotic damage.

Create Specter. The seething oblivion targets a corpse within 10 feet of it that has been dead for no longer than an hour, and died violently. The target's spirit rises as a deadly specter in the space of its corpse, or in the nearest unoccupied space. The specter is under the seething oblivion's control.

LEGENDARY ACTIONS

The seething oblivion can take 3 legendary actions, choosing from the options below. Only one legendary action option can be used at a time, and only at the end of another creature's turn. The seething oblivion regains spent legendary actions at the start of its turn.

Shift. The seething oblivion flies up to half its fly speed, without provoking opportunity attacks.

Hateful Lash. The seething oblivion makes a Necrotic Lash attack.

Create Specter (Costs 2 Actions). The seething oblivion uses its Create Specter ability.

"As the specter dissolved like smoke in the wind, I looked up to thank my savior. Its eyes (at least, I think they were eyes) met mine and... nothing. The thing simply did not regard me. It looked right through me, like I was less than nothing."

-Lana Wilfing, merchant, account of a bright wraith encounter

BRIGHT WRAITH

Medium undead, neutral good

Armor Class 18 (radiant form)
Hit Points 165 (22d8 + 66)
Speed 0 ft., fly 60 ft. (hover)

STR	DEX	CON	INT	WIS	CHA
6 (-2)	16 (+3)	17 (+3)	14 (+2)	19 (+4)	20 (+5)

Damage Vulnerabilities necrotic
Damage Resistances lightning, thunder; bludgeoning, piercing, and slashing damage from nonmagical attacks
Damage Immunities fire, poison, radiant
Condition Immunities charmed, exhaustion, grappled, paralyzed, petrified, poisoned, prone, restrained, unconscious
Senses darkvision 60 ft., passive perception 14
Languages the languages it knew in life
Challenge 9 (5,000 XP)

Incorporeal Movement. The bright wraith can move through other creatures and objects as if they were difficult terrain. It takes 5 (1d10) force damage if it ends its turn inside an object.

Radiant Form. The bright wraith's armor class is equal to 10 + its Dexterity modifier + its Charisma modifier (already included above). Additionally, it sheds bright light to a radius of 30 feet, and dim light for another 30 feet.

Redeeming Light. If a wraith or specter is slain by radiant damage dealt by the bright wraith, it reconstitutes on its next turn as a Bright Mote under the bright wraith's control. The bright wraith can't have more than 14 bright motes under its control at a time.

ACTIONS

Searing Touch. *Melee Weapon Attack:* +8 to hit, reach 5 ft., one creature. *Hit:* 36 (8d8) radiant damage. If the target is undead or a fiend, it must succeed on a DC 16 Constitution saving throw, or its hit point maximum is reduced by an amount equal to the damage taken. This reduction lasts until the creature finishes a long rest. The target dies if this effect reduces its hit point maximum to 0.

Radiant Burst (Recharge 5-6). The bright wraith emits a burst of radiant energy. Creatures within 30 feet of the bright wraith must make a DC 16 Constitution saving throw, becoming blinded for 1 minute and taking 45 (10d8) radiant damage on a failed save, or half as much damage on a successful one. A creature can repeat the saving throw at the end of each of its turns, removing its blindness on a success.

BRIGHT MOTE

Small undead, neutral good

Armor Class 14 (radiant form)
Hit Points 42 (12d6)
Speed 0 ft., fly 40 ft. (hover)

STR	DEX	CON	INT	WIS	CHA
1 (-5)	14 (+2)	10 (+0)	10 (+0)	10 (+0)	15 (+2)

Damage Vulnerabilities necrotic
Damage Resistances lightning, thunder; bludgeoning, piercing, and slashing damage from nonmagical attacks
Damage Immunities fire, poison, radiant
Condition Immunities charmed, exhaustion, grappled, paralyzed, petrified, poisoned, prone, restrained, unconscious
Senses darkvision 60 ft., passive perception 12
Languages the languages it knew in life
Challenge 2 (450 XP)

Incorporeal Movement. The bright mote can move through other creatures and objects as if they were difficult terrain. It takes 5 (1d10) force damage if it ends its turn inside an object.

Radiant Form. The bright mote's armor class is equal to 10 + its Dexterity modifier + its Charisma modifier (already included above). Additionally, it sheds bright light to a radius of 20 feet, and dim light for another 20 feet.

Redeeming Light. If a wraith or specter is slain by radiant damage dealt by the bright mote, the bright mote dies, and both the mote's and the slain creature's soul can pass on to the afterlife.

ACTIONS

Searing Touch. *Melee Weapon Attack:* +4 to hit, reach 5 ft., one creature. *Hit:* 18 (4d8) radiant damage. If the target is undead or a fiend, it must succeed on a DC 12 Constitution saving throw, or its hit point maximum is reduced by an amount equal to the damage taken. This reduction lasts until the creature finishes a long rest. The target dies if this effect reduces its hit point maximum to 0.

More specifically, our savior was a bright wraith, an undead spirit sworn to oppose its dark brethren. It had, it seemed, recently appeared on this material plane, and sought us out as potential allies. After we broke camp (we kept our boots next to the fire in the fruitless hope of drying all the swamp from them), it approached us.

"The foe is not far now. It knows you entered the swamp. It waits across the battlefield. You have disrupted its plans. Destroyed its lieutenants. The king. The lich. The wights."

"So you think we'll be useful in the fight to come?"

"It has been forced to abandon a number of its schemes, but it can still build an army. It wishes to destroy you personally. You have proven to be an annoyance, and this will cause the wraith to act rashly. Drawn away from its army, it will be vulnerable. This is your use."

I wondered what Thaddeus thought of this taste of his own, blunt medicine. He gave no indication.

"We're a distraction," he said.

"So we have to goad an enemy who wants to destroy all life on earth into attacking us, and just hope you come to the rescue?"

"Hope is not necessary," the glowing figure replied, encouragingly. "Go."

And so we went. The oppressive malaise only grew as we left our newfound ally behind. Thaddeus explained that bright wraiths do not exude an aura of hope to counter their darker cousins (this much I had worked out for myself), but there was still some comfort to be found in proximity to its power, seemingly uncaring as it was. Its absence made the scenery that much more oppressive.

We made our way through a broad valley between two hills. Scattered here and there, half sunk in the mud, we saw dinted helms and scraps of old mail, remnants of a great battle fought here; we were getting close. Even beyond the evidence of our eyes, our growing proximity to the wraith was quite clear. Each step felt heavier than the last, the growing weight of the task ahead of us pressing us down. Slumped with despair, even keeping our eyes fully open seemed a difficult task.

Atop it all was, what I can only describe as, a growing sickness in my very soul; a deep feeling that death surrounded me on all sides. Not the fear of death by violence or mishap, with which I had, unfortunately, become accustomed, but the very antithesis of what I felt beating in my breast; death that was aware of me, and hated every atom of my being. It made me think back fondly to my experience of ghostly possession, which was, by contrast, a relaxing bath.

As these feelings built to their grim crescendo, we caught sight, for the first time, of the horrible figure we had been hunting for so long. In the faint, faltering sun, it was darkness in darkness; a sucking void which light dared not illuminate. It lazily circled a charnel pit; either all those slain in whatever battle had taken place years ago had been piled here, or the fight was of such immediate brutality that hundreds, or thousands, died all together. Beyond, at the entrance to the valley, its army stood, waiting for their newest recruits. Ranks and ranks of the dead – zombies swaying like drunkards, still clad in the rusted armor they were raised in; skeletons, straight and alert, dotted about as unit commanders. Here and there, something stirred amongst the marshaled corpses – some whispered threat of darker, and more subtle, troops at the wraith's command. Clearly this was not the first such site it had visited, though it may well have been the largest; at a glance, it seemed that as many dead were scattered before the wraith as stood behind it.

Seemingly satisfied with its assessment of the area, the wraith extended a withered hand, the cold points of light which served as eyes flaring as it did so. A sick, greenish light began to suffuse the ground, and that crushing, grinding sense of wrongness began to grow, like the pressured rumble of a sound too low for hearing. Before the dead could begin to stir, Thaddeus was on the move.

He walked tall, sword drawn. It seemed a futile gesture. One could as well draw their sword against the storm for all the good it looked likely to do him. The shrouded figure tilted what passed for a head and, with horror, I realised we had been seen.

"Loach," it whispered, with a voice of knives, as it swept towards him like a fog bank. "You come to your death so willingly."

Thaddeus raised his sword in silent defiance.

"The arrogance of mortals. Your time is borrowed and brief. You are an accident that shall be corrected."

It drove forward, its claws (for want of a better word) flashing in the green twilight. Steel met with shadow as they clashed and, for a wonderful moment, I thought victory was in our sights. The wraith circled him continuously, enveloping him in thick, black fog, before unleashing a flurry of blows. What I initially took for caution revealed itself to be calculated patience; Thaddeus began to tire, and The Shrouded One did not.

It became clear, then, that this was no equal contest. The wraith was toying with him, as a cat might with a particularly amusing mouse. With ease, it swept through him. Thaddeus gasped and reeled, coughing up dark fog, and the wraith struck again, grabbing him around the wrist of his sword arm as he tried to defend himself. The flesh of his arm blistered and blackened as they made contact, the muscle sloughing away as if the limb aged centuries in a split second.

"You might kill me," Thaddeus panted, taking up his sword in his other hand, allowing the injured arm to hang uselessly. "There'll be others. Someone will stop you."

"And each of their failures will lend me strength. Behold – your failures made flesh." The Shrouded One lifted a hand, and each of the thousands of corpses standing in the distance stiffened, awaiting its command. As one, they took a step forward. The ground rumbled. "My legion shall scour this world, but you I shall deal with personally."

Darkness lashed forth from it, crackling whips of night. Thaddeus did his best to parry with his off-hand, but the onslaught was relentless. He was forced down to his knees, but still he fought back, though each strike, each block, was slower and weaker than the last. The wraith stretched out its hand. It seemed to be relishing the moment. Thaddeus could barely raise his head to meet its gaze. He leant heavily on his sword; I feared he wasn't able to maintain even his kneeling position without its support.

"Your spirit is strong. It will serve me well. Give in. You cannot hope to forestall the inevitable."

"Hope is not necessary," said the light in the darkness. It grew until it was searing.

The blackness swirled up against it, Thaddeus quite forgotten in its urgency. Light and dark clashed, as repellent to one another as oil and water. Within the blinding glare and cloying shadow, the figures of the combatants could be seen rending into one another; the bright wraith calm and methodical, our enemy scrabbling and clawing like a wild thing. It shrieked when they made contact, the light blistering through it, its form becoming ragged and torn.

The bright wraith grasped hold of our adversary's head with both of its hands. Tendrils of light and dark hissed and billowed like steam. The wraith let out a terrible, piercing howl, the fear and pain of unchallenged might made impotent in the face of greater power. Cut short as it was, it continued to reverberate. Even as I write, it feels fresh in my ears.

The darkness was gone. Only errant strands of smoke remained, which swirled together tighter and tighter until they formed an orb of glowing, pearlescent light, which lazily circled the bright wraith.

"It is done," it said.

For the first time, our focus turned to the army of dead off in the distance. A change had come upon them. With the wraith gone, they seemed restless. Some, at least, had noticed the bright light, or been alerted by the noise and began to shuffle forwards, all rank forgotten.

Thaddeus, looking little better than a corpse himself after his ordeal, stared blankly. He heaved himself to his feet, breathing heavily.

"It is done," it repeated. "Life is preserved. Lives are the concern of mortals."

With that, it was gone. We had no choice but to run with whatever strength remained to us. Our enemy was defeated, though it seemed our real test was only just beginning.

Zombies

rave dirt cakes its form like a picked-at scab, yet the details beneath the flaking crust are plain to see. One eye is clouded, and maggots writhe where the other would have sat. Reaching out a hand black with jellied, pooling blood, the creature opens its weeping sore of a mouth and heaves out a wordless exhalation of fetid air. Putting one bloated foot in front of the other clumsily, as if controlled by an inexpert puppeteer, it shambles forward.

Like skeletons, zombies are corpses animated by magic. However, they also possess an animalistic instinct to attack and feed which makes them harder to control, yet somewhat easier to predict. Beyond the fact of their animation, zombies are indistinguishable from mundane corpses, and are as varied in their appearance as that morbid panoply allows. Dependant on the manner of death, level of preservation, and amount of time elapsed between expiration and reanimation, zombies can be horribly bloated with noxious gases, crawling with scavengers, oozing with putrefaction, withered and near-skeletal, or they may display any number of grotesque physiological traits that go along with the grim process of decay. The only essential commonality is that there must be some level of flesh covering the bones in order for the zombie to

haul itself around for, while there is magic holding them together to a point, it is limited compared to that which knits together other types of undead, such as skeletons.

As zombies (and ghosts) are probably the most widespread varieties of undead, and therefore most likely to be encountered by a layman, there is not so much superstition surrounding them as practical solutions to deter and dispatch them. All cultures must deal with their dead respectfully, but it can be unwise to assume they will simply *stay* dead.

In rural locations, inhabitants will typically bury their dead a way out of the village boundary and will dig a moat between the gravesite and the community. Any risen dead, with their propensity to run in a straight line towards living victims, will suffer a sharp drop and remain trapped, to be dispatched at leisure.

In larger centers of civilisation, which have grown to overtake and surround formerly outlying burial sites, inhabitants often erect strong fences and employ guards to ensure the contents of their graveyards don't go wandering. Similarly, it has been suggested by some that the nobility's inclination towards grand mausoleums of stone to inter their dead is as much for practicality as it is to be a show of grandeur. A large stone structure, barred with iron, is as difficult to break out of as it is to break in: anything to avoid the indignity of seeing some revered ancestor shambling about, gnawing on the populace.

ORIGIN

Though certainly one of the most common forms of undead, zombies are potentially one of the least useful. Truly mindless, they will obey the will of the one who raised them to the best of their abilities but, given the extreme limits on their intelligence, options are limited. For this reason, zombies are generally only deliberately created by apprentice necromancers, or as fodder in the undead hordes of those more powerful. However, their creation is also a common side effect of powerful necromantic rituals bleeding into the surrounding area.

The magic used to raise a zombie reanimates the brain with limited functionality, allowing it to control the body's motor functions. While they are no stronger than their living counterpart, their inability to feel pain, and therefore the stresses and strains of pushing themselves beyond reasonable limits, allows even the most unremarkable zombie to accomplish feats of strength and endurance on par with a highly-trained warrior.

While enough damage to the limbs can stop a zombie from moving, a limbless zombie will still writhe and snap at anything it can reach. The only way to truly destroy a zombie for good is by removing the head or destroying the brain.

ENVIRONMENT

While animated by magic, and able to shrug off blows which would kill or incapacitate a creature capable of feeling, zombies are still corpses and, as such, still rot. The dark energies animating them will hold them together up to a point but, should so much rotting flesh slough off the zombie's form that it is unable to move, the magic is powerless to compel it otherwise. For this reason, zombies are more or less of a lingering threat depending on the environment; the natural preservative effects of cold or dry heat can keep the undead in a viable state almost indefinitely. On the other hand, zombies raised in more tropical latitudes will rot away very quickly, though their pervasive stench may linger for some time. Also, while frozen temperatures can certainly delay the process of decay, extreme cold can freeze the zombies entirely. In environments such as these, even if the creature is able to move, the dry, frozen skin and muscle will be frostbitten and brittle, and will soon flake away.

ROLEPLAYING ZOMBIES

Zombies are extremely limited in their interactions with other creatures, and entirely devoid of individual personality. They are sluggish to respond to stimuli, and easy to feint and mislead. Zombies are able to undertake tasks on the orders of their master, but will always go about them in the simplest and most literal way, and generally with a large amount of collateral damage, unless given explicit orders. Any other factors will be ignored while a zombie carries out its task, even factors which would endanger or destroy it.

COMBAT TACTICS

Zombies lack the intelligence for even the basic tactics shown by animals. They will attack whatever living being is closest to them, though they do have a preference for humanoid prey. Engaged by multiple foes, a zombie will flail, attacking at random rather than focusing on a single target.

Zombies have no sense of self-preservation, so will attempt the shortest path to a target, even if it means suffering deadly hazards which would be obvious to any other creature. Powerful necromancers can use this to their advantage; given enough zombies, almost any barrier becomes surmountable. Dozens of zombies can clog the mechanism of a trap, hundreds can dam an inconvenient river, and thousands might create a mound of bodies high enough to create a serviceable siege ramp.

PLAGUE-BORN ZOMBIES

A less common form of zombie, plague-born are the result of a virulent contagion animating the corpses of the infected, rather than necromantic ritual. Having been transformed into zombies at the point of death, they tend to be less advanced in their level of decay than other zombies. Indeed, were it not for their unnatural movements, feral bloodlust and, in most cases, horrific wounds, many would be indistinguishable from the living (albeit those living with a terrible illness).

Originating from a necromantic disease rather than being raised, plague-born have no master to serve and will attack any living being they come across. They are more reactive to external stimuli, and will flock towards bright lights or loud noises, often congregating in great swarms, descending on the source like crows on a carcass.

ORIGIN

Given their unique and difficult-to-replicate nature, it is theorised that all plague-born originate from a single source. Whether a botched attempt to raise a common zombie or a vindictive curse, we may never know and, given their frighteningly rapid proliferation, it is likely whoever was responsible is in no position to say.

The disease is transmitted through contact with infected blood. Bites are the most common - and most dangerous - form of exposure, though any form of contact with contaminated blood carries a risk. Those exposed contract a horrible disease which, upon their death, animates their corpse as a zombie. Should a plague-born remain animated for enough time (usually a few weeks to a few months), the disease ferments into a more virulent strain; those infected by one of these 'plague-hosts' reanimate with the ability to further spread the disease.

The disease acts quickly; depending on where a victim is bitten, death and subsequent transformation can take place in a matter of minutes, though the uncommonly resilient may last a day or longer. Fever and convulsions are rapidly followed by vomiting blood and an insatiable hunger and, finally, the afflicted slips into oblivion, reanimating within minutes.

ENVIRONMENT

Spreading as a contagion from host to host, plague-born zombies are more dangerous the more potential victims surround them. They are drawn to centers of civilisation as their best food source and means of proliferation.

When there is no obvious food source around, plague-born wander, directionless, until they find one, or until they disintegrate entirely. Very rarely, a plague-born might show some preference for locations and stimuli important to who it was in life. One might be drawn to wander the same streets it did in life, or appear fascinated by tools or clothing relevant to its former trade. While this might lure the unwary to hope that some remnant of a former loved one remains in the creature, the phenomenon is simply due to rote action in life (a process similar to 'bone memory' in skeletons), and any seeming interest is quickly ignored, should living prey present itself.

ROLEPLAYING PLAGUE-BORN

Plague-born behave in a similar manner to zombies left to their own devices, simply at a much faster pace, appearing jittery and unstable. They take orders far less readily than their sluggish kin, with any instructions constantly battling with the urge to bite and feed (and losing, more often than not).

COMBAT TACTICS

Like their common cousins, plague-born attack mindlessly, though they have a glimmer of animal cunning; at least enough to prefer attacking those who face an immediate threat to those who do not. They swarm towards intense stimuli, so any effect which produces loud noises or bright lights is sure to attract plague-born in the immediate area, and perhaps even those from further afield.

ZOMBIE NECROSIS DISEASE

Zombie necrosis is a disease carried by plague-born zombies and scavengers that feed on infected bodies. These creatures inflict the disease with their bite attacks.

Those infected by the disease almost immediately suffer shaking and fever as the infection rapidly spreads through their system. If the infected is resilient enough to keep the disease at bay for a time, they might begin to exhibit an insatiable, maddening hunger (though most die before this stage can take hold). When the disease is in its final stages, the victim vomits blood, which also seeps from their eyes and nose.

Creatures immune to the poisoned condition are immune to this disease. For every hour that elapses, a diseased creature's current and maximum hit points are reduced by 1d4. This reduction lasts until the disease is cured. If the creature's hit point maximum is reduced to 0, the creature dies. A creature that dies while afflicted with zombie necrosis reanimates 2d10 rounds later as a plague-born zombie.

ZOMBIE ENCOUNTERS

CR 1/2-6

d8	CR	Encounter
1	1/2	**Stray Corpses:** 2 Orc Zombies, 1 Hobgoblin Zombie
2	1	**Necromancer's Dregs:** 4 Human Zombies, 1 Elf Zombie, 1 Dwarf Zombie
3	2	**Cursed Tribe:** 3 Hobgoblin Zombies, 8 Goblin Zombies
4	2	**Stirring Graveyard:** 10 Human Zombies, 4 Elf Zombies, 2 Dwarf Zombies
5	3	**Onset Infestation:** 1 Plague-Born Human, 4 Human Zombies, 2 Elf Zombies, 1 Dwarf Zombie
6	4	**Afflicted Warband:** 3 Plague-Born Orcs, 8 Orc Zombies
7	5	**Contaminated Farm:** 1 Plague-Born Dog, 3 Human Zombies, 2 Zombie Dogs, 2 Zombie Horses, 7 Zombie Oxen
8	6	**Rotting Horde:** 2 Ogre Zombies, 2 Troll Zombies, 5 Orc Zombies, 3 Hobgoblin Zombies, 4 Goblin Zombies

CR 9-22

d6	CR	Encounter
1	9	**Deceased Hatchery:** 3 Young Zombie Dragons
2	10	**Infected Underkeep:** 1 Goblin Plague-Host, 2 Plague-Born Goblins, 1 Plague-Born Dwarf, 4 Goblin Zombies, 7 Dwarf Zombies
3	12	**Rapid Epidemic:** 1 Elf Plague-Host, 6 Plague-Born Elves, 8 Elf Zombies
4	16	**Plaguestricken Township:** 3 Human Plague-Hosts, 4 Plague-Born Humans, 2 Plague-Born Elves, 8 Human Zombies, 3 Elf Zombies, 2 Dwarf Zombies
5	19	**Tenacious Contagion:** 2 Dwarf Plague-Hosts, 5 Plague-Born Dwarves, 2 Plague-Born Trolls
6	22	**Giant Outbreak:** 1 Ogre Plague-Host, 1 Troll Plague-Host, 3 Plague-Born Trolls, 4 Plague-Born Ogres

Human Zombie

Medium undead, neutral evil

Armor Class 8
Hit Points 13 (2d8 + 4)
Speed 20 ft.

STR	DEX	CON	INT	WIS	CHA
14 (+2)	6 (-2)	15 (+2)	2 (-4)	7 (-2)	1 (-5)

Saving Throws Con +4, Wis +0
Damage Immunities poison
Condition Immunities poisoned
Senses darkvision 60 ft., passive Perception 8
Languages understands the languages it knew in life, but can't speak
Challenge 1/8 (25 XP)

Cadaverous Appearance. While the zombie is lying still, it is indistinguishable from a mundane decomposing corpse. It can still be detected by a *detect evil and good* spell, or similar magic.

Undead Fortitude. If damage reduces the zombie to 0 hit points, it must make a Constitution saving throw, with a DC of 5 + the damage taken, unless the damage is radiant or from a critical hit. On a success, the zombie drops to 1 hit point instead.

Actions

Slam. *Melee Weapon Attack:* +4 to hit, reach 5 ft., one target. *Hit:* 5 (1d6 + 2) bludgeoning damage.

Plague-Born Human

Medium undead, neutral evil

Armor Class 12 (natural armor)
Hit Points 68 (8d8 + 32)
Speed 25 ft.

STR	DEX	CON	INT	WIS	CHA
16 (+3)	6 (-2)	18 (+4)	2 (-4)	9 (-1)	1 (-5)

Saving Throws Con +6, Wis +1
Damage Immunities poison
Condition Immunities poisoned
Senses darkvision 60 ft., passive Perception 9
Languages understands the languages it knew in life but can't speak
Challenge 2 (450 XP)

Cadaverous Appearance. While the plague-born is lying still, it is indistinguishable from a mundane decomposing corpse. It can still be detected by a *detect evil and good* spell, or similar magic.

Grasping Horde. If a creature is grappled by more than one creature with this ability, it has disadvantage on ability checks to escape the grapple.

Undead Fortitude. If damage reduces the plague-born to 0 hit points, it must make a Constitution saving throw, with a DC of 5 + the damage taken, unless the damage is radiant or from a critical hit. On a success, the plague-born drops to 1 hit point instead.

Actions

Multiattack. The plague-born makes a slam attack. If it is grappling a creature, the plague-born can also make a bite attack.

Slam. *Melee Weapon Attack:* +5 to hit, reach 5 ft., one target. *Hit:* 7 (1d8 + 3) bludgeoning damage, and the target is grappled (escape DC 11). Until this grapple ends, the plague-born can't use its slam attack against another target.

Bite. *Melee Weapon Attack:* +5 to hit, reach 5 ft., one grappled creature. *Hit:* 10 (2d6 + 3) piercing damage. Additionally, living creatures must succeed on a DC 11 Constitution saving throw, or take 9 (2d8) necrotic damage and contract the zombie necrosis disease (p.192).

HUMAN PLAGUE-HOST
Medium undead, neutral evil

Armor Class 13 (natural armor)
Hit Points 133 (14d8 + 70)
Speed 25 ft.

STR	DEX	CON	INT	WIS	CHA
18 (+4)	6 (-2)	20 (+5)	2 (-4)	10 (+0)	1 (-5)

Saving Throws Con +8, Wis +3
Damage Immunities poison
Condition Immunities poisoned
Senses darkvision 60 ft., passive Perception 10
Languages understands the languages it knew in life, but can't speak
Challenge 8 (3,900 XP)

Cadaverous Appearance. While the plague-host is lying still, it is indistinguishable from a mundane decomposing corpse. It can still be detected by a *detect evil and good* spell, or similar magic.

Grasping Horde. If a creature is grappled by more than one creature with this ability, it has disadvantage on ability checks to escape the grapple.

Virulent Miasma. Creatures, other than undead and constructs, within 30 feet of the plague-host have disadvantage on Constitution checks and saving throws.

Undead Fortitude. If damage reduces the plague-host to 0 hit points, it must make a Constitution saving throw, with a DC of 5 + the damage taken, unless the damage is radiant or from a critical hit. On a success, the plague-host drops to 1 hit point instead.

ACTIONS

Multiattack. The plague-host makes two slam attacks. If it is grappling a creature, the plague-host can also make a bite attack.

Slam. *Melee Weapon Attack:* +7 to hit, reach 5 ft., one target *Hit:* 11 (2d6 + 4) bludgeoning damage, and the target is grappled (escape DC 15). Until this grapple ends, the plague-host can't use its slam attack against another target.

Bite. *Melee Weapon Attack:* +7 to hit, reach 5 ft., one grappled creature. *Hit:* 14 (3d6 + 4) piercing damage. Additionally, living creatures must succeed on a DC 16 Constitution saving throw, or take 18 (4d8) necrotic damage and contract the zombie necrosis disease (p.192).

LEGENDARY ACTIONS

The plague-host can take 3 legendary actions, choosing from the options below. Only one legendary action option can be used at a time, and only at the end of another creature's turn. The plague-host regains spent legendary actions at the start of its turn

Lurch. The plague-host moves up to 5 feet, without provoking opportunity attacks.

Attack (Costs 2 Actions). The plague-host makes one slam or bite attack.

Surrounded by the dead. Thought we could hold them off with fire. Now surrounded by burning dead and no oil for the lamps.

-last entry in the logbook of Whitehall garrison

ELF ZOMBIE

Medium undead, neutral evil

Armor Class 12
Hit Points 11 (2d8 + 2)
Speed 30 ft., Climb 10 ft.

STR	DEX	CON	INT	WIS	CHA
11 (+0)	15 (+2)	13 (+1)	2 (-4)	7 (-2)	1 (-5)

Saving Throws Wis +0
Damage Immunities poison
Condition Immunities poisoned
Senses darkvision 60 ft., passive Perception 8
Languages understands the languages it knew in life, but can't speak
Challenge 1/4 (50 XP)

Cadaverous Appearance. While the zombie is lying still, it is indistinguishable from a mundane decomposing corpse. It can still be detected by a *detect evil and good* spell, or similar magic.

Lesser Undead Fortitude. If damage reduces the zombie to 0 hit points, it must make a Constitution saving throw with a DC of 10 + the damage taken, unless the damage is radiant or from a critical hit. On a success, the zombie drops to 1 hit point instead.

ACTIONS

Bite. *Melee Weapon Attack:* +4 to hit, reach 5 ft., one target. *Hit:* 5 (1d6 + 2) piercing damage.

PLAGUE-BORN ELF

Medium undead, neutral evil

Armor Class 15 (natural armor)
Hit Points 52 (7d8 + 21)
Speed 35 ft., Climb 15 ft.

STR	DEX	CON	INT	WIS	CHA
12 (+1)	17 (+3)	16 (+3)	2 (-4)	9 (-1)	1 (-5)

Saving Throws Dex +5, Wis +1
Damage Immunities poison
Condition Immunities poisoned
Senses darkvision 60 ft., passive Perception 9
Languages understands the languages it knew in life, but can't speak
Challenge 3 (700 XP)

Cadaverous Appearance. While the plague-born is laying still, it is indistinguishable from a mundane decomposing corpse. It can still be detected by a *detect evil and good* spell, or similar magic.

Undead Flexibility. Standing up from prone costs only 5 feet of the plague-born's movement, rather than half its movement.

Lesser Undead Fortitude. If damage reduces the plague-born to 0 hit points, it must make a Constitution saving throw with a DC of 10 + the damage taken, unless the damage is radiant or from a critical hit. On a success, the plague-born drops to 1 hit point instead.

ACTIONS

Multiattack. The plague-born makes two bite attacks.

Bite. *Melee Weapon Attack:* +5 to hit, reach 5 ft., one target. *Hit:* 7 (1d8 + 3) piercing damage. Additionally, living creatures must succeed on a DC 11 Constitution saving throw, or take 9 (2d8) necrotic damage and contract the zombie necrosis disease (p.192).

One detail of note is the report of merfolk in the area, who claim to have come across a whale-fall some months after the ship's disappearance. Among the usual hagfish and scavenging crabs was a walking corpse, clad in the rotting remnants of sailor's garb, also feasting on the carcass. The merfolk understandably kept their distance, but the zombie's presence suggests an altogether darker fate befell the crew than a simple storm or pirate raid.

-report on the disappearance of trading vessel Mermaid's Purse

ELF PLAGUE-HOST

Medium undead, neutral evil

Armor Class 17 (natural armor)
Hit Points 90 (12d8 + 36)
Speed 35 ft., Climb 15 ft.

STR	DEX	CON	INT	WIS	CHA
12 (+1)	18 (+4)	17 (+3)	2 (-4)	10 (+0)	1 (-5)

Saving Throws Dex +7, Wis +3
Damage Immunities poison
Condition Immunities poisoned
Senses darkvision 60 ft., passive Perception 10
Languages understands the languages it knew in life, but can't speak
Challenge 8 (3,900 XP)

Cadaverous Appearance. While the plague-host is lying still, it is indistinguishable from a mundane decomposing corpse. It can still be detected by a *detect evil and good* spell, or similar magic.

Undead Flexibility. Standing up from prone costs only 5 feet of the plague-host's movement, rather than half its movement.

Leaping Pounce. The plague-host's long jump is 30 feet and its high jump is 20 feet, with or without a running start.

If the plague-host ends a jump within 5 feet of a Large or smaller creature, and then hits that creature with a bite attack, the target is grappled (escape DC 15). Until this grapple ends, the target is restrained and the plague-host's bite deals an additional 9 (2d8) slashing damage to the target on each hit.

Lesser Undead Fortitude. If damage reduces the plague-host to 0 hit points, it must make a Constitution saving throw with a DC of 10 + the damage taken, unless the damage is radiant or from a critical hit. On a success, the plague-host drops to 1 hit point instead.

ACTIONS

Multiattack. The plague-host makes two bite attacks.

Bite. *Melee Weapon Attack:* +7 to hit, reach 5 ft., one target. *Hit:* 11 (2d6 + 4) piercing damage. Additionally, living creatures must succeed on a DC 14 Constitution saving throw, or take 18 (4d8) necrotic damage and contract the zombie necrosis disease (p. 92).

LEGENDARY ACTIONS

The plague-host can take 3 legendary actions, choosing from the options below. Only one legendary action option can be used at a time, and only at the end of another creature's turn. The plague-host regains spent legendary actions at the start of its turn

Lunge. The plague-host moves up to 10 feet, without provoking opportunity attacks.

Bite (Costs 2 Actions). The plague-host makes one bite attack.

Elf zombies tend to be jittery and frenzied, retaining some of the natural speed they had in life, through with none of the attendant gracefulness.

Dwarf Zombie

Medium undead, neutral evil

Armor Class 8
Hit Points 22 (3d8 + 9)
Speed 15 ft.

STR	DEX	CON	INT	WIS	CHA
14 (+2)	6 (-2)	17 (+3)	2 (-4)	9 (-1)	1 (-5)

Saving Throws Con +5, Wis +1
Damage Immunities poison
Condition Immunities poisoned
Senses darkvision 60 ft., passive Perception 9
Languages understands the languages it knew in life, but can't speak
Challenge 1/4 (50 XP)

Cadaverous Appearance. While the zombie is lying still, it is indistinguishable from a mundane decomposing corpse. It can still be detected by a *detect evil and good* spell, or similar magic.

Dwarven Undead Fortitude. If damage reduces the zombie to 0 hit points, it must make a Constitution saving throw with a DC of 5 + the damage taken, unless the damage is radiant or from a critical hit. On a success, the zombie drops to 1 hit point instead. On a failure it is not immediately destroyed, but falls prone and remains conscious. While it has 0 hit points, the zombie can't regain any hit points, automatically fails any saving throws, and dies if it suffers a single hit that deals 5 or more damage. At the end of its next turn, the zombie dies.

Actions

Slam. *Melee Weapon Attack:* +4 to hit, reach 5 ft., one target. *Hit:* 5 (1d6 + 2) bludgeoning damage.

Plague-Born Dwarf

Medium undead, neutral evil

Armor Class 12 (natural armor)
Hit Points 85 (9d8 + 45)
Speed 20 ft.

STR	DEX	CON	INT	WIS	CHA
16 (+3)	6 (-2)	20 (+5)	2 (-4)	10 (+0)	1 (-5)

Saving Throws Con +7, Wis +2
Damage Immunities poison
Condition Immunities poisoned
Senses darkvision 60 ft., passive Perception 0
Languages understands the languages it knew in life, but can't speak
Challenge 3 (700 XP)

Cadaverous Appearance. While the plague-born is lying still, it is indistinguishable from a mundane decomposing corpse. It can still be detected by a *detect evil and good* spell, or similar magic.

Dwarven Undead Fortitude. If damage reduces the plague-born to 0 hit points, it must make a Constitution saving throw with a DC of 5 + the damage taken, unless the damage is radiant or from a critical hit. On a success, the plague-born drops to 1 hit point instead. On a failure it is not immediately destroyed, but falls prone and remains conscious. While it has 0 hit points, the plague-born can't regain any hit points, automatically fails any saving throws, and dies if it suffers a single hit that deals 5 or more damage. At the end of its next turn, the plague-born dies.

Actions

Multiattack. The plague-born makes a slam attack. If it is grappling a creature, it then makes a bite attack.

Slam. *Melee Weapon Attack:* +5 to hit, reach 5 ft., one target. *Hit:* 7 (1d8 + 3) bludgeoning damage, and the target is grappled (escape DC 11). Until this grapple ends, the plague-born can't use its slam against another target.

Bite. *Melee Weapon Attack:* +5 to hit, reach 5 ft., one creature the plague-born is grappling. *Hit:* 6 (1d6 + 3) piercing damage. Additionally, living creatures must succeed on a DC 13 Constitution saving throw, or take 4 (1d8) necrotic damage and contract the zombie necrosis disease (p.192).

Dwarf Plague-Host

Medium undead, neutral evil

Armor Class 14 (natural armor)
Hit Points 157 (15d8 + 90)
Speed 20 ft.

STR	DEX	CON	INT	WIS	CHA
18 (+4)	6 (-2)	22 (+6)	2 (-4)	12 (+1)	1 (-5)

Saving Throws Con +10, Wis +5
Damage Immunities poison
Condition Immunities poisoned
Senses darkvision 60 ft., passive Perception 11
Languages understands the languages it knew in life, but can't speak
Challenge 10 (5,900 XP)

Cadaverous Appearance. While the plague-host is lying still, it is indistinguishable from a mundane decomposing corpse. It can still be detected by a *detect evil and good* spell, or similar magic.

Dwarven Undead Fortitude. If damage reduces the plague-host to 0 hit points, it must make a Constitution saving throw with a DC of 5 + the damage taken, unless the damage is radiant or from a critical hit. On a success, the plague-host drops to 1 hit point instead. On a failure it is not immediately destroyed, but falls prone and remains conscious. While it has 0 hit points, the plague-host can't regain any hit points, automatically fails any saving throws, and dies if it suffers a single hit that deals 5 or more damage. At the end of its next turn, the plague-host dies.

Actions

Multiattack. The plague-host makes two slam attacks. If it is grappling a creature, it then makes a bite attack.

Slam. *Melee Weapon Attack:* +8 to hit, reach 5 ft., one target. *Hit:* 11 (2d6 + 4) bludgeoning damage, and the target is grappled (escape DC 12). Until this grapple ends, the plague-host can't use its slam against another target.

Bite. *Melee Weapon Attack:* +8 to hit, reach 5 ft., one creature the plague-host is grappling. *Hit:* 11 (2d6 + 4) piercing damage. Additionally, living creatures must succeed on a DC 18 Constitution saving throw, or take 9 (2d8) necrotic damage and contract the zombie necrosis disease (p.192).

Pestilent Discharge (Recharge 5-6). The plague-host spews a mix of infectious fluids in a 15-foot cone. Living creatures in the area must make a DC 18 Constitution saving throw, taking 13 (3d8) necrotic damage and contracting the zombie necrosis disease (p.192) on a failed save, or taking half as much damage on a successful one. Creatures immune to the poisoned condition are immune to this disease. Until the end of its next turn, the plague-host's melee weapon attacks deal an additional 4 (1d8) necrotic damage, and creatures have disadvantage on Constitution saving throws against disease inflicted by the plague-host's bite.

Legendary Actions

The plague-host can take 3 legendary actions, choosing from the options below. Only one legendary action option can be used at a time, and only at the end of another creature's turn. The plague-host regains spent legendary actions at the start of its turn

Lurch. The plague-host moves up to 5 feet, without provoking opportunity attacks.

Attack (Costs 2 Actions). The plague-host makes one slam or bite attack.

Combining the inherent toughness of a dwarf with the tenacity of their undead form, **dwarf zombies** are incredibly difficult to kill.

...make her see, understand how I feel... a few drops is all it... think I got the mixture right... she'll love me...hunger for me...

—bloodstained scrap of paper found by the well of an abandoned village

Goblin Zombie

Small undead, neutral evil

Armor Class 11
Hit Points 11 (2d6 + 4)
Speed 25 ft.

STR	DEX	CON	INT	WIS	CHA
8 (-1)	13 (+1)	15 (+2)	2 (-4)	5 (-3)	1 (-5)

Saving Throws Wis -1
Damage Immunities poison
Condition Immunities poisoned
Senses darkvision 60 ft., passive Perception 7
Languages understands the languages it knew in life, but can't speak
Challenge 1/4 (50 XP)

Cadaverous Appearance. While the zombie is lying still, it is indistinguishable from a mundane decomposing corpse. It can still be detected by a *detect evil and good* spell, or similar magic.

Horde Instincts. The zombie has advantage on a melee attack roll against a creature if at least two of the zombie's allies are within 5 feet of the creature, and the allies are not incapacitated.

Lesser Undead Fortitude. If damage reduces the zombie to 0 hit points, it must make a Constitution saving throw with a DC of 10 + the damage taken, unless the damage is radiant or from a critical hit. On a success, the zombie drops to 1 hit point instead.

Actions

Bite. *Melee Weapon Attack:* +3 to hit, reach 5 ft., one target. *Hit:* 5 (1d8 + 1) piercing damage.

Plague-Born Goblin

Small undead, neutral evil

Armor Class 14 (natural armor)
Hit Points 52 (7d6 + 28)
Speed 30 ft.

STR	DEX	CON	INT	WIS	CHA
9 (-1)	15 (+2)	18 (+4)	2 (-4)	7 (-2)	1 (-5)

Saving Throws Dex +5, Wis +0
Damage Immunities poison
Condition Immunities poisoned
Senses darkvision 60 ft., passive Perception 8
Languages understands the languages it knew in life, but can't speak
Challenge 3 (700 XP)

Cadaverous Appearance. While the plague-born is lying still, it is indistinguishable from a mundane decomposing corpse. It can still be detected by a *detect evil and good* spell, or similar magic.

Horde Instincts. The plague-born has advantage on a melee attack roll against a creature if at least two of the plague-born's allies are within 5 feet of the creature, and the allies are not incapacitated.

Lesser Undead Fortitude. If damage reduces the plague-born to 0 hit points, it must make a Constitution saving throw with a DC of 10 + the damage taken, unless the damage is radiant or from a critical hit. On a success, the plague-born drops to 1 hit point instead.

Actions

Multiattack. The plague-born makes two bite attacks.

Bite. *Melee Weapon Attack:* +5 to hit, reach 5 ft., one target. *Hit:* 9 (2d6 + 3) piercing damage. Additionally, living creatures must succeed on a DC 12 Constitution saving throw, or take 9 (2d8) necrotic damage and contract the zombie necrosis disease (p.192).

GOBLIN PLAGUE-HOST
Medium undead, neutral evil

Armor Class 16 (natural armor)
Hit Points 90 (12d6 + 48)
Speed 30 ft.

STR	DEX	CON	INT	WIS	CHA
11 (+0)	16 (+3)	19 (+4)	2 (-4)	9 (-1)	1 (-5)

Saving Throws Dex +6, Wis +2
Damage Immunities poison
Condition Immunities poisoned
Senses darkvision 60 ft., passive Perception 9
Languages understands the languages it knew in life, but can't speak
Challenge 8 (3,900 XP)

Cadaverous Appearance. While the plague-host is lying still, it is indistinguishable from a mundane decomposing corpse. It can still be detected by a *detect evil and good* spell, or similar magic.

Horde Instincts. The plague-host has advantage on a melee attack roll against a creature if at least two of the plague-host's allies are within 5 feet of the creature, and the allies are not incapacitated.

Tenacious Clinger. If the plague-host hits the same creature with at least two attacks on the same turn, it latches onto the target. The plague-host is considered grappled by the target with the following exceptions: The target cannot end the grapple at will, instead it must use its action to attempt a DC 14 Strength (Athletics) or Dexterity (Acrobatics) check, shaking the plague-host off and ending the grapple on a success. The plague-host can end the grapple at will.

Until the grapple ends, attack rolls against the target have advantage, and the target has disadvantage on attack rolls and Strength and Dexterity checks that are not made to attempt to shake the plague-host off.

Additionally, if two or more creatures with this ability are latched on to the same Large or smaller creature, the target is also grappled. If three or more creatures are latched on to the same Large or smaller creature, the target is also restrained and incapacitated.

Lesser Undead Fortitude. If damage reduces the plague-host to 0 hit points, it must make a Constitution saving throw with a DC of 10 + the damage taken, unless the damage is radiant or from a critical hit. On a success, the plague-host drops to 1 hit point instead.

ACTIONS

Multiattack. The plague-host makes two bite attacks.

Bite. *Melee Weapon Attack:* +6 to hit, reach 5 ft., one target. *Hit:* 13 (3d6 + 3) piercing damage. Additionally, living creatures must succeed on a DC 15 Constitution saving throw, or take 13 (3d8) necrotic damage and contract the zombie necrosis disease (p.192).

LEGENDARY ACTIONS

The plague-host can take 3 legendary actions, choosing from the options below. Only one legendary action option can be used at a time, and only at the end of another creature's turn. The plague-host regains spent legendary actions at the start of its turn

Scuttle. The plague-host moves up to 10 feet, without provoking opportunity attacks.

Bite (Costs 2 Actions). The plague-host makes one bite attack.

Though not much of a threat individually, **goblin zombies** become much more of a menace when allowed to coalesce into a swarm of gnashing teeth.

HOBGOBLIN ZOMBIE

Medium undead, neutral evil

Armor Class 8
Hit Points 13 (2d8 + 4)
Speed 20 ft.

STR	DEX	CON	INT	WIS	CHA
14 (+2)	6 (-2)	15 (+2)	2 (-4)	7 (-2)	1 (-5)

Saving Throws Con +4, Wis +0
Damage Immunities poison
Condition Immunities poisoned
Senses darkvision 60 ft., passive Perception 8
Languages understands the languages it knew in life, but can't speak
Challenge 1/8 (25 XP)

Cadaverous Appearance. While the zombie is lying still, it is indistinguishable from a mundane decomposing corpse. It can still be detected by a *detect evil and good* spell, or similar magic.

Undead Fortitude. If damage reduces the zombie to 0 hit points, it must make a Constitution saving throw with a DC of 5 + the damage taken, unless the damage is radiant or from a critical hit. On a success, the zombie drops to 1 hit point instead.

ACTIONS

Slam. *Melee Weapon Attack:* +4 to hit, reach 5 ft., one target. *Hit:* 5 (1d6 + 2) bludgeoning damage.

Bite. *Melee Weapon Attack:* +4 to hit, reach 5 ft., one grappled creature. *Hit:* 6 (1d8 + 2) piercing damage.

PLAGUE-BORN HOBGOBLIN

Medium undead, neutral evil

Armor Class 12 (natural armor)
Hit Points 68 (8d8 + 32)
Speed 25 ft.

STR	DEX	CON	INT	WIS	CHA
16 (+3)	6 (-2)	18 (+4)	2 (-4)	9 (-1)	1 (-5)

Saving Throws Con +6, Wis +1
Damage Immunities poison
Condition Immunities poisoned
Senses darkvision 60 ft., passive Perception 9
Languages understands the languages it knew in life, but can't speak
Challenge 2 (450 XP)

Cadaverous Appearance. While the plague-born is lying still, it is indistinguishable from a mundane decomposing corpse. It can still be detected by a *detect evil and good* spell, or similar magic.

Undead Fortitude. If damage reduces the plague-born to 0 hit points, it must make a Constitution saving throw with a DC of 5 + the damage taken, unless the damage is radiant or from a critical hit. On a success, the plague-born drops to 1 hit point instead.

ACTIONS

Multiattack. If it is not grappling a creature, the plague-born can make two bite attacks.

Slam. *Melee Weapon Attack:* +5 to hit, reach 5 ft., one target. *Hit:* 7 (1d8 + 3) bludgeoning damage, and the target is grappled (escape DC 13). Until this grapple ends, the plague-born can't use its slam against another target.

Bite. *Melee Weapon Attack:* +5 to hit, reach 5 ft., one grappled creature. *Hit:* 10 (2d6 + 3) piercing damage. Additionally, living creatures must succeed on a DC 12 Constitution saving throw, or take 4 (1d8) necrotic damage and contract the zombie necrosis disease (p.192).

"Gods, the years have not been kind to me, have they?"

—Runfolo Gastarne, ghost, upon seeing his own reanimated corpse

HOBGOBLIN PLAGUE-HOST
Medium undead, neutral evil

Armor Class 13 (natural armor)
Hit Points 133 (14d8 + 70)
Speed 25 ft.

STR	DEX	CON	INT	WIS	CHA
18 (+4)	6 (-2)	20 (+5)	2 (-4)	10 (+0)	1 (-5)

Saving Throws Con +8, Wis +3
Damage Immunities poison
Condition Immunities poisoned
Senses darkvision 60 ft., passive Perception 10
Languages understands the languages it knew in life, but can't speak
Challenge 8 (3,900 XP)

Cadaverous Appearance. While the plague-host is lying still, it is indistinguishable from a mundane decomposing corpse. It can still be detected by a *detect evil and good* spell, or similar magic.

Death Shriek (Recharge 5-6). As a bonus action, the plague-host utters an ear-splitting shriek that can be heard up to 500 ft away. Any other zombie, within 60 feet that can hear the shriek, can use its reaction to do one of the following:

- Move up to half its speed on the most direct path possible toward the shrieking plague-host.

- Make a single melee weapon attack against a creature within 5 feet of the shrieking plague-host.

Undead Fortitude. If damage reduces the plague-host to 0 hit points, it must make a Constitution saving throw with a DC of 5 + the damage taken, unless the damage is radiant or from a critical hit. On a success, the plague-host drops to 1 hit point instead.

ACTIONS

Multiattack. The plague-host makes two slam attacks. If it is not grappling a creature, the plague-host can instead make two bite attacks.

Slam. *Melee Weapon Attack:* +7 to hit, reach 5 ft., one target. *Hit:* 11 (2d6 + 4) bludgeoning damage and the target is grappled (escape DC 15). Until this grapple ends, the plague-host can't use its slam against another target.

Bite. *Melee Weapon Attack:* +7 to hit, reach 5 ft., one creature the plague-host or one of its allies is grappling. *Hit:* 14 (3d6 − 4) piercing damage. Additionally, living creatures must succeed on a DC 16 Constitution saving throw, or take 9 (2d8) necrotic damage and contract the zombie necrosis disease (p.192).

LEGENDARY ACTIONS

The plague-host can take 3 legendary actions, choosing from the options below. Only one legendary action option can be used at a time, and only at the end of another creature's turn. The plague-host regains spent legendary actions at the start of its turn.

Lurch. The plague-host moves up to 5 feet, without provoking opportunity attacks.

Attack (Costs 2 Actions). The plague-host makes one slam or bite attack.

Even after death, **hobgoblins** show rudimentary cooperation, attacking as a group rather than a collection of individuals.

ORC ZOMBIE

Medium undead, neutral evil

Armor Class 8
Hit Points 13 (2d8 + 4)
Speed 20 ft.

STR	DEX	CON	INT	WIS	CHA
16 (+3)	6 (-2)	15 (+2)	2 (-4)	7 (-2)	1 (-5)

Saving Throws Con +4, Wis +0
Damage Immunities poison
Condition Immunities poisoned
Senses darkvision 60 ft., passive Perception 8
Languages understands the languages it knew in life, but can't speak
Challenge 1/4 (50 XP)

Cadaverous Appearance. While the zombie is lying still, it is indistinguishable from a mundane decomposing corpse. It can still be detected by a *detect evil and good* spell, or similar magic.

Mindless Aggression. If the zombie uses the Dash action, and ends its movement within 5 feet of a creature, it can make a melee weapon attack against that creature as a bonus action. After making this attack, it can't move any further on that turn.

Undead Fortitude. If damage reduces the zombie to 0 hit points, it must make a Constitution saving throw with a DC of 5 + the damage taken, unless the damage is radiant or from a critical hit. On a success, the zombie drops to 1 hit point instead.

ACTIONS

Multiattack. The zombie makes two attacks: one with its slam, and one with its bite.

Slam. *Melee Weapon Attack:* +5 to hit, reach 5 ft., one target. *Hit:* 6 (1d6 + 3) bludgeoning damage.

Bite. *Melee Weapon Attack:* +5 to hit, reach 5 ft., one target. *Hit:* 6 (1d6 + 3) piercing damage.

PLAGUE-BORN ORC

Medium undead, neutral evil

Armor Class 12 (natural armor)
Hit Points 68 (8d8 + 32)
Speed 25 ft.

STR	DEX	CON	INT	WIS	CHA
18 (+4)	6 (-2)	18 (+4)	2 (-4)	9 (-1)	1 (-5)

Saving Throws Con +6, Wis +1
Damage Immunities poison
Condition Immunities poisoned
Senses darkvision 60 ft., passive Perception 9
Languages understands the languages it knew in life, but can't speak
Challenge 2 (450 XP)

Cadaverous Appearance. While the plague-born is lying still, it is indistinguishable from a mundane decomposing corpse. It can still be detected by a *detect evil and good* spell, or similar magic.

Mindless Aggression. If the plague-born uses the Dash action, and ends its movement within 5 feet of a creature, it can make a melee weapon attack against that creature as a bonus action. After making this attack, it can't move any further on that turn.

Undead Fortitude. If damage reduces the plague-born to 0 hit points, it must make a Constitution saving throw with a DC of 5 + the damage taken, unless the damage is radiant or from a critical hit. On a success, the plague-born drops to 1 hit point instead.

ACTIONS

Multiattack. The plague-born makes two attacks: one with its slam and one with its bite.

Slam. *Melee Weapon Attack:* +6 to hit, reach 5 ft., one target. *Hit:* 8 (1d8 + 4) bludgeoning damage, and the target is grappled (escape DC 12). Until this grapple ends, the plague-born can't use its slam against another target.

Bite. *Melee Weapon Attack:* +6 to hit, reach 5 ft., one target. *Hit:* 11 (2d6 + 4) piercing damage. Additionally, living creatures must succeed on a DC 12 Constitution saving throw, or take 9 (2d8) necrotic damage and contract the zombie necrosis disease (p.192).

ORC PLAGUE-HOST
Medium undead, neutral evil

Armor Class 13 (natural armor)
Hit Points 133 (14d8 + 70)
Speed 25 ft.

STR	DEX	CON	INT	WIS	CHA
20 (+5)	6 (-2)	20 (+5)	2 (-4)	10 (+0)	1 (-5)

Saving Throws Con +8, Wis +3
Damage Immunities poison
Condition Immunities poisoned
Senses darkvision 60 ft., passive Perception 10
Languages understands the languages it knew in life, but can't speak
Challenge 8 (3,900 XP)

Cadaverous Appearance. While the plague-host is lying still, it is indistinguishable from a mundane decomposing corpse. It can still be detected by a *detect evil and good* spell, or similar magic.

Mindless Aggression. If the plague-host uses the Dash action, and ends its movement within 5 feet of a creature, it can make a melee weapon attack against that creature as a bonus action. After making this attack, it can't move any further on that turn.

Aggressive Force. If the plague-host moves at least 20 feet straight toward a creature, and then makes a slam attack against that creature using its Mindless Aggression trait, the target takes an additional 21 (6d6) bludgeoning damage, and must succeed on a DC 16 Strength saving throw, or be knocked prone.

Undead Fortitude. If damage reduces the plague-host to 0 hit points, it must make a Constitution saving throw with a DC of 5 + the damage taken, unless the damage is radiant or from a critical hit. On a success, the plague-host drops to 1 hit point instead.

ACTIONS

Multiattack. The plague-host makes three attacks: two with its slam, and one with its bite.

Slam. *Melee Weapon Attack:* +8 to hit, reach 5 ft., one target. *Hit:* 11 (2d6 + 5) bludgeoning damage, and the target is grappled (escape DC 13). Until this grapple ends, the plague-host can't use its slam against another target.

Bite. *Melee Weapon Attack:* +8 to hit, reach 5 ft., one target. *Hit:* 14 (3d6 + 5) piercing damage. Additionally, living creatures must succeed on a DC 16 Constitution saving throw, or take 18 (4d8) necrotic damage and contract the zombie necrosis disease (p.192).

LEGENDARY ACTIONS

The plague-host can take 3 legendary actions, choosing from the options below. Only one legendary action option can be used at a time, and only at the end of another creature's turn. The plague-host regains spent legendary actions at the start of its turn.

Lurch. The plague-host moves up to 5 feet, without provoking opportunity attacks.

Attack (Costs 2 Actions). The plague-host makes one slam attack.

Orcs' natural aggression appears to be part of their very physiology, for their zombies seem to possess a heightened bloodlust.

"Be sure to include your freshest troops in the vanguard as you move forward. Not only are the newly-raised more durable, but this increases the chance of your foes coming across a familiar face. Any moment of hesitation in battle could well mean another soldier for your army."

-Shae-vash Shan, necromancer

OGRE ZOMBIE

Large undead, neutral evil

Armor Class 8
Hit Points 84 (8d10 + 40)
Speed 30 ft.

STR	DEX	CON	INT	WIS	CHA
19 (+4)	6 (-2)	20 (+5)	2 (-4)	7 (-2)	1 (-5)

Saving Throws Wis +0
Damage Immunities poison
Condition Immunities poisoned
Senses darkvision 60 ft., passive Perception 8
Languages understands the languages it knew in life, but can't speak
Challenge 2 (450 XP)

Cadaverous Appearance. While the zombie is lying still, it is indistinguishable from a mundane decomposing corpse. It can still be detected by a *detect evil and good* spell, or similar magic.

Undead Fortitude. If damage reduces the zombie to 0 hit points, it must make a Constitution saving throw with a DC of 5 + the damage taken, unless the damage is radiant or from a critical hit. On a success, the zombie drops to 1 hit point instead.

ACTIONS

Slam. *Melee Weapon Attack:* +6 to hit, reach 5 ft., one target. *Hit:* 11 (2d6 + 4) bludgeoning damage.

PLAGUE-BORN OGRE

Large undead, neutral evil

Armor Class 10 (natural armor)
Hit Points 184 (16d10 + 96)
Speed 30 ft.

STR	DEX	CON	INT	WIS	CHA
21 (+5)	6 (-2)	22 (+6)	2 (-4)	7 (-2)	1 (-5)

Saving Throws Con +9, Wis +1
Damage Immunities poison
Condition Immunities poisoned
Senses darkvision 60 ft., passive Perception 8
Languages understands the languages it knew in life, but can't speak
Challenge 7 (2,900 XP)

Cadaverous Appearance. While the plague-born is lying still, it is indistinguishable from a mundane decomposing corpse. It can still be detected by a *detect evil and good* spell, or similar magic.

Undead Fortitude. If damage reduces the plague-born to 0 hit points, it must make a Constitution saving throw with a DC of 5 + the damage taken, unless the damage is radiant or from a critical hit. On a success, the plague-born drops to 1 hit point instead.

Grappler. The plague-born has advantage on attack rolls against creatures it is grappling.

ACTIONS

Multiattack. The plague-born makes two attacks, only one of which can be a bite.

Slam. *Melee Weapon Attack:* +8 to hit, reach 5 ft., one target. *Hit:* 14 (2d8 + 5) bludgeoning damage. If the target is a Large or smaller creature, it is grappled. Until this grapple ends, the plague-born can't use this hand to make slam attacks against another creature. The plague-born can grapple up to two Medium or smaller creatures.

Bite. *Melee Weapon Attack:* +8 to hit, reach 5 ft., one target. *Hit:* 12 (2d6 + 5) piercing damage. Additionally, living creatures must succeed on a DC 18 Constitution saving throw, or take 9 (2d8) necrotic damage and contract the zombie necrosis disease (p.192).

OGRE PLAGUE-HOST

Large undead, neutral evil

Armor Class 12 (natural armor)
Hit Points 275 (22d10 + 154)
Speed 30 ft.

STR	DEX	CON	INT	WIS	CHA
23 (+6)	6 (-2)	24 (+7)	2 (-4)	7 (-2)	1 (-5)

Saving Throws Con +12, Wis +3
Damage Immunities poison
Condition Immunities poisoned
Senses darkvision 60 ft., passive Perception 8
Languages understands the languages it knew in life, but can't speak
Challenge 14 (11,500 XP)

Cadaverous Appearance. While the plague-host is lying still, it is indistinguishable from a mundane decomposing corpse. It can still be detected by a *detect evil and good* spell, or similar magic.

Grappler. The plague-host has advantage on attack rolls against creatures it is grappling.

Bursting Infection. If the plague-host dies, its bloated form explodes. Living creatures within 20 feet of the plague-host must succeed on a DC 20 Constitution saving throw, or take 9 (2d8) necrotic damage and contract the zombie necrosis disease (p 192). Creatures immune to the poisoned condition are immune to this disease.

Legendary Resistance (1/Day). If the plague-host fails a saving throw, other than a Constitution saving throw from its Undead Fortitude feature, it can choose to succeed instead.

Undead Fortitude. If damage reduces the plague-host to 0 hit points, it must make a Constitution saving throw with a DC of 5 + the damage taken, unless the damage is radiant or from a critical hit. On a success, the plague-host drops to 1 hit point instead.

ACTIONS

Multiattack. The plague-host makes three attacks: one with its bite and two with its slam.

Slam. *Melee Weapon Attack:* +11 to hit, reach 5 ft., one target. *Hit:* 15 (2d8 + 6) bludgeoning damage. If the target is a Large or smaller creature, it is grappled. Until this grapple ends, the plague-host can't use this hand to make slam attacks against another creature. The plague-host can grapple up to two Medium or smaller creatures.

Bite. *Melee Weapon Attack:* +11 to hit, reach 5 ft., one target. *Hit:* 16 (3d6 + 6) piercing damage. Additionally, living creatures must succeed on a DC 20 Constitution saving throw, or take 18 (4d8) necrotic damage and contract the zombie necrosis disease (p.192).

LEGENDARY ACTIONS

The plague-host can take 3 legendary actions, choosing from the options below. Only one legendary action option can be used at a time, and only at the end of another creature's turn. The plague-host regains spent legendary actions at the start of its turn.

Massive Sway. The plague-host moves up to 10 feet. During this movement, it can attempt to move into another creature's space. If it does so, the creature must make a DC 15 Strength saving throw. On a failure, the creature is pushed up to 10 feet in a direction of the plague-host's choosing. On a successful save, the plague-host ends its movement adjacent to the creature.

Slam (Costs 2 Actions). The plague-host makes one slam attack.

Those who have had the misfortune of spending time around **ogres** report that their zombies differ little from the living article, save for the smell.

Had another prankster in today. Seems he decided to surprise his friend by running at her moaning and covered in pig's blood. I know tensions are running high with the undead practically on our doorstep, and people need a release, but this kind of thing is going to get someone killed, if it continues. As it is, this one's lucky to be alive with a fractured skull. I suggest a public whipping, once he's on the mend, as an example to any other would-be comedians.

-letter from Hilde Vanster, physician, to Storrick Mazkhan, guard captain

TROLL ZOMBIE

Large undead, neutral evil

Armor Class 12 (natural armor)
Hit Points 80 (7d10 + 42)
Speed 25 ft.

STR	DEX	CON	INT	WIS	CHA
18 (+4)	6 (-2)	22 (+6)	2 (-4)	7 (-2)	1 (-5)

Saving Throws Wis +0
Damage Immunities necrotic, poison
Condition Immunities poisoned
Senses darkvision 60 ft., passive Perception 8
Languages understands the languages it knew in life, but can't speak
Challenge 3 (700 XP)

Cadaverous Appearance. While the zombie is lying still, it is indistinguishable from a mundane decomposing corpse. It can still be detected by a *detect evil and good* spell, or similar magic.

Foul Recovery (1/Turn). Whenever the zombie would take poison or necrotic damage, it instead takes no damage and regains a number of hit points equal to the total damage, up to 10 hit points.

Undead Fortitude. If damage reduces the zombie to 0 hit points, it must make a Constitution saving throw with a DC of 5 + the damage taken, unless the damage is radiant or from a critical hit. On a success, the zombie drops to 1 hit point instead.

ACTIONS

Multiattack. The zombie makes two attacks, only one of which can be a bite.

Claws. *Melee Weapon Attack:* +6 to hit, reach 5 ft., one target. *Hit:* 11 (2d6 + 4) slashing damage.

Bite. *Melee Weapon Attack:* +6 to hit, reach 5 ft., one target. *Hit:* 8 (1d8 + 4) piercing damage.

PLAGUE-BORN TROLL

Large undead, neutral evil

Armor Class 14 (natural armor)
Hit Points 175 (14d10 + 98)
Speed 30 ft.

STR	DEX	CON	INT	WIS	CHA
20 (+5)	6 (-2)	24 (+7)	2 (-4)	8 (-1)	1 (-5)

Saving Throws Con +10, Wis +2
Damage Immunities poison
Condition Immunities poisoned
Senses darkvision 60 ft., passive Perception 9
Languages understands the languages it knew in life, but can't speak
Challenge 8 (3,900 XP)

Cadaverous Appearance. While the plague-born is lying still, it is indistinguishable from a mundane decomposing corpse. It can still be detected by a *detect evil and good* spell, or similar magic.

Foul Recovery (1/Turn). Whenever the plague-born would take poison or necrotic damage, it instead takes no damage and regains a number of hit points equal to the total damage, up to 15 hit points.

Undead Fortitude. If damage reduces the plague-born to 0 hit points, it must make a Constitution saving throw with a DC of 5 + the damage taken, unless the damage is radiant or from a critical hit. On a success, the plague-born drops to 1 hit point instead.

ACTIONS

Multiattack. The plague-born makes three attacks: one with its bite, and two with its claws.

Claws. *Melee Weapon Attack:* +8 to hit, reach 5 ft., one target. *Hit:* 14 (2d8 + 5) slashing damage.

Bite. *Melee Weapon Attack:* +8 to hit, reach 5 ft., one target. *Hit:* 14 (2d8 + 5) piercing damage. Additionally, living creatures must succeed on a DC 18 Constitution saving throw, or take 9 (1d8) necrotic damage and contract the zombie necrosis disease (p.192).

TROLL PLAGUE-HOST

Large undead, neutral evil

Armor Class 16 (natural armor)
Hit Points 250 (20d10 + 140)
Speed 30 ft.

STR	DEX	CON	INT	WIS	CHA
22 (+6)	6 (-2)	25 (+7)	2 (-4)	9 (-1)	1 (-5)

Saving Throws Con +12, Wis +4
Damage Immunities poison
Condition Immunities poisoned
Senses darkvision 60 ft., passive Perception 8
Languages understands the languages it knew in life, but can't speak
Challenge 14 (11,500 XP)

Cadaverous Appearance. While the plague-host is lying still, it is indistinguishable from a mundane decomposing corpse. It can still be detected by a *detect evil and good* spell, or similar magic.

Foul Recovery (1/Turn). Whenever the plague-host would take poison or necrotic damage, it instead takes no damage and regains a number of hit points equal to the total damage, up to 20 hit points.

Undead Fortitude. If damage reduces the plague-host to 0 hit points, it must make a Constitution saving throw with a DC of 5 + the damage taken, unless the damage is radiant or from a critical hit. On a success, the plague-host drops to 1 hit point instead.

ACTIONS

Multiattack. The plague-host makes one attack with its bite, and two attacks with any combination of claw and foul limb attacks. It cannot make more than one attack with each severed limb.

Claws. *Melee Weapon Attack:* +11 to hit, reach 5 ft., one target. *Hit:* 20 (4d6 + 6) slashing damage.

Bite. *Melee Weapon Attack:* +11 to hit, reach 5 ft., one target. *Hit:* 19 (3d8 + 6) piercing damage. Additionally, living creatures must succeed on a DC 20 Constitution saving throw, or take 18 (4d8) necrotic damage and contract the zombie necrosis disease (p.192).

Foul Limb. *Melee or Ranged Weapon Attack:* +11 to hit, reach 10 ft. or range 30/90 ft., one target. *Hit:* 24 (4d8 + 6) bludgeoning damage. Additionally, living creatures must succeed on a DC 20 Constitution saving throw, or take 4 (1d8) necrotic damage and contract the zombie necrosis disease (p.192). Creatures immune to the poisoned condition are immune to this disease.

If the plague-host is not holding one of its own severed limbs when making this attack, it rips off one of its limbs first, dealing 13 (2d6 + 6) slashing damage to itself.

LEGENDARY ACTIONS

The plague-host can take 3 legendary actions, choosing from the options below. Only one legendary action option can be used at a time, and only at the end of another creature's turn. The plague-host regains spent legendary actions at the start of its turn.

Lurch. The plague-host moves up to 5 feet, without provoking opportunity attacks.

Claws (Costs 2 Actions). The plague-host makes one claws attack.

Trolls' immune systems, boosted by their extraordinary regeneration, react aggressively to the zombie contagion, often causing dramatic mutations in a vain attempt to fight off the disease.

YOUNG ZOMBIE DRAGON
Large undead, neutral evil

Armor Class 14 (natural armor)
Hit Points 114 (12d10 + 48)
Speed 30 ft., fly 40 ft.

STR	DEX	CON	INT	WIS	CHA
18 (+4)	8 (-1)	19 (+4)	2 (-4)	7 (-2)	1 (-5)

Saving Throws Con +7, Wis +0
Damage Immunities poison, necrotic
Condition Immunities poisoned
Senses blindsight 30 ft., darkvision 60 ft., passive Perception 8
Languages understands Common and Draconic, but can't speak
Challenge 5 (1,800 XP)

Cadaverous Appearance. While the zombie dragon is lying still, it is indistinguishable from a mundane decomposing corpse. It can still be detected by a *detect evil and good* spell, or similar magic.

Undead Fortitude. If damage reduces the zombie dragon to 0 hit points, it must make a Constitution saving throw with a DC of 5 + the damage taken, unless the damage is radiant or from a critical hit. On a success, the zombie dragon drops to 1 hit point instead.

ACTIONS

Multiattack. The zombie dragon makes two attacks: one with its bite, and one with its claws.

Bite. *Melee Weapon Attack:* +7 to hit, reach 10 ft., one target. *Hit:* 15 (2d10 + 4) piercing damage.

Claws. *Melee Weapon Attack:* +7 to hit, reach 5 ft., one target. *Hit:* 11 (2d6 + 4) slashing damage.

Rot Breath (Recharge 5-6). The zombie dragon exhales a squall of necrotic rot in a 30-foot cone. Creatures in the area must succeed on a DC 15 Constitution saving throw, taking 18 (4d8) necrotic damage on a failed save, or half as much damage on a successful one.

"We thought that we were doing well - we were barely holding on, but we were driving them back. Then a shadow blotted out the moon, and bile rained from the sky. We realized then that we'd be lucky if any of us saw the dawn."

-Baranthor, soldier, account of the defense of Atanarra

ADULT ZOMBIE DRAGON
Huge undead, neutral evil

Armor Class 15 (natural armor)
Hit Points 200 (16d12 + 96)
Speed 30 ft., fly 40 ft.

STR	DEX	CON	INT	WIS	CHA
22 (+6)	8 (-1)	23 (+6)	2 (-4)	9 (-1)	1 (-5)

Saving Throws Con +10, Wis +3
Damage Immunities poison, necrotic
Condition Immunities poisoned
Senses blindsight 30 ft., darkvision 60 ft., passive Perception 9
Languages understands Common and Draconic, but can't speak
Challenge 10 (5,900 XP)

Cadaverous Appearance. While the zombie dragon is lying still, it is indistinguishable from a mundane decomposing corpse. It can still be detected by a *detect evil and good* spell, or similar magic.

Undead Fortitude. If damage reduces the zombie dragon to 0 hit points, it must make a Constitution saving throw with a DC of 5 + the damage taken, unless the damage is radiant or from a critical hit. On a success, the zombie dragon drops to 1 hit point instead.

ACTIONS

Multiattack. The zombie dragon makes two attacks: one with its bite, and one with its claws.

Bite. *Melee Weapon Attack:* +10 to hit, reach 10 ft., one target. *Hit:* 17 (2d10 + 6) piercing damage. Additionally, living creatures must succeed on a DC 18 Constitution saving throw, or take 13 (3d8) necrotic damage and contract the zombie necrosis disease (p.192).

Claws. *Melee Weapon Attack:* +10 to hit, reach 5 ft., one target. *Hit:* 13 (2d6 + 6) slashing damage.

Tail. *Melee Weapon Attack:* +10 to hit, reach 5 ft., one target. *Hit:* 15 (2d8 + 6) slashing damage.

Rot Breath (Recharge 5-6). The zombie dragon exhales a squall of necrotic rot in a 30-foot cone. Creatures in the area must succeed on a DC 18 Constitution saving throw, taking 31 (7d8) necrotic damage on a failed save, or half as much damage on a successful one. A creature that fails its saving throw has its hit point maximum reduced by an amount equal to the necrotic damage taken. This reduction lasts until the creature finishes a short or long rest. If the creature's hit point maximum is reduced to 0, the creature dies.

LEGENDARY ACTIONS

The zombie dragon can take 1 legendary action, detailed below, at the end of another creature's turn. The zombie dragon regains the use of its legendary action at the start of its turn.

Tail. The zombie dragon makes one tail attack.

Ancient Zombie Dragon

Gargantuan undead, neutral evil

Armor Class 16 (natural armor)
Hit Points 385 (22d20 + 154)
Speed 30 ft., fly 40 ft.

STR	DEX	CON	INT	WIS	CHA
24 (+7)	8 (-1)	25 (+7)	2 (-4)	11 (+0)	1 (-5)

Saving Throws Con +13, Wis +6
Damage Immunities poison, necrotic
Condition Immunities poisoned
Senses blindsight 30 ft., darkvision 60 ft., passive Perception 10
Languages understands Common and Draconic, but can't speak
Challenge 17 (18,000 XP)

Cadaverous Appearance. While the zombie dragon is lying still, it is indistinguishable from a mundane decomposing corpse. It can still be detected by a *detect evil and good* spell, or similar magic.

Undead Fortitude. If damage reduces the zombie dragon to 0 hit points, it must make a Constitution saving throw with a DC of 5 + the damage taken, unless the damage is radiant or from a critical hit. On a success, the zombie dragon drops to 1 hit point instead.

Actions

Multiattack. The zombie dragon makes two attacks: one with its bite, and one with its claws.

Bite. *Melee Weapon Attack:* +13 to hit, reach 10 ft., one target. *Hit:* 17 (2d10 + 6) piercing damage. Additionally, living creatures must succeed on a DC 18 Constitution saving throw, or take 18 (4d8) necrotic damage and contract the zombie necrosis disease (p.192).

Claws. *Melee Weapon Attack:* +13 to hit, reach 5 ft , one target. *Hit:* 13 (2d6 + 6) slashing damage.

Tail. *Melee Weapon Attack:* +13 to hit, reach 5 ft., one target. *Hit:* 15 (2d8 + 6) slashing damage.

Rot Breath (Recharge 5-6). The zombie dragon exhales a squall of necrotic rot in a 30-foot cone. Creatures in the area must succeed on a DC 21 Constitution saving throw, taking 49 (11d8) necrotic damage on a failed save, or half as much damage on a successful one. A creature that fails its saving throw has its hit point maximum reduced by an amount equal to the necrotic damage taken. This reduction lasts until the creature finishes a short or long rest. If the creature's hit point maximum is reduced to 0, the creature dies.

Legendary Actions

The zombie dragon can take 3 legendary actions, choosing from the options below. Only one legendary action option can be used at a time, and only at the end of another creature's turn. The zombie dragon regains spent legendary actions at the start of its turn

Tail. The zombie dragon makes one tail attack.

Winged Lunge. The zombie dragon flies up to 10 feet.

Bite (Costs 2 Actions). The zombie dragon makes one bite attack.

It takes uncommonly powerful magic (or a particularly virulent strain of the disease) to resurrect a **dragon**, so such creatures typically exist under the thrall of a megalomaniacal necromancer who will have gone to great pains to raise one. The rare zombie dragons to arise on their own are heralds of disease, rot and woe.

ZOMBIE DOG

Medium undead, neutral evil

Armor Class 10
Hit Points 11 (2d8 + 2)
Speed 30 ft.

STR	DEX	CON	INT	WIS	CHA
14 (+2)	10 (+0)	13 (+1)	2 (-4)	11 (+0)	1 (-5)

Saving Throws Wis +2
Skills Perception +2
Damage Immunities poison
Condition Immunities poisoned
Senses darkvision 60 ft., passive Perception 12
Languages —
Challenge 1/8 (25 XP)

Cadaverous Appearance. While the zombie dog is lying still, it is indistinguishable from a mundane decomposing corpse. It can still be detected by a *detect evil and good* spell, or similar magic.

Keen Smell. The zombie dog has advantage on Wisdom (Perception) checks that rely on smell.

Pounce. If the zombie dog moves at least 15 feet directly toward a creature, and then hits it with a bite attack on the same turn, the target must succeed on a DC 12 Strength saving throw, or be knocked prone.

Undead Fortitude. If damage reduces the zombie dog to 0 hit points, it must make a Constitution saving throw with a DC of 5 + the damage taken, unless the damage is radiant or from a critical hit. On a success, the zombie dog drops to 1 hit point instead.

ACTIONS

Bite. *Melee Weapon Attack:* +4 to hit, reach 5 ft., one target. *Hit:* 5 (1d6 + 2) piercing damage.

PLAGUE-BORN DOG

Medium undead, neutral evil

Armor Class 13 (natural armor)
Hit Points 45 (6d8 + 18)
Speed 35 ft.

STR	DEX	CON	INT	WIS	CHA
16 (+3)	10 (+0)	16 (+3)	2 (-4)	13 (+1)	1 (-5)

Saving Throws Wis +3
Skills Perception +3
Damage Immunities poison
Condition Immunities poisoned
Senses darkvision 60 ft., passive Perception 13
Languages —
Challenge 2 (450 XP)

Cadaverous Appearance. While the plague-born dog is lying still, it is indistinguishable from a mundane decomposing corpse. It can still be detected by a *detect evil and good* spell, or similar magic.

Keen Smell. The plague-born dog has advantage on Wisdom (Perception) checks that rely on smell.

Pounce. If the plague-born dog moves at least 15 feet directly toward a creature, and then hits it with a bite attack on the same turn, the target must succeed on a DC 13 Strength saving throw, or be knocked prone.

Undead Fortitude. If damage reduces the plague-born dog to 0 hit points, it must make a Constitution saving throw with a DC of 5 + the damage taken, unless the damage is radiant or from a critical hit. On a success, the plague-born dog drops to 1 hit point instead.

ACTIONS

Bite. *Melee Weapon Attack:* +5 to hit, reach 5 ft., one target. *Hit:* 10 (2d6 + 3) piercing damage. Additionally, living creatures must succeed on a DC 13 Constitution saving throw or take 9 (2d8) necrotic damage and contract the zombie necrosis disease (p.192).

ZOMBIE OX
Large undead, neutral evil

Armor Class 10 (natural armor)
Hit Points 51 (6d10 + 18)
Speed 25 ft.

STR	DEX	CON	INT	WIS	CHA
19 (+4)	6 (-2)	16 (+3)	1 (-5)	6 (-2)	1 (-5)

Saving Throws Con +5, Wis +0
Damage Immunities poison
Condition Immunities poisoned
Senses darkvision 60 ft., passive Perception 8
Languages —
Challenge 1 (200 XP)

Cadaverous Appearance. While the zombie ox is lying still, it is indistinguishable from a mundane decomposing corpse. It can still be detected by a *detect evil and good* spell, or similar magic.

Charge. If the zombie ox moves at least 10 feet straight toward a target, and then hits it with a gore attack on the same turn, the target takes an extra 7 (2d6) piercing damage.

Undead Fortitude. If damage reduces the zombie to 0 hit points, it must make a Constitution saving throw with a DC of 5 + the damage taken, unless the damage is radiant or from a critical hit. On a success, the zombie ox drops to 1 hit point instead.

ACTIONS

Gore. *Melee Weapon Attack:* +6 to hit, reach 5 ft., one target. *Hit:* 11 (2d6 + 4) piercing damage.

ZOMBIE HORSE
Large undead, neutral evil

Armor Class 10 (natural armor)
Hit Points 30 (4d10 + 8)
Speed 35 ft.

STR	DEX	CON	INT	WIS	CHA
16 (+3)	8 (-1)	14 (+2)	1 (-5)	8 (-1)	1 (-5)

Saving Throws Wis +1
Damage Immunities poison
Condition Immunities poisoned
Senses darkvision 60 ft., passive Perception 9
Languages —
Challenge 1/4 (50 XP)

Cadaverous Appearance. While the zombie horse is lying still, it is indistinguishable from a mundane decomposing corpse. It can still be detected by a *detect evil and good* spell, or similar magic.

Charge. If the zombie horse moves at least 10 feet straight toward a target, and then hits it with an attack with its hooves on the same turn, the target must succeed on a DC 13 Strength saving throw, or be knocked prone.

Undead Fortitude. If damage reduces the zombie horse to 0 hit points, it must make a Constitution saving throw with a DC of 5 + the damage taken, unless the damage is radiant or from a critical hit. On a success, the zombie horse drops to 1 hit point instead.

ACTIONS

Hooves. *Melee Weapon Attack:* +5 to hit, reach 5 ft., one target. *Hit:* 8 (2d4 + 3) bludgeoning damage.

Zombie Bear

Large undead, neutral evil

Armor Class 11 (natural armor)
Hit Points 84 (8d10 + 40)
Speed 25 ft.

STR	DEX	CON	INT	WIS	CHA
21 (+5)	8 (-1)	20 (+5)	1 (-5)	9 (-1)	1 (-5)

Saving Throws Con +7, Wis +1
Damage Immunities poison
Condition Immunities poisoned
Senses darkvision 60 ft., passive Perception 9
Languages —
Challenge 2 (450 XP)

Cadaverous Appearance. While the zombie bear is lying still, it is indistinguishable from a mundane decomposing corpse. It can still be detected by a *detect evil and good* spell, or similar magic.

Undead Fortitude. If damage reduces the zombie bear to 0 hit points, it must make a Constitution saving throw with a DC of 5 + the damage taken, unless the damage is radiant or from a critical hit. On a success, the zombie bear drops to 1 hit point instead.

Actions

Multiattack. The zombie bear makes two attacks: one with its bite, and one with its claws.

Bite. *Melee Weapon Attack:* +7 to hit, reach 5 ft., one target. *Hit:* 9 (1d8 + 5) piercing damage.

Claws. *Melee Weapon Attack:* +7 to hit, reach 5 ft., one target. *Hit:* 12 (2d6 + 5) slashing damage.

Plague-Touched Rat

Tiny beast, unaligned

Armor Class 10
Hit Points 2 (1d4)
Speed 20 ft.

STR	DEX	CON	INT	WIS	CHA
2 (-4)	11 (+0)	11 (+0)	2 (-4)	10 (+0)	3 (-4)

Saving Throws Con +2
Damage Resistances poison
Senses darkvision 30 ft., passive Perception 10
Languages —
Challenge 0 (10 XP)

Insensitive to Pain. If damage reduces the plague-touched rat to 0 hit points, it must make a Constitution saving throw with a DC of 10 + the damage taken, unless the damage is from a critical hit. On a success, the plague-touched rat drops to 1 hit point instead.

Keen Smell. The plague-touched rat has advantage on Wisdom (Perception) checks that rely on smell.

Poison and Disease Resistance. The plague-touched rat has advantage on saving throws made to resist disease and the poisoned condition.

Actions

Bite. *Melee Weapon Attack:* +0 to hit, reach 5 ft., one target. *Hit:* 1 piercing damage. Additionally, living creatures must succeed on a DC 4 Constitution saving throw, or take 4 (1d8) necrotic damage and contract the zombie necrosis disease (p.192).

Swarm of Plague-Touched Rats

Medium swarm of Tiny beasts, unaligned

Armor Class 10
Hit Points 36 (8d8)
Speed 30 ft.

STR	DEX	CON	INT	WIS	CHA
9 (-1)	11 (+0)	11 (+0)	2 (-4)	10 (+0)	2 (-4)

Saving Throws Con +2
Damage Resistances bludgeoning, piercing, poison, slashing
Condition Immunities charmed, frightened, paralyzed, petrified, prone, restrained, stunned
Senses darkvision 30 ft., passive Perception 10
Languages —
Challenge 1 (200 XP)

Keen Smell. The swarm has advantage on Wisdom (Perception) checks that rely on smell.

Poison and Disease Resistance. The swarm has advantage on saving throws made to resist disease and the poisoned condition.

Swarm. The swarm can occupy another creature's space, and vice versa, and the swarm can move through any opening large enough for a Tiny rat. The swarm can't regain hit points or gain temporary hit points.

Swarm Insensitivity. If damage reduces the swarm to 17 or fewer hit points, it must make a Constitution saving throw with a DC of 5 + the damage taken, unless the damage is from a critical hit. On a success, the swarm is only reduced to 18 hit points.

If damage reduces the swarm to 0 hit points, it must make a Constitution saving throw with a DC of 5 + the damage taken, unless the damage is from a critical hit. On a success, the swarm drops to 1 hit point instead.

Actions

Bites. *Melee Weapon Attack:* +2 to hit, reach 0 ft., one target in the swarm's space. *Hit:* 7 (2d6) piercing damage, or 3 (1d6) piercing damage if the swarm has half of its hit points or fewer. Additionally, living creatures must succeed on a DC 10 Constitution saving throw, or take 9 (2d8) necrotic damage and contract the zombie necrosis disease (p.192).

Plague-Touched Raven

Tiny beast, unaligned

Armor Class 12
Hit Points 2 (1d4)
Speed 10 ft., fly 50 ft.

STR	DEX	CON	INT	WIS	CHA
2 (-4)	14 (+2)	10 (+0)	2 (-4)	12 (+1)	4 (-3)

Saving Throws Con +2
Skills Perception +3
Damage Resistances poison
Senses passive Perception 13
Languages —
Challenge 1/8 (25 XP)

Insensitive to Pain. If damage reduces the plague-touched raven to 0 hit points, it must make a Constitution saving throw with a DC of 10 + the damage taken, unless the damage is from a critical hit. On a success, the plague-touched raven drops to 1 hit point instead.

Mimicry. The plague-touched raven can mimic simple sounds it has heard, such as a person whispering, a baby crying, or an animal chittering. A creature that hears the sounds can tell they are imitations with a successful DC 10 Wisdom (Insight) check.

Poison and Disease Resistance. The plague-touched raven has advantage on saving throws made to resist disease and the poisoned condition.

Actions

Bite. *Melee Weapon Attack:* +4 to hit, reach 5 ft., one target. *Hit:* 1 piercing damage. Additionally, living creatures must succeed on a DC 4 Constitution saving throw or take 4 (1d8) necrotic damage and contract the zombie necrosis disease (p.192).

Swarm of Plague-Touched Ravens

Medium swarm of Tiny beasts, unaligned

Armor Class 12
Hit Points 36 (8d8)
Speed 10 ft., fly 50 ft.

STR	DEX	CON	INT	WIS	CHA
6 (-2)	14 (+2)	11 (+0)	3 (-4)	12 (+1)	4 (-3)

Saving Throws Con +2
Skills Perception +5
Damage Resistances bludgeoning, piercing, poison, slashing
Condition Immunities charmed, frightened, paralyzed, petrified, prone, restrained, stunned
Senses passive Perception 15
Languages —
Challenge 2 (450 XP)

Poison and Disease Resistance. The swarm has advantage on saving throws made to resist disease and the poisoned condition.

Swarm. The swarm can occupy another creature's space, and vice versa, and the swarm can move through any opening large enough for a Tiny raven. The swarm can't regain hit points or gain temporary hit points.

Swarm Insensitivity. If damage reduces the swarm to 17 or fewer hit points, it must make a Constitution saving throw with a DC of 5 + the damage taken, unless the damage is from a critical hit. On a success, the swarm is only reduced to 18 hit points.

If damage reduces the swarm to 0 hit points, it must make a Constitution saving throw with a DC of 5 + the damage taken, unless the damage is from a critical hit. On a success, the swarm drops to 1 hit point instead.

Actions

Beaks. *Melee Weapon Attack:* +4 to hit, reach 0 ft., one target in the swarm's space. *Hit:* 7 (2d6) piercing damage, or 3 (1d6) piercing damage if the swarm has half of its hit points or fewer. Additionally, living creatures must succeed on a DC 11 Constitution saving throw, or take 9 (2d8) necrotic damage and contract the zombie necrosis disease (p.192).

Swarm of Plague-Touched Roaches

Medium swarm of Tiny beasts, unaligned

Armor Class 12 (natural armor)
Hit Points 33 (6d8 + 6)
Speed 20 ft., climb 20 ft.

STR	DEX	CON	INT	WIS	CHA
3 (-4)	13 (+1)	12 (+1)	1 (-5)	7 (-2)	1 (-5)

Saving Throws Con +3
Damage Resistances bludgeoning, piercing, poison, slashing
Condition Immunities charmed, frightened, paralyzed, petrified, prone, restrained, stunned
Senses blindsight 10 ft., passive Perception 8
Languages —
Challenge 1 (200 XP)

Poison and Disease Resistance. The swarm has advantage on saving throws made to resist disease and the poisoned condition.

Swarm. The swarm can occupy another creature's space, and vice versa, and the swarm can move through any opening large enough for a Tiny roach. The swarm can't regain hit points or gain temporary hit points.

Swarm Insensitivity. If damage reduces the swarm to 15 or fewer hit points, it must make a Constitution saving throw with a DC of 5 + the damage taken, unless the damage is from a critical hit. On a success, the swarm is only reduced to 16 hit points.

If damage reduces the swarm to 0 hit points, it must make a Constitution saving throw with a DC of 5 + the damage taken, unless the damage is from a critical hit. On a success, the swarm drops to 1 hit point instead.

Actions

Bites. *Melee Weapon Attack:* +3 to hit, reach 0 ft., one target in the swarm's space. *Hit:* 10 (4d4) piercing damage, or 5 (2d4) piercing damage if the swarm has half of its hit points or fewer. Additionally, living creatures must succeed on a DC 10 Constitution saving throw, or take 9 (2d8) necrotic damage and contract the zombie necrosis disease (p.192).

PLAGUE SWARM INFESTATION

Some zombies are created from corpses that were fed upon by plague-touched animals. Many of the creatures may still inhabit and slowly feed on the body as it rises to undeath. Such an infested zombie does not appear significantly different from most other zombies, other than having especially ravaged flesh.

A zombie infested by a plague swarm, and the swarm inside it, are treated as a single creature with the zombie's normal statistics, except for the following ability:

Bursting Infestation. When the zombie dies, the swarm infesting it bursts from its body. Swarms of plague-touched rats, ravens, or roaches exit the body into the zombie's space, or a space within 5 feet of the zombie. The swarms roll their own initiative.

All swarms infesting a zombie are of the same type. The number of swarms exiting the body depends on the zombie's size:

Tiny - a tiny zombie cannot be infested

Small or Medium - 1 Swarm

Large - 1d4 Swarms

Huge - 1d8 Swarms

Gargantuan - 2d8 Swarms

THE ZOMBIE ARCHETYPE

This template can be applied to any beast, dragon, humanoid, or monstrosity. The following changes apply:

- **Ability Scores.** Unless its natural attribute is lower, the zombie's Intelligence score becomes 2 (-4), its Wisdom score becomes 7 (-2), and it's Charisma score becomes 1 (-5).

- **Type.** The zombies type becomes undead, and it loses all subtypes.

- **Alignment.** The zombie's alignment becomes neutral evil.

- **Slow.** Each of the zombie's speeds are reduced by 10 feet to a minimum of 10 feet.

- **Poison Immunity.** The zombie is immune to poison damage and the poisoned condition.

- **Mindlessness.** The zombie loses all Spellcasting and Innate Spellcasting abilities, but it retains other abilities that allow it to produce magical effects. Furthermore, the zombie loses proficiency with all tools, skills, martial weapons, and armor. It can no longer speak, but still understands the languages it knew in life.

- **Cadaverous Appearance.** While the zombie is lying still, it is indistinguishable from a mundane decomposing corpse. It can still be detected by a *detect evil and good* spell, or similar magic.

- **Undead Fortitude.** If damage reduces the zombie to 0 hit points, it must make a Constitution saving throw with a DC of 5 + the damage taken, unless the damage is radiant or from a critical hit. On a success, the zombie drops to 1 hit point instead.

- **Slam.** If the zombie has arms, it gains a slam melee attack that deals 1d6 bludgeoning damage, unless the zombie already has a claw, fist, slam, or tentacle attack. The zombie is proficient with this attack. A Large zombie deals 2d6 damage, a Huge zombie deals 3d6, and a Gargantuan zombie deals 4d6 damage with its slam instead.

- **Undead Nature.** The zombie doesn't require air, food, drink, or sleep.

Plague-born are created by zombies known as plague-hosts. They are generally more powerful than regular zombies, and capable of infecting creatures with a necromantic disease that slowly kills a victim and raises its corpse as another zombie. The same changes apply to plague-born as normal zombies, with the addition of the following:

- **Slam.** The zombie's slam attack deals d8s for damage, instead of d6s. Additionally, on a hit, the target is grappled (escape DC 10 + the zombie's Strength modifier).

- **Bite.** If the zombie has a beak or a mouth with teeth, it gains a bite melee attack that deals 2d6 piercing damage, unless the zombie already has a bite or beak attack. The zombie is proficient with this attack, but it can only target creatures it is grappling. A Large zombie deals 4d6 damage, a Huge zombie deals 6d6, and a Gargantuan zombie deals 8d6 damage with its bite instead.

Additionally, whenever the zombie hits with a bite or beat attack, if the target is a living creature it must succeed on a Constitution saving throw (DC 8 + half the zombie's proficiency bonus + the zombie's Constitution modifier), or take 9 (2d8) necrotic damage and contract the zombie necrosis disease (p.192).

- **Multiattack.** As an action, the zombie makes an attack with its slam. If it is grappling a creature, it then makes a bite attack. This ability does not replace any other multiattack routines; if it has several multiattack abilities, it can choose which one to use.

The bite went bad quickly, and it's beginning to stink.

Our endeavor started off well enough. Fleeing the scene of the battle ahead of the ravening horde of awakened dead, who suddenly found themselves bereft of leadership, we warned as many settlements in their path as we could. Our time was split between scouting, attempting to keep track of the fragmenting (in more ways than one) zombies, and aiding in the fortification and defense of whatever villages we encountered. Our victories did not come without cost, of course, but I shudder to think how much higher those costs could have been without our warnings. Thaddeus was still forced to favor his off-hand: the other remained withered and black. With practice, though, he was becoming more confident, and he would have plenty of practice in the following days.

So many terrible nights of fighting. The dead were relentless, while we grew ever more exhausted. Thaddeus had to remind me many times that there was no saving them, that they were nothing more than evil beasts in humanoid form but, still, their faces, contorted and raging as they might have been, once belonged to people. In this, those more decayed zombies were almost preferable, their features so disfigured by rot as to be barely recognizable, though they brought with them a horror all their own.

Eventually, though, it seemed that our efforts were beginning to make a dent. By evacuating the villages that we could, fortifying those who could not flee (and, regrettably, burning those we failed to defend), we deprived our enemy of fresh troops. Lacking any leadership, the horde became fragmented, and it became easier to trap and dispatch large numbers of them (knowing that they would never learn from their mistakes, we were not forced to be particularly creative).

We had almost finished clearing out another village. The inhabitants, at our urging, were making their way to the nearest walled town, spurred on by the sporadic attacks from the remnants of the horde. We had repelled one such attack the night before, with the help of a ragged militia of those who

had elected to stay behind to help move along any stragglers who were, for whatever reason, still unwilling or unable to leave. We suspected that last night's attack was the worst of it, and remained only to assure ourselves of this fact before moving on.

Dusk came again and, with it, another attack. Such was the experience of the past few weeks that the evening was unremarkable, overall. The dead surged forth against our defences, and we beat a fighting retreat with fire, sword, and whatever other weapons could be scrounged. Towards midnight, as Thaddeus rallied a counterattack, I heard sounds of a struggle from a nearby barn and, having been proven of little use on the front-line anyway, cautiously moved to investigate.

I was immediately assailed by the rot within. Bodies, of fallen allies and slain foes alike, had been piled within after last night's assault – Thaddeus and I had learnt quickly that it was best to gather and burn all we could before moving on. As I held a rag to my nose against the smell, I was met with a sight which, devoid of the horrific scenery, might have been amusing. A halfling was struggling mightily, tugging with all his might at a length of rope fastened to the collar of a large goat, who was clearly as unconcerned with her surroundings as she was uninterested in leaving them.

The halfling yelled with fear at my approach, but quickly saw that I was not, as luck would have it, dead. He hurried me over with a grubby paw, asked if I was "one o' them adventure-y types" and, before I could muster an answer, solicited my help in his endeavor as he "weren't goin' nowhere withou' our Bess", by which he meant the goat. As I began to explain that I was hardly better equipped to move the beast than he was, another figure entered the barn.

I would not want to face down an orc at the best of times. As it was, the creature's slack jaw (revealing tusks dripping with black bile), its foot-dragging shuffle, and the hollow moan emanating from its rancid mouth all told me that we were far from the best of times. It turned its ghastly face to the halfling and, with heedless fury, trampled a path over the scattered corpses to get at him. Time seemed to slow; the halfling's face frozen in panic, the goat bleating as it bolted, the orc's corpse barreling down upon us, and my hand found the haft of a pitchfork leaning against a wall. With strength I did not know I possessed (and still somewhat doubt I exhibited), I gave some semblance of a battlecry and charged, gripping the pitchfork like a spear.

The orc was heavier, but I was able to gain greater speed, and the impact pushed it back. It stumbled, uncoordinated, and I continued my charge, driving it back. With a shuddering impact, I drove it against the wall, the tines of the fork biting through rotting flesh and wood alike, to pin it in place. It howled, clawling wildly and snapping with its dripping fangs. Remembering Thaddeus' teachings, I looked for a blade to put an end to it, and found a sickle I thought would serve, still clutched in the hand of an unrecognizable corpse who had, presumably, wielded it last night. I wrenched it from the hand and swung.
Decaying as it was, the orc's neck was still thick with muscle, and a sickle is no headsman's axe. It took more chops than I would have liked.

Sweating and tired, I took a moment to savor my victory, small as it may have been. The halfling, wide-eyed, nodded a mute thank you. I took a breath. It was then that I felt a pinching, ripping pain. The corpse, whose sickle I had borrowed, had reared up and, perhaps taking exception to my acquisition, sunk its teeth deep into the flesh of my palm. I panicked and swung down, feeling the jolt up my arm as my blade bit into its skull, before it could get to its feet. I shouted for my companion to run, but he and his goat were already gone; one more zombie, it would seem, was the last straw. I was completely alone. I ran.

Later, I found Thaddeus. We had won another night. He said nothing about my hand, though he definitely saw it. Already it was puffy, inflamed, red, and difficult to miss. The villagers had moved on to safety. We burnt the barn, orc, pitchfork and all. Its crackling flames were brilliant in the darkness of midnight, throwing into deep relief the crags of Thaddeus' face, or the inscrutable mask he wore in place of one. I shivered against the cold regardless.

Thaddeus thought it safe enough to stay for the night, and he set up our camp in the sole stone structure the village had to offer: the fire-gutted ruin of an old farmhouse. The edges of the bite were beginning to turn black now, and it was weeping a foul-smelling fluid. Despite the sickness I felt upon looking at it, I was ravenous.

I can see Dorothea, clearer than Thaddeus somehow, calling to me. Says it's alright, or is that Thaddeus' hand on my shoulder? Thoughts come slowly. Writing is difficult.

The sun is beginning to rise. Not had breakfast.

So hungry.

I'm afraid

APPENDIX A: ANIMATED OBJECTS

The objects in this appendix may have been animated by any manner of undead and accursed creature, for any number of reasons. They are often associated with incorporeal creatures, such as ghosts, used as often to terrify, distract, and drive off would-be intruders as to do damage. Items might have been cursed by malevolent spellcasters to stand vigil and guard their lairs, or maybe possessed by a long-deceased spirit, desperate for any kind of corporeal existence. Areas ravaged by spiritual disturbance may, inadvertently, grant sentience to the most mundane of objects, which might have mixed feelings about the strange new world they are now cognizant of...

ANIMATED OBJECT ENCOUNTERS

d6	CR	Encounter
1	4	**Indignant Doll Collection:** 1 Haunted Doll, 6 Living Dolls
2	5	**Belligerent Armory:** 4 Animated Spiked Armors, 6 Flying Halberds, 4 Animated Longbows
3	8	**Crusading Miniature Collection:** 4 Miniature Infantry Regiments, 2 Miniature Soldiers, 4 Miniature Chariots
4	15	**Disgruntled Crop:** 1 Jack o' Lantern, 4 Hitched Scarecrows
5	19	**Unruly Treasure Hoard:** 1 Sentient Sword, 2 Enchanted Flying Swords, 1 Possessed Armor, 1 Giant Animated Armor, 2 Masterwork Animated Armors
6	26	**Rebellious Flotilla:** 3 Ghost Ships

LIVING DOLL

Small construct, unaligned

Armor Class 12
Hit Points 14 (4d6)
Speed 25 ft.

STR	DEX	CON	INT	WIS	CHA
6 (-2)	15 (+2)	11 (+0)	1 (-5)	4 (-3)	11 (+0)

Damage Vulnerabilities bludgeoning, thunder
Damage Immunities poison, psychic
Condition Immunities blinded, charmed, deafened, exhaustion, frightened, paralyzed, petrified, poisoned
Senses blindsight 60 ft. (blind beyond this radius), passive Perception 7
Languages —
Challenge 1/4 (50 XP)

Antimagic Susceptibility. The living doll is incapacitated while in an area of antimagic, such as an *antimagic field*. If targeted by a *dispel magic* spell, the doll must succeed on a Constitution saving throw against the caster's spell save DC, or fall unconscious for 1 minute.

False Appearance. While the living doll remains motionless, it is indistinguishable from a normal doll.

ACTIONS

Fist (Requires Unshattered Hand). *Melee Weapon Attack:* +4 to hit, reach 5 ft., one target. *Hit:* 2 (1d4) bludgeoning damage to both the target and the living doll, and the living doll's hand shatters.

Sharp Fracture (Requires Shattered Hand). *Melee Weapon Attack:* +4 to hit, reach 5 ft., one target. *Hit:* 5 (1d6 + 2) piercing damage.

HAUNTED DOLL
Small construct, neutral evil

Armor Class 14 (natural armor)
Hit Points 45 (10d6 + 10)
Speed 25 ft.

STR	DEX	CON	INT	WIS	CHA
6 (-2)	17 (+3)	13 (+1)	10 (+0)	12 (+1)	17 (+3)

Damage Vulnerabilities bludgeoning, thunder
Damage Immunities poison, psychic
Condition Immunities blinded, charmed, deafened, exhaustion, frightened, paralyzed, petrified, poisoned
Senses blindsight 60 ft. (blind beyond this radius), passive Perception 11
Languages —
Challenge 4 (1,100 XP)

False Appearance. While the haunted doll remains motionless and silent, it is indistinguishable from a normal doll.

Pitiful Cries. The haunted doll can constantly emit sorrowful cries, like those of a child weeping or crying for help. Adult humanoids who start their turn within 60 feet of the doll, and can hear it, must succeed on a DC 13 Wisdom saving throw against this magic, or be charmed by the doll until the start of their next turn.

While charmed in this way, during its turn, the creature must move directly toward the doll along the shortest safe path. Additionally, the doll has advantage on attack rolls against the charmed creature.

A creature that succeeds on three saving throws against the same doll's Pitiful Cries becomes immune to the effect.

A creature that fails on three saving throws against the same doll's Pitiful Cries becomes charmed for 24 hours.

Sneak Attack (1/Turn). The haunted doll deals an extra 21 (6d6) damage when it hits a target with a weapon attack, and has advantage on the attack roll, or when the target is within 5 feet of an ally of the doll that isn't incapacitated, and the doll doesn't have disadvantage on the attack roll.

ACTIONS

Fist (Requires Unshattered Hand). *Melee Weapon Attack:* +5 to hit, reach 5 ft., one target. *Hit:* 2 (1d4) bludgeoning damage, and the living doll's hand shatters.

Sharp Fracture (Requires Shattered Hand). *Melee Weapon Attack:* +5 to hit, reach 5 ft., one target. *Hit:* 6 (1d6 + 3) piercing damage.

Kitchen Knife. *Melee Weapon Attack:* +5 to hit, reach 5 ft., one target. *Hit:* 5 (1d4 + 3) piercing damage.

ANIMATED SPIKED ARMOR
Medium construct, unaligned

Armor Class 18 (natural armor)
Hit Points 32 (5d8 + 10)
Speed 30 ft.

STR	DEX	CON	INT	WIS	CHA
15 (+2)	10 (+0)	14 (+2)	1 (-5)	3 (-4)	1 (-5)

Damage Immunities poison, psychic
Condition Immunities blinded, charmed, deafened, exhaustion, frightened, paralyzed, petrified, poisoned
Senses blindsight 60 ft. (blind beyond this radius), passive Perception 6
Languages —
Challenge 1 (200 XP)

Antimagic Susceptibility. The armor is incapacitated while in an area of antimagic, such as an *antimagic field*. If targeted by a *dispel magic* spell, the armor must succeed on a Constitution saving throw against the caster's spell save DC, or fall unconscious for 1 minute.

False Appearance. While the armor remains motionless, it is indistinguishable from a normal suit of armor.

Spiked Form. If the armor is grappling, or grappled by, a creature, it can deal 5 (1d6 + 2) piercing damage to that creature as a bonus action.

ACTIONS

Slam. *Melee Weapon Attack:* +4 to hit, reach 5 ft., one target. *Hit:* 5 (1d6 + 2) bludgeoning damage, and the target is grappled (escape DC 12).

"Picked it up last market day. Loved her cute little dress. Seller seemed keen to be rid of it, to be honest..."

-Aradayle, baker (deceased)

GIANT ANIMATED ARMOR
Large construct, unaligned

Armor Class 17 (natural armor)
Hit Points 76 (8d10 + 32)
Speed 30 ft.

STR	DEX	CON	INT	WIS	CHA
19 (+4)	8 (-1)	18 (+4)	1 (-5)	3 (-4)	1 (-5)

Damage Immunities poison, psychic
Condition Immunities blinded, charmed, deafened, exhaustion, frightened, paralyzed, petrified, poisoned
Senses blindsight 60 ft. (blind beyond this radius), passive Perception 6
Languages —
Challenge 5 (1,800 XP)

Antimagic Susceptibility. The armor is incapacitated while in an area of antimagic, such as an *antimagic field*. If targeted by a *dispel magic* spell, the armor must succeed on a Constitution saving throw against the caster's spell save DC, or fall unconscious for 1 minute.

False Appearance. While the armor remains motionless, it is indistinguishable from a normal suit of armor.

ACTIONS

Multiattack. The armor makes two slam attacks. It can use Imprison in place of one attack.

Slam. *Melee Weapon Attack:* +7 to hit, reach 5 ft., one target. *Hit:* 11 (2d6 + 4) bludgeoning damage. If the target is a Medium or smaller creature, it is grappled (escape DC 15). The armor has two arms, each of which can grapple one Medium or smaller creature.

Imprison. The armor stuffs a Medium or smaller creature it is grappling into its hollow torso, which ends the grapple. While imprisoned, a creature is blinded and restrained and has total cover against effects and attacks from outside the armor. The armor can have no more than two creatures imprisoned at a time.

An imprisoned creature can use its action to attempt a DC 19 Dexterity (Acrobatics) or Strength (Athletics) check, escaping the armor on a success, falling prone in an adjacent space.

If the armor is destroyed, imprisoned creatures can escape using 10 feet of movement, exiting prone.

MASTERWORK ANIMATED ARMOR
Medium construct, unaligned

Armor Class 19 (natural armor)
Hit Points 91 (14d8 + 28)
Speed 30 ft.

STR	DEX	CON	INT	WIS	CHA
16 (+3)	11 (+0)	15 (+2)	6 (-2)	10 (+0)	6 (-2)

Saving Throws Con +5
Damage Immunities poison, psychic
Condition Immunities blinded, charmed, deafened, exhaustion, frightened, paralyzed, petrified, poisoned
Senses blindsight 60 ft. (blind beyond this radius), passive Perception 10
Languages —
Challenge 5 (1,800 XP)

Antimagic Susceptibility. The armor is incapacitated while in an area of antimagic, such as an *antimagic field*. If targeted by a *dispel magic* spell, the armor must succeed on a Constitution saving throw against the caster's spell save DC, or fall unconscious for 1 minute.

False Appearance. While the armor remains motionless, it is indistinguishable from a normal suit of armor.

ACTIONS

Multiattack. The armor makes three attacks: two with its halberd and one with its slam.

Halberd. *Melee Weapon Attack:* +6 to hit, reach 10 ft., one target. *Hit:* 8 (1d10 + 3) bludgeoning damage.

Slam. *Melee Weapon Attack:* +6 to hit, reach 5 ft., one target. *Hit:* 6 (1d6 + 3) bludgeoning damage.

"Thought if I got the enchantment right, I could save on the cost of a squire, you know, just have the armor follow me about by itself when I wasn't using it. Had to stop wearing it after it walked me five miles behind enemy lines. Managed to get it home, and now it's hacking up the east wing. I'm not sure how to make it stop..."

-Lord Welkhern Rost, on his set of animated armor

POSSESSED ARMOR

Medium construct, chaotic evil

Armor Class 19 (natural armor)
Hit Points 172 (23d8 + 69)
Speed 35 ft.

STR	DEX	CON	INT	WIS	CHA
20 (+5)	11 (+0)	17 (+3)	14 (+2)	13 (+1)	14 (+2)

Saving Throws Cha +6
Damage Vulnerabilities radiant
Damage Resistances acid, fire, necrotic
Damage Immunities cold, lightning, poison
Condition Immunities blinded, deafened, exhaustion, paralyzed, petrified, poisoned
Senses blindsight 60 ft. (blind beyond this radius), passive Perception 10
Languages understands Abyssal, but can't speak
Challenge 10 (5,900 XP)

Possession. The possessed armor can be donned like an ordinary suit of armor, functioning as a suit of +1 plate armor. While worn by a creature, the armor can't take actions and perceives through the senses of its wearer, in addition to its own blindsight. Resistances and immunities only apply to the armor itself, not the wearer.

If a creature dons or partially dons the armor, the creature must make a DC 19 Charisma saving throw. The creature is unaware that it is resisting possession. On a failed saving throw, the creature is possessed by the armor until targeted by a *dispel evil and good* spell, or similar magic. If the creature succeeds on the saving throw, it must make another saving throw each hour until it doffs the armor. While possessed, the creature is completely under the armor's control.

Aura of Evil Arcane. The armor, and any creature wearing it, can be detected by a *detect evil and good* spell, or similar magic, as though it were a fiend. It can also be detected by a *detect magic* spell, seeming to be a suit of +1 plate armor.

False Appearance. While the armor remains motionless, it is indistinguishable from a normal suit of armor.

Fiendish Dismissal. If the armor is targeted by a *dispel evil and good* spell, or similar effect, it must save as though it were a demon. If it fails its saving throw against the dismissal effect, the possessing demon is sent to its home plane for 1 hour, and the armor becomes a mundane suit of plate armor for that duration. If the armor is destroyed while the demon is banished, the demon is permanently banished.

Shadow Strikes. Melee weapon attacks made by the armor, or a creature wearing it, deal an extra 7 (2d6) psychic damage (already included in the armor's attacks).

ACTIONS

Multiattack. The armor makes three attacks, two with its halberd and one with its slam.

Halberd. *Melee Weapon Attack:* +9 to hit, reach 10 ft., one target. *Hit:* 10 (1d10 + 5) bludgeoning damage, plus 7 (2d6) psychic damage.

Slam. *Melee Weapon Attack:* +9 to hit, reach 5 ft., one target. *Hit:* 8 (1d6 + 5) bludgeoning damage, plus 7 (2d6) psychic damage.

GHOSTLY STAGECOACH

Huge construct, neutral evil

Armor Class 16 (natural armor)
Hit Points 178 (17d12 + 68)
Speed 40 ft., fly 40 ft. (hover)

STR	DEX	CON	INT	WIS	CHA
22 (+6)	8 (-1)	19 (+4)	2 (-4)	17 (+3)	1 (-5)

Saving Throws Str +11, Dex +5
Skills Perception +8
Damage Immunities poison, psychic
Condition Immunities blinded, charmed, deafened, exhaustion, frightened, paralyzed, petrified, poisoned, prone
Senses blindsight 60 ft., darkvision 120 ft., passive Perception 18
Languages understands Common, but can't speak
Challenge 15 (13,000 XP)

Legendary Resistance (3/Day). If the stagecoach fails a saving throw, it can choose to succeed instead.

Runover. If the stagecoach moves at least 20 feet in a straight line, it can move through other Large or smaller creatures' spaces. Creatures whose space it moves through must succeed on a DC 17 Dexterity saving throw, or take 36 (8d8) bludgeoning damage and be knocked prone. On a successful save, the creature takes half as much damage and isn't knocked prone.

Undead Weakness. If the stagecoach is targeted by an effect that turns undead, it must make a save against the effect. On a failed save, it is not turned, but is instead stunned until the end of its next turn.

ACTIONS

Multiattack. The stagecoach makes three attacks: two with its phantasmal hooves and one with its phantasmal whip.

Phantasmal Hooves. *Melee Spell Attack:* +11 to hit, reach 10 ft., one target. *Hit:* 14 (4d6) necrotic damage.

Phantasmal Whip. *Melee Spell Attack:* +11 to hit, reach 15 ft., one target. *Hit:* 9 (2d8) necrotic damage.

LEGENDARY ACTIONS

The ghostly stagecoach can take 3 legendary actions, choosing from the options below. Only one legendary action option can be used at a time, and only at the end of another creature's turn. The stagecoach regains spent legendary actions at the start of its turn.

Whip. The stagecoach makes a phantasmal whip attack.

Ghostly Rush (Costs 2 Actions). The stagecoach moves up to half its speed.

HITCHED SCARECROW
Medium construct, chaotic evil

Armor Class 14 (natural armor)
Hit Points 84 (13d8 + 26)
Speed 0 ft., fly 30 ft. (hover)

STR	DEX	CON	INT	WIS	CHA
18 (+4)	9 (-1)	15 (+2)	11 (+0)	10 (+0)	16 (+3)

Damage Vulnerabilities fire
Damage Resistances bludgeoning, piercing, and slashing from nonmagical weapons
Damage Immunities poison, psychic
Condition Immunities charmed, exhaustion, frightened, paralyzed, poisoned, unconscious
Senses darkvision 60 ft., passive Perception 10
Languages understands the languages of its creator but can't speak
Challenge 6 (2,300 XP)

Eerie Presence. A creature that starts its turn within 40 feet of a scarecrow, and can see it, must succeed on a DC 14 Wisdom saving throw, or be overcome with a magical uneasiness until the start of its next turn. While under this effect, the creature has disadvantage on attack rolls and ability checks.

A creature that is immune to being frightened is immune to the scarecrow's Eerie Presence. Similarly, a creature that has advantage on saving throws against being frightened has advantage on its saving throws against the scarecrow's Eerie Presence.

False Appearance. While the scarecrow remains motionless, it is indistinguishable from a mundane scarecrow.

ACTIONS

Mind Rend. The scarecrow magically fills the mind of a creature it can see, within 60 feet, with nightmarish visions that rend its psyche. The target must succeed on a DC 14 Wisdom saving throw, or take 27 (6d8) psychic damage.

Terrify (Recharge 5-6). The scarecrow emits a magical wave of terror. Creatures within 40 feet of the scarecrow must succeed on a DC 14 Wisdom saving throw, or be frightened for 1 minute. A creature that is under the effect of any scarecrow's Eerie Presence has disadvantage on the saving throw.

On its turn, a frightened creature must take the Dash action to move as far away as possible from the scarecrow. At the end of each of its turns, a creature can repeat the saving throw, ending the effect on itself on a success.

JACK O' LANTERN
Medium construct, chaotic evil

Armor Class 16 (natural armor)
Hit Points 135 (18d8 + 54)
Speed 40 ft.

STR	DEX	CON	INT	WIS	CHA
14 (+2)	21 (+5)	17 (+3)	13 (+1)	12 (+1)	22 (+6)

Damage Resistances fire; bludgeoning, piercing, and slashing from nonmagical weapons
Damage Immunities poison
Condition Immunities charmed, exhaustion, frightened, paralyzed, poisoned, unconscious
Senses darkvision 60 ft., passive Perception 10
Languages understands the languages of its creator, but can't speak
Challenge 8 (3,900 XP)

Eerie Presence. A creature that starts its turn within 40 feet of the jack o' lantern, and can see it, must succeed on a DC 16 Wisdom saving throw, or be overcome with a magical uneasiness until the start of its next turn. While under this effect, the creature has disadvantage on attack rolls and ability checks.

A creature that is immune to being frightened is immune to the jack o' lantern's Eerie Presence. Similarly, a creature that has advantage on saving throws against being frightened has advantage on its saving throws against the jack o' lantern's Eerie Presence.

False Appearance. While the jack o' lantern remains motionless, it is indistinguishable from a mundane scarecrow with a pumpkin head.

Lantern Light. The jack o' lantern emits dim light in a 20-foot radius. Creatures in this area, that can see the jack o' lantern's light, have disadvantage on saving throws against being frightened and any scarecrow's Eerie Presence.

ACTIONS

Multiattack. The jack o' lantern makes two claw attacks.

Claw. *Melee Weapon Attack:* +8 to hit, reach 5 ft., one target. *Hit:* 12 (2d6 + 5) slashing damage.

Fire Breath (Recharge 5-6). The jack o' lantern's head exhales a magical gout of fire in a 40-foot cone. Creatures in the area must make a DC 14 Dexterity saving throw, taking 28 (8d6) fire damage on a failed save, or half as much damage on a successful one. A scarecrow reduced to 0 hit points by this damage is not destroyed, but transformed into a scorched effigy with full hit points.

Scorched Effigy

Medium construct, chaotic evil

Armor Class 13
Hit Points 33 (6d8 + 6)
Speed 40 ft.

STR	DEX	CON	INT	WIS	CHA
13 (+1)	17 (+3)	12 (+1)	3 (-4)	11 (+0)	4 (-3)

Damage Resistances bludgeoning, and piercing from nonmagical weapons
Damage Immunities fire, poison, psychic
Condition Immunities charmed, exhaustion, frightened, paralyzed, poisoned, unconscious
Senses darkvision 60 ft., passive Perception 10
Languages understands the languages of its creator, but can't speak
Challenge 2 (450 XP)

Eerie Presence. A creature that starts its turn within 40 feet of the scorched effigy, and can see it, must succeed on a DC 7 Wisdom saving throw, or be overcome with a magical uneasiness until the start of its next turn. While under this effect, the creature has disadvantage on attack rolls and ability checks.

A creature that is immune to being frightened is immune to effigy's Eerie Presence. Similarly, a creature that has advantage on saving throws against being frightened has advantage on its saving throws against the effigy's Eerie Presence.

Scorched Form. A creature that touches the effigy takes 5 (1d8) fire damage. In addition, the effigy sheds dim light in a 10-foot radius.

Actions

Multiattack. The effigy makes two attacks with its scorched touch.

Scorched Touch. *Melee Spell Attack:* +5 to hit, reach 5 ft., one target. *Hit:* 7 (1d8 + 3) fire damage.

Made to guard the harvest,
And harvest's coming in.
They'll stitch you up and hitch you up,
And carve you with a grin.

A roughspun sack's your mantle,
Your crown, a hollowed gourd.
Hail the king of scarecrows,
A-nailed to his board.

-popular rhyme

Sentient Sword
Small construct, any alignment

Armor Class 18 (natural armor)
Hit Points 97 (15d6 + 45)
Speed 0 ft., fly 50 ft. (hover)

STR	DEX	CON	INT	WIS	CHA
16 (+3)	17 (+3)	16 (+3)	15 (+2)	17 (+3)	11 (+0)

Saving Throws Dex +8, Con +8
Damage Immunities all, except damage from the forge hammer the sword was created with
Condition Immunities blinded, charmed, deafened, frightened, paralyzed, petrified, poisoned
Senses blindsight 60 ft. (blind beyond this radius), passive Perception 13
Languages telepathy 60 ft.
Challenge 13 (10,000 XP)

Antimagic Susceptibility. The sentient sword is incapacitated while in an area of antimagic, such as an *antimagic field*. If targeted by a *dispel magic* spell, the sword must succeed on a Constitution saving throw against the caster's spell save DC, or fall unconscious for 1 minute.

Artifact Weakness. When hit by the forge hammer it was forged with, the sentient sword loses all damage immunities, except immunity to poison and psychic damage, for 1 minute.

False Appearance. While the sentient sword remains motionless, it is indistinguishable from a normal sword of its kind.

Legendary Resistance (3/Day). If the sentient sword fails a saving throw, it can choose to succeed instead.

Actions

Multiattack. The sentient sword makes three longsword attacks.

Longsword. *Melee Weapon Attack:* +8 to hit, reach 5 ft., one target. *Hit:* 7 (1d8 + 3) slashing damage. The sentient sword scores a critical hit on a d20 roll of 19 or 20, instead of only 20.

Legendary Actions

The sentient sword can take 3 legendary actions, choosing from the options below. Only one legendary action option can be used at a time, and only at the end of another creature's turn. The sword regains spent legendary actions at the start of its turn.

Attack. The sentient sword makes one longsword attack.

Jab (Costs 2 Actions). The sentient sword moves up to its fly speed in a straight line. It can make a longsword attack at the end of this movement. If the attack hits, it deals an additional 7 (2d6) slashing damage for every 10 feet moved.

Enchanted Flying Sword
Small construct, unaligned

Armor Class 18 (natural armor)
Hit Points 65 (10d6 + 30)
Speed 0 ft., fly 50 ft. (hover)

STR	DEX	CON	INT	WIS	CHA
15 (+2)	17 (+3)	16 (+3)	1 (-5)	5 (-3)	1 (-5)

Saving Throws Dex +5, Con +5
Damage Immunities poison, psychic
Condition Immunities blinded, charmed, deafened, frightened, paralyzed, petrified, poisoned
Senses blindsight 60 ft. (blind beyond this radius), passive Perception 7
Languages —
Challenge 4 (1,100 XP)

Antimagic Susceptibility. The enchanted flying sword is incapacitated while in an area of antimagic, such as an *antimagic field*. If targeted by a *dispel magic* spell, the sword must succeed on a Constitution saving throw against the caster's spell save DC, or fall unconscious for 1 minute.

False Appearance. While the enchanted flying sword remains motionless, it is indistinguishable from a normal sword of its kind.

Magic Weapons. The enchanted flying sword's weapon attacks are magical.

Actions

Multiattack. The enchanted flying sword makes three longsword attacks.

Longsword. *Melee Weapon Attack:* +7 to hit, reach 5 ft., one target. *Hit:* 9 (1d8 + 5) slashing damage.

Flying Halberd

Medium construct, unaligned

Armor Class 16 (natural armor)
Hit Points 22 (5d8)
Speed 0 ft., fly 40 ft. (hover)

STR	DEX	CON	INT	WIS	CHA
15 (+2)	13 (+1)	11 (+0)	1 (-5)	5 (-3)	1 (-5)

Saving Throws Dex +3
Damage Immunities poison, psychic
Condition Immunities blinded, charmed, deafened, frightened, paralyzed, petrified, poisoned
Senses blindsight 60 ft. (blind beyond this radius), passive Perception 7
Languages —
Challenge 1/2 (100 XP)

Antimagic Susceptibility. The flying halberd is incapacitated while in an area of antimagic, such as an *antimagic field*. If targeted by a *dispel magic* spell, the weapon must succeed on a Constitution saving throw against the caster's spell save DC, or fall unconscious for 1 minute.

False Appearance. While the flying halberd remains motionless, it is indistinguishable from a normal halberd of its kind.

Actions

Halberd. *Melee Weapon Attack:* +4 to hit, reach 10 ft., one target. *Hit:* 7 (1d10 + 2) slashing damage.

Animated Longbow

Medium construct, unaligned

Armor Class 15 (natural armor)
Hit Points 18 (4d8)
Speed 0 ft., fly 30 ft. (hover)

STR	DEX	CON	INT	WIS	CHA
10 (+0)	16 (+3)	11 (+0)	1 (-5)	5 (-3)	1 (-5)

Saving Throws Dex +5
Damage Immunities poison, psychic
Condition Immunities blinded, charmed, deafened, frightened, paralyzed, petrified, poisoned
Senses blindsight 120 ft. (blind beyond this radius), passive Perception 7
Languages —
Challenge 1 (200 XP)

Antimagic Susceptibility. The animated longbow is incapacitated while in an area of antimagic, such as an *antimagic field*. If targeted by a *dispel magic* spell, the longbow must succeed on a Constitution saving throw against the caster's spell save DC, or fall unconscious for 1 minute.

Animate Arrows. The animated longbow automatically animates any unattended arrows, appropriate for its size, that pass within 10 feet of it. The animated arrows become part of the longbow until it shoots them, at which point they become mundane arrows once more. The longbow can't animate more than 20 arrows at a time.

False Appearance. While the animated longbow remains motionless, it is indistinguishable from a normal longbow of its kind.

Actions

Longbow. *Melee Weapon Attack:* +5 to hit, range 120/600 ft., one target. *Hit:* 7 (1d8 + 3) piercing damage.

Flying Dagger

Tiny construct, unaligned

Armor Class 15 (natural armor)
Hit Points 17 (7d4)
Speed 0 ft., fly 50 ft. (hover)

STR	DEX	CON	INT	WIS	CHA
8 (-1)	16 (+3)	11 (+0)	1 (-5)	5 (-3)	1 (-5)

Saving Throws Dex +5
Damage Immunities poison, psychic
Condition Immunities blinded, charmed, deafened, frightened, paralyzed, petrified, poisoned
Senses blindsight 60 ft. (blind beyond this radius), passive Perception 7
Languages —
Challenge 1/2 (100 XP)

Antimagic Susceptibility. The flying dagger is incapacitated while in an area of antimagic, such as an *antimagic field*. If targeted by a *dispel magic* spell, the dagger must succeed on a Constitution saving throw against the caster's spell save DC, or fall unconscious for 1 minute.

False Appearance. While the flying dagger remains motionless, it is indistinguishable from a normal dagger of its kind.

Actions

Dagger. *Melee Weapon Attack:* +5 to hit, reach 5 ft., one target. *Hit:* 5 (1d4 + 3) piercing damage.

USHABTI

Medium construct, lawful evil

Armor Class 15 (natural armor)
Hit Points 32 (5d8 + 10)
Speed 20 ft.

STR	DEX	CON	INT	WIS	CHA
14 (+2)	10 (+0)	14 (+2)	6 (-2)	8 (-1)	6 (-2)

Damage Vulnerabilities fire or thunder
Damage Immunities poison, psychic
Condition Immunities blinded, charmed, deafened, exhaustion, frightened, paralyzed, petrified, poisoned
Senses blindsight 60 ft. (blind beyond this radius), passive Perception 9
Languages —
Challenge 1/2 (100 XP)

Cursed Resolve. If the ushabti starts its turn within 30 feet of one or more mummies, it regains a number of hit points equal to the highest Charisma modifier of the mummies.

False Appearance. While the ushabti remains motionless, it is indistinguishable from a normal wooden or clay statue.

ACTIONS

Ritual Blade. *Melee Weapon Attack:* +4 to hit, reach 5 ft., one target. *Hit:* 6 (1d8 + 2) slashing damage. If the ushabti is within 60 feet of a mummy, this attack deals an extra 3 (1d6) necrotic damage.

DIVINE TOMB GUARDIAN

Huge construct, lawful evil

Armor Class 18 (natural armor)
Hit Points 170 (15d12 + 60)
Speed 30 ft.

STR	DEX	CON	INT	WIS	CHA
22 (+6)	8 (-1)	19 (+4)	6 (-2)	14 (+2)	6 (-2)

Skills Perception +6
Damage Resistances cold, fire; bludgeoning, piercing, and slashing from nonmagical attacks
Damage Immunities poison, psychic
Condition Immunities blinded, charmed, deafened, exhaustion, frightened, paralyzed, petrified, poisoned
Senses blindsight 120 ft. (blind beyond this radius), passive Perception 16
Languages —
Challenge 11 (7,200 XP)

Divine Dedication. Every tomb guardian is dedicated to a different divine aspect, represented by the animal shape the statue's head is carved into. The aspect allows the guardian to innately cast a spell once per day, without requiring material components:

- **Cat.** *blade barrier*
- **Cobra.** *eyebite*
- **Crocodile.** *antilife shell.* The barrier created by the spell has a 30 foot radius.
- **Falcon.** *sunbeam*
- **Ibis.** *true seeing*
- **Jackal.** *circle of death.* Constructs and undead are immune to damage caused by the spell.

False Appearance. While the tomb guardian remains motionless, it is indistinguishable from a mundane stone statue.

ACTIONS

Multiattack. The tomb guardian makes two melee attacks.

Ritual Blade. *Melee Weapon Attack:* +10 to hit, reach 10 ft., one target. *Hit:* 19 (3d8 + 6) slashing damage, plus 14 (4d6) necrotic damage.

REACTIONS

Cursed Devotion. When a mummy within 5 feet of the guardian becomes the target of an attack, the tomb guardian can impose disadvantage on the attack roll. If the attack misses the mummy by 5 or more, it hits the guardian instead.

Miniature Infantry Regiment

Large swarm of Tiny constructs, lawful evil

Armor Class 14 (natural armor)
Hit Points 52 (7d10 + 14)
Speed 20 ft.

STR	DEX	CON	INT	WIS	CHA
8 (-1)	14 (+2)	15 (+2)	1 (-5)	10 (+0)	1 (-5)

Damage Resistances bludgeoning, piercing, poison, slashing
Damage Immunities poison, psychic
Condition Immunities blinded, charmed, deafened, exhaustion, frightened, paralyzed, petrified, poisoned, prone, restrained, stunned
Senses blindsight 30 ft. (blind beyond this radius), passive Perception 10
Languages —
Challenge 4 (1,100 XP)

False Appearance. While the regiment remains motionless, it is indistinguishable from a normal regiment of clay soldier miniatures.

Swarm. The regiment can occupy another creature's space, and vice versa, and the regiment can, as a swarm, move through any opening large enough for a Tiny soldier. The regiment can't regain hit points or gain temporary hit points.

Actions

Multiattack. The regiment makes two melee attacks. It cannot make both attacks against the same target.

Spears. *Melee Weapon Attack:* +4 to hit, reach 0 ft., one target in the regiment's space. *Hit:* 21 (6d6) piercing damage, or 10 (3d6) piercing damage if the regiment has half of its hit points or fewer.

Reactions

Devoted Army. If a creature in the regiment's space makes an attack against a mummy, the regiment can make a spears attack against that creature.

Miniature Soldier

Tiny construct, lawful evil

Armor Class 13 (natural armor)
Hit Points 2 (1d4)
Speed 20 ft.

STR	DEX	CON	INT	WIS	CHA
8 (-1)	14 (+2)	10 (+0)	1 (-5)	10 (+0)	1 (-5)

Damage Immunities poison, psychic
Condition Immunities blinded, charmed, deafened, exhaustion, frightened, paralyzed, petrified, poisoned, prone, restrained, stunned
Senses blindsight 30 ft. (blind beyond this radius), passive Perception 10
Languages —
Challenge 0 (10 XP)

False Appearance. While the soldier remains motionless, it is indistinguishable from a normal clay soldier miniature.

Actions

Spear. *Melee Weapon Attack:* +4 to hit, reach 5 ft., one target. *Hit:* 1 piercing damage.

MINIATURE CHARIOT
Small construct, lawful evil

Armor Class 13 (natural armor)
Hit Points 9 (2d6 + 2)
Speed 40 ft.

STR	DEX	CON	INT	WIS	CHA
12 (+1)	12 (+1)	13 (+1)	6 (-2)	8 (-1)	5 (-2)

Damage Immunities poison, psychic
Condition Immunities blinded, charmed, deafened, exhaustion, frightened, paralyzed, petrified, poisoned
Senses blindsight 60 ft. (blind beyond this radius), passive Perception 9
Languages —
Challenge 1/4 (50 XP)

False Appearance. While the chariot remains motionless, it is indistinguishable from a normal clay or wood miniature chariot.

Melee Shooter. The chariot does not suffer disadvantage when making ranged attacks while within 5 feet of a hostile creature.

ACTIONS

Multiattack. The chariot makes one attack with its bow, and one attack with its spear.

Spear. *Melee Weapon Attack:* +3 to hit, reach 5 ft., one target. *Hit:* 4 (1d6 + 1) piercing damage.

Bow. *Ranged Weapon Attack:* +3 to hit, range 30/60 ft., one target. *Hit:* 3 (1d4 + 1) piercing damage.

In the light of our torches, the statues seemed to watch us with unfriendly eyes as we continued on. Our presence in that sacred space was an affront they could only bear for so long.

-Howel Varcanon's account of his doomed expedition

GHOST SHIP

Gargantuan construct, any alignment

Armor Class 15 (natural armor)
Hit Points 507 (26d20 + 234)
Speed 0 ft., swim 35 ft.

STR	DEX	CON	INT	WIS	CHA
20 (+5)	4 (-3)	29 (+9)	6 (-2)	22 (+6)	15 (+2)

Skills Perception +12
Damage Immunities poison, psychic
Condition Immunities blinded, charmed, deafened, exhaustion, frightened, paralyzed, petrified, poisoned, prone
Senses blindsight 120 ft. darkvision 240 ft., passive Perception 22
Languages —
Challenge 21 (33,000 XP)

Crash. The ghost ship can move into another creature or object's space. If it does so, the target must make a DC 19 Dexterity saving throw, or take 88 (16d10) bludgeoning damage, and the ghost ship must succeed on a DC 15 Constitution saving throw, or take an amount of bludgeoning damage dependant on the target's size:

Medium or smaller: no damage

Large: 22 (4d10)

Huge: 44 (8d10)

Gargantuan 88 (16d10)

If the target is Huge or larger, the ship must then end its movement; otherwise, the target is moved to the nearest unoccupied space and the ship can keep moving. It cannot crash into the same target more than once each turn.

Damage Threshold (20). The ghost ship does not take damage from hits that deal a total of less than 20 damage each.

Deck. Huge or smaller creatures can occupy the ship's space, moving with the ship. While they're on deck, the ship cannot shake them off, make ranged attacks against them, or crash into them.

Legendary Resistance (3/Day). If the ghost ship fails a saving throw, it can choose to succeed instead.

Phantom Crew. The ghost ship has advantage on Wisdom (Perception) checks. Additionally, the ghost crew has a Dexterity score of 20 (+5), which the ship uses for ranged weapon attacks. For all other purposes, the ship uses its own Dexterity score. The ship does not suffer disadvantage when making ranged attacks while within 5 feet of a hostile creature.

Misty Wake. The ghost ship is shrouded in a cloud of mist that extends 90 feet from its space. Creatures and objects within the mist are lightly obscured from any creature more than 30 feet away, and heavily obscured from any creature more than 60 feet away. If the ship is targeted by an effect that turns undead, the fog dissipates for one minute, even if the ship succeeds on its saving throw against the effect.

Sailing Movement. The ghost ship cannot use the Dash action. Further, it can only swim at the water's surface, like a regular ship.

Undead Weakness. If the ghost ship is targeted by an effect that turns undead, it must make a save against the effect. On a failed save, it is not turned, but is instead incapacitated until the end of its next turn.

ACTIONS

Multiattack. The ghost ship makes two mangonel attacks, and one ballista attack. In place of any number of these attacks, the ghost ship can make one melee attack each with its ghostly weapons against a creature in its space. It cannot make more than one attack with its ghostly weapons against the same target.

Ghostly Weapons. *Melee Spell Attack:* +8 to hit, reach 0 ft., one target in the ship's space, *Hit:* 20 (4d8 + 2) necrotic damage, or 11 (2d8 + 2) necrotic damage if the ship has half its hit points or less.

Mangonel. *Ranged Weapon Attack:* +11 to hit, range 200/800 ft., one target. *Hit:* 32 (5d10 + 5) bludgeoning damage.

Ballista. *Ranged Weapon Attack:* +11 to hit, range 120/480 ft., one target. *Hit:* 21 (3d10 + 5) piercing damage.

LEGENDARY ACTIONS

The ghost ship can take 3 legendary actions, choosing from the options below. Only one legendary action option can be used at a time, and only at the end of another creature's turn. The ship regains spent legendary actions at the start of its turn.

Full Speed. The ghost ship swims up to 15 feet.

Ballista. The ghost ship makes one ballista attack.

VARIANT: AGE OF SAIL

Following the invention of cannons, naval artillery has become significantly more powerful. A ghost ship from this age is far more dangerous as a result.

An age of sail ghost ship has a Challenge rating of 24 (62,000 XP), swim speed of 45 ft., and replaces its multiattack, ballista and mangonel actions, and ballista legendary action, with the following:

Multiattack. The ghost ship makes three cannon attacks. In place of any number of these attacks, the ghost ship can make one melee attack each with its ghostly weapons against a creature in its space. It cannot make more than one attack with its ghostly weapons against the same target.

Cannon. *Ranged Weapon Attack:* +11 to hit, range 600/2,400 ft., one target. *Hit:* 44 (8d10) bludgeoning damage.

Legendary Actions

Cannon. The ghost ship makes one cannon attack.

"The Black Rose. She went down with all hands.
Aye, and came up with them too..."

-Bazokhan Baroo, sailor

APPENDIX B: PLAYER OPTIONS

These rules allow a player to create or modify a character based on the creatures presented in the previous chapters. As always, discuss with your GM before selecting a non-standard option.

MONSTROUS CLASSES

The following options allow player characters to pursue lichdom, as well as retain control after being transformed into a lycanthrope or vampire. The standard rules for multiclassing apply, with the exception that a character does not need to meet the Ability score prerequisites for their starting class in order to gain levels in a monstrous class. However, if the player wishes to multiclass into other classes, the usual prerequisites apply.

A character may choose to pursue the lich class once they meet the prerequisites. Both the lycanthrope and vampire class can only be accessed by those who have been bitten and infected; these are intended as alternatives to the character being taken over as an NPC under the GM's control. Gaining levels in these two classes is representative of becoming familiar with, and pushing the limits of, your new form.

LICH

Prerequisites: 5th level in any class with the spellcasting class feature, and a spell list that includes 9th level spells (this does not include subclasses that use another class's spell list), completed ritual to create a phylactery.

Level	Features
1	True Undeath, Phylactery
2	Spellcasting Mastery, Spellcasting Improvement
3	Spellcasting Improvement
4	Ability Score Improvement, Spellcasting Improvement
5	Spellcasting Improvement
6	Paralyzing Touch, Spellcasting Improvement
7	Spellcasting Improvement
8	Ability Score Improvement, Spellcasting Improvement
9	Deathly Resistance, Spellcasting Improvement
10	Phylactic Bond, Spellcasting Improvement

CLASS FEATURES

As a lich, you gain the following class features:

HIT POINTS

Hit Dice: 1d6 per lich level

Hit Points at Each Level: 1d6 (or 4) + your Constitution modifier per lich level

PROFICIENCIES

You gain no additional proficiencies.

PHYLACTERY

When you become a Lich at 1st level, you create a phylactery: any Medium, or smaller, object assembled from multiple parts, such as an amulet, a music box, or a hand mirror. As long as you have a phylactery, it contains your soul and allows you to rejuvenate from injuries.

If you are killed while your phylactery is within 500 feet of the place where you died, you begin rejuvenating. You gain a new body in 1d10 days. It appears within 5 feet of your phylactery and you gain the benefits of a long rest. If you don't have your phylactery in range at the time of your death, or it is destroyed before you rejuvenate, your death is permanent and you cannot be resurrected by any means (not even a *true resurrection* spell).

TRUE UNDEATH

Additionally, starting at 1st level, your type becomes undead rather than humanoid, you have resistance to necrotic damage, immunity to poison damage and the poisoned condition, and gain darkvision within 120 feet of you, unless you already have darkvision with a greater range.

Spellcasting Mastery

From 2nd level, you continue honing your mastery as a spellcaster. Choose a class that you have at least 5 levels in, with the spellcasting class feature, and a spell list that includes 9th level spells to be your Spellcasting Mastery class. You learn an additional cantrip from the spell list of that class.

Casting Improvement

Additionally, at 2nd level and every level thereafter, your spellcasting improves. Each time you gain this feature, you count as gaining a level in your Spellcasting Mastery class for the purpose of the Spellcasting class feature of that class.

For example, if you are a level 7 wizard and gain you reach 2nd level as a lich, choosing wizard as your Spellcasting Mastery, you count as a level 8 wizard for the purpose of your Wizard Spellcasting class feature, including learning new spells and the maximum level of spells you can learn and prepare.

Ability Score Improvement

When you reach 4th level, and again at 8th level, you can increase one ability score of your choice by 2, or two ability scores of your choice by 1. As normal, you can't increase an ability score above 20 using this feature.

Paralyzing Touch

Starting at 6th level, you can sap the warmth from other creatures with a touch, paralyzing them with your unholy energy. As an action, you can make a melee spell attack using the spell attack bonus of your Spellcasting Mastery class. On a hit, the attack deals 3d6 cold damage and the target must succeed on a Constitution saving throw against your spell save DC or be paralyzed for 1 minute. A creature can repeat the saving throw at the end of each of its turns, ending the effect on itself on a success.

Deathly Resistance

Starting at 9th level, you gain resistance to bludgeoning, piercing, and slashing damage from attacks not made with magical weapons. Additionally, you have advantage on saving throws against exhaustion and the charmed, frightened, and paralyzed conditions.

Phylactic Bond

At 10th level, you no longer need to be near your phylactery to rejuvenate. As long as you have a phylactery, you gain a new body 1d10 days after you died, independent of where your phylactery is.

LYCANTHROPE

Level	Features
1	Lineage, Beast Form, Beast Fangs, Lineage Feature
2	Gift of the Moon
3	Lineage Feature
4	Moon Flesh, Ability Score Improvement
5	Lineage Feature
6	Gift of the Moon
7	Lineage Feature
8	Moon Flesh (Resistance), Ability Score Improvement
9	Lineage Feature
10	Lineage Feature

CLASS FEATURES

As a lycanthrope, you gain the following class features:

HIT POINTS

Hit Dice: 1d8 per lycanthrope level

Hit Points at Each Level: 1d8 (or 5) + your Constitution modifier per lycanthrope level

PROFICIENCIES

You gain proficiency with unarmed strikes.

LINEAGE

Starting at 1st level, when you begin your lycanthrope progression, you gain a Lineage based on the type of lycanthrope you descend from: werebat, werebear, wereboar, werepanther, wererat, wereraven, weretiger, or werewolf.

You gain Lineage features at 1st, 3rd, 5th, 7th, 9th, and 10th level.

BEAST FORM

Also, starting at 1st level, you gain the Shapechanger subtype and the ability to use your action to transform into animal form, hybrid form, or back into your original humanoid form. When transforming between humanoid and hybrid form, your gear does not transform with you: it stays on your body, and fits both forms. When transforming to animal form, you can choose whether your gear falls to the ground in your space, or melds into your body and has no effect until you transform into humanoid or hybrid form.

Your statistics are the same in each form, except for the following changes:

- While in animal or hybrid form, you can attack using your Beast Fangs.
- Unless an ability of your subspecies specifies otherwise, your size in your animal form is Medium, regardless of your humanoid form's size, and your size in hybrid form is the same as in your humanoid form.

- You lose the ability to speak and cast spells while in animal form, and any actions that require hands are limited by your animal form.
- Each form gains additional features detailed in the description of your Lineage.

BEAST FANGS

Additionally, at 1st level, you gain a special, natural attack while you are in animal or hybrid form, known as Beast Fangs. You can make unarmed strikes using your Beast Fangs that, instead of the usual bludgeoning damage, deal damage and potential additional effects, dependant on your Lineage. These are detailed in the Beast Fangs ability of your Lineage. Additionally, whenever you hit a humanoid creature that is not already a lycanthrope with your Beast Fangs, that creature must succeed on a Constitution saving throw, or be cursed with lycanthropy.

You can attack with your Beast Fangs once per turn.

The DC to save against your Beast Fangs is 8 + your proficiency modifier + your Constitution modifier.

MOON FLESH

Starting at 4th level, you become resistant to ordinary weapons. As a bonus action, you can gain resistance to bludgeoning, piercing, and slashing damage from attacks not made with magical or silvered weapons until the start of your next turn.

You can use this feature a number of times equal to your Constitution modifier (minimum 1). When you finish a short or long rest, you regain all expended uses of this feature.

Starting at 8th level, you permanently have resistance to bludgeoning, piercing, and slashing damage from attacks not made with magical or silvered weapons.

ABILITY SCORE IMPROVEMENT

When you reach 4th level, and again at 8th, leveI, you can increase one ability score of your choice by 2, or two ability scores of your choice by 1. As normal, you can't increase an ability score above 20 using this feature.

If you have the werebear, wereboar, or weretiger Lineage, you must increase your Strength score, and if you have the werebat, werepanther, or wereraven Lineage you must increase your Dexterity score as much as possible each time you gain this feature. As long as you can increase the ability score in question, you can't choose any alternatives (including feats and other alternatives replacing your Ability Score Improvements).

GIFT OF THE MOON

At 2nd level, and again at 6th level, you can choose a gift from the Gifts of the Moon list.

LINEAGE

Every lycanthrope inherits the animalistic features of the lycanthrope that sired it, from the infamous werewolves to the elusive wereravens.

WEREBAT

Level	Humanoid Form Features	Hybrid Form Features	Animal Form Features
1		Beast Fangs, Bat Form	Beast Fangs, Bat Form
3		Sky Hunter (45 ft.)	Sky Hunter (45 ft.)
5		Bat Claws	
7	Bat Senses	Bat Senses	Bat Senses
9		Echolocation	Echolocation
10		Sky Hunter (60 ft.)	Sky Hunter (60 ft.)

BEAST FANGS

You can use your Beast Fangs to make a bite attack that deals 1d6 + your Strength modifier piercing damage. Additionally, your bite is treated as having the finesse weapon quality for all intents and purposes.

BAT FORM

When you become a werebat at 1st level, your beast form resembles a giant bat. While you are in animal or hybrid form, and not wearing armor, you have a fly speed of 30 feet.

Additionally, while in animal form, your size is Large.

SKY HUNTER

At 3rd level, your fly speed in hybrid and animal form increases to 45 feet. When you reach 10th level, it increases to 60 feet.

BAT CLAWS

Starting at 5th level, you can attack with your bat claws. While in animal or hybrid form, you can use your claws to make unarmed strikes that deal 1d4 + your Strength modifier slashing damage, instead of the normal bludgeoning damage. Additionally, your claws are treated as having the finesse weapon quality for all intents and purposes.

BAT SENSES

Beginning at 7th level, you gain a keen sense of hearing. You have advantage on Wisdom (Perception) checks that rely on hearing.

ECHOLOCATION

Starting at 9th level, you are able to perceive your surroundings using your beast form's echolocation. You have blindsight, within 60 feet of you, while you are in animal or hybrid form. You can't use your blindsight while you are deafened.

WEREBEAR

Level	Humanoid Form Features	Hybrid Form Features	Animal Form Features
1		Beast Fangs, Bear Form	Beast Fangs, Bear Form
3		Predatory Speed	Predatory Speed
5		Bear Claws	Bear Claws
7	Bear Senses	Bear Senses	Bear Senses
9		Climbing Claws	Climbing Claws
10		Powerful Fangs	Powerful Fangs

BEAST FANGS

You can use your Beast Fangs to make a bite attack that deals 1d10 + your Strength modifier piercing damage.

BEAR FORM

When you become a werebear at 1st level, your beast form resembles a large bear. While you are in animal or hybrid form, and not wearing armor, your armor class becomes 11 + your Dexterity modifier.

Additionally, while in animal or hybrid form, your size is Large.

PREDATORY SPEED

At 3rd level, your walking speed in hybrid and animal form increases by 10 feet.

BEAR CLAWS

Starting at 5th level, you can attack with your bear claws. While in animal or hybrid form, you can use your claws to make unarmed strikes that deal 1d8 + your Strength modifier slashing damage, instead of the normal bludgeoning damage.

BEAR SENSES

Beginning at 7th level, you gain a keen sense of smell. You have advantage on Wisdom (Perception) checks that rely on smell.

CLIMBING CLAWS

Starting at 9th level, you gain a climb speed of 30 feet while in hybrid or animal form.

POWERFUL FANGS

When you reach 10th level, your bite's damage increases by 1d10, and your claws' damage increases by 1d8.

WEREBOAR

Level	Humanoid Form Features	Hybrid Form Features	Animal Form Features
1		Beast Fangs, Boar Form	Beast Fangs, Boar Form
3		Hog Speed	Hog Speed
5		Charge	Charge
7		Gift of the Moon	
9	Relentless	Relentless	Relentless
10		Gift of the Moon	

BEAST FANGS

You can use your Beast Fangs to make a tusk attack that deals 2d6 + your Strength modifier slashing damage.

BOAR FORM

When you become a wereboar at 1st level, your beast form resembles a wild boar or warthog. While you are in animal or hybrid form, and not wearing armor, your armor class becomes 11 + your Dexterity modifier.

HOG SPEED

At 3rd level, your walking speed in animal form increases by 10 feet.

CHARGE

Starting at 5th level, you can charge with overwhelming force. While in animal or hybrid form, if you move at least 15 feet in a straight line toward a target, and attack with your Beast Fangs on the same turn, the target takes an extra 7 (2d6) slashing damage. If the target is a creature, it must succeed on a Strength saving throw, or be knocked prone. The DC for this saving throw is 8 + your proficiency bonus + your Strength modifier.

GIFT OF THE MOON

At 7th level, and again at 10th level, you can choose an additional gift from the Gifts of the Moon list.

RELENTLESS

Starting at 9th level, you become inured to pain. If you take an amount of damage equal to your level + your Constitution modifier, or less, that would reduce you to 0 hit points, you are reduced to 1 hit point instead.

WEREPANTHER

Level	Humanoid Form Features	Hybrid Form Features	Animal Form Features
1		Beast Fangs, Panther Form	Beast Fangs, Panther Form
3		Climbing Claws	Climbing Claws
5		Panther Claws	Panther Claws
7	Cat Senses	Cat Senses	Cat Senses
9		Nimble Hunter	Nimble Hunter
10		Pounce	Pounce

BEAST FANGS

You can use your Beast Fangs to make a bite attack that deals 1d6 + your Strength modifier piercing damage. Additionally, your bite is treated as having the finesse weapon quality for all intents and purposes.

PANTHER FORM

When you become a werepanther at 1st level, your beast form resembles a medium-sized wild cat, such as a black jaguar or leopard. Additionally, your walking speed in hybrid and animal form increases by 10 feet.

CLIMBING CLAWS

Starting at 3rd level, you gain a climb speed of 30 feet while in hybrid or animal form.

PANTHER CLAWS

Starting at 5th level, you can attack with your panther claws. While in animal or hybrid form, you can use your claws to make unarmed strikes that deal 1d4 + your Strength modifier slashing damage, instead of the normal bludgeoning damage. Additionally, your claws are treated as having the finesse weapon quality for all intents and purposes.

CAT SENSES

Beginning at 7th level, you gain a keen sense of smell and reflective eyes. You have advantage on Wisdom (Perception) checks that rely on smell, and gain darkvision within 60 feet of you, unless you already have darkvision with a greater range.

NIMBLE HUNTER

Starting at 9th level, your walking speed and climb speed, in animal and hybrid form, increase by an additional 10 feet.

POUNCE

When you reach 10th level, if you move at least 15 feet in a straight line toward a creature, and hit it with a claw attack on the same turn, the target must succeed on a Strength saving throw, or be knocked prone. If the target is prone, you can make a bite attack against it as a bonus action. The DC for this saving throw is 8 + your proficiency bonus + your Strength modifier.

WERERAT

Level	Humanoid Form Features	Hybrid Form Features	Animal Form Features
1		Beast Fangs, Rat Form	Beast Fangs, Rat Form
3		Gift of the Moon	
5		Gift of the Moon	
7	Rat Senses	Rat Senses	Rat Senses
9		Gift of the Moon	
10		Gift of the Moon	

BEAST FANGS

You can use your Beast Fangs to make a bite attack that deals 1d4 + your Strength modifier piercing damage. Additionally, your bite is treated as having the finesse weapon quality for all intents and purposes.

RAT FORM

When you become a wererat at 1st level, your beast form resembles a giant rat. You become proficient with the Stealth skill. Additionally, while you're in your animal form, your size is Small.

GIFT OF THE MOON

At 3rd level, and again at 5th, 9th, and 10th level, you can choose an additional gift from the Gifts of the Moon list.

RAT SENSES

Beginning at 7th level, you gain a keen sense of smell. You have advantage on Wisdom (Perception) checks that rely on smell.

WERERAVEN

Level	Humanoid Form Features	Hybrid Form Features	Animal Form Features
1		Beast Fangs, Raven Form	Beast Fangs, Raven Form
3		Sky Hunter (40 ft.)	Sky Hunter (40 ft.)
5		Raven Talons	Raven Talons
7	Mimicry	Mimicry	Mimicry
9		Sky Hunter (50 ft.)	Sky Hunter (50 ft.)
10		Gift of the Moon	

BEAST FANGS

You can use your Beast Fangs to make a beak attack that deals 1d4 + your Strength modifier piercing damage. Additionally, your bite is treated as having the finesse weapon quality for all intents and purposes.

RAVEN FORM

When you become a wereraven at 1st level, your beast form resembles an oversized raven. While you are in animal or hybrid form, and not wearing armor, you have a fly speed of 30 feet.

Additionally, while in animal form, your size is Small.

SKY HUNTER

At 3rd level, your fly speed in hybrid and animal form increases to 40 feet. When you reach 9th level, it increases to 50 feet.

RAVEN TALONS

Starting at 5th level, you can attack with your taloned feet. While in animal or hybrid form, you can use your talons to make unarmed strikes that deal 1d4 + your Strength modifier slashing damage, instead of the normal bludgeoning damage. Additionally, your talons are treated as having the finesse weapon quality for all intents and purposes.

MIMICRY

Starting at 7th level, you can can mimic simple sounds you have heard, such as whispering, screams of pain, or the cries of a wild animal. A creature that hears the sounds can identify them as imitations with a successful Wisdom (Insight) check. The DC for this check is 8 + your proficiency bonus + your Wisdom modifier.

GIFT OF THE MOON

When you reach 10th level, you can choose a gift from the Gifts of the Moon list.

Weretiger

Level	Humanoid Form Features	Hybrid Form Features	Animal Form Features
1		Beast Fangs, Tiger Form	Beast Fangs, Tiger Form
3		Gift of the Moon	
5		Tiger Claws	Tiger Claws
7	Tiger Senses	Tiger Senses	Tiger Senses
9		Gift of the Moon	
10		Pounce	Pounce

Beast Fangs

You can use your Beast Fangs to make a bite attack that deals 1d10 + your Strength modifier piercing damage.

Tiger Form

When you become a weretiger at 1st level, your beast form resembles a great cat, typically a tiger. Your walking speed in hybrid and animal form increases by 10 feet.

Additionally, while in animal or hybrid form, your size is Large.

Gift of the Moon

At 3rd level, and again at 9th level, you can choose an additional gift from the Gifts of the Moon list.

Tiger Claws

Starting at 5th level, you can attack with your tiger claws. While in animal or hybrid form, you can use your claws to make unarmed strikes that deal 1d8 + your Strength modifier slashing damage, instead of the normal bludgeoning damage.

Tiger Senses

Beginning at 7th level, you gain a keen sense of smell and keen, reflective eyes. You have advantage on Wisdom (Perception) checks that rely on sight and smell, and gain darkvision within 60 feet of you, unless you already have darkvision with a greater range.

Pounce

When you reach 10th level, if you move at least 15 feet in a straight line towards a creature, and hit it with a claw attack on the same turn, the target must succeed on a Strength saving throw, or be knocked prone. If the target is prone, you can make a bite attack against it as a bonus action. The DC for this saving throw is 8 + your proficiency bonus + your Strength modifier.

Werewolf

Level	Humanoid Form Features	Hybrid Form Features	Animal Form Features
1		Beast Fangs, Wolf Form	Beast Fangs, Wolf Form
3		Predatory Speed	Predatory Speed
5		Wolf Claws	
7	Wolf Senses	Wolf Senses	Wolf Senses
9		Gift of the Moon	
10		Gift of the Moon	

Beast Fangs

You can use your Beast Fangs to make a bite attack that deals 1d8 + your Strength modifier piercing damage.

Wolf Form

When you become a werewolf at 1st level, your beast form resembles a large canid, such as a gray or timber wolf. While you are in animal or hybrid form, and not wearing armor, your armor class becomes 11 + your Dexterity modifier.

Predatory Speed

At 3rd level, your walking speed in hybrid and animal form increases by 10 feet.

Wolf Claws

Starting at 5th level, your hybrid form's hands grow sharp claws. While in hybrid form, you can use your claws to make unarmed strikes that deal 2d4 + your Strength modifier slashing damage, instead of the normal bludgeoning damage.

Wolf Senses

Beginning at 7th level you gain keen senses of hearing and smell. You have advantage on Wisdom (Perception) checks that rely on these senses.

Gift of the Moon

At 9th level, and again at 10th level, you can choose a gift from the Gifts of the Moon list.

GIFTS OF THE MOON

When you gain access to a Gift of the Moon (at lycanthrope level 2 and 6, plus various other levels in some Lineages), you can choose from the list below. You can only gain each Gift of the Moon once.

BEAST HEART

While in animal form, you can speak to beasts similar to your beast form (for example, a werewolf could speak to other canines, and wererats could speak to rodents) as if under the effect of a *speak with animals* spell.

Additionally, you can innately cast *animal friendship* on these beasts, without requiring material components. Once you have done so, you can't do so again until you finish a long rest.

DIRE WOLF

You transcend your lineage, becoming a dire werewolf. Your bite's damage increases by 1d8 and your claws' damage increases by 1d4. Additionally, while in animal or hybrid form, your size is now Large.

When you curse a creature with lycanthropy using your Beasts Fang, that creature becomes a dire werewolf rather than a regular werewolf.

Prerequisites. werewolf Lineage, *Resilient Hide* Gift of the Moon, lycanthrope level 10

FERAL SCRATCH

When you use the Attack action to make an attack with a melee weapon, and have a claw or talon that is not holding an object, you can make one additional attack with your animal or hybrid form's claws or talons as a bonus action.

Prerequisite. werebat, werepanther or wereraven Lineage

FLYBY

You do not provoke opportunity attacks when flying out of an enemy's reach in animal or hybrid form.

Prerequisites. wereraven Lineage

HORRIFIC TRANSFORMATION

You can transform from your humanoid form into either your animal or hybrid form, as part of an action you use to make an Intimidate check. If you do, you have advantage on the check. If the check does not require the use of an action, you must use your action (or bonus action, if you have the *Quick Transformation* Gift of the Moon) to transform to gain this benefit.

NIGHT HUNTER

You gain darkvision within 120 feet of you.

NIGHT PROWLER

While in animal or hybrid form, you have proficiency with the Stealth skill. If you are already proficient, you instead gain expertise, doubling your proficiency bonus for Stealth checks.

PACK HUNTER

You have advantage on attack rolls with your Beast Fangs if at least one of your allies is within 5 feet of the target, and your ally is not incapacitated.

Prerequisites. werewolf Lineage

QUICK SHIFT

You can change between your humanoid, hybrid, and animal form as a bonus action, rather than as an action.

Prerequisites. lycanthrope level 6 or more

RESILIENT HIDE

Your beast hide becomes thicker and more resistant to attack. When not wearing armor in your beast or hybrid form, your armor class becomes 13 + your Dexterity modifier.

Prerequisites. werebear, wereboar, or werewolf Lineage

RUNNING LEAP

In animal or hybrid form, as part of your movement, and after a 10-foot running start, you can long jump up to 25 feet.

Prerequisites. werepanther, weretiger or werewolf Lineage

SLY FANG

When you use the Attack action to make an attack with a melee weapon other than your Beast Fangs, you can make a single attack with your Beast Fangs as a bonus action.

Prerequisites. werebat, wererat, or wereraven Lineage

SWIMMER

In animal or hybrid form, you have a swim speed equal to your walking speed, or 30 feet, whichever is lower.

Prerequisites. werebear, werepanther, wererat, or weretiger Lineage

Vampire

Level	Features
1	Vampire Weaknesses, Vampiric Fangs, Undeath
2	Vampiric Shapes
3	Blood Power
4	Ability Score Improvement
5	Blood Power
6	Regeneration
7	Blood Power
8	Damage Resistance, Ability Score Improvement
9	Blood Power
10	Misty Escape

Class Features

As a vampire, you gain the following class features:

Hit Points

Hit Dice: 1d8 per vampire level

Hit Points at Each Level: 1d8 (or 5) + your Constitution modifier per vampire level

Proficiencies

You gain proficiency with unarmed strikes.

Vampire Weaknesses

When you become a vampire at 1st level, you become susceptible to the following weaknesses:

- *Forbiddance.* You can't enter a residence without an invitation from one of the occupants. Once you have been invited into a residence, you can freely enter and leave.

- *Harmed by Running Water.* You take 20 acid damage when you end your turn in running water.

- *Stake to the Heart.* You are paralyzed if a piercing weapon made of wood is driven into your heart while you are incapacitated in your resting place. You remain paralyzed, and can't regain hit points, until the stake is removed.

- *Sunlight Hypersensitivity.* You take 20 radiant damage when you start your turn in sunlight. While in sunlight, you have disadvantage on attack rolls and ability checks.

- *Resting Place.* You are dependent on having a resting place. This must be a vessel large enough to contain your body and shield it from sunlight that is no more than one size category larger than you, such as a coffin.
  If you are reduced to 0 hit points while outside of your resting place, you cannot regain hit points until you are returned to your resting place.

In order to establish a resting place, you must finish a long rest inside the object. Upon finishing the long rest, you can attune the object as your resting place.
Otherwise, while you are not within your resting place, you don't regain expended hit dice when finishing a long rest except if you have hit a living, humanoid creature with a bite attack within the last 24 hours.

- *Vampiric Destruction.* Being reduced to 0 hit points by radiant damage from sunlight, acid damage from running or holy water, or decapitation while paralyzed by a stake to the heart, kills you instantly. This is regardless of whether or not you are in your resting place, and you cannot use your Misty Escape ability.

Vampiric Fangs

Additionally, at 1st level, you gain vampiric fangs. Once per turn, when you target an incapacitated or restrained creature, a creature grappled by you or one of your allies, or a willing creature with your unarmed strike, you can make a bite attack that deals 1d8 + your Strength modifier piercing damage, plus 2d6 necrotic damage, in place of the usual bludgeoning damage. The target's hit point maximum is reduced by a number equal to the necrotic damage it takes, and you regain an equal number of hit points.

The hit point reduction lasts until the creature finishes a long rest. If the creature's hit point maximum is reduced to 0 by your fangs, the creature dies.

Undeath

Finally, starting at 1st level, your type becomes undead rather than humanoid, you have resistance to necrotic damage, and you gain darkvision within 120 feet of you, unless you already have darkvision with a greater range.

Vampiric Shapes

Starting at 2nd level, you gain the shapechanger subtype. If you aren't in sunlight, or running water, you can use use an action to polymorph into a Tiny bat, a Medium wolf, a Medium cloud of mist, or back into your true form.

While in bat or wolf form, you can't speak and your statistics, other than your size and speed, are unchanged. Anything you are wearing transforms with you, but nothing you are carrying does. Additionally, you can only attack using your Vampiric Fangs. You revert to your true form if you die.

In bat form, your walking speed is 5 feet, and you have a flying speed of 40 feet.

In wolf form, your walking speed is 40 feet, and you can use your Vampiric Fangs against any target, not just one that is grappled, incapacitated, restrained, or willing.

While in mist form, you can't take any actions, speak, or manipulate objects. You are weightless, have a flying speed of 20 feet, can hover, and can enter other creature's spaces and stop there. In addition, you can pass through any space that air can pass through without squeezing but can't pass through water. You are immune to all non-magical damage other than radiant damage from sunlight.

Blood Power

When you reach 3rd level, and every two levels thereafter, you gain a power chosen from the Blood Powers list.

Ability Score Improvement

When you reach 4th level, and again at 8th level, you can increase one ability score of your choice by 2, or two ability scores of your choice by 1. As normal, you can't increase an ability score above 20 using this feature.

Regeneration

Starting at 6th level, as long as you have at least 1 hit point, and are not in sunlight, running water or paralyzed by a stake to the heart, you can use a bonus action to start regenerating. For 1 minute, you regain 3 hit points at the start of each of your turns. The regeneration ends early if you take radiant damage, acid damage from holy or running water, or you are reduced to 0 hit points. Once you have used this feature, you can't do so again until you have finished a long rest.

Damage Resistance

Starting at 7th level, you gain resistance to bludgeoning, piercing, and slashing damage from hits that are not caused by a magical attack.

Misty Escape

Starting when you reach 10th level, when you are reduced to 0 hit points by damage other than by the methods of Vampiric Destruction detailed in your Vampire Weaknesses, and you are outside your resting place, you immediately transform into your mist form.

While you are at 0 hit points in mist form, you can't transform into any other form or regain health. You must reach your resting place within 1 hour of transforming or you die. When you reach your resting place, you revert to your true form and become paralyzed until you regain at least 1 hit point.

Additionally, you can't be killed other than by the methods of Vampiric Destruction detailed in your Vampire Weaknesses.

Blood Powers

When you gain access to a Blood Power (at vampire level 3, and every 2 levels thereafter), you can choose from the list below. You can only gain each Blood Power once, unless specified.

Abominable Power

You gain the ability to use your Vampiric Shapes to transform into a Large vampire abomination. This form lasts for 1 minute or until you are reduced to 0 hit points or fall unconscious. In abomination form, anything you are wearing transforms with you, but nothing you are carrying does. Additionally, the following rules apply:

- You gain a fly speed of 40 feet, and resistance to all damage types except fire, force, psychic, and radiant damage, as well as acid damage from running or holy water.
- You can use your Vampiric Fangs against any target, not just one that is grappled, incapacitated, restrained, or willing.
- Your hands grow large claws. You can use your claws to make unarmed strikes that deal 2d8 + your Strength modifier slashing damage, instead of the normal bludgeoning damage.

Once you have transformed into abomination form, you can't do so again until you finish a long rest.

Prerequisites. vampire level 9 or more

Bloodied Hands

Your unarmed strikes, other than with your bite or claws, deal damage equal to 1d8 + your Strength modifier, instead of the normal damage. Additionally, when you hit a creature with this attack, you can choose to grapple it instead of dealing damage. The grapple succeeds automatically, but the creature can use its action to try to escape the grapple as normal.

Charm

You can cast *charm person* at will, without expending a spell slot. Your spellcasting ability for this spell is Charisma.

Prerequisites. Charisma 13 or higher

Dark Celerity

As a bonus action, you can double each of your speeds until the end of your turn. Once you have used this power, you can't do so again until you finish a short or long rest.

Dark Thirst

The necrotic damage dealt by your Vampiric Fangs increases to 4d6.

Master of Shapes

You can change forms using your Vampiric Shapes as a bonus action, rather than as an action.

Prerequisites. vampire level 5 or more

Mystic Study

You continue honing your mastery as a spellcaster. Choose a class with the spellcasting class feature that you have at least 1 level in. You count as gaining a level in that class for the purpose of the Spellcasting class feature of that class. You can choose this Blood Power more than once.

For example, if you are a level 5 sorcerer and you gain this power for the first time, choosing sorcerer, you count as a level 6 sorcerer for the purpose of your sorcerer Spellcasting class feature, including learning new spells and the maximum level of spells you can learn.

Prerequisites. Spellcasting class feature

Spider Climb

You can climb difficult surfaces, including upside down on ceilings, without needing to make an ability check.

Swift Fangs

While you are grappling a creature, you can use a bonus action to make an attack against that creature with your Vampiric Fangs. You can still only use your Vampiric Fangs once per turn.

Prerequisites. *bloodied hands* blood power

Water Resistance

You no longer take acid damage from running water.

PLAYER RACES

Some of these races contain optional 'racial feats' that can be taken as an alternative to ability score improvements in addition to those found in the core rulebooks.

AWAKENED DEAD

Necromancers raise volumes of zombies and skeletons as mindless servants however, sometimes, something goes awry, and the corpse awakens with all its memories of life intact. These awakened dead are usually swiftly disposed of if they do not immediately swear fealty to their reanimator but, sometimes, these unfortunate souls are unnoticed, or manage to escape. Left on their own, confused and trying to return to a facsimile or a normal life, the awakened dead will often find themselves rejected by the living, even if they bear no ill intent.

Ability Score Increase. One ability score of your choice increases by 1.

Age. Awakened dead do not grow, age, or die of old age. Zombies decompose over the years, though this does not adversely affect them until they deteriorate to such a degree as to become non-functional.

Alignment. Awakened dead can be of any alignment.

Size. Awakened dead are the same size as they were in life. Your size is your choice of Medium or Small.

Speed. Your base walking speed is 30 feet.

Undead. Your type is undead, rather than humanoid. You do not require food, drink, sleep, or air. You still need to rest for 8 hours to gain the benefits of a long rest.

Undead Resistance. You are immune to poison damage and the poisoned condition.

Darkvision. You have darkvision within 60 feet of you.

Subrace. Awakened dead are animated as either zombies or skeletons.

Languages. You can speak, read, and write Common and one other language of your choice.

SKELETON

Ability Score Increase. Your Dexterity score increases by 2.

Skeletal Fragility. You are vulnerable to bludgeoning and radiant damage

No Flesh. You are immune to exhaustion and necrotic damage

ZOMBIE

Ability Score Increase. Your Constitution score increases by 2.

Undead Fortitude. If damage reduces you to 0 hit points, make a Constitution saving throw with a DC of 5 + the damage taken, unless the damage is radiant, or from a critical hit. On a success, you drop to 1 hit point instead.

Ghast

Although ghasts retain many feral traits, some individuals have levels of intelligence and personality on par with other mortal races. Some ghasts are the result of cannibalistic humanoids coming into contact with mutagenetic ghoul saliva, while others are the result of generations of ghouls devouring intelligent prey. Neither origin is socially acceptable, and their monstrous appearance, deathly stench, and hunger for flesh make it hard for them to pass unnoticed in civilized society, where they are widely hated.

Ability Score Increase. Your Strength score increases by 2, and your Constitution score increases by 1.

Age. Ghasts do not grow, age, or die of old age. They reach adulthood as living creatures, before becoming ghasts, or emerge fully formed from a larval state.

Alignment. Ghasts strongly tend toward both chaotic and evil.

Size. Ghasts are the same size of their race in life, although they tend to be emaciated and lighter. Your size is Medium.

Speed. Your base walking speed is 30 feet.

Undead. Your type is undead, rather than humanoid. You also do not require food, drink, sleep, or air. You still need to rest for 8 hours to gain the benefits of a long rest.

Ghoulish Hunger. Although you do not require food to survive, you constantly hunger for humanoid flesh. If you have not fed on a humanoid body within the last 24 hours, you must succeed on a DC 15 Wisdom saving throw when you start your turn aware of the presence of a humanoid corpse, or a living humanoid creature, within 600 feet of you. On a failed save, you lose control of your hunger and must spend your turn consuming the nearest humanoid corpse. If there is no corpse within range that qualifies, you must instead spend your turn trying to attack the nearest living humanoid creature, to the best of your ability. You do not have to use any limited use abilities or consumable items in this attempt, but you must take the shortest safe route available toward the target, and use your action to consume it or attack it with a weapon, spell, or your Ghoulish Weapons.

Ghoulish Resistances. You are immune to poison and necrotic damage and the poisoned condition, but are vulnerable to radiant damage.

Ghoulish Weapons. You can use your bite and claws to make unarmed strikes. Your bite deals piercing damage equal to 1d8 + your Strength modifier, instead of the normal damage, and your claws deal slashing damage equal to 1d6 + your Strength modifier.

Darkvision. You have darkvision within 60 feet of you.

Keen Smell. You have advantage on Wisdom (Perception) checks that rely on smell.

Stench. As a bonus action, you can release your ghast Stench. All creatures within 5 feet of you must succeed on a Constitution saving throw or become poisoned until the end of their next turn. The DC for this save is equal to 8 + your proficiency bonus + your Constitution modifier. On a successful saving throw, the creature is immune to your Stench for 24 hours. You can use this feature a number of times equal to your Constitution modifier (minimum 1). You regain all expended uses of this feature when you finish a long rest.

Languages. You can speak, read, and write Common and one other language of your choice.

Optional Racial Feats
Paralyzing Claws

Prerequisites: ghast

The touch of your claws can paralyze the living.

When you hit a creature, other than undead, with your claw attack, you can expend one use of your Stench ability to force the target to make a Constitution saving throw against your Stench ability's save DC. On a failed save, the target is paralyzed for 1 minute. The target can repeat the saving throw at the end of each of its turns, ending the effect on itself on a success.

MONGRELFOLK

Pariahs in almost every society, it is no mystery why many mongrelfolk turn to an adventuring life. For many, risking life and limb is the only way they can hope to achieve any modicum of respect (or even a kind word) from the general populace.

Ability Score Increase. Your Constitution score increases by 2 and your Strength score increases by 1.

Age. Mongrelfolk have unpredictable life spans, some dying of old age when they are no more than 50 years old, while others live for up to two centuries. Most reach maturity in their early to mid teens.

Alignment. Mongrelfolk can be of any alignment.

Size. Mongrelfolk are mutated humanoids of various origins. Your size is your choice of Medium or Small.

Speed. Your base walking speed is 25 feet.

Prominent Deformities. You can have up to 6 features from the mongrelfolk deformity table (p.79), determined randomly by rolling a d4 and d10 each. You may add +10 to the result of no more than half of the d10 rolls, chosen after you have made the rolls. The d4 determines the location of each deformity (head, torso, arms, or legs) and the d10 determines the specific deformity. Alternatively, you can choose your deformities, but no more than half of the chosen deformities may be chosen from the table results from 12 to 20.

You can choose the same deformity up to twice but, if you do so, you must take an additional deformity from among *single cyclopean eye*, *open lesions*, *crooked arm*, or *withered leg*.

Languages. You can speak, read, and write Common and one other language of your choice.

Wight

Wights are almost universally evil and obviously monstrous. As such, they are vilified by the living population, even among many evil creatures, as a wight's hatred for the living doesn't discern by alignment. Despite this, wights retain much of their personality and memories after death (though they do tend to fade over time), making them one of the more varied and individualistic undead.

Ability Score Increase. Your Constitution score increases by 2, and your Charisma score increases by 1.

Age. Wights do not grow, age, or die of old age. They reach adulthood as living creatures, before becoming wights.

Alignment. Wights are almost exclusively neutral evil.

Size. Wights are the same size of their race in life. Your size is Medium.

Speed. Your base walking speed is 30 feet.

Undead. Your type is undead, rather than humanoid. You do not require food, drink, sleep, or air.

Wight Resistances. You are immune to poison and necrotic damage and the poisoned condition, but are vulnerable to radiant damage.

Darkvision. You have darkvision within 60 feet of you.

Life Drain. You can use your action to make a special, unarmed strike that uses your Charisma modifier for attack and damage rolls, and deals 1d6 necrotic damage, instead of the normal damage. On a hit, the target must succeed on a DC 13 Constitution saving throw or its hit point maximum is reduced by an amount equal to the damage taken. This reduction lasts until the target finishes a long rest. If the creature's hit point maximum is reduced to 0 by this effect, the creature dies.

A humanoid, or beast, slain by this attack rises 24 hours later as a zombie under your control, unless the creature is restored to life, or its body is destroyed. You can have a maximum number of zombies equal to your level under your control at one time.

Sunlight Sensitivity. While in sunlight, you have disadvantage on attack rolls, as well as on Wisdom (Perception) checks that rely on sight.

Turn Resistance. You have advantage on saving throws against any effect that turns undead.

Languages. You can speak, read, and write Common and one other language of your choice.

Optional Racial Feats

Relentless Hatred

Prerequisites: wight

Your hatred for the living inexorably drives you toward your goals.

When you take this feat, you gain immunity to exhaustion.

Deathless Flesh

Prerequisites: wight, *Relentless Hatred* feat, 12th level or higher

As your power grows, your flesh becomes resilient to mundane forms of damage.

When you take this feat, you gain resistance to bludgeoning, piercing, and slashing damage from non-magical sources that aren't silvered.

Player Templates

Death doesn't have to be the end! The following templates can be applied to an existing player character upon their death, at the GM's discretion, to turn them into a ghost or revenant. These templates grant the character new abilities, but also strip certain features that are normally inherent to player characters, such as the ability to gain levels.

Becoming a Ghost

If a player character dies with unfinished business, and the GM and player agree, the character may return as a ghost. While they are a ghost, the character cannot pass on to their afterlife, or be resurrected by any means.

Before becoming a ghost, agree with your GM on the parameters of your unfinished business and how to complete it. As a ghost you gain the following features:

Ghost Form. Your soul leaves your body and reforms as a ghost. Your ghostly form retains clothing, armor, and weapons you regularly carried, or wore, in life. You retain the AC granted by any such armor, but you cannot doff the armor, and you no longer benefit from the magical effects of any items. If you drop any items that are part of your ghost form, the dropped item disappears and reforms on your form at the start of your next turn.

You can still make attacks with weapons that are part of your ghostly form, however, these attacks deal necrotic damage instead of the normal damage, and you use Charisma instead of your Strength or Dexterity for attack and damage rolls.

Your Strength score becomes 5. However, when you become a ghost, you may choose to increase your Charisma score to what your Strength score was before you died.

Undead. Your type becomes undead, rather than humanoid. You no longer require food, drink, sleep, or air. You no longer grow or age, and you can no longer gain experience or levels.

Incorporeal Movement. You gain a fly speed equal to your walking speed, and the ability to hover. You lose all other special speeds, and your walking speed becomes 0 ft. You can move through other creatures and objects as if they were difficult terrain. If you end your turn inside an object, you take Xd10 force damage, where X is equal to half your level.

Ghostly Resistance. You become immune to exhaustion, and to the charmed, frightened, grappled, paralyzed, petrified, poisoned, prone, and restrained conditions.

You gain resistance to bludgeoning, piercing, and slashing damage from non-magical sources, as well as acid, fire, lightning, and thunder damage and immunity to cold, necrotic, and poison damage.

Ethereal Sight. You lose all your natural modes of vision, and gain darkvision within 60 feet of you. Additionally, you can see 60 feet into the Ethereal Plane, when you are on the Material Plane, and vice versa.

Etherealness. As an action, you can enter the Ethereal Plane from the Material Plane, or vice versa. You remain visible on the Material Plane while you are in the Border Ethereal, and vice versa, but you can't affect, or be affected, by anything on the other plane.

Horrifying Visage. As an action, you can warp your features into a terrifying countenance. Living creatures within 60 feet of you, that can see you, must succeed on a Wisdom saving throw or become frightened for 1 minute (the DC is equal to 8 + your proficiency bonus + your Charisma modifier). A frightened target can repeat the saving throw at the end of each of its turns, ending the frightened condition on itself on a success. If a target's saving throw is successful, or the effect ends for it, the target is immune to your Horrifying Visage for the next 24 hours. Once you have used this feature, you can't do so again until you finish a short or long rest.

Unfinished Business. If you complete your unfinished business, your ghostly form moves on to the afterlife. You die and can't be resurrected by any means.

If you are destroyed before your unfinished business is completed, you cannot be resurrected by any means, but your ghost can be recalled to the material plane by a *wish* spell. If you do not want to be recalled, you must succeed on a Charisma saving throw against the caster's spell save DC to resist the spell. If you successfully resist, the spell's material components are not consumed.

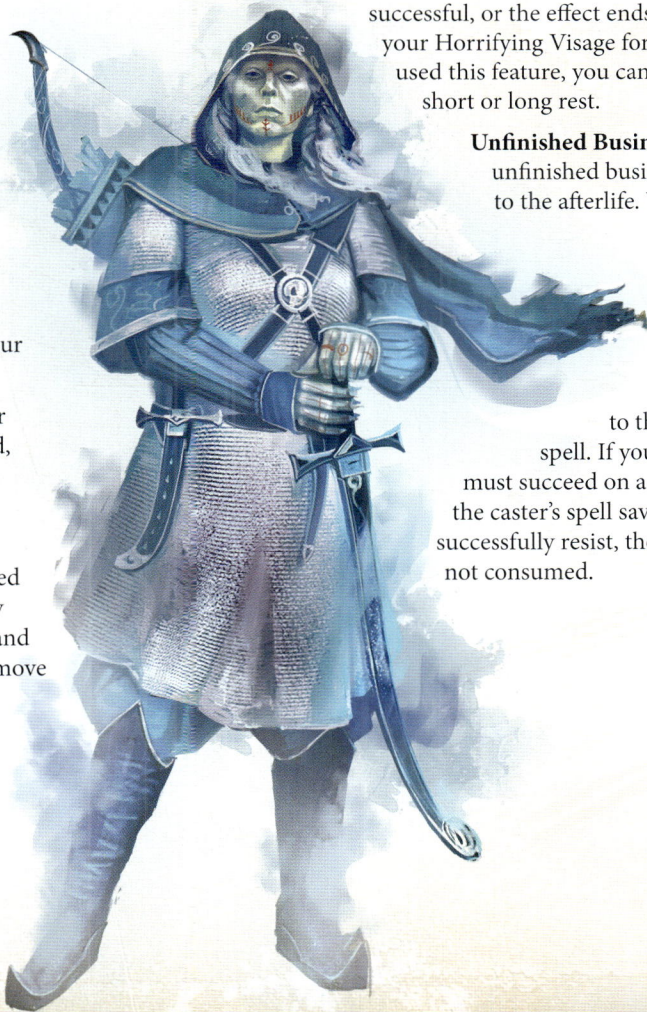

Becoming a Revenant

If a player character is unjustly murdered, they may wish to seek vengeance against those who inflicted this injustice upon them. If the GM and player agree, the character may return as a revenant. While they are a revenant, the character cannot pass on to their afterlife, or be resurrected by any means.

Before becoming a revenant, agree with your GM on the reason for, and target or targets of, your revenge. As a revenant you gain the following features:

Undead. Your type becomes undead, rather than humanoid. You no longer require food, drink, sleep, or air. You no longer grow or age, and you can no longer gain experience or levels.

Revenant Resistances. You become immune to exhaustion, and the charmed, frightened, paralyzed, poisoned, and stunned conditions.

You gain resistance to necrotic and psychic damage, and immunity to poison damage.

Regeneration. You regain a number of hit points equal to half your level at the start of each of your turns. If you take fire or radiant damage, you cannot regenerate on your next turn.

Darkvision. You gain darkvision within 60 feet of you, unless you already have darkvision with a greater range.

Vengeful Strikes. When you make a weapon attack against the target of your revenge, or a creature that is trying to protect the target from you, you roll the weapon's damage dice one additional time and add the result to the total.

Turn Immunity. You are immune to effects that turn undead.

Vengeance Seeker. You innately know the distance and direction of any and all creatures against whom you seek revenge, even if the creature and you are on different planes of existence. If all the creatures die, you learn of their deaths and lose your Regeneration ability.

Without Rest. If you are killed, you reanimate with full hit points after 24 hours. If your body has lost parts, it regenerates from the head, and any lost body parts are restored when you reanimate. If your head is destroyed, you can't reanimate and your soul is forced to the afterlife.

Revenge. If you, or one of your allies, slay all targets of your revenge, your purpose as a revenant is complete. You lose your Regeneration and Without Rest abilities and you die.

If your soul moves on to the afterlife for any reason, you can't be resurrected by any means.

APPENDIX C: LAIR MAPS

Use these maps as inspiration for encounters involving the creatures found in the previous chapters.

INDEX

MONSTERS IN ALPHABETICAL ORDER

CR	Creature	Page
3	Werebat	63
10	Werebear Devotee	65
7	Werebear Protector	64
3	Werepanther	66
2	Wereraven	67
4	Werewolf Mauler	68
8	Wight Champion	167
7	Wight Despoiler	170
7	Wight Hunter	164
5	Wight Malignant	169
4	Wight Tracker	163
4	Wight Warrior	166
3	Wisp of Yearning	178
5	Young Zombie Dragon	210
2	Zombie Bear	214
1/8	Zombie Dog	212
1/4	Zombie Horse	213
1	Zombie Ox	213

MONSTERS BY CHALLENGE RATING

CR	Creature	Page
0	Miniature Soldier	230
0	Plague-Touched Rat	214
1/8	Hobgoblin Zombie	202
1/8	Human Zombie	194
1/8	Mongrelfolk Mite	76
1/8	Plague-Touched Raven	215
1/8	Zombie Dog	212
1/4	Dwarf Zombie	198
1/4	Elf Zombie	196
1/4	Goblin Zombie	200
1/4	Living Doll	220
1/4	Miniature Chariot	231
1/4	Mongrelfolk	76
1/4	Mummified Baboon	96
1/4	Orc Zombie	204
1/4	Skeletal Dog	130
1/4	Skeleton Archer	125
1/4	Skeleton Infantry	123
1/4	Skeleton Warrior	121
1/4	Stunted Ghoul	23
1/4	Zombie Horse	213

CR	Creature	Page
1/2	Flying Dagger	228
1/2	Flying Halberd	228
1/2	Mongrelfolk Thug	77
1/2	Skeletal Riding Horse	130
1/2	Ushabti	229
1	Animated Longbow	228
1	Animated Spiked Armor	221
1	Goul Gnawer	23
1	Mongrelfolk Warrior	77
1	Phantom Servant	9
1	Swarm of Plague-Tocuhed Roaches	216
1	Swarm of Plague-Touched Rats	215
1	Tomb Hound	96
1	Traversing Specter	138
1	Zombie Ox	213
2	Bitter Ghast	30
2	Bright Mote	187
2	Garghoul	24
2	Ghostflame	177
2	Horrific Countenance	10
2	Ogre Zombie	206
2	Phantom Hound	11
2	Plague-Born Dog	212
2	Plague-Born Hobgoblin	202
2	Plague-Born Human	194
2	Plague-Born Orc	204
2	Possessive Consciousness	12
2	Scorched Effigy	226
2	Silhouette Shadow	114
2	Skeleton Marksman	125
2	Skeleton Pikeneer	123
2	Skeleton Soldier	121
2	Swarm of Cursed Snakes	97
2	Swarm of Plague-Touched Ravens	216
2	Wereraven	67
2	Zombie Bear	214
3	Plague-Born Elf	196
3	Eyeless Stalker	25
3	Mongrelfolk Brute	78
3	Mummified Murderer	89
3	Mummy Acolyte	91
3	Mummy Soldier	87

Legal Appendix